HOPE
FOR THE
BEST

VANESSA LAFLEUR

BQB

Virginia

Published in the United States by BQB Publishing
(an imprint of Boutique of Quality Books Publishing Company, Inc.)
www.bqbpublishing.com

978-1-945448-61-4 (p)
978-1-945448-62-1 (e)

Library of Congress Control Number: 2020932095

Book Design by Robin Krauss, www.bookformatters.com
Cover Design by Rebecca Lown, www.rebeccalowndesign.com
First editor: Olivia Swenson
Second editor: Caleb Guard

PART 1

SUMMER OF 2090

CHAPTER 1

The northernmost part of the city stood impossibly still in a motionless state of decay. Another storm crawled along the horizon waiting for the perfect moment to attack with torrential rain and destructive winds. Dark, disintegrating buildings lined both sides of the street in what at one time had been a busy business district. Walls bowed toward the littered street, roofs sagged and crumbled onto rotting floors, and the windows that weren't boarded up stared out as empty voids of darkness, sightless eyes that offered the false hope of a place to hide, to rest, to think.

Lareina's worn tennis shoes slapped rhythmically against cracked concrete. Resilient, creeping weeds reached for her ankles, while heavy, thudding bootsteps echoed between the buildings, urging her forward and strengthening her determination to elude Detective Galloway. She didn't bother to glance over her shoulder; she already knew he barreled toward her, not catching up, but not slowing down either.

Over the past week, she had run from one end of the city to the other in an attempt to circumvent the detective. To her advantage, she had spent two years living on the streets of San Antonio, and her knowledge of the city gave her an edge in the high-stakes game of hide-and-seek. She knew what time of the day she could avoid bystanders, where she could lose Galloway in a crowd of people, and places she could hide when caught off guard.

Empty storefronts blurred by in a rush of faded color. Gusty winds whistled through spaces between the damaged buildings, plastering her long hair over her eyes and blurring her vision. Although these challenges didn't slow her down, outrunning the detective wasn't an option. Three of her strides equaled one of his, and although she was quick, endurance to continue at that pace wasn't on her side.

Only hours earlier she'd woken up, warm and comfortable, to the sound of soft rain on the roof of the public library. It was her second Galloway-free day, and she was starting to think maybe she'd lost him. Luckily, she had planned her escape routes ahead of time and managed to climb through a basement window. It had given her a head start, but not enough to escape the detective permanently.

Lungs burning, legs aching, heart racing, Lareina knew she needed to stop and rest, if only for five minutes. Abruptly, she made a right turn into an alley that cut between the buildings to the next block, dodging overturned trash cans, empty crates, and split bags of trash years overdue for collection. Feeling lightheaded, she searched the alley for a dark corner, a crevice in the wall, or anything to hide under. Up ahead, a chest-high chain-link fence divided the alley in half.

On the other side of the fence, cluttered with old mattresses, dumpsters, and other unidentified rotting debris, she spotted her chance to hide, to rest, to lose the detective. Gasping for air, she propelled herself over the fence, darted down the alley, and squeezed herself into the space between a crumbling brick wall and a disintegrating mattress.

Heart knocking against her chest as frantically as a wild bird caught in a net, she forced herself to breathe in short, silent gulps. She raised her hand to her chest and outlined the shape of the strange pendant that hung from a chain around her neck, concealed beneath her t-shirt. She pictured the pendant's polished black surface with white letters S-P-

E-R-O across the bottom. Absentmindedly, she traced the smooth, flat object. A slanted edge led to a rounded arch at the bottom, then back to a second slanted edge that ended in a point joining it to the first. Sometimes it reminded her of a teardrop and sometimes a slice of pizza, depending on her mood.

She didn't know what it was, only that Galloway wanted it more than anything. Poor Susan's last garbled plea echoed in her head: *Protect the pendant. Never let anyone . . . know . . . find . . . warn him.* The girl had gasped those last words as a wound to her abdomen turned green grass red. She died because of the pendant now dangling icily against Lareina's skin.

Escape Detective Galloway, and you'll be free, she reminded herself. *Then you can find out what the pendant is and either throw it into the river or sell it for all it's worth.* The musty smell of the old wet mattress stifled her sinuses. Pinching her nose so she wouldn't gag or cough, she pushed a strand of long black hair away from her face and tugged at the side seam of her jeans, which were three inches too long for her short stature. Crouched on the soggy ground, she listened to a cricket chirp, flinched with each drip of cold water against her arm, and squeezed her eyes shut.

During her two-day library reprieve, she had forestalled her longing to get lost in the world of a book and instead had gathered every book on jewelry in the library's catalog. She read up on valuable pendants made of diamonds, rubies, and pearls. She read about costume jewelry meant to imitate its more expensive counterpart. She flipped through picture after picture, so many she felt sure she could distinguish a real diamond necklace from a fake, but nothing resembling her pendant appeared in the books. According to all of her research, it couldn't be valuable. It couldn't be worth a week of Galloway's time to retrieve, but still, he found her.

Water dripped onto her back and she shrugged in response to the tingling sensation. She wished she had spent time reading books about falling in love, traveling the world, winning a war—anything but jewelry. Her research had been pointless, and in her seventeen years of life she had barely begun to read the millions of books in existence. The realization that she might never read another book, that she might never walk out of the alley, crashed over her like an immense wave, pulling her under and preventing her from ever reaching the surface. She couldn't remain still much longer and, more importantly, couldn't let Galloway win.

Resting her cheek against a brick wall, she noticed red powder around her feet, accumulating as the manmade stone crumbled over time. Leave San Antonio? It was no longer an option but a requirement for survival. She felt no attachment to the city; there was no building she called home, and there were no people she would miss. It was too easy for Galloway to find her there, but if she kept running until those familiar streets disappeared behind her, she could vanish into the population of any city she chose.

Footsteps crunched across the gravel alley and her muscles tensed.

One step. Two steps. Three.

What will happen if he gets the pendant?

Four. Five.

How does he keep finding me?

Six steps. Seven.

If he sees me, I'm trapped.

She tilted her head to the left and spotted his oversized black boot through the gap between the mattress and the wall. Holding her breath she gripped the pendant tightly in one hand. She could keep herself still and her breathing quiet, but nothing could calm her desperate thoughts.

Galloway glided past the mattress, sending pebbles splashing into the puddles behind him. "I know you're here. Come on out and I won't hurt you." He glanced up and down the alley, walked another six feet, and flipped up the lid of a dumpster with a bang. He peered inside, glanced around again, then lowered himself into a push-up position and surveyed the space beneath.

Knowing he wouldn't leave an inch of the alley unsearched, Lareina slipped out of her hiding place and edged along the cold brick that made up one side of the alley, back toward the fence she jumped minutes earlier. Each shuffle step pushed her further away from her hiding place, out into the open, and visible to the detective if he turned around. Her only comfort came from the sight of his back moving away from her. She wanted noise to muffle her footsteps, but Galloway searched silently as he peered into crevices and behind piles of debris.

Holding her breath, she tiptoed backward with one arm stretched behind her, feeling for the fence as she inched away from the detective. A deafening crunch echoed through the alley.

Looking down at her feet, she cringed and lifted her shoe off a long-ago discarded plastic bottle. Galloway froze at the far end of the alley. She froze too, unable to take her eyes off the back of his head. *Don't turn around.* She mouthed the words in a silent prayer, unwilling to make another sound. A crow cawed in the distance, a breeze ruffled the trash spilling out of rotted plastic bags, and time didn't move.

Galloway's voice floated down the alley before he turned cautiously. "I don't want to hurt you." He held his hands out, palms down in front of him as if trying not to startle a deer. "I don't care about all of the things you've stolen. Just give me the pendant and you're free."

"Is that what you told Susan?" She slid one foot back across the gravel.

"Yes, but she wouldn't listen, and the people I work for aren't patient." He took a step forward. "I can't waste any more time chasing that thing."

"Since when do you work for other people?" Her feet twitched inside of her shoes. "I don't believe you."

"It's complicated." His shoulders sagged slightly as if to prove the weight of his problem, but his lips tightened into a straight line. "I got mixed up in something I want to get out of. You have to believe me when I tell you that thing won't make you any money. It'll only bring you misery."

"Then why do these people you're working for want it?" Her hands clenched and unclenched. Every muscle twitched in preparation to run.

"It's a matter of national security." His hand lowered toward his belt.

Springing backward, she leaped for the fence, and caught the top edge with her foot, enough to propel her over. She hit the ground with a splash and sprinted back toward the street with Galloway trailing a half block behind her.

She tore down the littered road, hurdling a couch left by looters and darting past a half-collapsed building that spilled bricks onto the sidewalk. Only one more block and she would see the bridge that would link her to an abandoned neighborhood. A quick dash across overgrown soccer fields would give her the advantage of rows and rows of houses offering endless places to hide and a chance of losing Galloway.

Glancing behind her she noticed the detective keeping pace but not getting any closer.

Feet sliding across gooey mud, she skidded to a stop. Right in front of her, where the bridge should have been, a rushing river swallowed her only link to freedom. Chunks of concrete had eroded from the edge of the bridge, and only the flat top of the guardrail stood above the water. It trembled in the middle where it had lost its concrete anchor. Torrential rains of the past week combined with above-normal rainfall over the summer had led to extreme flooding throughout the state.

Stepping forward into the current, she gripped the guardrail as knee-deep water threatened to sweep her off her feet. Just ahead, white torrents cascaded across the surface, foaming as they caught on submerged concrete barriers. The bridge shook, quickly being overpowered by the flood's tremendous force.

Another glance back revealed Detective Galloway lumbering ever closer. If she didn't move, he would capture her; if she didn't hurry, the bridge would be gone. Shivering, she hoisted herself onto the four-foot guardrail that once stood between people on the sidewalk and the trickle of a creek below. Ignoring her trembling hands, she stood up and swayed from side to side.

It's just like the balance beam on a playground, or walking along the top of a retaining wall, she tried to convince herself. Galloway shouted behind her, but she couldn't make sense of what he said over the roaring water—or was that the sound of blood pumping in her ears? She slid one foot in front of the other. Although only thirty yards ahead, the bank of the creek seemed a mile away as she struggled to maintain her balance.

"Have you lost your mind?" Galloway's voice came so

clearly through the deafening rush of water that she worried he had followed her onto the rail. "You'll get yourself killed out there."

The guardrail bounced beneath her and groaned with every step as she crossed the unsupported middle section. As she attempted to turn her head toward the detective, her left foot slid partially down the side of the thin beam. Flailing her arms, she leaned far to the right and managed to find her balance again.

"You have to move," she whispered over the roar of water. "You can't stay here."

Shaking, she looked down at the water lapping fiercely two feet below her shoes. She took a deep breath and stepped forward.

CHAPTER 2

Never had Lareina known relief like reaching the end of that guardrail. Leaping as far from the edge of the water as possible, she sank shin deep into mud along the saturated creek, but she didn't care. She would have one more day of freedom and one more day to live.

Turning around, she spotted Galloway standing, hands pressed against the top of his head, across the water. Another chunk of the bridge collapsed and the guardrail bobbed wildly. He made no attempt to come after her. His eyes, surrounded by puffy eyelids and dark circles, scrutinized the scene as his lips stretched into a thin flat line.

"Your precious pendant is safe." She stood tall as she shouted at him, the adrenaline of her stunt and the reality of her freedom racing through her body. "And if you want it, you'll have to take it because it belongs to me now."

As she turned away from the water, she heard him yell, "I'll find you no matter where you run. I'll always find you."

The threat constricted muscles in her shoulders and jaw, but instead of turning around she walked toward the promised shelter of houses on the horizon. Galloway could try to follow her, but the flooding would give her time to disappear while he looked for a way around the obstacle. Gray clouds piled in from the west, tumbling past one another and swallowing those too slow to keep up. The creek would only swell with the rain overnight, and she laughed out loud at the perfect timing of the approaching storm.

Kicking mud off her shoes, she imagined the comforts of the house she would sleep in that night. A soft pillow, somewhere dry to rest, and some clean clothes were the only luxuries she needed. In the city she slept in libraries and churches—the only places she felt safe and could be alone. All abandoned buildings in the city had been looted, but she'd heard rumors that houses outside of the city tended to be not only empty of people, but still stocked with supplies left behind by their owners.

Although the economic downturn began when she was too young to remember, she had felt its affects all her life. She guessed it was the reason her parents had abandoned her, why so many children had been left to a system unprepared to provide for their needs. Every new home for children she was sent to seemed to have less food and more orphans assigned to a room than the one before. By the time she was twelve, a fuel shortage nearly doubled the population of cities across the country. People couldn't afford to commute far for work, and they wanted to live close to the best hospitals, restaurants, and entertainment. A few years later, when the fever started, the overpopulation of urban areas allowed it to sweep through like a wildfire.

Only six in ten survived the flu-like virus that started out as a cough and ended in a high fever. The vast majority of survivors were between the ages of ten and twenty-five. Lareina took comfort that at seventeen she fell in that age group, but still she worried she couldn't beat such a formidable illness without anyone to take care of her. Unfortunately it didn't show any signs of dying out, so she feared it was only a matter of time.

Cutting across overgrown playing fields, she could make out the shapes of tree houses and deteriorating trampolines behind the wood fences outlining backyards. How different would her life have been had she grown up in a house with green grass, a trampoline, parents and siblings? Maybe she would have learned to play the piano so beautifully people would have traveled miles to hear her in concert. Maybe she would have studied medicine and found a cure to the dreaded fever. She definitely wouldn't have turned out to be the thief and fugitive she'd become.

The houses that had appeared as black silhouettes against the gray sky from across the bridge became gloomy two-story homes with dark windows. They differed in the color of their siding and the locations of chipping paint but were otherwise identical. She remembered stories of desperate homeowners unable to sell their houses located too far outside of city limits to be valuable. To protect what they had left in case their fortunes or the economy turned, they transformed their homes into burglar traps before fleeing to the city.

"They like to hide nets under the leaves," a boy named Joe had told her once. She had been huddled around a trashcan fire under an overpass with a dozen other children who had run away from children's homes or replacement families. The others, hardened after being on their own for years, looked at Joe with a mixture of disbelief and disregard. They knew the rules.

There is no friendship. Trust no one. Share nothing.

"Sometimes turning on the kitchen sink triggers an explosion that can take your hand right off," Joe exclaimed. No one listened. Joe claimed to loot houses, hauling the goods into town and selling them for any profit he could make. Lareina and others like her didn't dare leave the city, focused more on surviving the cold winter than Joe's stories, which they considered to be nothing more than fantasies.

But only twelve then, she had listened. She had been on her own for a month. Perhaps it was that she didn't know the rules, or the earnestness in Joe's voice made her stop and listen. "The worst are the pits," he told his wide-eyed audience of one. "You never see them until you're face-first in the dirt."

Her cautious eyes immediately noticed how the field behind the houses had rectangular sections that sunk lower than the ground around them. Some areas had completely dropped away, exposing rotted edges of blue tarp still staked into the ground above. Easing closer to the nearest backyard, she tested the ground in front of her with one foot before putting her weight on it. She didn't believe anyone could really lack the observation skills to fall for such an obvious trap, but the uncertainty of what she might miss had kept her in the city. Now Galloway had forced her from the place where at least she knew the rules to survive.

Clouds approached, thickening, darkening, and blotting out the ever-dimming light. Ten feet to the fence, then the safety of an overgrown backyard, then the warmth of any house she chose.

A snapping sound drew her attention upward to a red-and-white striped tarp blowing in the wind. Once the roof of a treehouse, it lifted, twisted, fell, and her memory did the same. Nearly eight years earlier in a place almost a thousand miles away, she had spent summer evenings watching fireworks and fall afternoons reading books in a treehouse almost identical to the one in front of her. Although she had lived in the Maibe, Nebraska, Home for Children, she spent most of her time with Rochelle Aumont, the only friend she had ever made in her life. For that brief year, she had been given a childhood.

A mosquito hummed near her ear. She swatted it away and stepped forward.

To her left an open pit swallowed up the ground, daring any visitor to take another step. Large chunks of tarp shivered on stakes after being torn away at strategic cuts when strained under too much weight. She edged closer to investigate. Thunder rumbled in the distance as she looked into the pit.

Something orange stood out against the dull mud in gray light. When it moved she took a cautious step forward, sending little clumps of earth rolling into the hole. A boy with a dirt-smudged face and mud-speckled blond hair stared up at her.

"Hey, are you all right down there?" She leaned forward as far as she could without tumbling over the edge.

The boy scowled up at her and rolled his eyes in a way that involved his entire head. "Does it look like I'm all right?"

She shrugged and turned away from the pit, ready to find some shelter before the storm crawled any closer. Interacting with other people would only be done for necessity of survival. *Trust no one. Share nothing.*

"Wait." The small voice sounded so different from the first that she had to look again to verify only one boy sat in the trap. "I'm hungry and I hurt my ankle."

Any gruffness had fizzled from his voice and deflated from his stature. He winced as he pulled his knees up to his chin. Pathetic, terrified, and desperate. Would he die if no one else came along to help him? She imagined herself in the same situation, Galloway's face hovering above, and shivered.

"I'll be right back." She turned and maneuvered through a rotted section of fence into the knee-high grass of a backyard gone wild. "Don't worry, I'll get you out."

Easing around the yard to avoid any other traps, she maneuvered to the tree house she had noticed earlier. Barely visible through lush grass, hid the remnants of an old tire swing. She ripped the tire away from tangled weeds and surveyed the frayed rope attached to the end. It would have to be good enough. She hoisted the tire and walked awkwardly back to the pit as the wind picked up intensity, gusting out of the north, complementing sharp lightning that streaked through the darkening sky. Although she anticipated it, each roar of thunder sent a tremor through her body.

She set the tire down at the edge of the pit and lowered the rope. When the boy gripped the frayed end, she wrapped her arms through the tire and leaned back with all of her weight. Nothing happened.

"You're going to have to help me," she shouted against the wind. "Try to climb up the side."

Hugging the tire as if it were a teddy bear, she pulled. Tension on the rope slackened and she took a step back. Inch by inch she stepped away from the pit. With one last tug, she stumbled backward and the boy sprawled onto the grass.

Lareina sat on the soggy ground, too drained and proud of her ingenuity to remember fear. She remained still, head bent forward, watching as the wind lifted strands of her long black hair.

The boy crawled toward her without letting his left ankle touch the ground. He tilted his head to the side and curly blond hair flopped over his forehead. "Are . . . are you all right?" His voice trembled with uncertainty.

She smiled and nodded. "Yeah, just resting."

He settled next to her, injured ankle stretched in front of him, and extended his hand. "I'm Nick Ziel."

She shook his hand politely, but an introduction didn't come readily to her lips. Was it safe to tell this boy her name? Would he know she was a wanted fugitive? She didn't even have a last name to give him.

Nick's puzzled expression let her know she had hesitated

too long. She nodded and smiled to buy another second, to think of the kind of person she wanted to be, then met his puzzled eyes and replied, "Nice to meet you, Nick. My name is Rochelle Aumont."

The image of a smiling eight-year-old girl with kind green eyes flashed through her mind. Lareina had only been ten years old for a week when she said goodbye to Rochelle. The last day of the eleven months and fifteen days that she had lived in the Maibe Home for Children was one of the few times she'd cried in the past ten years. It felt wrong to steal an old friend's name, but it was too late to change her mind. Nick let go of her hand as the first raindrops landed on her face.

"It's starting to rain," he complained. "We have to get up onto a porch before we get soaked."

"What's the rush?" She laughed. "You could use a shower anyway."

Wide brown eyes, thin nose, and pointed chin all nodded forward to observe his clothing. A deepening frown warned her that he hadn't appreciated the comment.

"Me? How about you?" he shot back.

She had momentarily forgotten about the muddy grime that had accumulated on the worn jeans and baggy t-shirt she had nabbed from a fire escape rail as they dried. Rain poured heavier and, for the second time in less than an hour, she decided to leave Nick on the ground and find herself shelter for the night. She had pulled him out of the trap, and now he had his freedom and could fend for himself. Standing, she started toward the house.

"Hey, you aren't going to leave me here?"

"Why shouldn't I?"

"I can barely put any weight on my ankle. I need your help," he pleaded.

Sighing, she returned to his side, offering her hand. "Then let's go."

He took her hand and she pulled him to his feet. Though he stood a head taller than her, he was slighter than she first thought, and she awkwardly supported the weight his leg couldn't as they stumbled through a deluge of water to the front porch of the nearest house. She helped him to a rotting wicker chair and tried the door. Locked, as expected, but she considered that less of a deterrent and more of an annoyance. After locating her lock picking tools in her bag, she knelt and inserted a pin into the keyhole on the doorknob.

"What are you doing?" Nick asked as she worked on the lock.

"I'm going to open this door."

Thunder rumbled and a stiff wind splattered raindrops against their drying faces.

"You can't do that."

A streak of lightning momentarily lit the sky. She tried the knob. Not quite.

"Of course I can. Just give me a few more minutes."

"No, I mean we can't just break into someone's house."

She stopped working and turned to Nick. Words weren't enough to express all she understood but he didn't seem to comprehend. "It's dangerous out here. We need a safe place to stay until the storm moves through."

Folding his arms across his chest, he leaned back in the chair. "I know how dangerous it is. I've been doing this for three weeks now."

Lareina laughed. "You've been falling into pits for three weeks?"

"No, that's the first pit I've fallen into." He met her

amused smile with a glare. "I mean I've been away from home and surviving on my own just fine."

Ignoring him, she turned back to her task. In another minute, the lock clicked and with a light nudge, the door swung open.

"I'm not going in there." He folded his arms across his chest.

"Come on, Nick, I can see you shivering."

"Nothing you say is going to convince me to do something illegal." The intensity of his scowl let her know just how much he disapproved of her actions. His attitude bounced from one hemisphere of her brain to the other, gaining speed, creating heat, simmering inside her head.

"Illegal." She spat the word back at him. "Is that going to be your last thought when you get struck by lightning? How old are you, Nick?" She forced a normal breath, kept a calm expression on her face, but felt her feet move closer to the open door.

He leaned forward. "Seventeen."

"In that case . . ." She pointed to the dark sky beyond the porch. "There's a storm." She pointed into the dark interior of the house. "There's shelter." The wind gusted noisily, and she yelled to be heard over it. "You're plenty old enough to make a decision."

His scowl vanished and he looked out at the black sky as if surveying the clouds for the first time. "Fine," he surrendered. "Let's go inside."

Lareina exhaled, willed her shaking hands to be still and took Nick's arm. Once inside, she kicked the door shut with her foot, locking the storm outside. They entered a comfortable living room furnished with a blue couch and two matching recliners. It appeared untouched by the elements—no dripping ceiling or flood-saturated carpet. Through a second doorway, the kitchen greeted them, pristine and ready for someone to prepare a meal. No broken windows, no scattered possessions, undefiled by looters. Its proximity to the city should have made it one of the first targets, but perhaps it had been more recently abandoned. She shivered, thinking the family may have spent their final evening in the room where she stood only a few weeks earlier.

A low rumble in her stomach drove her thoughts back to the more immediate requirements of survival. The last meal she had eaten was early that morning and had consisted of half of one of the precious candy bars stashed in her backpack.

"Have you eaten anything today?" She helped Nick over to the kitchen table.

"No, I ran out of food yesterday, and I ran out of money last week."

"Why does that not surprise me?" Lareina laughed, then regretted expressing her opinion out loud. Nick, on first impression, came across as pathetic, naïve, and inept at staying alive, but insulting the stranger trapped under the same roof for the night constituted reckless behavior.

He pushed her arm away and sat down heavily on a chair.

Sighing, she leaned against the table. "I'm sorry. It's been a long day and I'm not so good at this."

"At what?" Nick rolled his eyes. "Having a conversation? Have you forgotten how to talk to people or do you just think you're above all their rules?" He made a sweeping gesture with his hand and brought it to rest on the top of his head.

Reading his mood didn't come easy in the minutes she'd known him, but his posture slackened with his last sentence.

"I don't dislike people." She brushed her fingers through

the knots at the ends of her hair. "I just don't trust them. Very few of them have given me any reason to."

Nick nodded and slouched. The suspicion in his eyes momentarily vanished, and she found her own emotions reflected in his expression: fear, uncertainty, and desperation. For the first time, she recognized their similarities. They both traveled alone, both wore dirty clothes, both hesitated to trust another human being. Each of them wandered through a broken world filled with starvation, riots, disease, and the fear of war around every corner.

"I'm sorry. I was rude before. Thank you for helping me." He rested his cheek on the table and all of his hair shifted, hiding half of his face.

Lareina knelt next to him and rolled the left leg of his jeans up to his knee. A swollen bulge the size of a large peach replaced his ankle.

"This is going to hurt," she warned, and pulled his shoe off before he had time to protest.

Nick cried out and clutched the seat of the chair. "What are you doing?" he demanded through clenched teeth.

Shifting the chair next to him so it faced him, she lifted his injured leg onto it. "I'm just trying to help." She stood and walked over to the cupboards. Inside she found white plates, matching bowls, and glasses—items she expected, but not what she hoped for.

"What are you doing now?"

She crossed the room and opened the doors to a floor-to-ceiling pantry. "I'm looking for supper, and I think I found it." Reaching into the back corner of the darkness, she pulled out a can of chicken noodle soup, a nearly empty bag of raisins, and a bottle of salad dressing. Pushing the bottle back onto the shelf, she announced, "Soup and raisins it is."

"Mmm, something warm sounds great." All accusation faded from his voice.

"It does," she agreed. "Too bad no one has been paying the electric bill."

Nick didn't say another word as she divided the soup and raisins into separate bowls and carried them to the table. Lifting a spoonful of soup to her lips, she closed her eyes and tried to imagine warm steam tickling her face and soothing her dry throat.

He gagged after his first bite. "How old is this?"

Fantasy shattered, she opened her eyes and lowered the spoon. "What?"

"The soup. Did you look at the date on the can? It tastes like it's been in that cupboard for half a century." Dropping his spoon in the bowl, he slid it away.

"I don't look at the dates. Expired food is the least of our problems." She shrugged and swallowed another mouthful.

Eventually, he decided he was hungry enough to eat the slightly metallic tasting soup and managed to swallow it by pinching his nose. Even with that strategy, he grimaced and complained about the probability of food poisoning.

Lareina ignored him, letting her eyes drift across countertops and through a doorway leading into a dark room. The house looked huge from the outside, and she imagined four large bedrooms, all decorated with curtains and matching bedspreads, all with their own bathrooms that contained long, deep bathtubs. Bedrooms meant clothes. According to the stories, every house contained excess clothing. With her hunger satisfied, the discomfort of her sopping clothes clinging to her skin demanded her full attention.

"Where are you going?" he asked when she was halfway to the door.

"Upstairs to find some dry clothes."

"Rochelle, this isn't our house. All of this stuff belongs to someone else."

The new name felt more authentic with every passing minute. She could feel herself slipping into a new life, shedding her old problems, and running toward something bright. There would be no going back, only forward. She continued toward the door. "No one's coming back here, Nick. They're all gone."

Gone. All gone. Those words echoed through her head and followed her up the wide stairway. *The saddest notions are those that are true.* She had read that phrase in a book, but she couldn't remember which one.

Silently, she padded across the soft carpet and into the first room at the top of the stairs. Never in her life had she encountered so much pink. The walls were painted pale pink, the bedspread matched, and even the carpet, although a darker shade, shared the color scheme. Three dolls sat on the bed and a pile of teddy bears guarded the corner.

Gliding over to the bed, she picked up a doll wearing a green dress. She had never owned a doll, or much more than the clothes on her back for that matter. The air grew thicker, heavier, almost painful to force into her lungs as she thought of the little girl who once slept in that room.

"Please let her be safe out there," she whispered. After carefully replacing the doll exactly where she had found it, she wandered across the hall.

In the next room clothes covered the floor; sheets, pillows, and blankets spilled off the bed to add to the chaos. Two posters—one depicting a man holding a basketball and the other a guy balancing a soccer ball on his knee—covered one wall.

She pulled a t-shirt out of the closet and held it up. *Perhaps a little big for Nick,* she thought, *but at least it's dry.* After a quick search of the room she also found a pair of sweatpants, a pair of jeans, and a clean pair of socks.

Leaving her new finds for Nick in a pile at the top of the staircase, she crossed the hall, passed a bathroom, and entered the last room. It was simple enough with white walls, beige carpet, and a green comforter on the neatly made bed. Two dressers lined one wall, but she headed to the closet. One side contained button-up shirts, black slacks, and an assortment of ties in different patterns. The other side housed skirts, slacks, blouses, and dresses hanging according to color. Selecting a pale blue dress, she held it up in front of her. She didn't allow herself to look in the mirror because she would want to keep the dress, but it wouldn't help her to survive. Instead, she returned it to the closet and chose a belt from a hook then reluctantly closed the door and crossed the room.

Each drawer of the dresser revealed new surprises. Jeans, t-shirts, shorts, sweaters—all stuffed the drawers so full she had to yank them open. Leaving her old clothes in a pile on the carpet, she dressed in the clean, dry t-shirt and jeans she chose from the assortment. Sitting down in front of the dressing table mirror, she picked up a brush and ran it through her tangled hair. The reflection looking back at her was exactly who she expected to see—the same long black hair, the same thin face, and the same wide brown eyes.

But I'm not Lareina anymore.

"Hello. My name is Rochelle Aumont," she whispered. A smile formed on her lips. She liked the way the name sounded and the freedom that accompanied her new identity. The name conjured memories of warmth, the promise of family, and a forced goodbye from the only place she'd ever wanted to stay.

Would they welcome her back if they found out she became a thief and fugitive? Would they remember her eight years later? Would they even be there anymore? She closed her eyes and saw the blue-and-white stripes on the awning above the candy store, felt warm sunlight filtering through green trees in the park, smelled cookies baking at Rochelle's house. She opened her eyes and felt a slight disappointment at finding herself back in a dark bedroom with only her reflection for company.

"I'll go back there," she whispered to the mirror. Rochelle would remember her—she had promised. Even if Galloway followed her outside of San Antonio, he would stop before she got to Nebraska. "I'll be safe and warm. I'll have a family." A family—the one thing she couldn't steal from the market, the one thing she wanted more than anything else. "Everything I want is out there, and it's time for me to start running toward it." Her mirror image smiled and nodded in agreement.

CHAPTER 3

To distract herself from the storm outside, Lareina explored the house. She made several trips downstairs to deliver dry clothes and then blankets to Nick. Framed photos in the hallway captivated her as she observed a family of four laughing, celebrating, and enjoying life together. The contradiction between those pictures and her own memories transformed the cozy house into a reminder of her own lack of a family.

When she came down the stairs, Nick was resting on the couch covered by a blanket. His leg rested on a pile of pillows propped up on the coffee table. His head rested against the back of the couch, eyes closed, chest rising, falling, rising, falling. After all of his protesting about stealing and breaking the law, he sat on someone else's couch, wrapped up in someone else's blanket, and wore someone else's clothes. She almost felt proud.

He looked comfortable, as if he'd lived there for years, while she couldn't be still without an uneasy feeling creeping through every cell of her body. Whether it stemmed from the storm beating against the windows or the thought that ghosts of the former occupants watched her examine their things, she couldn't be sure.

"There doesn't seem to be anything unusual about this house," she announced, walking into the living room. She wanted to wake Nick, to hear another human voice that would chase away the ghosts and distract her from the clamor outside.

Nick opened his eyes and sat up straighter. "Did you hope to find something more valuable than an old can of soup?"

Sinking into a recliner, she turned sideways to see him. Why wouldn't he—why wouldn't anyone—expect a thief to steal at every chance presented? Nevertheless, she couldn't prevent contempt from sliding into her voice. "No, I just wanted to get to know the people who used to live here. Curiosity isn't a crime, Nick."

"And rummaging through their things is polite," he muttered.

She turned away and leaned her head against soft fabric. There had to be a way to turn the conversation toward something they could agree on. "So, what inspired you to become a runaway?"

"A runaway from what?" His voice rose in confusion with each word.

Lareina laughed and leaned forward. "The Orphan Redistribution Institution, of course. You know, ORI. You don't have to be ashamed. I'm one of them too."

Nick's eyes narrowed in a way that made her want to travel back in time and avoid asking that question. A second ticked by on the wall clock, then two, then twenty.

"I'm not running away from anything and I'm not one of you."

She slumped back in the chair and closed her eyes. The words he hadn't vocalized—*I'm better than whatever you are and you better not forget it*—stung worse than any he had spoken. Tears welled in her eyes, a few of them landing in warm drops on the back of her hand. Rarely did anything make her cry, and never did she allow anyone to see her tears. *Remain silent. Slow breath in, slow breath out.*

After several minutes of silence, Nick cleared his throat.

"I'm sorry. I didn't mean it to come out that way." Only a low rumble of thunder replied. Those words weren't enough and she couldn't guarantee she had control over her voice. He continued, his voice small again. "My family died last month from the fever so I decided to come to Texas and find an old friend. She's the closest thing to family I have left."

"I'm sorry to hear that." She turned her face away from Nick, not wanting to see him cry. "It can't be easy to be on your own so suddenly."

A minute passed before he answered. "It's definitely been rough, but once I find my friend everything will be okay."

At least you have one person, she thought. *And at least you know what it feels like to have a family at all.* She remembered the thin file she'd walked from New Orleans to San Antonio to see. It had taken her three years to find out where she came from and locate the New Beginnings Home for Children. Two weeks passed before she convinced the director to let her see the file.

An entire lifetime of questions had tickled the tips of her fingers as she opened the tan folder. Inside she found a document listing her name and a physical description of her two-year-old self. Beneath that, a clipped newspaper article.

Toddler Discovered in Pasture

A child estimated to be two years old was discovered walking around a pasture north of town. When asked, she told authorities her name is Lareina. She hasn't given a last name or any indication of her parents' whereabouts. Lareina is currently in the custody of the New Beginnings Home for Children. If anyone has any information regarding the parents or guardians of this child, please contact the sheriff's office.

The date, written in faded ink at the bottom of the page, was August 2, 2075.

She had shaken the folder, examined the description document and newspaper clipping, held them up to the light, read them each a dozen times, searched the floor around her feet, but nothing new materialized.

Her questions had no answers. Her life began at age two, if the authorities had estimated correctly. She had no birthday, no family, no last name. No one cared that she existed and no one would notice when she ceased to exist.

"I'll be able to find her, right?" Nick's question interrupted her disheartenment.

A flash of lightning brought the room back into focus and Lareina back into the present. For a second she wanted to tell him no, to dash his hopes, to make him feel what she felt, but she didn't want anyone to experience such stifling isolation.

She cleared her throat but kept her face turned away from Nick. "What's her name?"

"Ava Welch. We used to live right next door to each other in Omaha, but her family moved away a few years ago. Her dad was some kind of scientist and I think he was transferred to San Antonio." He seemed to be talking to himself, reconstructing events from memory.

"You're from Omaha?" she asked with interest, this time turning to face him.

"Yeah, why?"

"I used to live a few hours away from there." Finally, something in common. "How long have you been looking for Ava?"

"Since my train got here three weeks ago."

"You had money for a train ticket?" She sat up, forgetting about her tears.

"I had enough to get here and apparently enough for two weeks of food and supplies, but now . . ."

"I was afraid at first too, but all you get for begging is hunger, and the mosquito bites and sunburns aren't worth sleeping outside."

"If you're such an expert, how long have you been a . . . runaway?" Nick sounded both annoyed and hesitant to use her terminology.

"Since I was twelve, so five years now."

"Is living like this really better than what you're running from?"

"The institution doesn't pay families to host orphans in their homes, and the laws about orphan treatment aren't enforced." She shook her head and lowered her voice. "Replacement families make us work to repay the resources we use. For any reason, they can decide to ship you off to a home for children or another replacement family that needs temporary housekeepers and gardeners. They barely feed you, and sometimes lock you in the basement or attic so you can't escape. I'm not any worse off now than I was then, and at least I'm free."

A low rumble of thunder shook the house. Both of them jumped.

Lareina walked over to the window and stared out at the dark sky. She couldn't see anything except during brief bursts of lightning. "Maybe we should have found a house with a basement."

"It's just a thunderstorm. Get some sleep." Nick squirmed into position so his legs stretched across the couch and his head rested against the softest pillow from upstairs.

Back in the recliner, she pulled a light blanket up to her chin. It wasn't really cold, but the blanket was comforting.

"Good night, Nick."

"Good night, Rochelle."

Despite the comfort of a warm, dry shelter, sleep didn't come easy. She remembered trying to fall asleep in an attic in Minnesota as a storm raged outside; she remembered her first night as a runaway, sheltering in a yellow tunnel slide at the park; she remembered the thrill that energized her fingers like a superpower when she picked her first lock. She tried to remember her parents, tried to picture their faces, tried to understand how she wound up alone in a pasture, but despite the vivid memories haunting her mind, she had no memories to answer the most important questions always lapping against the edges of her brain.

The warmth of sun on her face invited Lareina to open her eyes. Sitting up inch by inch, she glanced around the room. Outside, a bright sunrise in a blue sky brightened the neighborhood. Nick slept on, a blanket tangled around his feet, pillow slipping halfway to the floor.

Based on the angle of the sun's rays on the carpet, it was seven o'clock, no later than eight. Leaning forward, she slid slowly off the chair to avoid waking Nick.

Illuminated by daylight, the room felt small, cramped, like a trap. She tiptoed across the floor and slipped out the front door. Fluffs of cotton glittered in sunlight as they drifted on the cool breeze. Breathing in the rain-cleaned air—like cool water against sunburned skin—brought her a sense of calm and hope.

She walked down the street, past quiet houses still untouched by the decay she knew would creep in with destructive fingers. A windstorm would pry off a shingle or smash a tree branch through a window, allowing rain to drip into attics and bead across windowsills. Mold would find a home along with squirrels and raccoons. Fall breezes would send leaves skittering across kitchen counters and carefully made beds. Roofs would collapse, foundations would crack, and soon the neighborhood would be an unrecognizable heap of rotten wood and broken furniture.

Windows glinted in the morning sun, and she imagined a man stepping out to pick up his newspaper, a woman jogging down the street pushing a stroller, a car pulling out of a driveway to carry its driver to work. What should be. What would never be again.

Turning away, she let the image fade from her mind. She wanted to keep walking, to get far away, to enter the horizon glowing with sunlight that promised a never-ending day of clear travel weather. Instead she turned back, took her time walking down the street, continued through the front door of her temporary residence, and tiptoed past Nick.

In the kitchen, she found the bag of raisins, popped them into her mouth one at a time, and wondered if Galloway found a way across the torrent of water. She wondered how far he would follow her. She wondered how long she could outrun him. She wondered too many things that would spoil the gift of a sunny cool day in the middle of summer.

"Rochelle?" Nick called from the living room. She stuffed a handful of raisins into her mouth and focused on chewing. "Rochelle? Are you still here?" His voice grew louder then faded to a whimper. "Rochelle?"

She walked to the doorway carrying the bag of raisins. He sat straight up on the couch, and when his glance landed on her, he leaned back and took a breath, a glimmer of a smile playing at the corners of his mouth. Patches of curly hair stuck up like antennas stretching out of his skull while the rest lay smashed flat against his head.

"I thought maybe you left already." His voice was a low hum of drowsiness and relief.

Surprised at Nick's response to her presence, she crossed the room, sat down on the coffee table across from him, and offered the bag of raisins.

"Thanks." He smiled and pulled out a handful.

"How's your ankle?"

He flexed his left foot up and down then twisted it left and right. "I think it's feeling better."

"You think you'll be okay to walk on it?" The muscles in her neck and shoulders slackened as the weight of obligation lifted away.

Nick chewed and swallowed a handful of raisins then reached for another. "Yeah, I'll be all right."

"That's great news." The perfect weather and uncertainty about Galloway's whereabouts made her eager to start walking. "It's been great meeting you, but I have to keep moving."

"Wait, what's the rush?" He dropped his raisins on the coffee table and swung his legs off the couch. His uncombed hair and wide eyes made him look like a frightened child.

"I have friends expecting me." She'd never see Nick again— what would it matter if he knew the truth? But she heard the hesitation in her voice and immediately regretted it.

"What are you running from?" Concern spilled out of his voice. Concern for her safety or his own?

"I'm running from a detective," she admitted.

Leaning away from her, he pushed deep into the cushions as if he couldn't get far enough away. "I should have known," he whispered. "What did you do?"

Lareina rolled her eyes. "I didn't do anything."

He folded his arms across his chest and studied her. "I don't believe you."

"You shouldn't. But don't worry about it. I'm leaving and you'll never see me again." She picked up her backpack, secured both straps over her shoulders, and was halfway to the front door before Nick spoke.

"Wait, Rochelle. Maybe we could travel together for a while. Where are you headed?"

"I'm going north." She didn't want to leave him with any specific information in case Galloway interviewed him, and she certainly didn't want him tagging along.

"Oh," he sighed. Was he disappointed? "I have to stick around San Antonio to find Ava."

"We're going in opposite directions."

"I guess so. Are you sure you'll be all right out there, all alone?"

Sun splashed across the top of the couch, growing brighter, warmer, urging action while it lasted. Her foot tapped lightly against the floor, matching the staccato rhythm of the clock, reminding her of time slipping through her fingers like water. Would *she* be okay? She hadn't been the one to fall into a trap.

But also . . . had anyone ever cared whether she would be all right?

"I can take care of myself." She took another step toward the door. "Will you be okay?"

Nick nodded and looked down at his ankle, his face slightly red from a lingering sunburn she hadn't noticed the night before. He had no food, less money, and his will to survive wasn't strong enough to justify stealing.

Shrugging her bag off her shoulders, she caught it by the strap, reached inside and fished out three of her six candy bars. The ones she had planned to save for her most desperate moment of starvation. She could manage.

"Here." She held out the candy, golden wrappers glinting.

His eyes shifted, eyebrows raised, mouth opened, and she could see the protest rising within him, but just as abruptly it faded. He reached out and accepted the candy bars.

"Thanks. I really couldn't have made it without your help." Nick forced a smile and Lareina replaced her bag. She met his glance and matched his smile, then turned away and passed through the door without looking back.

Down the front walk, up the street, one block, two blocks, three, six. *Distance makes goodbye easier,* she told herself as she started north toward Austin. Sometimes on stormy days she had sat in the library looking through books of maps, plotting routes to a new life. She hadn't been brave enough to leave San Antonio in the two years since she'd arrived there searching for her family. Another city would offer food and shelter, voices and sounds. She could find a job, make some money, and forget about Galloway as she prepared to travel north to the only people she knew cared about her.

CHAPTER 4

After hours of misery under the sweltering August sun, Lareina decided to find shade and try traveling at night. Walking under the stars brought her a sense of peace, and she told herself the darkness would cloak her from Galloway. She dozed through the day and woke in the late evening as locusts began their buzzing decrescendo. When the first morning light streaked the sky with pink ruffles, she found the shadow of a tall tree and tried to rest.

Fortunately the weather remained clear, but the consequences of previous storms found her in the form of a washed out bridge and one section of a northbound road still deep under water. When she couldn't continue forward, she backtracked to the nearest intersection and tried a new route. For four nights, she walked over cracked concrete, taking directions from sparsely placed signs pointing her toward Austin.

The sweltering heat of the day made her sleep restless. Most days she couldn't keep her eyes closed for longer than thirty minutes at a time before Susan's hopeless face floated into her dreams, desperate and pleading.

Protect the pendant. Warn him.

Then she would sprint through a nightmare. Galloway chased her across an open field, but her feet didn't carry her any farther away from him. He grew closer and closer while she ran over the grass, trapped on a conveyor belt.

I'll find you no matter where you run.

She sat up gasping and drenched in sweat as if she'd

been running for hours. The leaves above her shimmered in lowering rays of the sun, fluttering against each other in the soft breeze. A symphony of crickets chirped in the grass all around her. Pulling the top of her shirt over her face, she wiped the sweat from her forehead, then slid it back down, making the landscape visible once again. Closing her eyes against the dull ache across her forehead, she coughed to temporarily relieve the feeling of sandpaper in her throat. For the two weeks she'd carried the pendant, her greatest fear had been Galloway finding her. Now that fear intertwined with the possibility of getting too sick to keep moving and dying alone. No one would ever know her story. No one would notice she was gone.

Bracing her hands against the tree's sturdy trunk, she pushed herself to her feet, scooped up her bag, and limped forward on blistered feet, determined to reach civilization. She hadn't seen a house, a person, or even a dog for three days. Cotton drifted lazily on the breeze. A tree branch creaked.

Lareina resolved to take better care of herself: eight hours of sleep, three meals a day, the most nutritious food she could find. She scanned the landscape for her usual foraging suspects: wild berry bushes, fruit trees, dandelions. None appeared on either side of the crumbling road she followed.

The familiar sound of rushing water caught her attention. She rubbed her watery eyes and examined the road ahead, fearing more flood damage, but an unbroken ribbon of concrete stretched ahead of her as far as she could see.

Relieved to find a functioning bridge, she paused to watch the swollen creek swoosh along below her like a slow-moving train. Large rocks obstructed the flow in places, slowing the water down and causing it to foam as it lapped over the obstacles. Starvation or fever? Which would be worse? Did she have a choice? She flattened the back of her hand against her forehead, but it didn't feel any warmer than usual.

Splunk . . . splunk . . . splunk.

Waist-high grass swayed in the breeze as far as she could see on both sides of the creek. Wispy clouds turned orange against the hazy blue of a late evening sky.

Splunk . . . splunk.

The unfamiliar sound took a moment to register in her tired mind. An auditory trick? An echo? She scanned the path of the creek looking for jumping fish, but instead glimpsed a rock fling itself out of the grass and into the water with a *splunk.* She waded into the grass to investigate.

Not far from the bridge, one rock and then another splashed into the muddy water. Rubbing her forehead, she walked forward.

Splunk . . . splunk . . . splunk . . . splunk.

A small hand clutching a rock let go at the top of the arch, sending it into the creek. One more step and the hand attached to an arm, and finally a little girl, not yet tall enough to see over the grass that swayed around her. Even with footsteps crunching toward her, the girl remained too preoccupied with her activity to notice.

"Hello," Lareina said when she stood four steps away.

"Hi," the girl replied, calmly turning toward her.

A child estimated to be two years old was discovered walking around a pasture. The words of the article haunted her. Had she been afraid? Had she been crying when they found her? Or had she been oblivious like this little girl, sure someone would come along to take her home.

"What are you doing out here all by yourself?"

"I'm lost." The little girl suddenly sounded a bit frightened as if she just remembered.

Hunching down on one knee, Lareina positioned herself at eye level with the child. Helping the little girl could mean a day of lost travel, and the risk of Galloway catching up with her. She let her eyes follow the creek off into the distance, then brought them back to the whimpering child. *Just walk away,* she told herself. *She's probably been abandoned out here, and you can't take care of her.*

As she stood, the words on the initial document in her file flashed through her mind.

Child's Name: Lareina (last name unknown)

Birthdate: Spring of '73 (estimated)

Status: Abandoned at two years of age. No success locating the parents. No note left with the child. No evidence the child will ever be reclaimed.

She tried not to, but she always pictured her parents somewhere warm and sunny, swaying in a hammock and sipping lemonade without her. *How could they just leave me?* That question had repeated in her mind for as long as she could remember. The two people who were supposed to love her more than anything in the world had left her to fend for herself. With no further leads in her file and nowhere to go, she had remained in San Antonio for two years.

Never had she shared her story with anyone else. They would make fun of her. They would blame her. It was her own weakness allowing herself to be hurt by parents she'd never met and her own failure that they didn't love her. The loneliness felt like a stack of bricks on her chest, like a blanket pulled away on the coldest winter day, like an eternal field of grass she couldn't see past.

She rested her left knee on the ground once more. "What's your name?"

"Abbie," the girl whispered.

"My name is Rochelle. Come on, I'll help you find your family."

She extended her hand and Abbie grasped it tightly. The amount of trust the child displayed surprised her. *She doesn't know any better,* she reminded herself, then wondered if she had trusted her rescuer long ago.

Hand in hand through fading daylight, they walked down a path of trampled grass that the child must have followed. Abbie chattered away, telling stories about her parents and sisters. Nodding and responding when the girl looked up, Lareina silently prayed that whoever they found wanted their child back. She wanted Abbie to have time to make more happy memories, memories that she would be old enough to remember.

Thousands of fireflies twinkled as they hovered over the grass. All shades of blue faded from the sky and stars glowed overhead.

A firefly brushed against Abbie's cheek and she giggled. "If you catch one and it lights up in your hand, you get to make a wish."

Lareina smiled despite the pulsing twinge behind her eyes. "That sounds pretty neat. Have you ever caught one?"

Abbie held her hand tighter and swung their arms up and back as she skipped along. "One time. I wished for a kitten, and the next day my sister Amy found four kittens under our porch."

"Whoa, you wished for one and got four. You must be magic."

She reached out and swiped a firefly from the air while Abbie talked about her kittens. If only magic did exist. In the cool night air with stars shining above and firefly lights drifting all around, she tried to believe in magic, in wishes, in hope for something better. A soft glow emanated from inside her loosely clenched fist. *I wish I didn't have to run alone.* She opened her hand and a dimming glow floated off through the darkness, surged bright one more time, then vanished into the glittering grass.

The field opened onto a muddy dirt road with traces of gravel down the middle. "I know where we are," Abbie squealed. "My house is this way." She took off quickly, skipping down the road and pulling her new companion along behind her. They only walked for a few minutes before the outline of a small, cabin-like blue house appeared in the miles of flat darkness. Bright lights glowed in the two front windows framed by white shutters and window boxes displaying blooming flowers.

"There she is," a small, high-pitched voice yelled from somewhere ahead. The shadowy silhouettes, one tall and two much shorter, moved down the front walk toward them.

Abbie pulled Lareina up to the house. A woman with frizzled brown hair wearing a yellow sundress watched them approach Two little girls, who appeared to be about five and seven years old, hid behind their mother, peering out curiously at the stranger holding their sister's hand.

Suddenly feeling self-conscious about her appearance, Lareina smoothed her hair away from her face. Over the past four days, she hadn't paid much attention to cleanliness besides brushing her teeth and occasionally washing her face. Her hope had been to arrive in Austin within two or three days, but as much as she hated to admit it, after all of the backtracking and searching for a way around swollen waterways, she was hopelessly lost.

The little girl ran to her mother, who scooped her up and held her tight. "Abbie Mae, don't you ever wander off and scare me like this again."

She whispered something in her mother's ear and the woman turned back to the unkempt teenager who had brought her daughter home.

"Thank you. We were frantic looking for her." The woman had a warm, comforting voice, the kind of voice Lareina imagined her own mother would have.

"It was no problem."

"My name is Sarah, this is Annie and Amy, and I guess you've already met Abbie."

She smiled. "It's nice to meet all of you. I'm Rochelle."

"You shouldn't be out here all by yourself." Sarah's concern showed in the creases of her forehead and the preoccupied frown forming on her lips. She didn't see an orphan, a thief, or a fugitive standing in front of her, but a little girl traveling through the dangers of darkness alone.

"I'm actually on my way to Austin to meet my family." The lie was much more acceptable than the truth.

"We haven't had supper yet. Why don't you come on in and eat with us," Sarah offered.

"I should really keep moving." Although spoken politely, the words came out flat. Hunger gnawed at the ever-growing void in her ribcage. The promise of food triumphed over any fear of judgment or determination to reach the city by morning.

"Nonsense, you look half-starved and exhausted, plus it's awfully dangerous around here at night. Why don't you spend the night here and start out again in the morning?"

Clearly Sarah wouldn't take no for an answer unless Lareina could come up with a more urgent reason requiring her to travel at night. She tried to formulate a story of a sick grandpa or a need to deliver money to save her starving siblings, but her headache weakened her resolve. She nodded and allowed Sarah to usher her into the little house, which felt refreshingly cool.

Although she offered more than once, Sarah refused any help with preparing dinner. Instead Lareina sat at the table and watched the girls clothe their dolls in lacy, velvet dresses. She rested her elbow on the table and used her hand to support her chin. Sarah lit a fire in the old stove, dumped two jars of liquid into a pot, and stirred while it heated. The entire time, she talked about the floods, her garden, and her husband, who had traveled to the city to trade for supplies.

"How far is Austin from here?"

"At least half a day of walking if you know all the trails." Sarah glanced back at the table. "Are you all right, honey? You look awfully pale."

"I have a bad headache. I might be getting sick." Her stomach twisted with the thought that she might have exposed such kind people to something terrible like the fever.

Sarah didn't recoil or ask her guest to leave. Instead, she crossed the room and rested a cold hand against her forehead. "Well, you aren't running a fever—that's a good sign. You might have a cold, but I bet you just need a good meal and some rest."

The reassuring words calmed her fears but couldn't relieve the aching that streaked across her temples. With the necessity of pretending removed, she rested her head on her arms and closed her eyes. *What would I do if I were alone in a field right now? What if I were running from Galloway?* The questions pounded in her head despite every attempt to push them away.

CHAPTER 5

After dinner, which was some of the best food Lareina had eaten in months, the girls disappeared into another room. Sarah walked over to the sink, pushed the faucet up, and let water surge into a large pot. It echoed with a metallic ring as if someone struck a bell. "Does your head feel any better?"

"I can barely tell it even hurt." She could still feel a dull ache behind her eyes, but the throbbing had subsided. "You were right. I guess I was just hungry."

Sarah carried the full pot over to the stove and hoisted it onto a burner, then returned to the sink and began to fill another one. "You just stay right there and rest. I can tell you aren't completely well yet. I'll have this water heated up for your bath in a little while."

"You don't have to go through the extra work for me, Sarah. It's getting late and I don't want to keep you up." She needed Sarah to go to sleep so she could sneak out and keep walking.

"Oh honey, I have three kids under the age of eight. I don't usually get much sleep." She laughed. "How long has it been since you've seen your parents?"

Watching Sarah walk back and forth from the sink, to the stove, to the little bathroom off the kitchen provided time to fabricate the perfect story. "About a year. I was staying in San Antonio with my grandma for a while, but now my cousin is going to stay with her."

"It must be difficult to have so many miles between your family like that."

"Oh, it is. No matter where I am, I always miss someone."

Finally, Sarah led her into the bathroom where a full tub of water waited. "Take your time." She placed some towels on the counter and left the room.

In less than a minute, Lareina removed her stiff clothes and sank into the warm water that seemed to simultaneously support and engulf her. Minutes passed and she remained still, letting the water lap against her chin, the pendant shifting slightly against her chest. Reaching for the oddly shaped necklace, she cringed with the memory of how it had become hers.

Three weeks earlier she had been standing in the market surveying a bakery cart from which she hoped to snatch a loaf of bread.

"Excuse me." The voice behind her exuded confidence and contained a musical quality like wind chimes in a soft breeze. "Could you help me find someone I'm looking for? I'll pay you."

The girl wore black slacks and a blazer with her blond hair twisted back into a bun and pale skin accustomed to shelter. She would pay three hundred dollars to the person who helped her find a Dr. Iverson, an old friend of her father's. She hadn't seen him in three years, but she had to ask him a question.

Three hundred dollars. Enough money to buy food for a year, to pay for a hotel room and take dozens of warm showers, to buy new shoes that didn't pinch her toes. Lareina knew her way around the city better than she knew her own shadow and eagerly agreed to what sounded like the easiest money she would ever make.

The girl introduced herself as Susan Andrews with a slight hesitation and a pitch that rose when it should have fallen. She was lying about something, but everyone lied about little things.

Every morning the two of them met outside of Susan's hotel and they worked to find the home of the elusive Dr. Iverson. Within a year's time he had moved from a mansion in a gated neighborhood, to a smaller house outside of San Antonio, to a hotel room on the south side of the city, to an apartment at the center of San Antonio. Lareina became frustrated after the third building they approached, only to find out the doctor didn't live there anymore. She herself was homeless and didn't move that much. Was this doctor involved in something illegal? Selling guns to criminals? Writing false prescriptions? Scamming people through his medical practice? By the fourth day of searching, she wanted five hundred dollars to cover any risks.

"It's not what you think," Susan explained. She looped her finger through a chain on her neck and slipped the pendant from inside her shirt. "This is what I have to talk to him about."

Lareina barely glanced at the little black triangle that looked like plastic children's jewelry. "What is it?"

Susan's eyes darted up and down the sidewalk in front of the crumbling apartment building, Dr. Iverson's last known address. She squeezed the pendant against her palm before it vanished beneath her shirt. "That's what I have to find out. You have to trust me that it's important."

Together they walked up to the front of the building and into a long hallway of doors. They found apartment 28B at the end of the hallway. Susan knocked once and the door slid into the room. She gasped and froze with her hand still poised to knock. The color drained from her cheeks, leaving her freckles pronounced like drops of ink sprinkled across new snow.

Taking a step forward, Lareina peered around the doorframe. A few feet in front of them, a large red splotch stained the carpet.

"We have to get out of here now," Susan whispered before rushing back down the hall. In a narrow alley, she slumped against a wall and slid to the ground. "It's too late." She shivered in a tiny huddle with her arms wrapped around her knees. "It's too late."

Lareina's breathing quickened as she tried to grasp the kind of trouble this stranger had involved her in. She wanted to walk away but couldn't protect herself without understanding the situation. "You have to tell me what's happening so we can figure out what to do next." Sliding to the ground, she put a hand on Susan's arm.

"You saw the blood." Her typically melodic voice shook and became a muffled clash of cymbals. "They already got him and now nothing will stop them from coming for me." She finally looked up but her blank eyes seemed to stare at something through the brick wall in front of them.

A sweltering summer sun beat down on Lareina, forming beads of sweat across her forehead, but she shivered. She tried to swallow, but all moisture had evaporated from her mouth, maybe her entire body. "Who will come for you?"

Susan shook her head and rubbed a hand through her hair, pulling blond strands loose to flap across her face. "The man, Russ Galloway. He claimed to be a detective, but he works for them. He wanted to talk to my dad about a project he worked on six years ago. He killed my parents." She tried to catch her breath in wheezing gasps. "He'll do anything to get the pendant."

"Why don't you just give it to him?" The pendant didn't have any inherent worth that she could see. A loaf of bread would be more valuable.

Susan shook her head and gripped Lareina's wrists so tight she thought her bones would snap. "No. My dad sent me away with it so they wouldn't find it. He said it would be the end of everything, of all of us . . . and his eyes. I'd never seen him . . . scared in my life, but when he gave this to me . . ." She looked down and blinked away a tear. "You can never tell another person about this."

"I won't." The promise rose out of fearful uncertainty.

Releasing her grip, Susan fell back against the wall, sobbing with her forehead against her scrunched knees.

"But I don't want to be a part of any of this." Standing, she brushed off her clothes, took a few steps toward the street, and then turned around. Sighing, she sank back down to the ground and waited until her acquaintance's sobs faded to whimpers.

"I left everything at the hotel . . . all of my money." Susan sniffled. "I can't go back there. It might be a trap."

"Maybe I can—"

"No," she interrupted. "If he's been watching us then he'll recognize you. It's too dangerous."

"But he is a detective. He's caught me stealing before and let me off with a lecture. He'll just think—"

"I said no." Susan's eyes narrowed. "You have to believe me." She slid her hand into her pocket and finally took a full breath. "I have my train ticket, but it's for three days from now." She looked to her only ally, helplessly.

"I'll help you hide until you can get a train out of the city." How could she abandon someone so unequipped to survive? After all, she wished someone had been there to guide her through the times she felt alone and hopeless.

Susan stretched her legs out in front of her and stared at her shoes. "I won't be able to pay you before I leave."

"You can get the money to me when you're safe."

For three days they crept through the city, sneaking from alley to alley, hiding in the shadows, ghosts traveling the streets unseen by any human eyes. On the last night they sat crouched behind a dumpster in a cluttered alley. Susan often complained of hunger and an inability to sleep. She wasn't used to going without, but stealing enough food for even one person often proved difficult.

"I haven't told you the worst part of the story." Her voice shook, barely audible over the rumble of a nearby air conditioner. "My dad had two of these pendants once. They were in a jewelry box in his desk when I was a kid, and I took them for friendship necklaces. When we moved I put this one back, but he didn't realize the other one was missing until a few months ago."

"You mean there's another one of these?"

"More than that, I think. Dr. Iverson should have had one." She shifted her weight and rested her head against her knees. "My friend is out there and he has no idea what kind of danger he's in because of me."

Lareina pulled her feet closer to her body to avoid drips falling from a window air conditioner above. "You didn't know."

"I loved him, I think, but we had to move away. We just left in the middle of the night so I never got to say goodbye. I didn't know it was because of the pendants."

Another air conditioner clattered to life, a car rumbled down the street, a dozen dogs barked in staccato yelps then yielded to the sirens of a police car screaming in the distance. For a long time they both remained silent.

"Lareina?"

"Yeah?"

"If something happens to me, you won't let him have the pendant, right?"

"Nothing's going to happen."

"But if it does?"

"I won't let him have it."

The next day Galloway spotted them at the train station. They made it to the tree line but Susan wasn't accustomed to running. She wasn't fast enough to escape the detective's bullets.

CHAPTER 6

Lareina dressed in the clean clothes from her bag and carefully rearranged the pendant so it would be hidden under her shirt. Since the day Susan's bloody fingers had pressed it into her hand, she hadn't taken it off for fear it would be lost or stolen.

"I won't let him have it." Speaking the words out loud renewed the promise. "I'll never tell anyone."

Stepping out of the bathroom, she yawned and walked into the living room where Sarah placed a sheet and pillow on the couch. Standing in the doorway, backpack resting on the ground beside her, she imagined her head sinking into the feather pillow. Only for a minute and then it would be time to go.

Sarah turned around and smiled. "Oh there you are," she exclaimed. "I hope you'll be comfortable sleeping here. It took me a while to find an extra pillow."

"It looks really comfortable compared to my bed." Her back still ached from the lumpy ground she'd tried to sleep on earlier that day. *I can't stay. I can't stay.* The words repeated over and over in her mind, but her feet shuffled to the couch, and she sank down into the cool fabric. A blanket draped over her from her feet to her chin. Light faded from the room and outside crickets trilled their lonely song.

Twigs and washed out clumps of grass swirled through the murky torrent of a swollen creek. The constant roar of rushing water became a rumbling echo as it poured beneath a railroad bridge and lapped against the support beams. Glancing down at the map in her hand, Lareina smiled at Sarah's cartoon drawing of the structure right in front of her.

Only an hour earlier Sarah had packed a huge bag of deer jerky and a loaf of freshly baked bread. She wanted to send more but couldn't squeeze even the smallest morsel more into Lareina's backpack already stuffed with her belongings. She hugged Sarah and the girls each twice before they walked her down to the end of the dirt road, then her footsteps padded along alone as she waved goodbye to the strangers who had treated her like family.

A pulsing *clack-clack-clack* resonated in the distance. She watched the tracks as the ground rumbled, then a harsh whistle announced the coming train that rattled past her. One, two, three . . . The outflow of air from the rushing train twisted her hair around and across her face. Twenty-three, twenty-four, twenty-five . . . Sunlight glinted off glass in passenger cars revealing the figures of people traveling in comfort. Thirty-seven, thirty-eight, thirty-nine . . . The last car rushed past and a still silence settled over the landscape.

Thirty-nine cars carrying people, food, soap, coffee, and clothes. Each person, each item, had a destination, a place to go where someone waited. The beginning of an idea bloomed as the retreating train punctured the horizon. Trains had been a constant, a familiarity she'd come to expect no matter where the ORI sent her to live. She traveled by train whenever they transferred her to a new Home for Children or replacement parents. However, since running away from her last Home for Children, she hadn't been able to afford a ticket and had been too scared to risk stowing away. In the best-case scenario she would be sent to the nearest home for children. She could also be arrested. And then there was the possibility she would be killed on the spot. It all depended on who discovered her.

I could travel so much faster, without blisters, without worrying about Galloway catching me. She wondered how far north the tracks could take her and remembered the little train station in Maibe always swarming with people. *Could Galloway find me a thousand miles away? Is he even following me anymore?* She hadn't encountered him since the flooded bridge almost a week earlier, which offered hope that he would never find her again.

An arrow on Sarah's map prompted her to cross the railroad bridge and follow the tracks the rest of the way to Austin. During the next hour, two more trains raced along the tracks, both traveling away from Austin. The dewy grass soaked her feet, causing her wet shoes to slap with each step. Her worn right shoe gaped in the front leaving her toes exposed, and her left shoe had been fraying its way to the same fate for weeks. She would need to find new ones soon.

After miles of traveling in the scorching August sun without seeing a house or even a shed, the speck of a structure appeared on the horizon. It morphed from a windmill to a tree to a little blue house sitting eight feet off the railroad tracks.

Vines climbed the walls in thick tangles that pried beneath siding and edged through broken windows. She hesitated before testing the doorknob. A few wispy vines stretched across the doorway, but the rest looped to the side, as if pushed there. Stepping back, she listened to silence. A gust of wind lifted waxy leaves then dropped them back into place. Perhaps the vines had grown that way, unable to grasp any surface in the recess of the doorway. Perhaps someone slept inside or worse, waited to attack an intruder. Caution or courage? Blistered, chafed feet or the chance to find shoes without holes?

One twist of the knob and the door swung forward with a pitiful whimper. After a minute of watchful stillness, she walked into a sparsely furnished living room animated by shadows. Vines rustled in the windows, a tree branch scratched across crumbling shingles, and a train trilled in the distance. Empty cupboards, empty closets, and empty rooms greeted her as she searched the first floor. Frustrated, she ran to the top of the stairs.

In the room straight ahead, a box of brand-new shoes sat on the floor, open and waiting. Her confusion morphed into panic as Galloway's familiar scent of cinnamon woven with cedar reminded her of the dangers like a rumble of thunder alerts one to an oncoming storm. Her pulsing heart sank and her mouth went dry. Downstairs, footsteps pounded across the wooden floor. Time to plan, to think, to breathe dwindled with each footfall. *If something happens to me, you won't let Galloway have the pendant, right?*

The first stair groaned in an explosion of red fragments of sound. Darting into the room, she slammed the door shut as Galloway crashed against it from the other side. It bowed forward but held long enough for her to slide a single hook lock into place.

"Open this door." His voice rammed through the thin barrier between them. "You're trapped. There's nowhere for you to run."

She backed away from the door and picked up the pink-and-gray running shoes. Tags dangled from the shoelaces displaying a large black six. Exactly her size. Exactly what she needed.

"How did you know I needed new shoes?" It took less than

a minute to slip out of her tattered sneakers and pull the new ones onto her feet.

"They looked pretty pathetic when you pulled that tightrope routine last week. I figured you'd find a way to follow the railroad tracks." The detective laughed a low chuckle.

Determined to escape, she unlocked the window and attempted to shove the bottom upward. Her hands slipped and her shoulder knocked hard against solid glass. Outside, a large tree branch squeaked against the windowpane. The window didn't move. She examined the sill and found a nail jammed through.

Why did you choose the only room with glass in the window? Because you needed shoes. How could you walk into such a simple trap? Never again.

"Just slide the pendant under the door," Galloway threatened. "If I have to break this door down, you'll spend the rest of your life in a San Antonio prison."

"What are you going to do with it?" Her main goal was to keep him talking, but if she got answers in the process, all the better. She tried to pry her fingers under the window.

"I've already told you. It's not for me." The gruffness in his voice softened. "I'm under orders to retrieve that pendant by any means necessary."

Squeezing her fingers beneath the nail, she pulled upward. Her fingers burned, but the nail didn't move. She tried twisting the nail, then wiggling it back and forth. It didn't budge. "So when you killed Susan you were only doing your job?"

He stopped beating at the door. Either he had a new plan or the conversation was working to distract him.

"Yes, but I don't want anyone else to die over this thing," he shouted through the door. "I'm running out of time and they won't be as patient with me as I'm being with you."

Her fingers felt numb and tingly. The nail wasn't loosening. She had to keep stalling. "What do they need the pendant for?" She scanned the room for anything she could use to escape. The closet was empty and the only furniture was an old bed with musty blankets and a wooden chair.

"To protect the world from something worse than you can imagine." The usual bluntness returned to his voice, but Lareina, a practiced liar, noticed a telling change in pitch. It betrayed an emotion in Galloway that she never expected to discover.

"Funny, Susan told me the worst would happen if you got your hands on it." In the hallway, Galloway was silent. She crept to the chair and dragged it to the window, then fumbled to disengage the inside screen.

"What are you doing in there?" His voice dripped with impatience.

A muffled scraping filtered into the room and one hinge wobbled. He would remove the door before she could escape. *Talk to him. Distract him. Buy some more time.*

"What kind of detective are you? How could it take you an entire week to catch up with me?" she taunted.

"I'll admit you're pretty clever, but my plan was to get ahead of you and here we are."

She picked up the chair and smashed it through glass.

"What was that?" he shouted, but panic replaced anger.

"Thanks for the shoes."

Tearing a blanket from the bed, she tossed it over shards of glass on the sill before slipping through the window. Propelling herself from one sturdy tree branch to another, she scrambled over slick bark, swinging to the ground in seconds. Before the detective set foot outside the house, her new shoes met the ground and launched her forward.

Any disappointment for being outwitted vanished as her feet came back to life, floating over the ground in the only new shoes she'd ever owned. A sharp right turn through an overgrown field led into a thick grove of trees. It didn't matter where she was; her only priority was escaping the detective. Lareina didn't turn around, didn't flinch at twigs that scratched her face, didn't give up on pushing her feet through the tangle of slippery brush, but she felt Galloway's angry determination slither through the trees after her.

Sun filtered through a thick canopy, creating shadows across the ground. She sped out of the trees and into a park on the edge of a disintegrating town. Cutting across the small dirt parking lot, she rushed onto a bigger road that once upon a time was a quaint main street. Now, pieces of shingles, torn plastic bags, and broken furniture littered the cracked blacktop. A few more blocks and dilapidated houses with crooked awnings and shutters lined the street. The overhang of a porch rested against a house at a ninety-degree angle, and telephone poles strained against wires like dominoes ready to fall. The illusion of a slanted town made her dizzy and she couldn't catch her breath.

Keep running? Find a place to hide? How close is he?
Protect the pendant.

Stumbling to her right, she caught her balance and took off down another residential street, this one with larger yards. The road here was more deteriorated, and she had to watch her feet to avoid turning an ankle in the large potholes. Only when the road opened into a cul-de-sac did she realize that she was trapped.

Her feet skidded across loose rocks and sand covering the eroded pavement as she abruptly stopped. Crooked houses, storm-damaged trees, and decrepit fences blocked any escape.

She looked back up the road, afraid Galloway would appear at any time. There had to be a way out, a place to hide.

Out of place in its normalcy, the house directly ahead stood straight and retained all of its shingles. The only apparent defect was a hole in the latticed fencing around the bottom of the front porch.

Diving through the opening, she crawled back to the house's concrete foundation. Scrunching herself into the darkest corner, she clutched the pendant in her hand.

Light faded from the sidewalk, a cat crouched against the lattice then scurried away, dry leaves and dirty paper somersaulted down the street, but heavy black boots never clomped up to the house and Galloway's ranting shouts didn't disturb the peaceful evening. Using her backpack as a pillow, she drifted in and out of sleep. In her dreams, fields and towns rushed by through the window of a train. In her nightmares, Galloway gripped her ankle and dragged her from beneath the porch. Hours passed before morning sun found its way through the diamond-shaped gaps in the latticed fencing. Even as she crawled out, she scanned the street suspiciously.

"Hey, what are you doing under my porch." The small but powerful voice originated directly above her.

Startled, she froze and looked up at a boy, who appeared no older than eight, with his hands on his hips, staring down at her. She stood up and chased crumbled leaves from her clothes with one swipe of her hand. Although she towered a foot over the child, he didn't indicate the slightest sign of intimidation.

"I needed a place to sleep."

"Are you homeless?" The boy leaned forward with his arms

draped over the porch railing and observed her with eyes that reminded her of a rabbit's.

"I guess I am." Smiling, she considered all of the homes that never seemed to last.

The boy turned when the front door creaked open and two young girls walked out. They were just kids, the oldest about twelve and the younger one no older than ten.

"Who are you talking to, Shawn?" the older girl asked.

"This homeless girl," Shawn answered, gesturing. He turned to Lareina and added, "I'm protecting my sisters until my parents get back." Shawn clenched his hands into fists, as if ready to fight anyone who walked onto his property.

"Where did your parents go?"

"Austin to find food because we don't have any," the younger girl chimed in.

"They left yesterday and we don't know when they'll get back, but we're really hungry," the older girl explained.

Out of habit Lareina looked down the street behind her, but of course there was no one there. She sat down on the porch steps and unzipped her backpack, then pulled out the loaf of bread and the bag of dried deer meat Sarah had given her a day earlier. Berries and vegetables she'd found along the way had supplied most of her meals, allowing her to conserve the provisions in her bag. With their mouths slightly open, the children fixated on the food.

"I'll exchange this for some information," she said, looking at Shawn. "What's the fastest way to Austin from here?"

"If you walk back out to the main road and take a right, it's only four miles to the edge of the city, but there's a lot of fever there." Shawn seemed proud of his vast knowledge.

Four miles—that was closer than she could have hoped. "Is there a train station?"

He nodded. "Yeah, trains stop in the city all the time, but they might not let people on anymore because they're in quarantine."

She extended her hand to Shawn for a firm handshake. "Thank you, sir. You've been very helpful."

Reaching over the railing, she handed the food to the oldest girl. Stifled gasps and astonished smiles eased her regret at giving away an entire week of meals. *I can fend for myself and they can't,* she reminded herself as she slipped her backpack onto her shoulders.

"I hope your parents get back safely," she added before leaving the children behind. As she hurried down the street, away from the cul-de-sac, she hoped to pass a couple walking back toward home, but no one appeared.

CHAPTER 7

The main road continued for a mile or so until it merged with a cracked highway lined by waist high grass. Rusty green signs pointed Lareina toward her destination. Three miles to Austin, two miles—the faded outlines of numbers counted down. One more mile to food. One more mile to shelter. One more mile to crowds of people to blend into.

Swishing meadows dotted with lonely houses blurred against the horizon until mailboxes, retaining walls, and hundreds of houses surrounded her. A rabbit popped out of an overgrown median, scurried across the street, then disappeared into another wall of grass. Ahead, the tallest points of overpasses and skyscrapers rose against the sky and glittered in the scorching sun.

A man stumbled down the highway toward her. She maintained her course and focused her eyes on the other side of the road.

"You're going the wrong way," the man muttered. "Everyone wants out of the city." He stared straight ahead and talked to shimmering waves of air. "You'll catch the fever. Thousands of people are already dead. They can't even keep up with burying the bodies."

Her pace quickened until she jogged, then broke into a sprint. She needed food and a train station. The man couldn't be right. The way he acted, he had to be crazy. Up ahead an exit ramp merged with the highway. Out of breath, she held her hands over her head, gasping for air as heat shimmered off the pavement. The city's tallest buildings obliterated a flawless blue sky with their dark hulking forms. A gray haze hovered over the city like a curtain of death. She could survive on the food she had, maybe scavenge a little more, but if she caught the fever . . .

The fever had been terrorizing the country for about three years and the world longer than that. It didn't have a season like the flu and although there had been hope for a vaccine it had never become a reality. After the initial outbreak in Asia, some experts believed the danger had passed, but they were wrong. The fever continued to pop up in communities that had been spared at first, wiping out the adult population and creating a leadership vacuum. It was extremely contagious, spreading as easily as the flu and turning communities against each other as each family fought for their own survival.

A patch of wildflowers struggled to grow through thick weeds on the side of the road. Empathizing with the plants, she squeezed her eyes shut to block out the sun that seemed to grow hotter and brighter. Blisters on her feet sent a stinging ache through her body.

I'll rest for a while, she decided, *and when I wake up, I'll figure out whether it's safe to enter the city.* Lareina walked down the exit ramp and turned right toward distant houses. She followed the road until abandoned structures with rotted siding and loose shutters surrounded her. *Which one would make the best shelter?* House number one: shattered windows. House number two: half-collapsed roof. House number three: someone sitting on the front steps?

Through the remains of a picket fence, she observed the only other person besides the crazy man she'd encountered all day. Slumped forward with his hands clasped across his knees and his face buried in his arms, he appeared to be asleep or at least resting. Maybe grieving. *They can't even keep up with burying the bodies.*

Taking a step back, she cleared her throat loudly. The boy didn't look up.

"Please don't be dead," she whispered as she inched up the narrow front walk, stepping over knee-high weeds sprouting through cracks in the pavement. A few feet away, she paused and cleared her throat again. "Hey, can you help me with directions?"

The boy's absolute motionlessness argued against hope. A gust of wind ruffled the tips of his brown hair and tugged at the collar of his polo. Her hands grew slippery with sweat, but she couldn't pull herself away without knowing. After a moment of hesitation, she pressed her hand against his shoulder.

He jumped to his feet like he rested on springs. "What happened? Who are you?" He didn't sound angry or frightened, just groggy.

"I'm sorry, I didn't mean to scare you."

Squinting against the sunlight, he studied her through sparkling blue eyes. With a hasty flick of his arm, he pressed a hand over his head, pushing thick hair flat against his scalp. "I must have fallen asleep."

The boy, who towered over Lareina by almost a foot, let his hand slide down his face then sat on the step where she originally spotted him. His hair sloped, hanging longer on the left side than the right, revealing that his last haircut had probably been his own attempt to maintain a connection to civilization. He stretched his long legs down three steps and leaned back, resting his elbows against rotting planks behind him.

"I'm really sorry, you weren't moving and I just thought . . ." Her voice disintegrated into the wind.

A smile revealed a row of perfect white teeth. "It's okay. It's a relief that someone still shows concern for strangers. I'm Aaron Swanson, by the way."

"I'm Rochelle Aumont." Put at ease by Aaron's confident smile, she sank onto the step beside him. "Are you from Austin?"

"No, but I was in the city yesterday." The sun spread in long strips between each house, and squirrels chattered noisily in a nearby tree. Aaron's smile vanished as he peered back at the city. "I used to work with a doctor, so I came to help. They're turning patients away from the hospital, but they said I don't have enough training to be of any assistance. They're just . . ." He took a long breath in and let it out. "They're just letting people die."

"And the trains?" A cloud drifted over the sun.

"The tracks north of town washed out with the storm last week. Some lucky people made it onto southbound trains yesterday, but that's all over now. The city is under quarantine and last I heard they're having a hard time finding anyone willing to bring supplies in by train or truck." Aaron shook his head. "People who've already had the fever are extremely unlikely to contract it again, but they're all too superstitious to believe that medically proven fact. They aren't brave enough to help others even if their risk of getting sick is less than five percent."

No train tracks. No food. The air stood still. Lareina squeezed her eyes shut then opened them again, but nothing changed. "So it's true. The fever is in Austin."

Leaning forward, he clasped his hands over his knees. "It's devastating Austin. People are afraid to leave their houses, the sick are being left on front lawns, and bodies are piling up on the sidewalks. But they said I would just get in the way at the hospital." His voice collected volume then ended abruptly. He stared down at his hands. His shoulders heaved forward with each breath. "What kind of world is this, Rochelle?" he asked in a barely audible whisper. "How can people not even try to help their own family?"

Her life had always been one of fear and uncertainty, even before the fever. Hadn't people always prioritized their own well-being? Yet the intensity of disbelief in Aaron's eyes suggested the possibility of something different.

She shook her head. "They see what's happening, they've heard the stories, and they don't want to die." A question formed on her lips about his courage to enter an infected city, his daring to work in a hospital filled with contagious patients, but the question didn't have time to materialize.

A jarring dissonance of shouting reverberated down the street. Birds flapped into the air, and locusts stopped buzzing. The two of them looked at each other, wide-eyed, then down the street in each direction. More shouts, maybe from the next street over. But before she could discuss it with Aaron, the boy sprang to his feet, dashed into the street, and rounded the corner, leaving his bag behind. Picking up both bags, she followed the commotion.

"Where's your food?" one voice shouted as she drew near.

"Give me your bag," yelled another.

A string of swearing.

At least three different voices spoke, but there could be others. Lareina paused to pull her bag open and fish around inside for the most valuable item she'd ever stolen. Her hand brushed its cool, smooth surface. Pulling it out, she jogged through a fenceless backyard, both bags bouncing on her back.

As she emerged onto the sidewalk, a circle of six boys taking turns kicking someone on the ground came into view.

Aaron approached the circle and shouted something she couldn't hear over the wild yelling. One tall, broad-shouldered boy from the circle lunged forward and Aaron took a swing at him. The boy blocked Aaron's punch and shoved him to the ground.

Squeezing her hand tighter around the gun, she aimed at the perfectly clear sky above her, took a shaky breath, and fired. The deafening sound bounced off walls and crashed through the air. Seven sets of eyes turned to her as commotion faded to silence. She aimed the gun at the group of boys and tried to steady her trembling hands.

"Everyone clear the area," she barked, managing to keep her voice steady. One second, two, three. No one moved. Four seconds, five, six . . . she hoped they didn't have weapons of their own but didn't lower her gun. Seven seconds, eight, nine, and one ragged boy backed away, followed by another, then the rest. They vanished around houses and behind fences. The tallest one spat on the ground before picking up a dirty gray backpack and loping off down the street and out of sight.

Forcing her stiff arms to bend, she lowered the gun, slid the safety into place, and zipped it back into her bag. Aaron stumbled to his feet, clutching his shoulder and never taking his eyes off the girl he just met. The other boy lifted his face from the ground. Blood trickled out of his nose and stood out in grotesque red splotches on his face.

"Nick?" She immediately recognized the suspicion in his eyes.

His face twisted into a grimace. "Rochelle?"

Although her stomach turned somersaults at the sight of blood, she nodded. *Breath in, breath out. Ignore it and help Nick.*

"You two know each other?" Aaron glanced back and forth between them.

A cloud rolled over the sun and the world dimmed. Letting both bags slide to the ground, Lareina knelt next to Nick, trying to examine the extent of his injuries. Bracing his feet against the grass, he slid a few inches away from her.

"We met briefly about a week ago, but only for a day." She sat back on her heels.

"You never mentioned the gun you keep in your bag," Nick accused.

She rolled her eyes and reached for his arm, but he pulled it back. "It's not something I go around bragging about. Plus it just saved your life."

He winced but managed to sit up on his own. "It saved my life for now."

"If I wanted you dead I would have just left you in that pit."

"I can tell you two have a lot to talk about, but I don't think this is the best place for an argument." Aaron scanned the landscape, forehead creased with worry.

"Aaron's right. Nick, are you coming with us or not?" She tried to ignore the blood, but had to look away after a moment.

Nick slouched, blinking his eyes as if someone shined a flashlight into his face. "Yeah, I'll come," he surrendered in a sigh of defeat.

Aaron and Lareina retrieved their bags then each took one of Nick's arms and pulled him to his feet. The three of them lumbered back into the labyrinth of houses.

"All right, which one looks like a good place to spend the night?" Her inspection of each building included a quick check for an intact roof and panes of glass in the windows.

"We're breaking into someone's house?" Aaron sounded more intrigued than uncertain.

"Obviously you haven't known Rochelle for long."

She ignored Nick even though she wanted to let go of his arm and send him tumbling to the ground. "I'll unlock the door. We aren't going to damage anything."

At the end of the block, an olive green, three-story house stood taller than all of those around it. Bay windows adorned the outside and all glass remained intact. She pulled the boys along, up four steps, and onto the front porch.

Boards creaked under their feet. A gust of wind tinkled through wind chimes hanging beneath the eaves. She examined the lock—a simple one, thankfully—selected a pick from the set she carried in her bag, and in a minute had the door open. An elaborate staircase with a solid wooden banister drew her eye up through a collage of family photos in golden frames that turned a corner at the landing and continued out of sight. The lowering sun beamed through the open door, illuminating a long hallway, glinting off a mirror on the wall, and erasing shadows to reveal doorways on each side of the passage stretching deep into the house.

Nick rubbed his forehead with the back of his hand. Perhaps he had a headache from the scuffle or more likely developed one from the thought of breaking into another house. Aaron stepped inside, pulling Nick along with him.

"This place is huge. The people who lived here must have been rich." His feet squeaked against the wood floor. He stopped at a bench in the foyer, lowered Nick onto it, then slipped his own shoes off and pushed them under the bench. "It's bad manners to tromp around someone else's house in your shoes, right?"

Lareina nodded and slipped out of her own shoes, crossing the floor in her socks.

"It feels weird to be in someone else's house without them knowing," Nick muttered.

Aaron strode to the staircase. "I'm going to find a first aid kit. I'll be right back." Without waiting for an answer, he swung around the banister and bounded up the stairs.

His feet creaked lightly through the ceiling overhead. She knew curiosity would keep him upstairs exploring for a while. At least he could make the best of a bad situation, unlike Nick.

Lareina closed her eyes and flipped a light switch on the wall, but when she opened them, the only light filtered through three rectangles of glass in the front door. The bench creaked when she sat down next to Nick, and she wondered why she even bothered to believe an abandoned house would have electricity.

Nick shifted his weight with a quick, agonized burst of breath. Silence filled the house and stagnated in the air between them.

"I thought you were going to stay in San Antonio?" She just wanted to hear sound, anything, even her own voice.

"So did I," he groaned. "Obviously that didn't go according to the plan."

Turning toward him, she tried to come up with something comforting to say, but even shadowy darkness couldn't obscure the drying blood. She turned away, focused on the rounded spokes of the banister, and swallowed to calm the gagging feeling rising in her throat.

"Are you okay?"

"I'm fine, I just can't look at blood. Sometimes I throw up when I see it."

"So you're not a murderer then?"

A smile brightened his voice. It was a joke rolled into a

serious question. He suspected she'd done something terrible, but hadn't she? She'd accumulated a lifetime of lying, stealing, and cheating people out of money or food.

"Definitely not." She pictured the blood on Susan's shirt and shivered.

Silence returned, but not absolute. Every twenty seconds or so a dull *drip-drip* called out from somewhere close. At first it didn't even register, but the longer she listened, the faster her heart beat.

"Do you hear that?" she finally whispered.

"Uh-huh, what is it?"

As she shuffled across the floor the beautiful sound became louder and more defined. She leaned against the banister and listened. To the right and under the stairs? She pulled open a little door that led through the paneling under the staircase, and in the limited light made out the shapes of a sink and toilet. A smile formed across her lips as she stepped up to the dripping faucet, twisted the handle, and released a rushing stream of water.

"We have running water," she shouted, skipped out of the bathroom, and slid back onto the bench. "We have running water."

Nick squinted up at her, still rubbing his forehead.

"We won't have to go look for water to drink." She dug through her bag to find the flashlight. "We can wash our clothes and take showers. It might be cold, but who cares?" Her hand closed around a plastic tube and she pulled the flashlight from her bag. Pointing it at the wall, she flipped the plastic slider up and a weak beam of light blossomed into a yellow circle on the wall. Standing, she held a hand out to Nick.

"Where are we going?"

"To wash away the blood so I can have an actual conversation with you."

Without argument, he took her hand and limped to the little bathroom. Standing in the doorway, she held the flashlight as he splashed water over his face, through his hair, and up his arms.

"Is that better?" In the narrow shaft of light, a cut stretched across his forehead near his hairline and a dark blue bruise formed beneath his left eye.

"Much better."

Together they walked into the next room down the hall. A large green area rug covered the wooden floor in front of a couch with a chair positioned on each side. Two shelves piled with books filled one corner of the room, while a little table holding a white vase with pink flowers painted across the top adorned the other. Nick lowered himself onto the couch inch by inch, and winced when his body came in contact with the cushions. He held the bottom of his shirt out, examining the stains with a frown, and revealing a blackening bruise crawling across his ribcage.

"I had a clean shirt in my bag." He leaned back all the way. "I guess it belongs to someone else now."

"I can find you another clean shirt." Lareina smiled and sat down next to him.

"You'll steal me a clean shirt."

"Let's call a truce. Just for tonight, we won't argue."

He closed his eyes and took a breath. "Agreed."

CHAPTER 8

Footsteps pounded down the stairs. Aaron appeared in the room carrying a small plastic tote. "This place is even bigger than it looks from outside." He set the tote on a chair and pulled out a bottle of rubbing alcohol, band aids, and a needle and thread. "There's eight rooms upstairs and another five on the third floor."

"Whoa, what do you have sewing stuff for?" Nick slid a little closer to Lareina.

Aaron poured some rubbing alcohol into a glass then dropped the needle and a section of thread in after it. He rubbed his thumb across his forehead to mirror where Nick's wound slashed an angry red gash across his skin. "The abrasion on your head."

Nick pressed his hand against his forehead then pulled it back. "It's fine. It's not even bleeding."

"Until it breaks open while you sleep, never fully heals, and eventually gets infected," Aaron warned.

Nick's eyes went wide. "You are hearing this, right? Your friend wants to stick a needle into my forehead."

Lareina rested her hand on Nick's shoulder. "He's not exactly my friend. I only met him a few minutes before you did."

"Is that supposed to make me feel better?"

Aaron held the needle up to the light, struggling to thread it. "I assure you it won't go all the way through."

"It's okay, Nick. He used to work at a hospital."

Turning so his back faced Aaron, he whispered, "How do you know?"

"Because he told me," she mimicked in a hushed voice.

"You met him an hour ago. You don't even know his name is really Aaron."

She swallowed over a lump forming in her throat. Would she let someone she just met stitch her forehead? Absolutely not.

"I know it seems scary." The words were more appropriate to comfort a little boy instead of someone her own age. "But you only have two options. You can let Aaron help you or you can figure out how to get antibiotics when you get an infection."

Nick winced, took a breath, and slowly turned until he faced forward.

"Lie back on the couch and relax," Aaron instructed. "Rochelle, sit right there and hold his hand. Nick, if you feel much discomfort squeeze Rochelle's hand and I'll stop, okay?"

"Okay?" His voice sounded faint.

Aaron pushed the curtains aside then shook his head. "Has anyone seen a flashlight around here?"

"I have one."

After retrieving it, she sat on the edge of the couch and aimed the beam of light at Nick's forehead. She squeezed his hand once for reassurance then focused her attention on the shelf of books while Aaron worked. They were all strangers who never would have met under normal circumstances, but at least for a moment, they all needed each other.

"Are you still okay, Nick?" Aaron asked.

"I barely feel anything."

The sun sank lower, draining light from the room. Aaron finished and Nick stretched out comfortably on the couch.

After covering Nick with a light blanket from a nearby chair, Lareina explored the kitchen—no food—and the second floor. She unpacked her bag in one of the bedrooms, but it felt quiet and lonely. When shadows filled the house and it became impossible to ignore the pendant's icy touch against her skin, she gathered a few blankets and carried her empty bag downstairs, planning to find food in the morning. After making herself a bed on the living room floor, she checked on Nick then drifted into a restless sleep.

Birds chirped loudly in the dim light. Lareina kicked her blanket aside and sat up. Her head ached and she felt damp with sweat. Despite the stifling, humid air, Nick slept soundly on the couch and Aaron rested comfortably in one of the big recliners, the side of his face pressed against the back cushion.

She tiptoed out of the room and down the long hallway. In the kitchen, wooden cupboards lined three walls and a sink waited for someone to wash dishes. A toaster, a blender, a radio, and a roll of paper towels lined the counter near a refrigerator. She imagined living in the house, coming downstairs to eat breakfast with her parents and siblings, watching movies with them in the living room, and setting the dining room table for a family of six.

Knowing the cupboards were empty from the previous day's inspection, she found a glass, filled it with water, and swallowed it slowly. It would have to be enough until they could get some food.

A light rustling and the soft murmuring of voices drifted in from the living room. By the time she picked her way back down the dark hall, Aaron was folding his blanket, and Nick sat on the couch, leaning forward with his face in his hands.

"Good morning, guys. How are you feeling Nick?"

"Like I got beat up," he mumbled without moving.

Aaron shrugged. "I told him he'd be stiff until he moves around a little bit."

Lareina sat next to Nick, considered putting a hand on his shoulder, then changed her mind. "There isn't any food in the kitchen. One of us is going to have to find some."

Nick's head popped up to reveal the stitching on his forehead, a cut on his lower lip, and an angry bruise below his left eye. Under different circumstances, he could have won a prize for the best zombie costume.

"You mean you're going to find berries or wild plums in the ditches, right?"

"I haven't had a lot of luck with that." Aaron stuffed his hands into his pockets.

"I think our best option is to shop in Austin." She stood and stretched her arms behind her. "After we've all had something to eat then maybe we can search out a good place for gathering."

"Don't forget Austin is under quarantine," Aaron warned. "Maybe I should go. I've already had the fever so I have immunity."

"How exactly are we going to shop? Does anyone have money?" Nick looked from Lareina to Aaron. The contrariness she was used to slid back into his voice.

Aaron shoved his hands into his pockets. "Good point."

One . . . two . . . three. Don't lose patience with him. "I'll find a way to get some money."

"You're going to steal money," Nick accused.

Her hands clenched into fists at her sides and she locked eyes with him in a staring contest that neither of them intended to lose. Sunlight filtered through the open blinds, encasing them in golden luminosity. Frustration defeated patience.

"I'm trying to keep us alive. If you want to starve then go try to gather berries."

"What about the people you're stealing from? How are they supposed to survive?"

"What do you know about survival?" Her voice rose to a shout, so she took a breath to get it under control then looked right at Nick. "Oh, that's right—you tumble into traps and get robbed."

He stood, bent forward at first, then slowly straightened his back. "At least I know the difference between right and wrong. No wonder you're the orphan no one wanted."

The words knocked her back a step. She couldn't breathe, couldn't speak. Nick didn't move and if he regretted his words, she couldn't tell.

"I'm going for a walk."

Aaron stepped in front of her. "Hold on. I don't think it's a good idea for you to go into the city. Especially not alone."

There was a whole world out there away from Nick, crowds of people to blend into and blocks of towering skyscrapers to hide among. She pushed past Aaron and collected her bag in the foyer. "I go wherever I want."

Aaron followed her through the front door. His footsteps creaked across the porch as she made her way down the front walk. "Are you coming back?" he shouted after her.

She stopped and turned back for a second. He stood with his hands on the railing, leaning forward. Unable to reply for fear her voice would break, she turned and hurried away.

The usual impulse to survive and the need to get far away from Nick smothered any fear of the fever. Lost in annoyance and frustration, her feet carried her through quiet neighborhoods, then past deserted shops and skyscrapers, into an empty ghost city where Austin, Texas, should have been. A sheet of paper swirled down the street in a dusty gust of hot wind before catching around the base of a pole. Blazing sun scorched the city from a hazy blue sky, making it more comfortable to remain, whenever possible, under the awnings of shops or in the shadows of buildings.

She walked up and down the streets in search of an outdoor market, like the kind she stole from in San Antonio. Very few people ventured outside, but those who did held cloth over their noses and crossed to the other side of the street to avoid meeting each other. Every few blocks she glimpsed stacked shapes swathed in white sheets at the curb. The sight caused her to quicken her pace, afraid the wind would rip the sheet away before she rushed past.

She shivered despite the broiling sun on her back, and the seriousness of the fever collided with the wounded pride that had driven her away from safety. She'd never been in an infected city. Until now she had only read terrifying accounts in the paper. Lareina mopped sweat from her forehead with the sleeve of her shirt. *You don't know the difference between right and wrong. No wonder you're the orphan no one wanted.* She would have walked across the entire continent to escape Nick's judgmental accusations, so she had catapulted herself into a place where nothing but a white sheet stood between the living and the dead. Run away and escape the fever or stay and avoid starvation? Either option seemed like a death sentence.

Traffic lights creaked back and forth in the wind, flies buzzed around overflowing garbage cans, and a truck rumbled up the street with six white sheets stacked in the back. Turning the corner, she pressed her back against the warm brick of a building. She squinted up at skyscrapers stretched toward the shimmering blue sky. A strange apprehension rose within her, drying out her throat and tying knots in her stomach. If people weren't sick, they were scared. And scared people were dangerous.

Walking faster, she tried to focus on the spotty shadows dotting the sidewalk. Occasionally, curtains would flutter as she passed, invisible people peeking from dark windows. The doors of dress shops and restaurants displayed signs with CLOSED printed in large black letters. She wanted to leave, to forget what Nick said, to return to the huge house with bay windows and running water.

Blinking back a tear, she crossed the street, and trudged down the shaded walking path of a park. She sank onto a bench, and covered her face with her hands. Only days earlier it seemed so easy to jump onto a train and wake up in Maibe. People wouldn't judge her there; she wouldn't tell them what she had done. But there were no trains, at least not in Austin.

The pendant slapped against her chest when she lifted her head. Accepting it had been a mistake that would forever steal her freedom and her future.

Across the park, through neatly trimmed trees and shrubs, she noticed a sprawling building, the entire front wall made of glass so clean that it glinted in the sunlight. She stood and crept closer to the unexpected but welcome sight. The appearance of the building caught her attention, but the stream of people entering and leaving beneath a sign that read "Penny's Grocery" captivated all of her hope. Women wearing bright sundresses and wary expressions held the hands of children with masks over their noses and mouths.

Life had to go on. There would be survivors, the trains would return, and those who remained would bring the city back to life. Humanity would rebound as it always had.

Her relief only lasted until she realized that an indoor market would make her method of shopping much more difficult than it had been outdoors. She sat between two bushes, trying to formulate a plan as she watched a woman with two little boys leave the building as a man wearing a white shirt and blue tie entered. As he pulled the glass door open, he reached back and pushed a protruding wallet deeper into his back pocket.

Target in sight, she stood, patted the dust from her clothes, and crossed the street. Huge red letters painted on the side window announced

FINAL INVENTORY SALE
SHOP WHILE YOU STILL CAN

A blast of cool air welcomed her into the chaos of shoppers grabbing what they could in dim light. Some rushed through the store avoiding close proximity to other customers. Some chatted through masks as they reached for the last loaves of bread on the shelf. Some strolled up and down the aisles as if they'd never heard of the fever or refused to believe it was in the city.

For a few seconds the man seemed to have eluded her, but then she spotted his white shirt turning into a nearby aisle. Quickening her pace enough to catch up but maintaining enough of a distance to avoid suspicion, she followed the man to the back of the store, where he stopped in front of a glass display counter. Walking up next to him she imitated the way he peered through the glass at different cuts of raw meat.

"The steaks here are really good. The way things are,

this might be my last chance to enjoy one," he said without looking up.

Lareina nodded. "It's pretty scary."

"It's better not to think about it." Smiling sympathetically, he leaned over the case. "What're you here for?"

"Oh, it's my brother's birthday and my mom wants to surprise him with the best dinner we can manage. I'm not sure what I'm looking at though."

That was all it took, and the man was off, pointing out various cuts of meat and reminiscing on the special occasions when he had eaten them. Pretending to be interested, she watched the brown tip of his wallet in her peripheral vision. She had done it hundreds of times, but picking pockets always made her nervous. The proximity to her target meant a greater chance of getting caught, but she had little choice if she wanted to leave the store with some food.

"So that one there is a T-bone steak?" she interrupted, pointing directly in front of her.

He turned away and pointed to the other end of the case. "Oh no, those are way down on that end."

With one smooth motion, she slipped the wallet out of his pocket. He didn't react as she slid her hand behind her back.

"Can I help you, sir?" a man asked from behind the counter. If he had witnessed her crime, he didn't say anything.

The man looked at Lareina. "Excuse me a minute?"

Lareina nodded and as the man discussed his order with the butcher, she unfolded the wallet behind her back and felt the wad of bills. *Don't get greedy,* she reminded herself. *You can only fit so much food in your bag anyway.* Unable to see how much the bills were worth, she pulled out three and slipped them into her back pocket. Then, folding the wallet shut, she waited until the man leaned forward to take his package and let the wallet fall behind him. He heard it hit the floor, but she leaned down to pick it up before he could.

"Here, sir, this slipped out of your pocket."

"Thank you, I wouldn't want to lose that," he replied with a smile.

"Sure thing."

He waved then hurried off to the front of the store.

Walking away from the meat counter, she pulled three crisp ten-dollar bills from her pocket.

CHAPTER 9

By the time Lareina left the grocery store, her backpack hung low, the straps straining to hold four pounds of apples, three boxes of granola bars, two boxes of crackers, a loaf of bread, twelve bananas, one jar of peanut butter, and a jar of jelly. A few blocks from the grocery store, all sound ceased except for the rumbling truck prowling the streets to carry the dead away. Across a long intersection, a sign pointed north toward Dallas, and beyond Dallas, Maibe. A right turn would lead back to Nick and Aaron. Were they pacing across the area rug, worrying about her, wondering whether she would decide to come back?

The preposterous fantasy made her laugh. As much as she never wanted to see Nick again, she'd left her extra clothes, lock picks, and gun back at the house. She turned right.

Searing heat rose from the sidewalk in shimmering waves. Gusts of wind funneled between the buildings, twisting her hair around and plastering it against her face. The sky shimmered clear and blue up ahead, but on the western horizon columns of dark clouds flashed with lightning. Her parched mouth begged for water to wash away the grit of dirt lodged there by the wind, but she didn't want to stop. Faded billboards, overpasses, and closed businesses disappeared behind her as she followed the road into a residential neighborhood. She guessed she had walked about three of the four or so miles between the center of the city and the olive-green house.

"Almost there," she whispered over and over again. "Just one more mile."

"Water, please, water," a muffled voice whimpered.

No one else walked on the street. The wind? No, she'd distinctly heard a plea for water.

"Please, water," the voice groaned a little louder. Something blue moved against a green lawn.

One step, then another. She eased closer to a man huddled in a blue blanket, shivering where he sat on the lawn in front of a brick house. Lights glowed inside and a curtain fluttered.

"Please, I'm so thirsty," he begged. His thin body shook violently and beads of sweat lined the crown of his forehead. "Water . . ." He broke into a rasping cough that caved his body into itself.

Lareina reached her hand back and pulled a half empty bottle of water from the front pocket of her bag. She wanted to back away, to escape the most dangerous person she'd met all day, to return to the previous day when the fever was just a story in a newspaper, too distant to affect her. Instead she twisted the cap off the bottle and leaned down, placing it in the man's hand.

"Is your family inside?" she asked.

He didn't sit up, but tipped the bottle sideways and sipped slowly at the water. "I don't want them near me." He reached out and gripped her wrist so tight it hurt. His eyes burned into hers. "Keep them away from me."

She yanked her wrist back with such force that she tumbled backward. He collapsed against the blanket and watched her with frightened eyes. He knew he would die, alone on his front lawn, but he didn't believe he had another choice.

"I'm s-sorry." She stood and backed away, glancing from the man to the imprints of fingers on her wrist until her shoes left the spongy grass and landed on solid concrete. A low clap of thunder rumbled in the distance—the storm was close.

Lareina sprinted down the sidewalk despite thick, humid air and her heavy bag slamming against her back with every other step. She hurdled tree branches without stopping and skirted corners without slowing. When the olive-green house came into view, she stopped so abruptly that she almost fell forward. On wobbling legs she approached the porch, gasping for air and forcing her feet to shuffle forward.

Thunder roared in the distance and lightning painted a shadow tree across the house. Pausing to push tangled hair out of her face, she listened to the urgent clanging of the wind chime. The front door swung open and Aaron appeared in the doorway with a relieved smile on his face.

"Rochelle, where have you been? We thought you weren't coming back."

Without answering, she walked into the house and let her bag slide onto the bench in the foyer, then walked to the staircase. "There's food inside," she said on her way up the stairs.

"Where are you going?" Aaron's voice sounded far away.

"I'm not hungry."

Her feet found the landing and she bounded up the last six steps into a long hallway with polished wooden floors. A tree branch outside beat against the house with each gust of wind, but no footsteps followed on the stairs. She locked herself in the first bedroom where she had left all of her stuff the day before and rushed into the connected bathroom where she slumped into the bathtub. Any trace of the imprints left by feverish fingers had vanished from her wrist.

I'll die here, she thought. *I'll get sick and die all alone like that man, like all of those people wrapped in white sheets.*

Tears welled in her eyes but she didn't cry. Instead she stripped off her sweat-soaked clothes, letting them fall into the bathtub, and turned on the water. The shower spluttered before icy water cascaded over her. Every instinct screamed for her to escape the torturous cold, but she forced herself to remain still. She pulled a bottle of soap from a basket suspended in the shower, dumped the whole thing over her head, and scrubbed her skin until it turned crimson. Ten minutes passed before she felt satisfied that all of the fever germs had washed down the drain. After wrapping herself in a towel she washed her clothes out, hung them over the shower rod, and returned to the bedroom.

She picked up a brush off the dresser and stood in front of a mirror that hung on the back of the door, carefully untangling her wind- and water-knotted hair. Thunder rumbled loud enough to rattle knickknacks on a shelf above the bed. In flashes of lightning, she thought her lips looked blue, but despite uncontrollable shivering, she told herself she wasn't sick. In the closet she found a large t-shirt and sweatpants. The garments hung on her thin frame, but she decided they were good enough until her own clothes dried.

Still shaking, she picked up a blanket stretched across the foot of the bed and wrapped it around herself. The pendant sat against her chest like an ice cube, but she couldn't take it off. Thunder cracked outside, rattling the windowpane. Lareina ran to the door, reached her shaking hand toward the knob, then yanked it back.

Nick would be down there and she didn't want to face him, but she didn't want to be alone. The fever, the pendant, Nick, Galloway, the endless storms—she despised them all. A gust of wind slammed leaves and twigs against the window. She pulled the door open and stumbled down the stairs. A candle glowed in the foyer, casting flickering shadows on the wall. More shivering light and the comfort of human voices emanated from the living room where both boys sat on the floor with a game of Battleship between them.

Aaron looked up first. "Rochelle, are you okay?"

The room slid left, grew longer, then shorter. Her legs bent, too wobbly to hold her weight. Then Aaron's arm looped around her, guided her across the room, and helped her sit down on the couch. When she opened her eyes both boys studied her as if she were an abstract painting in a museum. Look but don't touch. Ask questions but never find answers.

"I shouldn't have g-gone into the city," she stammered.

Nick thrust his hands into his pockets.

Aaron leaned forward. "What happened? Are you hurt?"

She closed her eyes and saw white sheets fluttering in the wind, filling the beds of trucks, lined up and down sidewalks. Tears rushed to her eyes and she didn't try to stop them, didn't try to hide them.

"I saw a man dying on his front lawn," she explained. "He needed water so I gave him mine. He grabbed my wrist and now I'm shivering and my head hurts." Her voice fragmented into a dozen pieces, lost in the deafening thunder and wind outside.

Aaron shook his head. "You don't have the fever. You wouldn't show symptoms for at least two to three days after exposure."

"But I'm so cold." She pulled the blanket tighter around her shoulders.

"How long did you stand in the shower?" He gently touched the back of his hand to her forehead. "You're ice cold. There's no way you're running a fever."

Hands twisted the clouds above and a torrent of rain

crashed against the roof. Windows creaked and the house groaned.

"That man is outside in the storm," she whispered. New tears flooded her eyes.

Nick looked down at his socks, and swayed slightly back and forth.

Aaron put an arm around her. "You did everything you could for him. Most people wouldn't have even stopped."

She nodded, sniffled, closed her eyes, and let her head rest against Aaron's shoulder.

"Nick, can you go get her something to eat?"

Footsteps padded across the floor, softer and softer, until she couldn't hear them anymore. Lareina sat up and tried to wipe tears away with the sleeve of her shirt. Aaron handed her a box of tissues.

"Are you feeling better?"

She wasn't, but she nodded anyway. "I'm sorry about this." She wiped her cheek and wadded the wet tissue in her hand.

Aaron smiled. "I have three little sisters. Tears don't scare me."

Tears had always been a sign of weakness, a reason for ridicule, an unforgivable offense until now. "Where is your family?"

"California. We didn't have a lot of money so a year ago I went to Los Angeles to find a job. That way my parents had one less person to feed and I could send money back."

Trying to ignore the storm that ripped through the neighborhood, she shivered and folded her legs under her. "So how did you get to Texas?"

The smile in his eyes faded and his head slumped into his shoulders a little. "For a while I was working at a hospital, or kind of training with a doctor, I guess. He died two months ago, and none of the other doctors wanted an eighteen-year-old kid with less than a high school education hanging around. They told me there were no training programs in California and suggested I try heading east. One of them felt bad enough for me that he bought me a train ticket to Houston, where there used to be a training program . . . but now there isn't, and I'm here still trying to become a doctor."

"What about your family?"

Aaron shrugged. "They probably think I'm dead."

"But you could write to them." She couldn't imagine having a family and then walking away as if they didn't exist.

"Maybe one day."

Soft footsteps approached in the hall, and Nick returned carrying a dish and glass of water. He held out a plate containing a peanut butter and jelly sandwich surrounded by slices of apple.

"I can get you something else," he offered. "I wasn't sure what you would like."

"No, it's okay." She ate while a torrent of rain pounded against the house. After finishing her dinner, she curled up on the pile of blankets she'd left on the floor and closed her eyes against the cacophony outside.

Cool air brushed her face. She walked through a gray city with gray buildings and gray trees. A white sheet fluttered to the ground, and when she looked down at the sidewalk she found it was piled so high with people wrapped in white sheets that she couldn't continue forward. The sheets moved as people tried to kick and fight their way out, but no one escaped. Then everything around her turned white and squeezed tighter and tighter until—

"Rochelle. Rochelle, can you hear me?"

Her eyes shot open and she sat up, forcing air into her

lungs. Nick knelt on the floor beside her. A crisp breeze drifted through the open window. She looked around the room trying to orient herself, then noticed the blanket tangled around her leg and frantically kicked it away.

"You're okay, it was just a nightmare," Nick comforted.

"Yeah, I know. Where's Aaron?" She rubbed her eyes with the back of her hand. They felt heavy and crusty.

Nick sat down and stretched his legs across the floor. "He found a fishing pole in the garage and said he knew where he could catch fish. He told me to let you rest."

"What time is it?"

"Early in the afternoon." He jumped up. "You have to be hungry. What would you like? A sandwich, apple, granola bar, banana, all of the above?"

Lareina fell back onto her pillow and closed her eyes. "It's okay, Nick, I'm not hungry."

"You just rest. I'll figure something out."

When his footsteps faded, she got up, walked into the little bathroom to splash water on her face, then returned to the living room and knelt on the couch. The coolest afternoon air since April flowed through the open window. Outside were the remains of the storm: large branches littered the entire front yard and a tree had fallen across the street, pinning part of a fence to the ground.

"All right, lunch is served," Nick announced from the doorway.

Reluctantly she turned around and sank into the couch. She didn't have the patience to be in the same room with him or pretend that she could tolerate his sanctimonious attitude.

A sandwich, cut diagonally in half, and slices of apple filled the plate gripped in his hand. He sat down and lowered it to the cushion between them. After a moment of awkward silence, he said, "It's beautiful outside. Feels like October instead of August."

One bite of the sandwich sent its smooth, rich texture sliding along her tongue. "What is this?"

He grinned. "Peanut butter and banana."

She eyed the sandwich suspiciously. "That sounds disgusting."

"You thought it was good before I told you what it was," he teased. "Come on, you get your protein and potassium all in one sandwich."

"You aren't going to tell me you were studying to be a nutritionist?" She took another bite and swallowed.

"It's something my mom used to say." He shrugged, all lightheartedness gone from his expression. "That was my favorite food when I was a kid."

Nick had a favorite food, and she was lucky if the adults in her life remembered to feed her.

He shifted his weight and twiddled his thumbs nervously. "Rochelle, I'm really sorry about what I said yesterday. I didn't mean that, I just got mad and . . ."

Wind chimes clanged loudly outside and a breeze that smelled like roses drifted into the room. A ticking clock and the dripping bathroom sink combined to form a rhythmic beat. Nick watched his thumbs link and pull apart over and over. He looked remorseful, but how long would it last?

"You must have meant some of it. You've been suspicious of me since the moment we met."

He sat up straighter. "That's not true. You helped me and gave that guy water yesterday. You can't be all that bad."

Lareina finished her sandwich and started eating apple slices. She turned her face toward the window, let the refreshing air calm her, and waited for Nick's judgment.

"It's just, I grew up with really strict parents. If I had ever taken anything without paying for it, they would have killed me. I like talking to Rochelle Aumont, but hanging around Rochelle the thief makes me nervous."

"You make it sound like I'm two different people."

He leaned forward and light caught the bruise under his eye, revealing three shades of purple and four of blue. "Sometimes it seems like you are. You break the laws, but you do everything else right like giving me food before you left San Antonio. It's just . . . hard for me to fit all of that into one person."

Her eyebrows furrowed in confusion. Nick rubbed his hand across his forehead and shook his head.

"I think you're a good person," he started again, "but when I eat food you've stolen, I feel like an accomplice and I don't want to get in trouble. I don't want you to get in trouble either. I just wish the world was different."

Finally something she could agree with. Although the apology felt a little like an accusation, she smiled. "Me too, but it's not going to change, so I have to do whatever it takes to keep us alive."

"But if it did . . . change," he insisted, "then you would stop?"

"It won't change."

"But if it did?" He waited, his eyes staring into hers, searching for the truth.

"I would like nothing more than to never steal again." She said the words before she had time to think about them, but they felt true.

Nodding, he extended his hand. "Friends then? I promise to stop jumping to conclusions about you."

Slowly, she slid her hand forward and took his. "I promise to stop teasing you about falling into that pit."

Nick laughed, a resonating peal that sounded like church bells. She leaned her head against the couch and let her heavy eyelids slide closed. Despite sleeping all night and halfway through the day, her head felt heavy and her legs ached. "I'm still tired. You don't think I'm getting the fever?"

"No, you just need more rest."

She wanted to open her eyes, to examine his face for honesty, to lift her head off the cushion, but she struggled against weariness pulling her into the darkness of nightmares. "What if it is . . . the fever?"

"You're only seventeen. People under twenty-five almost always recover."

It took so much energy and effort to gather, find, steal enough food to survive each day. "I would starve to death." She remembered the man, dying alone while his family hid inside, and shivered.

An arm slid behind her shoulders, lifted her, and lowered her until her head sank into a pillow and her body rested against soft cushions. "Aaron and I wouldn't let you starve." The words repeated over and over in her mind as she spiraled back into sleep.

CHAPTER 10

Through a second-floor bedroom window, the sky glowed softly then brightened to hues of pink and blue as if someone pulled a tinted lens over the glass. Lareina sat on the window seat, knees drawn up to her chin, cheek rested against the glass. For her entire life she'd been focused on the horizon, running toward the sun, away from it, never succeeding in catching it or escaping herself. At first she didn't have a choice and the ORI administrators moved her against her will. Then she walked to San Antonio with the hope of finding her family but never uncovered the lead to take her to a new city. Galloway forcing her out of San Antonio made her realize she'd become a victim of her own life instead of taking charge and fighting for what she wanted. If she couldn't have the family she was born into then she would find a new one.

She needed to continue north, to Maibe and the people who were the closest to family she had ever known, but she wanted to say goodbye. It had been dark when she woke up on the couch with blankets tucked around her. Not wanting to wake the boys, she'd tiptoed upstairs and searched until she found clothes close enough to her size that they earned a spot in her bag, replacing worn or dirty counterparts. She changed into her jeans and t-shirt, now dry on the shower rod, and pulled her bag over her shoulder. Then she noticed the sunrise and sat down to watch it, to wait for Nick and Aaron to wake up, to delay her departure.

A door squeaked down the hall and footsteps padded to

the stairs. She took one last look at the sprawling blue sky stretching for miles before meeting the ground. Freedom and danger. Hope and dread. Her stomach tightened.

I can stay a little longer, she decided. *Galloway doesn't know where I am or he would have confronted me by now, right? He won't find me if I stay here—he can't search every house in Texas. I can stay and rest for a few more days. Maybe I can even catch the train north when the tracks are fixed.*

Feeling good about this decision, she left her backpack on the bed and crept down the stairs. Nick still slept, but she found Aaron with his back to her as he filled a glass with water in the kitchen. The food from her bag stretched across the island counter: boxes of granola bars next to boxes of crackers, then peanut butter and jelly, bread, and finally bananas and apples.

Aaron turned and a smile spread across his face. "Hey, long time no see."

"I guess I slept through most of yesterday." She pulled out a stool and sat down in front of the food.

"Nick told me you ate lunch then fell asleep talking to him." He crossed the room and placed his glass on the counter before touching the back of his hand to her forehead. "No fever. I declare you one hundred percent healthy." He smiled and sat down on the stool next to her.

Sun streamed through the window, glinted off the toaster and brightened pale yellow walls. She pulled a granola bar from a blue-and-white box then peeled the wrapper back. "That's a relief. Did you catch any fish yesterday?"

His eyes lit up, changing to a brighter shade of blue. "No, but today is going to be the day. Even better, the grill out back works and there's fuel in the garage. None of us are going to Austin for a few weeks until things calm down."

She nodded and took a bite of her granola bar. Chocolate chips melted in her mouth and slid over her tongue like silk. "I never want to go back to Austin again, but I can't stay here. I have to keep moving. I think the train is my best bet to get north."

"You can stay for a week or two. By then Austin will be in fever recovery, they'll repair the tracks, and I'll walk to the train station with you."

Lareina smiled. She felt safe at the house with people who cared about her health and her plans. Couldn't she let herself pretend she had a family? Just for a week? "That makes sense."

"Would you mind helping Nick out with gathering some fruits and vegetables? We'll get tired of eating just fish, and he didn't have much luck finding anything yesterday."

She hesitated. "Have you seen anyone around outside?"

"Not one person since we've been here." He picked up an apple, tossed it from one hand to the other, then set it down on the counter. "Is it true that you're a fugitive?"

The granola bar wrapper crinkled softly as she folded it over and over between her fingers. "There's a detective trying to find me."

Instead of the fearful reaction she expected, he just tilted his head, eyes narrowing slightly. "What does he think you did?"

She unfolded the wrapper and began to pull it apart one section at a time. Aaron didn't suspect her of a violent crime. If anything, he acted curious. She felt the pendant against her skin and pulled the neckline of her shirt up to ensure that it remained hidden.

"I guess I just took something from the wrong person."

The hallway floor creaked, announcing Nick's entrance.

"Good morning, guys." He pushed a flap of blond hair away from his eyes, walked to the other side of the counter, and pulled the loaf of bread and peanut butter across to him. He tried to spread peanut butter on a slice of bread while simultaneously shaking hair out of his eyes, making his companions laugh. Finally he walked over to the sink, and slicked it back with water.

"You need a haircut or a headband," Lareina joked.

He took a bite of his breakfast. "Yeah, one or the other."

Aaron walked to the door and pulled a khaki fishing hat from a hook on the wall. "Are you going to find some food today, Nick? I mean something that's actually edible?"

"Count on it." He replied as if he'd been challenged to a free throw contest. A smile brightened his face. "Are you going to catch any fish?"

After opening the door and stepping out, Aaron stuck his head back inside. "So many we won't be hungry for days."

"You aren't planning on leaving here today?" Nick stumbled over a hidden branch, but maintained his balance. He led the way to an area he had found at the end of his foraging the day before that he thought would be promising.

Lareina pretended not to notice. "I can wait a week or two, but not any longer. You'll want to go and find Ava soon too, before winter comes."

Absentmindedly, he rubbed a hand across the stitches on his forehead then pushed his hair out of his eyes. "That's a fruit tree, right?" He pointed off to the right then hurried in that direction.

Holding up one hand to shield her eyes from the sun,

she spotted an eight-foot tree straining under the weight of hundreds of round purple fruits.

"It's a plum tree," she shouted.

By the time she caught Nick, he had already pulled ten plums from a branch and placed them in his canvas tote bag.

"Don't fill your bag all the way. We can always come back for more."

He took a bite of the plum in his hand. "Should we keep walking this way?"

"Yeah, I think this tree is a good sign."

The two of them continued for another quarter mile into an area with thick tree cover. Lareina shuffled her feet forward with her eyes on the trees, watching for familiar leaves.

"There, that one." She walked up to the tree and placed her hand against its trunk. Fruit with a skinny neck and rounded bottom dangled about five feet above her head.

Nick turned in circles with his head tilted all the way back. "What is it?"

"Don't tell me you've never seen pears."

"I've never seen pears." He reached an arm above his head then jumped toward the lowest fruit, but his fingers didn't even graze the bottom. "How are we going to get them down?"

"Can you catch?"

"Yeah, but . . ."

Wrapping her hands around the lowest branch, she braced her feet against the trunk and hoisted herself into the tree. Leaves brushed her face as lightly as butterflies and a feeling of freedom swept through her.

"Don't climb too high," he shouted from below. "Aaron doesn't have the supplies to fix a broken arm."

She pulled a pear off the tree and dropped it into open air.

The fruit plummeted and plopped to the ground in front of Nick's shoes.

"I wasn't ready yet. Try again."

Lareina rolled her eyes, glad he couldn't see her. "All right, here it comes." She dropped another pear. Nick took a few steps forward and it landed directly in his hands.

The pear collection became a game requiring Nick to dart around under the tree and catch falling fruit, sometimes two at a time, until he collapsed out of breath. "All right, Rochelle. The bag is getting heavy. You can come down now."

Balancing in a fork, high up in the tree, she looked between leaves at a landscape dotted with trees and bright clusters of wildflowers. "Are you sure you don't want to come up? You should see this."

"Maybe next time. I have to get back with this stuff before Aaron gets back with the fish or he gets to start the next game of Battleship."

She descended a few branches, then swung herself down in front of him. "That would be tragic. We better go." Grinning, she brushed imaginary dust from her jeans.

Nick laughed and picked up the bag full of fruit. They walked back to the house, taking a different route to scout out areas for future foraging. The trees faded behind them and swaying grass enveloped them just as it swallowed houses, fences, and sidewalks. Keeping her eyes on her feet to avoid tripping over a hidden root or tangle of brush, she at first ignored the few plants embedded in the grass. Thick stems with rounded leaves became more numerous, poking up through the rising and falling green ocean. She stopped, crouched down, and held a leaf in her hand to get a better look. Following the row, she spotted plants on the edge with brown, shriveling leaves.

"What are you doing?" He turned to watch her.

"This must have been someone's garden once. I think I found potatoes."

"I will definitely win if I bring potatoes back. Where are they exactly?" he asked, crouching down next to her.

"They grow underground." She couldn't stifle her laugh.

Nick looked over at her with his head tilted as if waiting for her to declare it all a joke. "How do you know this stuff?'

For a second, her mind carried her back to a summer afternoon in Maibe. She pictured Mrs. Aumont's tiny backyard garden, produce of every kind growing in the fenced in square.

She smiled at him and shrugged. "I read a lot."

"I'm glad you paid attention. I guess we better start digging."

Lareina wiggled her shoe into the mushy ground. "We need a shovel."

"There's no time for that." He knelt down next to one of the plants and pushed mud to the side with his hands, piling it up on either side of the plant. His hair flopped over his eyes and he pushed it back with grimy fingers.

"You're getting all dirty."

"I'll take a shower later. Are you going to help or not?"

Muck enveloped the tip of her shoe and she cringed. "I'll hold the bag since I already picked pears and everything."

"Fair enough." He reached into his newly dug hole, pulled a potato out of the ground, and held it up. Tiny and pathetic, but a potato nonetheless.

"Who needs the city," Nick exclaimed when their feet returned to concrete. He was filthy from digging potatoes but still laughing and joking. "We could live off the land forever."

She wanted to point out that he didn't know potatoes grew underground and wouldn't have been able to tell the

difference between a pear tree and an oak tree without her
help, but instead she smiled. They carried a bulging bag
through overgrown lawns to the back of the house where
Aaron worked to scrub gunk out of a rusted grill.

"How many fish did you catch?" Nick called from across
the yard.

Aaron looked up. "Five." He crossed his arms over his
chest. "Your bag looks a lot heavier than yesterday."

"We have pears and plums." Lareina nodded her head
toward Nick. "And potatoes."

He pushed his hair back and held his grimy hands up,
palms out. "I dug them with my bare hands. It took hours,
and Rochelle didn't help." He feigned exhaustion and flopped
onto the deck.

She hauled the bag up three stairs and let it rest next to
his head. With her hands on her hips, she shook her head. He
grinned up at her, his bruise and stitches invisible beneath
layers of dirt, his hair sprawled around his head like the rays
of a cartoon sun.

Aaron smiled. "That's amazing. We'll have a feast tonight."

Nick put one hand under his head. "When is supper,
anyway?"

"Go take a shower." She took his other hand and pulled
him into a sitting position. "Then I'll cut your hair. Then we'll
have supper."

He stood and took a few steps toward the door. "Can I
trust you to cut my hair?"

"You haven't regretted trusting me so far."

Nick pulled the door open. "You have a point."

"And look at the bright side. It can't get any worse than it
is now."

He scrunched his nose, stuck his tongue out, and disappeared into the house.

Lareina hauled all of the food inside and rinsed it in the sink before lining it up on the counter next to their few remaining supplies from the city. More bread and some eggs would be nice, but she had no intention of going back. It took her ten minutes to find a comb and scissors—bathroom, third floor—and by the time she got back outside, Nick was already there helping Aaron with the grill.

A comfortable breeze spread the fragrance of flowers and enough sun filtered through trees to brighten the backyard. She rested her arms on the deck railing and looked out at waist-high grass that lapped at a wooden fence. Spindly weeds grew tall and thick through every crack of a cement pad next to a rotting garden shed. Vines climbed over the shed, up the side of the deck, and all the way to the top of the house. It was only a matter of time before this house, like the rest, succumbed to nature.

Nick and Aaron talked to each other and the grill squeaked and groaned every time they moved it, but all of that faded to background noise. Closing her eyes, she slid back in time. The swaying grass became a trimmed green carpet and the garden shed, freshly painted white with blue trim, stood wide open to reveal a lawn mower and rakes inside. Lilacs lined the back fence and a trampoline filled all space on the cement pad. A family—parents and four children—sat on the deck, eating ice cream, laughing, and enjoying a typical summer evening before typical vanished forever.

Were they in the city, hiding from the fever? Did they sleep in a cramped house with relatives in the country? Were they alive?

"That's it. That's it. It's working," Aaron whooped.

Jolted back to reality, she turned in time to see the boys high five in front of small flames that flickered inside the grill.

Nick noticed the scissors in her hands and obediently walked toward her. "When is the last time you gave someone a haircut?"

Closing one eye and tapping a finger against the side of her face, she pretended to think about it. "Um, never."

He sank down onto the bottom step. "Well, that's encouraging."

"If Nick doesn't have any bald spots when you're done, you can cut my hair too," Aaron joked.

Lareina sat down two steps above Nick. He flinched when the scissors snipped through the first bunch of hair.

"Hold still, or you are going to have bald spots." She continued bit by bit, trimming the hair at the back of his neck, over his ears, across his forehead and then at the top of his head. When she finished, she stepped in front of him, drew in a sharp breath, and clapped a hand over her mouth.

"What?" His wide eyes darted between Lareina and Aaron watching with amusement from his place in front of the grill. "Is it really bad?" He jumped up and bent low enough to see his reflection in the porch windows. Leaning his head one way then the other, he slid his hand back over his hair. "It looks good, like the way it used to. Why . . ."

When he turned around, all three of them burst out in the carefree laughter that leads to watering eyes and stomach aches.

"She . . . got you . . . Nick," Aaron gasped out between bouts of laughter.

The rest of the evening passed that way. They feasted on a delicious meal, laughed, joked, told stories of the best times they could remember, and when all light faded from the sky, they retreated to the living room where Lareina read a book and the boys continued their Battleship tournament.

Their days continued in similar fashion. Aaron went fishing. Lareina and Nick scoured the neighborhood for food. They returned to the places they already knew then continued further. They found wild berry bushes and the remains of gardens filled with clusters of tomato plants, giant zucchini, and hidden onions. They ate breakfast together, snacked through lunch, then ate supper on the deck. Those were rare days of contentment, free of worry and fear.

One rainy day a week into their stay, Lareina sat in the living room, her elbow on the windowsill. A dull glow from outside barely lit the room enough for her to decode words in *The Book of Conversation Starting Questions* she'd pulled from the shelf.

Aaron rested with his elbows against the floor, his chin propped on his hands as he studied a medical book he'd discovered in the attic.

Nick sprawled across the couch, his head hanging off the cushion so he got an upside down view of the room. "We've been sitting here for hours. I'm so bored."

"Read a book," Aaron suggested. "There are plenty of them here."

Nick pulled his head back onto the couch but didn't make an effort to move any further.

"What was your childhood hobby?" She lowered the book and laughed at the questioning looks on the boys' faces. "I have a book of conversation starters here, I might as well make use of it."

"Fishing," Aaron volunteered. "But you guys probably already guessed that. I used to go every day. My mom would get mad because I would sneak out before I washed the dishes or took out the trash."

Nick rolled over onto his stomach. "I played baseball every day there wasn't snow on the ground. I even tried to play in the house once, but I broke my mom's favorite lamp." He cringed at the memory. "I thought I would play baseball in college, but I guess that won't be happening."

A silence descended on the room, magnifying the *thtock, thtock* of a clock in the hall and raindrops splashing against the window.

"What about you Rochelle?" Aaron asked. "What kept you entertained ten years ago."

"I don't know." Her life was a maze of chores, cold basements, hot attics, and constantly moving to a new place. Did she ever have spare time? What did she do with it? "I guess I liked to play with locks. When I was six or seven years old, I found a padlock on the ground and finally got it open two weeks later. I would lock my bag to the leg of my bed so the other kids at the Home for Children wouldn't drag it off and take my stuff while I slept."

"You have to have something happier than that."

"Nick," Aaron warned.

"No, he's right." She wanted a real story, a good memory like baseball and fishing. "I tried sewing once. My friend was really good at it. She could make dresses out of old jeans and curtains." The memory made her smile. "I made a square pillow with crooked stitching."

Nick beamed. "All right, now we're getting somewhere. What's the next question?"

She pulled the book close to her face and squinted at the small font. "What is your greatest fear?"

"Definitely spiders," Nick exclaimed. "They bite, they

jump out from dark corners, and they crawl across your face while you sleep."

Lareina laughed but wished her greatest fear could be so simple. She didn't like feeling trapped in small spaces, thinking about catching the fever terrified her, storms had always made her uneasy, and looking at the pendant gave her a sense of foreboding. "Being caught by the detective," she lied. *Never finding a family,* she thought. That would be worse than all of the others combined.

They looked to Aaron, who stared down at the book in front of him. "Being a failure," he muttered. "Ever since I was a little kid, I told my parents I would become a doctor and take care of them and send them money. They expected me to get perfect grades in school, and I did. But since getting into medical school is practically impossible, I've been trying to find another way."

She lowered the book to her lap. "Is that why you won't write to them?"

He nodded without looking up.

"You should just tell them you are a doctor." Nick touched the fading pink cut on his forehead. "I'm convinced."

"You're studying right now. You'll be a doctor one day, a good one."

"What's the next question?" Aaron analyzed the checkered pattern on the rug.

"If you could choose a superpower, what would it be?"

Nick sat up. "When was this book written anyway?"

She flipped to the front and held the book to the light. "The first date is twenty thirty."

"That's old," Nick exclaimed. "Forget old, it's ancient."

Aaron slid his book forward and sat up. "Or maybe it's history."

"Who studies history anymore?" He watched water droplets slither down the glass. "People don't even know if they'll live to see tomorrow."

Gloom slipped back in and Lareina wanted to continue the distraction for just a little while longer. "If I could choose a superpower, I would want super speed."

Nick swung his feet to the floor. "I would want to fly. Nothing would stand in my way and I could travel even faster than you."

"I want the ability to memorize all of this." Aaron picked up his book and slid it onto his lap. "And understand how to use it."

Lareina closed her book and looked out at the gloomy afternoon. Sometimes she imagined that new leaders would emerge and fix the world or at least restore it to the way it was during better times. But maybe it wouldn't save her or Nick or Aaron. Maybe they already lacked the education and skills they would need to survive in any world except the one around them. They were part of an entire generation, slipping through the cracks, ignored, neglected, abandoned. The generation that would be responsible for saving civilization or tipping the world into inescapable chaos.

CHAPTER 11

The moon chased the sun in a never-ending cycle of light fading to darkness and darkness brightening to light. The trio woke up, ate breakfast together, and scavenged the surrounding land for food. Nick and Aaron played Battleship or a new game they made up involving dried up bottles of nail polish and windmill trinkets that they moved across the squares of the area rug in a complicated flurry of rules that never allowed either of them to move all of their pieces to the other side. Lareina read books about medieval royalty, detectives solving mysteries, men and women fighting wars, and lawyers finding evidence just in time to save clients from a life of imprisonment. In the evenings, she walked a half mile to the nearest train tracks and watched until dark, but not one train passed by.

One morning she stepped outside and sat down on the bottom step of the front porch. A cool north wind swirled into long-forgotten flowerbeds and pulled out crunchy brown leaves trapped there a year earlier. The wrecked neighborhood appeared much as it had when they arrived, except the leaves on partially severed branches had withered into skeleton arms. Another flurry of wind sent some wrappers and papers skittering down the street. A tree limb stopped them at the end of the front walk.

She stood and approached the fallen branch. Two wrappers from candy bars, three grocery receipts, and a page from a newspaper fluttered as the wind plastered them around scarred bark. Careful not to tear it, she peeled the ragged, yellowed newspaper from its trap.

In smeared ink, the top of the paper displayed the date as 9-2-2090. September. It had been mid-August when she left San Antonio. She flipped the page over.

Trains in and out of Austin Stalled until the New Year

As Austin's latest epidemic eases, a new challenge faces the city. Last month's flooding has washed out several miles of railroad track north of Austin. Four key railroad bridges have also been reported destroyed in the eastern half of the state. Plans are being made to transport supplies to isolated communities. The public is asked to be patient as repairs are made. Due to major railroad damage throughout the country, there is a shortage of materials. Please postpone any plans to travel by train until the new year.

There wouldn't be a train for months. Not until the middle of winter. She folded the paper and put it in her pocket, all the while gazing down the road that would take her on her first steps to Maibe. The main reason she had delayed traveling was for the chance to catch a train. But it had all been a fantasy, a futile dream that she could be home by the end of summer. Now she had miles of walking ahead of her with winter quickly approaching.

Lareina rushed into the house and pounded up the stairs to the room she had claimed as her own. She tossed her backpack onto the bed and began shoving clothes, brush, flashlight inside.

"Rochelle, what's going on?" Aaron stood in the doorway.

"The trains aren't coming." She tossed a pair of socks into her bag. "I have to go."

"What are you talking about? How do you know that?"

She handed the article to him and watched as he read it. "There won't be trains out until January. I can't wait that long. I should have been out of here weeks ago."

Lowering the tattered paper, he nodded. "This is a setback, but we can figure it out." He turned toward the door. "Nick, come up here for a minute."

Shoving her bag aside, she sat down on the bed with her legs folded under her as Nick's footsteps creaked up the stairs.

"What happened now?"

Lareina explained the situation as he stared down at the article in Aaron's hand. "In another month we won't be able to find food and we're not close enough to the city to get our food there daily."

Aaron rested his arm on a dresser. "Are any of us going to the same place?"

Nick frowned. "I need to find Ava, but I'm not sure where to look." His head dropped. "I should have probably left a week ago, but I don't think I know how to survive out there."

Aaron shrugged. "I'm not sure I do either, but I think the three of us together handle it pretty well." He looked at Lareina, eyebrows raised.

She leaned forward with her elbows on her knees. "I'll travel with you guys, but I have to go north." Her destination would remain confidential. She wanted to trust them, but what if they learned the truth about her? What if, in the future, they had a reason to betray her?

"I have an idea." Aaron tossed the article aside. "A year and a half ago every state was required to do a census. It doesn't mean it's entirely accurate, but wherever Ava was at that time should be on record. The article says the fever has burned itself out in Austin, so let's go there, check the census, and figure out which direction Nick should be traveling. From there we'll decide what to do next."

Nick cocked his head, considering. "Where do they keep the census records? I didn't even know there was a census."

"The head of household usually fills out the information. And I'm not sure where the records are kept, but Austin is the capital, so they have to be in the city somewhere. We'll ask around when we get there."

Now Nick nodded enthusiastically. "That's the only real plan I've had since I started looking for Ava. I definitely need help from you two if I'm ever going to find her. Let's take our time packing and leave tomorrow morning. Right, Rochelle?"

Two sets of eyes waited for her to verify the plan. She felt anxious about leaving, apprehensive about staying, and unprepared to travel in a group on foot. But Aaron's plan was solid. "We'll leave tomorrow."

For hours she wandered around the house, collecting small items that she hoped the homeowners wouldn't miss if they ever came back to collect their belongings. A gold-colored bracelet, long forgotten in the bottom of a shoe box; a watch in the kitchen junk drawer that looked like an expensive Timetale but upon closer examination turned out to be a worthless Timetail. She pulled jackets from the backs of closets, preparing for more rainy weather and cooler fall temperatures. She packed, unpacked, and repacked, utilizing every inch of space in her and Aaron's bags so they could carry every ounce of food and supplies with them.

PART 2

FALL OF 2090

CHAPTER 12

The pavement felt harder and the sun blazed hotter after a week and a half of floors beneath her feet and a roof over her head. Aaron and Nick trudged along behind as Lareina retraced her steps from the grocery trip.

"Where do you guys want to go after Austin?" Nick's voice crashed through her thoughts.

"There is absolutely no reason to go west, unless you want to get caught up in the water wars," Aaron reported. "I guess I'll keep going north to Dallas. Try to find work."

Her plans shifted like a teeter-totter inside her head. She wanted to stay in a city where she knew she could always find food. She wanted to leave Texas. She never wanted to see Galloway again. She didn't want to walk all the way to Nebraska, but her memory always carried her to that little town with a park and a bakery. Nick and Aaron were as close to being her friends as anyone had been since she lived in Maibe. Now that they were traveling together, she had to start trusting them with at least some information.

"I want to go back to Maibe."

"Maybe where?" Aaron asked.

She kicked a loose rock, sending it skittering down the street. "Maibe, Nebraska."

Aaron shoved his hands into the pockets of his jacket. They couldn't fit anything more in their backpacks, and Lareina's fifteen-minute lecture on the perils of winter without proper clothing convinced the boys to bundle up despite the summerlike heat.

Aaron shrugged to reposition his bag. "If Nebraska is just a maybe, then where else?"

"No, the town is called Maibe." She laughed. "It's some guy's last name, the founder of the town, I think. I didn't pay attention to that lesson."

Nick caught up to her and kept pace alongside her. "The place you learned to sew, right?"

"That's the last place I would go," Aaron interjected. "All of the people and civilization are east in places like New York."

"I heard part of the East Coast broke off the continent and sank into the ocean, like Atlantis," Nick stated in a low voice as if it were a secret.

"Who told you that?" She rolled her eyes. "There is no way that really happened."

"Someone else told me . . ."

"You can't believe everything you hear, Nick."

"Whatever. Once I find Ava, I'll just live wherever she decides."

"If I can't find work in Dallas, I'm heading east," Aaron declared.

Lareina sped up her pace so she led the group again. After another thirty minutes of walking, the three of them entered a city transformed. Compared to the ghost town the city had been a week and a half earlier, now it practically bustled. Outdoor markets had popped up in the middle of streets, wherever shipping trucks dropped off food and other provisions, and were being perused by cautious adults, some of them wearing masks or cloth tied over their nose and mouth. Many looked not too much older than she was. Each face she passed seemed dull and worn, and few people made eye contact.

She led Nick and Aaron toward the park she had visited

on her first trip to the city. A large market had materialized across the entire block, flocked with crowds of people buying groceries. No one they encountered appeared to be sick, but she didn't want to look too closely for fear of brushing shoulders with a shivering stranger displaying the earliest symptom of the sickness. Instead, she surveyed the area for unwatched goods—her instincts to take food when she could get it were hard to restrain—but people swarmed every corner of the market.

"Do you know where I can find census results?" Nick canvassed the area, asking anyone who would listen.

She left him to it, giving her attention to a woman selling baked goods from a nearby cart. Cookies, cupcakes, slices of pie—it all looked delicious, but too many watching eyes made it too risky to justify stealing.

"Maybe I know something. What will you trade me to find out?" a gruff voice replied. It wasn't the statement itself, but the threatening desperation dripping from it that warned her to turn around. Ten feet away, a man clutched the collar of Nick's shirt in his fist while Nick stood there, helpless and stammering.

"I d-don't have anything to t-trade."

"Hey, let go of him." She struggled to keep her voice steady and calm as she sprang toward them.

The man turned toward her, pulling Nick along with him. She decided he couldn't be much older than her, maybe three or four years, but he was thin and dirty as if he had been living on the street, unsuccessfully, for a long time.

"Not without a trade," the man insisted.

"I don't have anything to trade," Nick repeated in a shaky whisper.

What had she pilfered from the house that this man might

find valuable? She reached into the pockets of her jacket and felt the rough outline of a book of matches, the cool metal of a couple of coins, the fake golden bracelet that she might be able to sell as real, a box of toothpicks, and the thin outline of a watch band. With a sigh, she pulled the watch from her pocket and held it up in front of her, contorting her face into a mask of fear and naiveté.

"I'll give you this Timetale watch if you'll let him go. It was my father's, it's all I have left . . . Please."

The man examined her as if trying to determine the watch's worth from the appearance of its owner. Then he held out one hand, still clutching the front of Nick's shirt with the other.

"On three," the man directed.

Lareina nodded.

"One," he began.

"Two," she counted, lowering the watch toward his palm.

"Three."

She dropped the worthless watch into the man's open hand; he pushed Nick toward her and ran off. The force of Nick crashing against her threw her off balance, but he caught her elbow and kept them both standing.

"Are you all right?"

"Yeah." He took a long breath. "Was that watch really . . ."

A smile quirked at her lips. "It wasn't real. I found it in the junk drawer."

"You lied about it," he exclaimed in a hushed voice, eyebrows lowering. Then after a pause, "And you stole something unessential from the house."

"Yes," she said, taking his arm. "Now let's get out of here before you find any more trouble."

"You have to stop. Rochelle, you're going to get caught one

of these days and then what are you going to do?" he protested as she pulled him down the sidewalk.

Keeping her arm linked with Nick's, she stopped and looked across the busy marketplace. "You're the one who has to be careful because one day I'm not going to be close enough to rescue you. But for now we need to find Aaron. When did you see him last?"

"Not since we first got to the market." He tilted his head and squinted one eye. "I think."

"Think harder. We have to find him." She watched light fade from above. "And find a place to sleep tonight."

"Hey guys, over here."

They turned at the same time, trying to locate the source of Aaron's voice. Standing on her tiptoes, she strained to see over the streaming crowd of people surrounding the busy stands.

"Come on, his voice came from this way." Nick pulled her through an impatient line of customers waiting to buy fruit.

Keeping pace with him, she glanced from her feet to the sidewalk, trying to locate Aaron without slipping off the curb. Finally they spotted him waving from across the street.

With Nick right beside her, she followed Aaron around the corner, through an alley, and to the back of a building with an arched doorway. He stopped and pointed proudly. "We should be safe here tonight, and there's a little shelter in case it starts to rain." Steps beneath the archway led up to a set of padlocked double doors that were clearly no longer in use. A wide, smooth top step stretched back into a sheltered entrance secluded from the bustle of the market.

Nick stepped inside and sat down. He squirmed back into the alcove then rested his head against one of the doors. "It's perfect."

Lareina sat down next to him. "Good work, Aaron. This place couldn't be better if I'd found it myself."

Beaming, he leaned back against the door and slid down next to her. They had stayed at the olive-green house long enough to eat lunch then snacked on berries and plums, which wouldn't keep well in their backpacks during their walk. Something about exploring the market, verifying other people still populated the Earth, had given her the rush of adrenaline she needed to temporarily forget that she hadn't slept well the night before. Now, exhaustion settled in, and the three of them didn't say another word.

Distant shouts of "Five minutes until closing" floated down the alley. The one sound she wanted to hear, a wailing train whistle off in the distance, remained absent. Nick's head slid against her shoulder and Aaron breathed steadily beside her. She sighed, rested her head against Nick's, and closed her eyes.

Lareina stepped out of the pawn shop, where she had managed to sell the gold bracelet for twenty-five dollars, ignoring the certainty that an unsuspecting stranger would be conned into buying it for a couple hundred. She wound her way through a maze of sidewalks to the building that housed census records. The building that had taken a day and a thousand repetitions of the same question to locate. The building that Nick had entered three times each day for the last week, inquiring about Ava Welch, but being told only proven family members would be given access to such information.

Nick and Aaron sat near the bottom of wide front steps leading up to thick lobby doors. The city had only grown busier the longer they'd been there, and now crowds of people rushed up and down the sidewalks, some of them carrying briefcases, some of them carrying purses or backpacks, all of them with some place to go. Sometimes she felt like the fever had never been in the city at all—and then she would see a woman crying on a bench clutching a picture of a deceased loved one, or hear a little boy asking his father why his mother had to live with the angels because he missed her.

She sank down next to Nick. "Any luck?"

"No." His face dropped into his hands. "I'm never going to find Ava."

He had grown increasingly discouraged with each passing day. At first he had been determined to find someone in the building who would help him, then he thought he might be able to sneak in and look it up for himself, and finally he decided persistence would be the only way he could win.

An ambulance siren blared from somewhere in the city, someone shouted something unintelligible from a corner down the street, and Lareina drew her knees up to her chin.

"What did they tell you today?"

Nick rubbed a hand over his eyes. "The usual: that I have to give them my identification number to prove my relation to Ava."

Aaron stretched one leg down to the next step. "There has to be another way we can approach this."

There were plenty of different approaches, but what if the census placed Ava in San Antonio like Nick suspected? Lareina could never go south of Austin without risking Galloway finding her. If Nick decided to go back to San Antonio, she would never see him again. Deep down, that made her hesitant to help him.

She felt her own heart sink when he turned to her with dull, hopeless eyes. He deserved to know the truth.

"Who's at the desk inside?"

"A young guy, older than us but not by much. I think his nametag said Corey."

She stood. "Come on, Aaron."

"Where are we going?" He scrambled to his feet before she could answer.

"To find out where Ava is. Nick, wait here. We'll be back as quick as we can."

Building a story in her head, she jogged to the top of the steps, then waited for Aaron to catch up.

"What exactly are we doing?" He watched her with that same curious, fascinated look he had when she told him she was a fugitive.

Taking Aaron's arm, she led him to the side and waited as two men entered the heavy doors. "You're going to be my brother while we're inside. Can you follow my lead?"

His eyes shimmered a brilliant shade of bright blue, and a grin formed across his face as if she had suggested they go skydiving or mountain climbing. "Sure thing."

Aaron held the door and she entered the musty smelling building. Their hollow footsteps thudded too loudly, echoing in the open reception area. The only person in sight sat at a desk about thirty feet in front of them, staring at a computer screen. Wide hallways led in each direction and a closed door divided the wall behind the desk. When Aaron stepped up beside her, she looked over at him and he nodded. They approached the desk.

The lone receptionist, a stocky young man with a square face, didn't look up.

Lareina cleared her throat. "Excuse me. Could you help us with something?"

The man glanced up at them, lips set in an angry line. His name tag did say Corey.

She smiled and his scowl vanished. "How can I help today?" His voice came out friendly—a complete contrast to his appearance.

"I'm Lucy Welch and this is my brother John." She nodded toward Aaron. "We're looking for my sister Ava. I hoped maybe you could give us the lead we need."

Corey tapped his fingers against the keyboard with a soft series of clicks. "I'm not exactly authorized to give out information like that."

"Please, we're desperate to find her." She leaned in closer to the desk and let panic seep into her voice. "You have to understand, she moved down here with our parents three years ago, while we stayed in Missouri with Grandma and Grandpa, but once she was settled our parents came home and we haven't heard from Ava since. Right, John?"

"That's right. Our parents are at home waiting for us to send news. We're terribly concerned." Aaron spoke calmly with a hint of restrained desperation, adding to the story as if it were the truth.

Corey glanced at his computer screen then leaned forward with his elbows on the desk. "You know, it's strange that you're asking about Ava Welch. I've had a guy come in here every day for a week trying to talk me into telling him where she is."

Lareina stood up straight and gasped, a hand over her mouth. She turned to Aaron, whose eyes went wide in his best imitation of shock.

"You haven't told him anything, have you?" she insisted.

"No, of course not," Corey assured. "Is there some kind of problem?"

"Let me guess, this guy is about five-six, blond hair, brown eyes." She pressed her finger against her forehead at her hairline. "He has a scar right about here?"

"That's exactly how he looks," Corey exclaimed.

"Oh no, John, he's going to find her."

"Now don't panic, Lucy. We'll find her first."

Corey glanced from Aaron to Lareina. "What exactly is going on here?"

"My sister moved to Texas to get away from that guy. He was her ex-boyfriend and he tried to kill her even though she had a restraining order against him. We have to find her and get her home where she'll be safe."

"Don't worry, we'll get this all straightened out." Corey typed something with a fluttering click of fingers across the keyboard. "All I need is an identification number from either one of you to verify that you're family."

She needed a nine-digit number, anything to make Corey believe her story. For a second, she glanced up at the ceiling as if trying to remember. "Nine, eight, five," she recited, "Two, five. Two, seven, eight, one."

He typed each number as she said it, and Lareina held her breath, preparing an excuse for her identity not matching whoever might pop up on the screen. A minute passed and Aaron shifted his weight from one foot to the other. Another minute passed in uncomfortable silence.

"This system has been slow ever since the fever came through," Corey said with a grunt after three minutes. "Let me go check our census files and see if I can find the information you need."

"Thank you. You have no idea how much we appreciate it." She took a breath and smiled.

Corey returned the smile as he slid his chair back. Then he unlocked the door behind him and vanished through it.

Aaron stepped up to the desk and craned his neck around to see the computer screen. He touched a few keys on the keyboard then stepped back again, folded his arms across his chest, and waited silently.

After two minutes, the silence grew heavy. She wanted sound. Shouting, sirens, thunder—anything would be better than the empty silence that surrounded her and threatened to bury her at any second. A door slammed deeper in the building, a shoe squeaked across newly waxed floors, then the door Corey had disappeared behind creaked open.

He approached the desk with a blue notecard flapping in his hand. "Our last records show Ava Welch living in Dallas at the address listed on this card." He held it out to Lareina.

She took the card and slipped it into her pocket. Dallas. That meant Nick had to go north. They would all be traveling in the same direction. She gave Corey a genuine, relieved smile. "Thank you, we really appreciate this."

"I'm sure that dirtbag ex-boyfriend will come back tomorrow, and we'll be ready for him when he does." He returned to his seat behind the computer. "Don't worry—he won't be bothering your sister again."

Aaron shook Corey's hand. "You've done a great thing. Our family can't thank you enough."

Together, Aaron and Lareina left the building, rushed down the stairs, found Nick, and ushered him into an ally.

"What happened?" he asked. "Do you know where she is?"

"I can't believe that worked." Aaron's hands shook with excitement and fear. "Whose identity number was that?"

"No one's, for all I know. She leaned back against a brick wall. It felt cool against her back. "In a game like this, it's not about what's true, but what you can make someone believe."

She pulled the card out of her pocket and held it out to Nick with a grin.

He snatched it from her hand. "Dallas! She's in Dallas. I can go north with you guys. How did you manage to get this?"

"We became John and Lucy Welch," Aaron bragged. "Oh, and Nick? I would stay far away from that building for a while."

Nick just shook his head. "I don't think I want to know any more."

"I have one more surprise." Lareina pulled the twenty-five dollars out of her pocket. The boys stared at the bills with wide eyes and dangling jaws.

"Where did you get that?"

"Don't ask questions." Nick held up his hand. "Let's just go buy some supper."

The three of them walked back to the market and bought loaves of bread, bags of raisins and almonds, peanuts, and beef jerky, freshly picked peaches and green beans. When their bags were bursting at the seams, they spent the rest of the money on sandwiches and cookies that they ate back at the alcove where they'd spent every night since arriving in the city.

As they settled in for the night, Lareina closed her eyes and wondered whether Galloway had come to Austin. Was he searching for her as she tried to fall asleep? Would anyone recognize her if he showed them a picture? Would he follow her two hundred miles to Dallas?

CHAPTER 13

Lareina wanted to put as many miles between herself and San Antonio—and therefore Galloway—as quickly as possible, but the walk to Dallas proved to be even more frustrating than her walk to Austin. They tried to follow main roads with rusted signs pointing them in the right direction, but flood-ravaged bridges sent them on long detours. Each time they circumvented the obstacle and returned to the main road, they only found another missing bridge or river over the road. Sometimes heavy storms forced them to seek shelter in abandoned buildings or thick tree cover for an entire day. A walk that should have taken one week stretched into two. As September came to an end, blisters plagued their feet and hunger gnawed at their stomachs.

One night, resting in a field of tall grass, Lareina stared up at a sky plastered with shimmering stars. Nick slept using the other half of her bag as a pillow. She could feel the top of his head touching the top of her head, and she felt safer knowing whatever happened she didn't have to face it alone. Aaron slept a few feet away, barely visible through a screen of grass.

She had almost drifted off contemplating the infrequent houses they'd passed that day when Aaron began thrashing and muttering in his sleep. He had regular nightmares that usually lasted only a minute or two, but his frantic movements lasted longer than normal. Walking over to Aaron, she knelt beside him, placed her hand on his shoulder, and shook him. He shot into a sitting position, breathing rapidly and looking around trying to establish his location.

"It's okay, Aaron, it's okay. You were having a nightmare."

He rubbed a hand across his forehead as his breathing calmed. "I know. It's always the same."

"Maybe it would help to talk about it?"

Aaron nodded but didn't say anything. The moon illuminated wispy clouds racing north, and she wished they would take her along.

"When I left home, I was scared and then I got sick . . . with the fever. I probably would have died . . . but a man came along and found me shivering in the hospital parking lot."

Nodding, Lareina folded her legs beneath her and waited.

"He took me inside . . . he was a doctor who worked at that hospital." Aaron smiled. "When I got better, I told him I had always wanted to be a doctor, and he started teaching me how to treat the fever, appendicitis, pneumonia . . . Dr. Liner said I had a gift for treating patients and could be a doctor in no time if I just kept studying."

Crickets, cloaked in darkness, chirped a late-night concert. Nick murmured something in his sleep then rolled onto his side.

Aaron's smile sank and vanished. "But then he was gone—a sudden heart attack. To everyone else, I was just a kid . . . in their way." He cleared his throat and looked up at the sky. "When I left California, I was confident I could find a teaching hospital or at least a mentor, but I can't find anything. Rochelle, I'm wasting so much time . . ."

"You'll figure it out. You're studying right now, so you're already ahead." She tried to sound comforting.

Shaking his head slowly, he rested his forehead against the palm of his hand. "I turned eighteen last month. I should have been taking classes months ago. What about my family?"

"Write to them." She leaned back on her hands and

stretched her legs out in front of her. "If they really do care about you then they'll just be happy you're alive."

"Of course they care about me." His voice vanished into his hand as it slid from his forehead to his chin. "But I don't want to disappoint them. They could be starving right now because I don't have the money to help them."

Any clouds from earlier had vanished across the horizon. "At least you have a family to disappoint."

His slumped shoulders straightened and his eyes lifted to meet hers. "You're right. I'm sorry. I didn't mean . . ."

A hint of light accentuated the horizon. She scrunched her knees up to her chin. "It's okay. I'm over it. Just don't be so hard on yourself."

"I'll try." He looked up toward the glitter-speckled sky. With his hand he traced a path toward the ground. "That's a shooting star. Better make a wish."

Nodding, she rested her chin on her knees, but didn't make a wish. A lifetime of wishing and thousands of failed attempts added up to enough proof that wishes didn't come true. Or maybe she just didn't deserve to be granted even the smallest of requests.

"We should probably try to catch a few more hours of sleep." Aaron's suggestion sounded like an apology.

The dying star had vanished, but a translucent curtain painted the eastern skyline misty shades of pink.

"You're right."

After trudging back to her nest of grass, she squeezed her eyes shut but couldn't fall back to sleep. When the sun became unbearably warm against her closed eyelids, she flopped a hand over her face. A soft breeze shivered through rasping grass. Pools of sunlight encroached on shadows. Another warm autumn morning. She stretched her legs straight out in front of her and wondered how much longer the warm temperatures would last. Finding her shoes next to her in the grass, she pulled them onto sore feet, already protesting another long day of walking. Nick mumbled something and turned his face away from the rising sun before slipping back into sleep.

Reluctantly, she stood, tiptoed past a sleeping Aaron, and knelt beside a stream that cut through the pasture. In any normal year there wouldn't be water there at all, but with record rainfall over the past two summers, runoff had created new streams and lakes. For a minute she stared at its shimmering surface, then scooped some into her hands and splashed it onto her face. Three weeks had passed since they'd left the house with running water and Lareina wondered when she would find a working shower again, then tried to remember the last time she'd changed her clothes. The dry grass rustled behind her and Aaron approached with a toothbrush in his hand.

"Morning," Aaron said sleepily.

"Morning."

She trudged back to their camp where Nick sat up, stretching his arms toward the sky. He rubbed the back of his hand against his sunburned face. "How can it be morning already," he groaned.

"Just be thankful it's still warm." She sat, pulled a brush out of her bag, and began to work the knots out of her hair.

"Maybe we should take a break," he suggested. "We could find a shady spot, relax, pretend we're eating ice cream."

She dropped the brush back into her bag and zipped it shut. "We're getting low on food again. We better find some today."

"What are we going to do during the winter when—"

A rustling in the grass interrupted him, and a moment later Aaron crawled into view. "There's a man coming our way," he whispered.

Lareina stood up halfway to see over the grass. She heard the trampling crunch of footsteps before she noticed the tall man two hundred yards in the distance rushing toward them.

It was Galloway.

She ducked back down to eye level with Nick and Aaron, breath already hitching in panic. "He found me. We're going to have to run."

"We need a plan," Aaron whispered.

"All right, Nick, you run for that clump of trees," she gestured to a dark mound in the near distance, "and hide. Aaron, run north as fast as you can and then when the coast is clear, circle back and meet Nick in the trees. I'll run west." She pulled her backpack onto her shoulders. "Galloway will follow me, and I'll meet up with you guys when I can." For a few seconds, she just looked at them, carefully memorizing each feature of their faces. She didn't intend to return and risk leading Galloway right back to them. The pendant was her problem and she had to deal with it alone.

"Are you sure—"

She cut him off. "There's no time. Ready?"

Nick looked at Aaron, who nodded.

"Go."

The three of them scattered in different directions. Lareina bounded through the grass, cringing each time her sore feet hit the ground. For a full minute, she focused on pumping her arms and legs as fast as possible. When her heart felt like it would burst, she slowed a bit, listening to determine Galloway's proximity. She didn't hear the expected swish of trampled grass or snapping twigs behind her.

Gripped by panic, she spun around without stopping. Her feet slid forward and her hands temporarily touched the ground, but somehow she stayed standing. Looking toward the tree line, she spotted Nick just disappearing behind the foliage, and as she feared Galloway right behind him.

No. No. No. No. The word repeated through her mind as she sprinted toward Nick, faster than she'd ever run in her life. Her thoughts battled in tempo with her pace. It didn't make sense. Galloway wanted the pendant, the one slapping against her collarbone with a violent sting. Was he going to use Nick as bait to lure her in? Why bother when she was already in his sight? Would Galloway hurt Nick? Probably not. But what if he did? Fighting against every screaming instinct in her head, she sprinted into the trees.

Leaves slid across her face as she entered into the shadowy world of trees clustered so tightly together they blocked out all sunlight. The shattering crack of two gunshots echoed under the thick foliage. Stopping abruptly, she gripped a tree to steady the swaying world, and listened. Her heavy breathing muffled the buzzing of flies and hissing of wind through crisp leaves. Ahead came the unmistakable crashing of someone stumbling through thick brush. A cry of pain that sounded like Nick.

Slipping silently through the trees, trying to catch her breath, she came to the top of a steep embankment. In an area cleared by a fallen tree, she spotted a flash of blue as Nick tumbled down the hill. Frantically, she scrambled down after him, clinging to thin trees as her feet slid over partially decayed leaves and loose stone.

When he saw her coming, he tried to stand up, but staggered and collapsed again. No Galloway in sight, but he couldn't be far behind. She gripped Nick's hand tightly, pulled him to his feet, and slipped into the shadows of a cave-like opening eroded into the embankment they had just come down. She shrugged her backpack off, lowered it to the ground behind her, and squirmed back into the opening until she felt the earthen wall cool against her back. Nick started to mumble, but she clapped her hand over his mouth and pulled him into the dark void beside her.

"Shhh, it's okay," she assured, but kept her hand in place.

The darkness thinned and shapes materialized around them. Roots hung down like thick spider webs. Remnants of an old footbridge crossed right overhead to the other side of a stream that trickled past their hiding place.

Nick shivered but didn't attempt to speak again. Raising a finger to her lips, Lareina removed the hand intended to keep him quiet. She slipped her hand into his and together they waited, frozen. Feet stomped across the intact section of the bridge above until the detective's black boots came into view. Nick squeezed her hand, an act of comfort, camaraderie, and terror. After what felt like hours but was probably only thirty seconds, the detective backed away and the crashing disturbance of brush grew fainter. Nick took a breath, his grasp loosened, and his hand slipped back to his side.

"Are you okay?" she whispered.

"I don't know." He examined his arms and legs as if he expected to find a bullet hole. "I thought you said he would follow you."

"I thought he would. I'm so sorry—"

"You came back for me," Nick interrupted.

"Usually I'm the one being chased. I was feeling kind of left out." She shrugged.

A half smile formed on his lips, but his eyes remained wide with terror. After waiting another ten minutes and not hearing anything, the two of them stepped into the light. Grass stains splashed across Nick's jeans and scratches crisscrossed his face, but otherwise he seemed to be unhurt.

"Will he come back?"

Lareina looked back at the creek, the direction Galloway had run. "When he doesn't find us, he'll double back and try again."

"But how did he find you? We've been careful."

Touching her fingertips to the neckline of her t-shirt, feeling the thin chain hidden just out of sight, she shivered. "He's probably been watching us for a while, and he thought you could help him. You and Aaron should go to Dallas. I'll go in a different direction and—"

"No way," he interrupted. "This is too dangerous for you to do alone. Aaron and I will protect you."

"Nick . . ."

He shook his head. "No arguing. Come on, we should find Aaron."

Nick led the way through cool shadows, and she followed in silence, not sure what else to say. She thought of Susan lying on the ground, color draining from her face, light fading from her eyes, and blood soaking the grass. Where would they ever be safe?

"He's really after you for stealing? That's it?" Nick stopped, turned around, and studied her as if they'd just met. A deep wrinkle formed in the space between his eyes. "He was shooting at me. What did you take?"

The pendant grew heavier around her neck. *You can never tell another person about this.*

"Come on, Rochelle. I'll help you, but I deserve to know what this is all about."

He watched her, waiting for a response. Hadn't she wanted to know once? Didn't she regret it? *You have to tell me what's happening so we can figure out what to do next.* Her voice echoed back to her through time and she wished she'd never spoken those words out loud.

"I took a necklace." She shrugged. "I guess it was really valuable to him."

"A necklace?" Nick scoffed. "That's what this is all about? That guy must be insane."

It had been close enough to the truth that she didn't even have to disguise her body language or facial expression. She had taken a necklace, but not from Galloway, and that was all she had done.

Footsteps rustled loudly in the grass. They turned at the same time, each poised to run, but relaxed when they realized it was only Aaron coming toward them.

"Are you guys all right?" He asked when he got closer. "I heard gunshots."

"We're all right." She glanced over at Nick. "Just a few scrapes."

"You really do have a detective after you," Aaron said in a hushed voice. "For a while I thought you just told us that so we'd be afraid of you, but he was right there." He smiled and watched her with a kind of respectful awe.

Nick glanced around them in every direction. "We should get out of here before he comes back."

Together, they exited the trees back into morning sunlight. Orienting himself so the sun was on his right, Nick led them north and Lareina, lost in thought, walked alongside Aaron.

Like every other day, her feet ached, but any sense of security had been wiped away with the appearance of Galloway. Every snapping twig sounded like his heavy boot, every humming insect echoed like his voice in the distance, every tree on the horizon lurked like his silhouette waiting for her to walk into a new trap.

CHAPTER 14

Pulling the sides of her jacket together, Lareina zipped it against the cold wind relentlessly gusting into her face. She fought her way through it as strenuously as if she swam against a powerful current. Nick and Aaron toiled along behind her, feet dragging, heads bent to keep the wind out of their eyes.

"I'm so hungry," Nick groaned. "I wish I had a grilled cheese sandwich or a piece of chocolate cake."

"Stop talking like that," Aaron snapped. "You're just making everything worse."

A raindrop splashed against her nose and another trickled through her hair. She shoved both hands into her pockets. The week had started with heavy rain that stalled them for three days, they got lost twice in their quest to bypass submerged roads, and they had to slow down for two days after Nick sprained his ankle.

"I'll talk about whatever I want," Nick challenged.

Lareina pulled her hood over her head, but the wind pushed it back down. October had started with unusually cold and gloomy weather.

"Not if I can do anything about it," Aaron threatened.

"Then do something about it."

She spun around to Aaron's hand clenching Nick's collar and Nick's fist poised in the air.

"Stop it," she shouted, squirming between them and pushing Nick's fist back down to his side. "Don't you two think we have enough problems without us fighting each other?"

Aaron backed up and folded his arms across his chest, standing perfectly still except for his chattering teeth. Nick stared down at his shoes. The constant mist charged forward with each gust of wind.

"I'm sorry, Nick."

"I'm sorry, Aaron."

She looked from one dirt-streaked face to the other and only saw hopelessness, hunger, and exhaustion. They'd run out of food the day before and had been going on slim rations for days before that. The cold made sleeping difficult, and they were all tired of walking. Twice that day they had passed abandoned structures, but food was their priority, so they continued walking.

"The next town we come to, we'll stop and find a real shelter." She put a comforting hand on Aaron's arm, but didn't feel encouraged by her own words as she shivered. "It'll just be a little while longer, then we can rest. Okay?"

"Okay," Aaron agreed. "We can make it a little further. We're probably almost there."

Lareina turned to Nick, standing stiff against the wind as it ripped at his jacket. "How about you, Nick?"

"Shhh, listen," he whispered.

Raindrops pattered against their jackets and through the grass, but something louder sliced through the gloom. It started as nothing more than the undertone of a wail that grew to an echoing roll that rose and fell on the wind before becoming the familiar blaring of a train's whistle.

The three of them smiled as its outline appeared on the horizon, hurtling toward them, then rumbling past only twenty feet away with an icy blast of air. How long had they been walking near the railroad tracks without realizing it?

"We must be closer to a town than we think," Aaron exclaimed.

"Trains run through here," Nick mused. "That means we can take a train to Dallas."

"That means they have bridges." She took off running after the vanishing train and heard Nick and Aaron wheezing behind her. It felt good to run, to feel tingling warmth return to her hands and feet, to know she was closer to civilization than she had been in months.

It only lasted minutes before she stopped, face bent toward her knees, as the wintry air burned in her heaving lungs. When Nick and Aaron caught up, she continued at their pace.

As afternoon transitioned to evening the temperatures plummeted, a steady rain began to fall, and a fierce wind howled around them.

"We have to find some shelter." Aaron's breathing sounded rough and labored. "We'll die of hypothermia out here."

"There isn't any shelter." Nick's words echoed Lareina's thoughts. "We're in the middle of nowhere."

"We'll keep walking until we find some." She felt determined to keep moving, to find warmth, to stay alive.

"But I'm so tired." Nick sank down into the grass and wrapped his arms around his knees. "Let's just catch our breath for a minute."

Stomping her feet and breathing into her cupped hands chased away a little of the encroaching numbness.

Aaron shook his head. "Not yet. Rochelle, help me." She took one of Nick's arms and Aaron the other.

Together they pulled him to his feet. With a nudge, Nick started walking again. Aaron stumbled forward. Lareina linked her arm through his, keeping pace alongside him.

"W-we have t-to keep m-moving or we won't m-make it to m-morning." Aaron seemed to be talking to himself as he fought against the wind.

Nick began to tell stories about Christmas when he was a little boy. Lareina felt dizzy and numb. She tightened her grip on Aaron's arm and only heard some of Nick's words.

"My friends and I built a snowman . . . The tree was too tall to fit in the living room . . . One year mom made pancakes instead of ham . . . The best ornament was red with gold trim . . ."

Sometimes she closed her eyes for a few minutes, hoping a house would appear when she opened them, but the sky only grew darker. Sometimes Aaron stumbled over his feet and she helped him keep his balance. Minute after minute, she fought the compulsion to give in and rest for a minute.

"Rochelle, I can see lights." Nick's booming exclamation startled her.

Every part of her shivered, including her brain. Teetering between lucidity and fuzzy confusion, she didn't immediately comprehend what he meant. With great effort she opened her bleary eyes.

Nick grasped her arm and pointed ahead. "Right there, do you see them?"

She blinked, thinking it could be a mirage, but the little squares of yellow light remained. "I see them. Aaron, look."

"Mmmhmm."

"It can't be very far. Come on," Nick encouraged.

With agonizingly slow progress, they approached the property. The ranch-style house sat all alone with no shed, no barn, not even a doghouse.

"We can't just knock on the door," she told Nick as they

stood just beyond the circle of light cast by the windows. "And obviously there are people in there."

"I know, it looks warm. I'll just talk to them. What's the worst that could happen?"

"Nick . . ." Apprehension built inside her. Anyone could be behind that door. Maybe they were nice people, maybe they would shoot anyone who stepped onto their property, or maybe Galloway waited for her, knowing she had run out of options.

Though she tried to hold back, Nick took her arm and pulled her up the front steps to the door. The three of them huddled together, hoping to absorb even the slightest draft of heat from inside. Nick raised his hand and rapped three quick knocks against the wooden door. Aaron's head wobbled back and forth between his shoulders and Lareina clutched his arm tighter.

The door pulled back to reveal just a thin sliver of light, then swung in all the way. An older woman, curled white hair piled on top of her head and a pink dress that scraped the floor, looked out at them.

"Hi." Nick's voice shook with his shivering. "We g-got caught in the rain and w-wondered if we could step in and warm up for a m-minute?"

The woman looked out at them and pity spread across her face. "Of course, dear. You three come right in." They stumbled inside and the woman helped each take off their dripping jackets to hang on a coat tree in the entryway. Then she led her guests through a cozy living room to a kitchen in the back of the house. She gestured toward a table that filled half of the tiny room.

"Go ahead and sit down. I'll get you something warm to

drink and something to dry off with. I'm Cornelia, by the way."

Lareina pulled two chairs close together and sat down next to Aaron, keeping one arm around him. His head rested on her shoulder, so she couldn't be sure whether she shivered or absorbed Aaron's shaking. Nick pulled up a seat on the other side of the table, rubbing his hands over his arms. Cornelia filled a pot with milk and placed it on the stove.

"You three look half frozen. What are you doing out in this weather?"

"We're on our way to Dallas." Lareina's voice shook.

"Dallas," Cornelia exclaimed. "You still have another fifty miles to go."

Nick tried to dry his face with his soaked sleeve. "We would have been there a long time ago if the roads weren't all washed out."

Cornelia eyed Aaron's shivering form. "I'll get a blanket for him."

"Are you okay, Aaron?"

"I will be in a minute."

Nick shivered from across the table. "We really could have died out there."

"We almost d-did," Aaron corrected. "We have t-to be m-more careful."

Cornelia provided dry clothes—one of her own house dresses for Lareina and faded, patched shirts and pants that appeared to have been worn by a man much larger than Nick or Aaron. She noticed a hint of sadness in Cornelia's eyes as she handled the clothing, but didn't want to ask what had happened to its owner. Cornelia cooked them a warm meal then showed the boys to their room and Lareina to a room of her own where she tucked herself into a soft bed and slept until the smell of breakfast drew her back to the kitchen.

After plates of pancakes, at least fifty thank yous, and Cornelia's directions to a train station only a mile up the road in New Lake, Lareina, Nick, and Aaron walked through another gray morning. The rain had stopped falling, at least temporarily, and a constant bellowing of distant trains revitalized her hope. New Lake, according to Cornelia, was a community that had risen out of empty grassland three years earlier when the first report of the fever came to Texas. People who could afford it abandoned their homes in the overpopulated city where the fever spread quickly and moved to the more isolated community.

The air still held a permeating chill, but with dry clothes and her jacket zipped, she could tolerate it. Her backpack sagged, stocked with three bottles of fresh water and the lunches Cornelia had packed in brown paper bags.

"Dallas has to be full of hospitals, right?" Aaron considered as they walked. "I mean, cities need doctors, and they have to train new ones, right?"

"No doubt." She readjusted the straps on her shoulders. "And they'll be thrilled when you walk through the doors."

"I'll study my anatomy book on the train." It had been the only item Aaron took from the house outside of Austin. He debated it for hours, putting it in his bag, then taking it out and returning it to the shelf, just to carry it back down the stairs again. Finally she had convinced him the homeowners would be happy to let him have it, since he was studying it in order to save lives. Reluctantly, he had zipped it into his bag, but he studied it every time they stopped to rest, staring at images depicting the inside of hearts and human skeletons in dim moonlight.

Nick followed behind with the blue note card clutched in his hand, reading Ava's last known address over and over. Lareina imagined what it would be like when they saw each other again. Hugging, laughing, days of talking about old memories, and then a future, maybe a scary future, but one Nick and Ava could walk into together. What would it feel like to have someone walk hundreds of miles to find you when you hadn't talked in two years? It seemed magical, like a fairytale. She admired Nick for taking the risks he did to find his old friend, and felt a twinge of jealousy that she didn't have anyone to do the same for her.

"There it is," Aaron announced softly.

From their position atop a slight incline, the town of New Lake spread out in front of them. Paved streets lined with little white houses branched out into a maze of exact duplication. They looked at each other and smiled before making their way down into the town.

"How do people know which house is theirs?" Nick glanced from one side of the street to the other as they weaved toward the thundering whoosh of a train.

Aaron pointed to one of the front porches with three steps leading up to the door and a little overhang like every other porch. "They have numbers."

The little black numerals nailed above doors counted up as she passed—1021, 1022, 1023, 1024. They turned the corner—932, 933, 934. A train rumbled by in little flashes of brown and red between houses.

They came out onto the town's main street running parallel to the railroad tracks. Two women left a building, labeled Market, with baskets over their arms. A man entered the hardware building and two young girls looked into the window of a dress shop. The cold, quiet train tracks beckoned from across the street and behind a chain-link fence.

Nick looked at the fence and sighed. "Now what?"

Lareina ignored him and continued walking down the street, past a bakery, a flower shop, a bank, and a restaurant until she spotted what she wanted—a one-story building with wood paneling for the front that displayed train departure times in the window. She pulled the door open and walked inside. Nick and Aaron caught up to her as she observed a sleepy-looking man sitting behind the counter.

"Well, I didn't expect anyone to come in on a miserable, gray day like today," he grumbled.

Stepping forward, she ignored the negative tone of his voice, and clasped her hands on the counter. "We'd like to buy three tickets to Dallas."

"Would you now?" The man leaned back in his chair. "It's always amusing how pretty little girls think they can just get whatever they want handed to them."

Her hands clenched into fists.

"Hey, how about showing a little respect to your customers." Aaron stepped forward and stood protectively beside her.

Nick stood at her other elbow.

The man yawned. "I can be respectful, but it won't help you a bit. We only run one passenger train to Dallas per week, and they're all booked until December."

"That can't be right." She barely recognized her own faltering voice. They could walk the fifty miles to Dallas in three days if they could avoid the rain, getting lost, and potential setbacks. She wouldn't wait two months for a train.

"There has to be something else," Nick demanded. "It's urgent that we get to Dallas."

The man chuckled, a greedy, excited laugh. "I'm not entirely unreasonable. I could sneak you into a cargo car, but it'll cost you."

"How much?" Aaron asked.

Lareina didn't want to make a deal with this man. She wanted to walk out, climb the fence, and sneak onto a waiting train from the other side of the tracks. After almost two months of trying, she still couldn't convince Nick that survival meant breaking the rules, and the best solutions rarely involved spending money or making deals.

"Forty dollars for three tickets."

"Forty dollars?" Nick's voice sounded far away.

"If you don't have enough money, perhaps you have something to trade?" The man's eyes glanced at each one of them, examining their faces for signs that they held anything of value.

Nick and Aaron shrugged, knowing they had nothing, but they were forgetting about one important asset. An image of Galloway hovered through Lareina's mind: his cold eyes and shrewd expression. *I'll find you. Wherever you go, I'll always find you.* They were lucky he hadn't found them again, but the more time they spent walking, the better chance they gave him. Trading with the ticket booth manager would mean wounded pride, but it would only last for a few hours. Being caught by Galloway would be the end of her freedom, possibly forever.

She reached into her bag, slipping her hand under the food and clothes until she felt cool metal—the gun that could protect her, that could save her, that could be worth trading to get to Dallas. "Would you trade for a gun?"

The man smiled and touched all of his fingertips together on top of the counter. "Depends what it looks like."

She didn't glance at Nick or Aaron, but took a step forward, slid the gun out of her bag, emptied the magazine, and placed it on the counter. The ticket booth manager picked it up, turned it over in his hands, and nodded.

"Very nice. If you're willing to leave it behind, I'll get the three of you on a train."

Her shoulders sagged as she glanced at her travel companions. Nick nodded and Aaron linked his hands behind his back.

"It's a deal." She closed her eyes and took a breath. "When do we leave?"

"A cargo train will stop here for loading at seven this evening. I need all of you to be here by six. Until then, enjoy New Lake. There's a nice coffee shop down the street."

Would the man be there at six? Would there be a train at seven? She didn't know if she could trust him, but what other choice did she have? With her eyes on her shoes, she walked through the door and around the building, where she sank to the ground. Her bag felt light and empty as she looked out at desolate railroad tracks. Then Nick and Aaron were there, pulling her to her feet and down the sidewalk with them.

"Thanks, Rochelle," Nick said. "I know that was a tough trade, but I'm so relieved we don't have to walk in the rain anymore."

She nodded, but thoughts of Galloway haunted her as they entered the coffee shop, ordered hot chocolate with their last few dollars, and ate parts of the lunches Cornelia had packed. The shop was warm and quiet with tables that stood so high off the floor even Aaron's feet dangled above the ground. A fireplace lit one corner, surrounded by chairs covered in blue fabric and shelves of books. On any normal day, Lareina would have gravitated to that corner, but it didn't give her a good angle to view the door, and she imagined Galloway sneaking in before she had time to escape. Trapped. She would be trapped, but so would Nick and Aaron. Not because they'd done anything to deserve it, but because they were with her. She had implicated them in a dangerous situation, just as Susan had done to her.

"Rochelle, are you okay?" Aaron sat across the table from her, but she barely noticed him. "Don't you want some of your hot chocolate?"

She took a sip from the large blue mug. "I'm just tired."

It had to end. She had to separate herself from Nick and Aaron before Galloway killed one of them. Too often she thought of Nick's narrow escape from Galloway and imagined him bleeding out on the ground like Susan. They wouldn't be so lucky the next time and she knew there would be a next time. Nick and Aaron didn't deserve to die because they chose the wrong travel companion. Protecting the pendant was her responsibility, and as much as she yearned to remain a part of this group, the pendant sentenced her to a life of isolation.

Nick looked up from the notecard in his hand, eyes bright. "It seems too good to be true. This time we're actually going to Dallas. I'm going to see Ava again."

Nothing had been easy since Susan told her about the pendant, and she couldn't believe that after months of struggles everything would suddenly work in her favor. Galloway had to be lurking around New Lake. Over and over she surveyed the coffee shop and every face of every customer. He could be on the train. He could be waiting in Dallas, or on the other end of the phone with the ticket booth manager. Aaron's eyes met hers and his eyebrows slid toward his forehead.

"Can you stop worrying so much?" Aaron leaned back in

his chair. "We made it. We're going to Dallas and everything will be great."

"Of course it will." She smiled and tossed her untouched sandwich back into her bag. "I'm going for a walk. Sitting still is just making me nervous."

Nick jumped up. "Can I come with you?"

"Do whatever you want."

They left Aaron at the coffee shop and walked through a maze of streets in the foggy afternoon. For a long time, neither of them spoke, and Lareina distracted herself by looking for slight differences among the identical houses. One had chipped paint around the windows. One had a window box, ready for summer flowers. One had a blue rock on the front porch.

"Rochelle, do you think Ava will be happy to see me?" Nick's voice sounded so small in the quiet street.

"Why wouldn't she?"

"Because I haven't seen her for two years. What if she doesn't even recognize me?"

"Then you'll either take the time to catch up or you'll move on."

He stopped walking. "Move on to what?"

Linking her arm through his, she pulled him along beside her. "To whatever comes next. Don't worry about it right now. I'm sure she'll be flattered when she hears about all you've been through to find her."

Verbalizing her own fears didn't come so easily. Once again they walked in silence. Back at the coffee shop, they waited with Aaron for the hands of the clock to divide its face in half. Then they returned to the oppressive little ticket sales building.

"Sit on this bench and don't look suspicious," the ticket

booth manager ordered. "When the car is loaded and the loaders are all busy with the next one, I'll signal. You'll all get in the car. The door will stay open, so stay hidden in the back and don't let anyone see you or I'll lose my job over this."

The three of them sat and silently watched men dressed in brown pants and blue shirts carry and cart boxes into each boxcar. She kept her eyes on the end of the train. Soon, no one swarmed in or out and the loading process moved away from them. The ticket booth manager stepped out of the shadows and waved.

"There he is." She looked up and down the loading dock, but there was no one there to see them. "Let's go."

They scrambled across the open area and snuck into their designated freight car. Large containers piled with glass bottles and scraps of metal surrounded them.

"Over here," Aaron whispered.

Lareina and Nick followed his voice deeper into thick darkness. Between a stack of boxes and the wall of the car remained a gap big enough for three people to squeeze into.

"Perfect." She slid into the gap and sat down next to Aaron. Her shoulder pressed against his and her knees brushed her chin.

Nick sank down beside her. "Now what?"

"Now we wait," Aaron whispered.

Raindrops drummed above, voices shouted outside, and Lareina's foot fell asleep. The train didn't move.

"Why do we have to be in here with all of the trash?" Nick tried to stretch his legs, but his toes caught on the box in front of him before his feet slid two inches.

Aaron leaned forward so he could see Nick. "Because they aren't worried about anyone robbing this car, which means they won't pay any attention to it."

A gust of wind gently lurched the train from side to side. Rain pounded harder against the roof. Still, they didn't move.

"At least we're out of the rain." She put her backpack on her knees and rested her forehead against it.

Nick squirmed and folded his legs under him. "I bet it's really cold out there."

"Freezing, but there's room to move out there," Aaron grumbled.

The train groaned and lurched, shifting all of the boxes. Slowly they slid forward, bumping along the tracks and picking up speed, the rumbling becoming so loud they didn't try to talk. Nick crawled over to the corner and stretched out his legs. Lareina moved over to give Aaron more room and closed her eyes, but couldn't find a way to prevent her head from bouncing against some part of the train. After fifteen minutes of trying to get comfortable, she realized Aaron and Nick had both, somehow, fallen asleep. She crawled to the door where a knee-high panel stood as a barrier to anything sliding out. Silvery stars blurred against the sky as she sped beneath them. The train slowed for a small town, sped up, slowed down again. Considering her options, she slid the pendant out of hiding, lifted it close to her face, then twirled it between her fingers. Could she tell Nick and Aaron about it? No. Were they in danger even without knowing? Definitely. Would she continue to expose them to such risks?

"No," she whispered out loud. The train slowed slightly, and guilt continued to plague her.

Turning away from the dark landscape blurring by outside, she observed Aaron slumped sideways, half hidden behind the boxes, and Nick sleeping peacefully curled up in the corner. They would be better off without her. She had to run alone or she would never escape. Despite the aching behind her eyes, the feeling of sandpaper in her throat, and the weight of dread in her legs, she stood.

The clack between each bump increased with every second. Unsteadily, she approached the doorway's edge with her backpack in one hand.

"I'm sorry," she whispered without turning around.

With a quick fling of her arm, she swung her backpack out into the grass beside the tracks. Then, without hesitation, she sprang forward, catapulting herself away from shelter, safety, and the two people who had almost been her family.

CHAPTER 15

Her shoulder slammed against the ground first and she somersaulted twice to displace the force. Tangled weeds and matted grass didn't offer as much cushioning as she had convinced herself they would. Sitting up slowly, a little stunned, she assessed her condition: no broken bones, perhaps a few scratches and bruises, but nothing serious. The train clacked away, unaffected by Lareina's departure. Aaron and Nick would wake up far too late to narrow down her location. They had their own goals to pursue anyway.

She stood up, dusted off her clothes, and walked along the track until she located her backpack. Out in the open, she found herself exposed to a bone-chilling wind that lifted her hair off her neck and swept her open jacket away from her body. Zipping her jacket, she picked her way through the waist high grass, away from the train tracks. Light from a town ahead should have drawn her like a moth to a porch light, but fear of Galloway on her trail steered her clear of civilization. Instead of walking toward safety and warmth, one step at a time, she traipsed deeper into the frigid darkness.

She distracted her mind from the discomfort of walking by counting her footsteps. Counting was easier than thinking about Galloway, or Susan, or the pendant like frost against her skin. There was nothing to see but grass—no trees, no houses, not even a bush. Under normal circumstances that wouldn't be a problem, but lightning flashed on the horizon. A low rumble of thunder announced the storm's close proximity.

Shivering, she shoved her hands deeper into her pockets.

The temperature continued to drop and her jacket proved insufficient to protect her from the icy wind. Although her feet ached and she wanted to sleep, she couldn't stop until she found shelter. A bright streak of lightning flashed through the darkness. She dropped to the ground, and clasped her hands over her head, sure that it struck the ground right in front of her. Only seconds later, a crash of thunder shook the ground. Lareina scrambled to her feet and ran. Logic told her outrunning the storm would be impossible, but her animal brain urged her on. Her numb feet slapped against the ground and every breath tore through her lungs like razor-edged snowflakes.

Tangled grass caught at her feet as a cold raindrop splashed against her face. Then one splattered her hand and another collided with her forehead. Raindrops thudded all around her, and she forced her feet forward. Individual drops of moisture became a wind-driven wall of water. She staggered forward, lost her footing, and plummeted into swampy grass. Soaked, shivering, and out of breath, shaky arms pushed her body upward until she once again stood against the storm.

One step, two steps, three . . . Another step closer to home, shelter, anything with a roof. She tried to forget her numb fingers, throbbing ears, uncontrollable shivering, and chattering teeth. *Don't think, just walk,* she told herself.

The diminishing storm offered little comfort; it had already done its damage. She forced her feet forward and extended her hands to the gentle mist that had replaced the punishing rain. Absolute silence fell over the soaked landscape. Any leftover drizzle ceased. Lareina raised her face to the sky, but before she could enjoy the moment of peace, a sharp, hard object fell from above, striking just below her left eye. The force of it dropped her to her knees.

No one, human or animal, heard her cry out in pain. Eyes blurring with tears, she reached toward the stinging injury then pulled her hand away, stained with warm, sticky blood. Something white glimmered against the dark ground in front of her. She picked up the jagged, golf ball–sized chunk of ice and turned it over in her hands. An arrhythmic *thud . . . thud, thud . . . thud* echoed around her.

Water splashed out of puddles, displaced by the oversized, frozen raindrops hurtling down from the sky. The intensity increased from a random thud here and there to a constant drumming. Another chunk of ice splashed mud onto her hand, breaking her daze, and motivating her to get on her feet again. With no other options, she sprinted through the ambush of hail.

She scanned the horizon for a tree, a bush, anything that could offer a little shelter, but knee-high grass stretched out around her for miles. As a last resort to protect herself, she pulled her backpack off and held it over her head as ice pellets carpeted the ground, creating a slippery, crunchy barrier for her to navigate. Ignoring the burning in her lungs, she ran blindly with no destination in sight. Her aching feet begged her to stop, but she couldn't stand out in the middle of a hailstorm.

Her foot caught on something and she fell forward, her elbows crashing against a hard surface that banged with her impact. With each burst of lightning, she examined the slightly slanted, rough surface beneath her. It consisted of two panels attached to a metal handle.

She surveyed the area for a house, a tree, any sign of civilization, but there was nothing. She wondered how a storm cellar could exist without anything else around it. Shivering, she wondered how many natural disasters had ravaged the area in recent years. A large hailstone landed near her hand on the storm door and shattered into tiny crystals.

Reaching for the handle, she noticed a rusty chain attached to a padlock. She took the chain in her hand and pulled, but it didn't break. Slamming it back down, she listened to the unending clamor around her. The padlock may have been rusting in the elements since before she was born, but it still managed to lock her out. With both hands, she desperately rummaged in her bag for her lock picking tools, found one with her fingertips, and inserted it into the lock while hail crashed all around her.

She pictured the first lock she'd solved years earlier to keep herself calm as she worked. The padlock sprang apart. Lareina flung the door open, plunged into her miraculous shelter, and pulled the door down tight against the icy barrage above.

Sitting on a cold concrete step, she waited for her heartbeat and breathing to return to normal. As dark as the sky had been, the storm cellar was a black void in comparison. Thuds from the hail echoed eerily through the shelter and her inability to see anything only made her more anxious. Then, she remembered the flashlight in her backpack. Violent shivering slowed her attempts to unzip her bag and locate the desired object by touch. Finally, she pulled it out and slid the switch forward.

A white beam of light perforated the darkness. Tired and stiff, she hobbled down the stairs. Even with light, there wasn't much to see in the little room. Some makeshift shelves stood against the back wall. Moving the light from the bottom shelf upward revealed each was empty—until her beam reached the top and illuminated five fabric cylinders. She reached up and, using the tips of her fingers, pushed one of the lightweight objects toward the front of the shelf. It fell to the floor with a soft *thump* and bounced to a halt against her feet.

She reached down and touched the smooth, soft material. *Sleeping bags,* she thought with a smile. The first good news since she'd left the train. Her fingers were so numb she could barely grip anything, but she managed to pull two more sleeping bags from the shelf, unroll them, and pile them in the middle of the room.

Lareina placed her flashlight on the shelf to chase away as much darkness as possible. She unzipped her jacket and slowly pulled her arms out of the sleeves, cringing every time heavy material touched her bruised skin. The dripping jacket plopped to the floor and her arm slid into the sliver of light. Black and blue and covered in welts, it looked like the arm of some grotesque creature. She pulled it back from the light and closed her eyes.

"It's n-not that bad," she whispered through chattering teeth. "It'll be b-better tomorrow."

After slipping out of her shoes, she removed the rest of her clothing, being careful to avoid standing in the light so she wouldn't see more of her injuries. Despite her shivering, she took the time to hang her dripping clothing from the shelf to dry for the next day. Then, too exhausted to concern herself with anything else, she placed one sleeping bag on top of another and wriggled inside the top tube of material. She pulled the third sleeping bag over her and turned the flashlight off.

Warmth from the sleeping bags brought her shivering to a more tolerable level, but this was her first night alone in some time, so despite her exhaustion strange sounds in the darkness kept her awake. *Thump . . . clank, drip . . . thump . . . thump, drip.* Her flashlight made the cellar much less ominous, but she couldn't afford to drain the batteries. Lacking any other sources of comfort, she tugged the top sleeping bag over her head like she had done with blankets as a child.

Her thoughts drifted back to Maibe. It wasn't the place she had been born, and she had only lived there for a year, but it was the only place she'd felt a sense of belonging.

"I just want to go home," she whimpered, and hunkered deeper into her bed.

CHAPTER 16

Squeezing her backpack strap in her hand, Lareina squinted ahead at a line of trees interspersed with the shadowy outlines of buildings. As she drew nearer, what she thought had been a town became a house surrounded by sheds and a barn. She understood the risks she faced by stepping onto that property, but continued her course anyway. As much as she wanted to avoid contact with people, she couldn't survive much longer without help. The sight of a house gave her hope that she hadn't been walking in circles after all, but also beckoned as a possible shelter from increasingly treacherous weather.

The past three days had left her lost, exhausted, and out of food. Rain drenched her and the nighttime temperatures were uncomfortably cold. Afraid of hypothermia, she barely slept and didn't rest for more than an hour at a time.

Although a thick cover of clouds hid the sun from view, she guessed the time to be early afternoon as she crunched through ankle deep leaves to the nearest shed. Flattening herself against a cool metal wall, she peeked around the corner and surveyed the house. Every pane of glass reflected the outside world, smooth and unbroken. The roof wasn't missing one shingle. That house represented warmth, dry clothes, and possible food. With everything she desperately needed waiting only feet away, she lost patience for caution, for surveillance, or for reason.

She took a teetering step away from the shed, but crunching

gravel sent her scrambling back for cover. Breathing rapidly, she looked out across the yard. The house, several sheds, and a thick perimeter of trees all looked the same until movement near the barn caught her eye. First she noticed familiar black boots. Her eyes moved upward to dark blue jeans, a red flannel shirt, and then the face that stalked her nightmares. Galloway looked toward the house. He had caught up with her, but he didn't know it yet. *I'm still in control*, she told herself. *I just have to hide until Galloway leaves and then walk in the opposite direction.*

Heart pounding against her chest, she struggled to keep her panicked breathing quiet. Every part of her wanted to run, but she knew that remaining absolutely still would be her best chance to escape. She flattened herself against the shed and held her breath, curious and nervous about Galloway's next move. She squeezed the pendant tightly against the palm of her hand.

Galloway stomped up hollow stairs to the farmhouse's front door. He knocked loudly, impatiently, then waited, shifting his weight from one foot to the other. Seconds passed before he pounded more persistently. The door opened just enough for someone to peek out.

Holding up his badge, he announced, "Detective Russ Galloway. I have a few quick questions."

The door opened wider and a tall, thin man stepped out onto the porch.

"What can I help you with, Detective?"

Galloway handed the man a sheet of paper and asked, "Have you seen this girl? She's wanted for murder and I have reason to believe she's nearby."

The man shook his head. "No sir. It's pretty quiet out here. I never have visitors."

"You wouldn't mind if I take a look around your property, just to ensure your safety?"

"No sir, not at all. I don't want any criminal wandering around my place," the man said, surveying his yard suspiciously.

If only he knew, Lareina thought. She edged to the farthest end of the shed as Galloway began his search. Her stomach growled and a cold gust of wind cut through her jacket like it was a t-shirt. The lost opportunity for food and shelter brought tears to her eyes, but she blinked them away. Maybe she could escape Galloway, but that left her with the choice of death by starvation or exposure to the elements, whichever came first.

"I know you're here somewhere. Why don't you just make it easy and come out of hiding." Galloway looked down at something in his hand then held it out in front of him like he was trying to pick up a signal.

Is he using some kind of tracking device? Like in a spy novel? Is that how he keeps finding me? But it didn't make sense. He had never been close enough to plant anything. Her chest constricted as she stared down at her mud-splattered shoes. There was no other explanation. Fighting against every instinct screaming in her head, she slipped one foot free and then the other. The cold, wet ground seeped through her socks.

She narrowed her focus to the space surrounding her in search of another hiding place and a way to get there without anyone spotting her. Galloway would surely check every inch of the farm, so she couldn't remain stationary. Two more sheds stretched toward a thin line of trees that separated the farm from a pasture. A second clump of trees sprouted just beyond that. It wouldn't be much cover, but if she could make it to that last cluster of trees, she would have a chance to escape and once again lose Galloway.

Taking a deep breath, she tried to persuade her heartbeat to slow to normal. Galloway squatted near the front porch, shining his light through the lattice screen. Darting forward, she slipped silently into the shadows projected by the second shed. She held her breath and waited, but no footsteps approached. One more shed, then thirty yards of exposed space before the shelterbelt's arms of protection embraced her.

Something soft and warm grazed her hand. She let out a silent gasp of surprise. A golden retriever wagged its tail at her. Dogs didn't scare her, but their friendly nature could easily reveal her hiding place.

Lareina waved her hands in front of her. "Shooo. Go away," she whispered.

The dog just stretched its front paws forward and made a high-pitched whining sound.

"Shhh," she scolded and edged another step along the wall. A low, rumbling growl radiated from the animal. Their eyes met, but the dog didn't share her sense of caution. He let out a loud bark then continued, growing louder by the minute.

Crunch . . . Scrape . . . Crunch-scrape. Galloway's boots rushed across the gravel driveway toward her. She didn't wait for him to enter her line of vision. Without looking back, she sprinted toward the tree line.

"Hey! Stop!" Galloway's voice boomed right over her shoulder.

She didn't have to turn to know Galloway followed close behind her, growing nearer every minute. But, without the city's labyrinth of alleys and hidden alcoves, she didn't know how to evade her pursuer. The reverberating echo of a gun bounced around her and a section of wet pasture splattered up her leg.

"The next one'll be in your arm if you don't stop," Galloway called, out of breath.

She began swerving back and forth, refusing to make herself an easy target. Shaky from hunger and clumsy from cold, her refuge appeared to be miles away, when in reality, it was only thirty feet. It seemed inevitable her legs or lungs would give out any second.

Another bang tore across the pasture as a searing pain sliced across her right arm, just below the shoulder. She staggered forward and crashed against spongy ground, but immediately scrambled to her feet. Galloway caught her bag and yanked her backward. Feet sliding against thick mud, she used the ground as a springboard and slammed all of her weight back against him. The force threw him off balance and they landed with a splash in the saturated sludge.

Lareina disentangled her arms from twisted backpack straps and tried to pull away, but Galloway clenched her left wrist. Hoping the mud would make her arm slippery, she heaved away from him, but he only gripped her tighter, slamming her back against the ground. She lifted her face and twisted sideways just as he reached for her other arm. Without time to think, she pulled her leg forward and kicked hard, aiming for his nose.

He released her wrist with a curse, hands going to his face. Lareina slid away from him, scrambled to her feet, and resumed running.

"You'll pay for that," Galloway growled. She didn't look back. Stiff, shaking, stumbling, her feet shuffled forward under wobbly legs.

He still had her backpack, but she had the pendant, and

that was enough. She would replace everything else later. Darting into the brush, she felt every rock and twig under her unprotected feet, warm blood trickled down her arm, and she fought her way through punishing branches that scratched her face and snagged her clothes.

Scanning her surroundings, she spotted a tangle of thick bushes and lunged into them. Her next step found her flailing through open air before splashing into a trench of frigid water. Patches of gray swirled and mixed with thick, angled branches as the world rotated left and then back again. Shadowy silhouettes of twigs trembled against a darkening sky. Enough light streamed in for her to determine she had fallen into an old drainage ditch screened by the bushes she had planned to hide in. At one time it probably directed water beneath a gravel road, but time and lack of traffic had allowed the rain and brush to erase any evidence of civilization from history. Dazed and out of breath, she crawled deeper into the culvert and flattened herself into the mud, hoping Galloway wouldn't discover her accidental refuge.

Her arm throbbed, cold mud seeped through her clothes, and time passed, but fear held her captive. The familiar shape of the pendant in her hand stood between sense and insanity. Logic begged her to give up, but hope wouldn't let her die there, alone. She promised herself that once she was free of Galloway, she would find someone who cared about her, someone to call family, and stay with them for the rest of her life. That hope provided the final surge of strength she needed.

Holding her injured arm tight to her chest and gripping roots and brush with her other hand, she pulled herself out of the ditch. Already exhausted from the short climb, she fell to her knees and stared up at the night sky, irritated that she had lost hours of daylight and warmth.

Lareina shivered as violently as the trees against icy gusts of wind. Her wet clothes and hair made the temperature feel twenty degrees colder, and every step required more energy than she could muster. Dizziness spun the world into an unfamiliar place, so the glimmer of light ahead was surely nothing more than a hallucination. But with each step, she moved closer and closer to the unwavering glow until she realized the little squares of light came from hundreds of windows. Buildings stood just out of her reach beyond a tall, concrete wall. She drew nearer, pressing her hands against solid blocks, looking for a way to get inside, her last chance for food and warmth.

What if Galloway is inside? What if he's been here with one of those posters? What kind of people live inside of a wall? The questions deteriorated any courage she had built up. Cautiously, she took a few steps back and looked around, but everything remained dark and quiet. She had to find a way to see over the wall, to know if anyone waited on the other side. Continuing forward, her foot caught something and she stumbled forward. A five-gallon bucket stuck up out of the grass. She turned it upside down and stepped onto it, but it wasn't enough; the wall succeeded in its mission to keep her out. The bucket tilted beneath her feet and she shifted her weight to balance it, but the sloping ground aided gravity.

Lareina and the bucket crashed to the ground. Every instinct screamed for her to run, but she couldn't move. Her arms and legs felt so numb she couldn't even guess whether she was injured in the fall. *This is it*, she thought. *Either Galloway will catch me or I'll freeze to death right here.* Low voices shouted, close and far away at the same time, and footsteps squished toward her. Huddled against the wall, holding her breath, and trying to stifle her shivering, she could only hope for the best as a flashlight beam found her.

"Who are you? What do you want here?" The voice was male, but its owner had to be young, maybe younger than her. Soggy footsteps slurped forward through thick mud.

Already caught and too exhausted to move, she could only wait to face the person behind the voice, prepare to accept the consequences, and perhaps take her last breath of freedom. Rallying all of her energy, she tilted her head sideways and opened her eyes. Two silhouettes hovered over her, fading in and out of focus like ghosts. She rubbed a hand over her face.

The taller one kept a flashlight aimed at her and the other held his gun in front of him, ready to defend whatever he guarded.

"Answer the question," the boy holding a gun demanded.

"I-I-I'm lost." She shivered so hard she could barely speak.

The two guards remained in position, studying the ragged intruder.

"Get up," the boy with a flashlight ordered.

She knew the two strangers would continue to view her as a threat until she proved herself harmless. It wouldn't be difficult in her condition, but still she intended to put on a good show. Bending her left elbow, she propped herself a few inches off the ground before collapsing. The flashlight beam came closer, but she could only shiver and curl her knees to her chest. A hand grasped her arm, lifted it, then dropped it. Pain surged from her elbow to her wrist, and she let out a weak yelp.

"She's hurt," the guard with the flashlight exclaimed. "Her

sleeve is soaked with blood." Whether the guard expressed concern or fear, she couldn't surmise from his dull, stiff voice.

"She must have enemies," the other guard whispered, a hint of panic in his voice. "We should get out of here."

If they left her out in the cold, she would die before morning, but if they determined she was a threat, she might not survive another hour. Feeling the situation slipping out of her control, she tried to lift her head from the ground without success.

"We can't leave her out here." The beam of light quivered slightly. "She'll die out here."

"If this goes wrong, it's on you," the other warned. "You can explain it to the president."

"Just shut up and keep your eyes open for the enemies you're worried about."

His words sounded louder and closer to her ear and then she felt herself being lifted, held against him, cold air blocked from her body as they moved through the mist. A new panic gripped her mind and stole her breath. Where would they take her? What would she encounter on the other side of the wall? Not wanting to pose any kind of threat, she fought the desire to open her eyes and remained as limp as possible.

Minutes later, the rain stopped and the air around her instantly rose thirty degrees. It felt like Cornelia's kitchen or the front porch of the olive-green house in early morning sun.

"We found her outside. She's in pretty bad shape."

"Dr. Avery, report to room 303."

"Take her down the hall to room 106. I'll get a doctor there as soon as I can."

The unfamiliar voices, beeping, buzzing, and gagging smell of disinfectants put her on edge. The only place she could associate with that overwhelming smell was a hospital.

It brought back memories of the broken leg she'd suffered at six years old. Her mind grasped for a way to escape, but nothing came to her.

"You'll be all right," the sympathetic guard said. "Just hang in there."

The strong arms that held her loosened and lowered her. Soon her back met a hard surface and her head sank into something soft that sounded like walking on dry leaves.

She kept her face turned away from the door even after she heard it click shut. Her hands and feet ached with a prickly tingling as the room's warmth chased away any numbness. Breathing slowly to calm herself, she positioned her good arm so she would be ready to defend herself the minute she heard the first squeak of a door opening.

Only a few moments passed before the knob clicked once then again. She sat up quickly and swung around on the exam table. It was too quick and the ceiling sank to the floor as everything spun around her. Lareina squeezed her eyes shut and pressed a hand against her forehead.

"Rochelle, is that you?"

CHAPTER 17

The immediate relief at hearing the familiar voice felt like a rope being tightened around her lungs had let go and she could breathe again. She opened her eyes and her vision came back into focus to reveal Aaron's kind face right in front of hers. It had been three days since she'd left him on the train, but already his eyes seemed brighter, less sunken, and his cheeks had lost their familiar pallor. He wore a white coat that matched the rest of the room, all a blinding, clean white. Lareina looked down at her hands, arms, and clothes all caked with mud. No wonder such hesitance gripped his voice. How could he possibly recognize her?

"Aaron, it's me," she whispered through chattering teeth.

For a moment she forgot about her aching arm, and tried to sit up, but the pain surged back and dizziness returned. Whimpering, she fell back against crinkling paper that covered the exam table.

Aaron put one hand on hers and another, warm, against her forehead, but watched her with a mixture of concern and confusion. "It's okay, you're safe now. Rochelle, what happened to you?"

She tried again to sit up, and this time Aaron slipped an arm behind her shoulders. "Galloway almost caught me, but I got away, for now." Shivering, she looked around the small, windowless room. Panic seeped through her body although she tried to swallow it down. Being trapped in the tiny white room, with no idea what waited outside and no escape route, increased her anxiety. "What is this place?"

"You're in a hospital at a place called Oak Creek." Aaron rested a gloved hand lightly on her shoulder. "Don't worry. I'll get you fixed up and you'll be just fine." He glanced at her arm while she stared at the spotless, white wall.

Aaron helped her out of her filthy jacket and she fought back the instinct to sob as the material pulled away from her wound.

"I'm sorry," he apologized, already examining the injury.

"Is it bad?" She sniffled, fighting back tears.

"No. The bullet just grazed you. But I have to clean it up or it'll get infected." With his arm still behind her, Aaron slowly lowered her until her head once again rested against the pillow. "Close your eyes. I'm just going to gather a few supplies."

A rustling sound, like alley cats in a dumpster, followed the high-pitched running of water that filled a container with a hollow echo. Lareina focused on breathing in and out. The entire day felt like a hallucination that began as a nightmare and ended like a dream. Could Aaron's presence be nothing more than a trick of her mind? She considered pinching herself to find out, but her throbbing arm seemed enough punishment to prove the reality of an old friend treating her wound in a strange hospital.

The room grew eerily silent. "Aaron, you're still here, right?"

His hand touched hers. "I'm right here. I'm going to wash the dirt away from your wound. I'll be careful, but it might hurt a little."

She opened one eye in time to see a white cloth and bowl of soapy water in gloved hands. Swallowing hard, she braced herself for the pain; it hurt enough already. Aaron dabbed it with the washcloth and she felt the bullet rip across her skin all over again. Unable to remain still, she squirmed as far away as she could get without plunging off the exam table.

"It hurts," she whimpered.

He reached for her arm again but she pulled it away.

"Rochelle, you have to let me do this or you'll be dealing with a serious infection by the end of the week."

Lareina looked at Aaron through watery eyes. She was in no position to argue, and he was just trying to help.

"Sorry. I'm ready now."

He squeezed her hand. "Take a deep breath. I'll do this quick. So, what happened to you on the train? We woke up and you were gone."

Staring at the colorless ceiling, fragmented through tears, she focused on Aaron's voice. "I started to think about Galloway and how he shot at Nick, and I jumped off the train before either of you could talk me out of it."

"We were worried about you. It looks like we were right to worry."

"Everything went wrong. I don't think I could have made it much longer," she muttered through her grimace.

"No need to worry anymore."

As he worked on her arm, Aaron relayed events of the past few days. He and Nick had woken when the train stopped at Oak Creek and found themselves staring down the barrel of a rifle. They were hauled inside the walled community that seemed to be connected to the rest of the world only by railway. After hours in what could only be described as a prison cell, Nick and Aaron had both been questioned by a President Whitley. When the president found out about Aaron's medical experience, he sent him straight to the hospital. Ever since, Aaron had been taking orders from the other doctors, who trusted him to care for less serious patients.

"Where's Nick?"

Aaron finished stitching the wound. "They said something about his skill set being perfect for the new project. They sent him to the barracks . . . I think that's what they called it. I'm not really sure what they do over there, and I haven't had a chance to talk to him yet. I don't leave the hospital much." His voice became excited and hopeful. "This is the experience I've been hoping for, Rochelle. I'm learning so much."

Lareina shivered involuntarily.

"Don't worry. This is a good place. You never have to worry about food or shelter here." He examined her arm and nodded. "All done for now. You can look at it."

She glanced at the clean six-inch band of skin on her arm. In the middle was a two-inch raised ridge of neat stitches. Though it wasn't bloody, the sight of the wound made her nauseous and she looked away. "Thanks, Aaron."

He extended his arm toward her and she slipped her hand into his. With Aaron's help, she stepped down from the exam table. He led her into an empty hallway, up one flight of stairs, and into a bigger room with a window and a bed, then showed her the door that led into a bathroom.

"Go ahead and get cleaned up and then I'll bandage your arm. I have to go check on a few patients but I'll be back." He took a step toward the door then glanced over his shoulder. "I'll make sure you get dinner and recommend that your questioning be held off until you're rested."

Before she could process his words, he rushed out of the room and she stood alone, barefoot on the shiny wooden floor. Taking Aaron's advice, she went into the tiny bathroom, flipped on the light, and took a look at herself in the mirror. A pale, tired reflection stared back through the glass. Her cheekbones looked like they were about to poke out of her skin, leaves and twigs stuck out of her tangled hair, and her eyes looked huge in her dirt smudged face. It had always been a point of pride to keep up with hygiene no matter where she slept.

Slipping out of her filthy clothes, she discarded them in a pile on the floor. For the first time in almost three months, she took off the pendant. Thick mud caked its surface, and she felt lighter without it weighing her down. After rinsing it under the faucet, she hung it on a hook to dry. Reaching into the shower, she twisted the knob to hot. The rush of scalding water forced her to pull her hand back.

She turned the knob back to warm and took her time showering, enjoying the clean scent of soap and scrubbing away layers of dirt that had accumulated on her skin. Feeling alert and refreshed, she dried herself and dressed in the hospital gown hanging on the door. The pendant reflected light ominously from where it hung next to the sink. *Just leave it there. Someone else can find it and deal with all of the problems.*

He said it would be the end of everything, of all of us. Susan's words. The promise she'd made. Lareina reached shaking hands toward the pendant and returned it to its place around her neck, then shuffled to the bigger room.

A dull throbbing returned to her head, so she decided to rest until Aaron came back. She got into bed and pulled the warm blankets up to her chin, letting any memories of violent shivering fade away. Somewhere between sleep and consciousness, a door groaned, something clattered beside her, and footsteps padded away. Too tired for fear or curiosity, she didn't open her eyes. If it weren't for the delicious aroma of a warm supper, she wouldn't have opened them at all, but her growling stomach held more influence than her fatigue.

After the door closed, she counted to twenty then opened her eyes. On a folding table next to the bed she found a tray of baked chicken, mashed potatoes, green beans, and a bowl of peaches. She pulled it onto her lap and ate the food without tasting much of it in the two minutes it took her to swallow everything edible on the tray.

When she finished, Lareina slid back onto the pillow. Water dripped in the bathroom—one drop, two drops, three drops. No footsteps in the hallway. Aaron had to come soon. He said he would. Even though he seemed a little more distant, she couldn't blame him. She had left him and Nick. Seven drops, eight drops, nine drops. Rain against the window added to the count. Ten drops, eleven drops. Her eyes closed. Twelve drops. She drifted into sleep.

A welcome brightness prompted her to open her eyes to gray daylight filtering through the curtains of her hospital room. She turned her face away from the window and closed her eyes to drift back to sleep. For a minute she did, until a knock on the door followed by the sound of its squeaky hinges startled her awake.

"Hey, how are you feeling?" Aaron carried a small gray bag and put it on the floor at the foot of her bed.

Squirming into a sitting position, she stretched her stiff arms carefully. "Better, I think."

"Good. You were so sound asleep when I came back last night, you didn't even wake up when I bandaged your arm."

An involuntary shiver shook her body. The number one rule of survival was to be alert at all times. Galloway could have walked into the room and she wouldn't have even known he was there.

"Can I check your arm?" Aaron asked, interrupting her thoughts.

She nodded and watched as he carefully unwrapped the bandage. "Aaron, is there a way out of here . . . of Oak Creek?"

He frowned as he turned her arm to examine his work. "We came in through a guarded gate. I'm not sure about other entrances or exits." He paused to meet her eye. "But after everything you've been through out there, why would you want to leave?"

"Because I'm not sure I'm safe here either."

Aaron gently taped down the edges of the new bandage. "Don't worry. In a few days, you won't even consider leaving. I know I don't want to leave. I'm really making a difference here." His eyes were bright and excited.

Whether her view of Oak Creek matched Aaron's was yet to be determined. It would be a welcome relief to stop running and stealing just to survive, but she didn't want to settle for the first nice place that came along. She wanted to be home. She wanted a family.

"There's some clothes for you in that bag." He pointed to the floor just beyond the bed. "Someone from security will be here in a couple of hours to escort you to your orientation questioning."

She sat up straight. "What does that mean?"

"It's nothing to worry about." Aaron smiled and shrugged. "Relax, Rochelle. This is a good place. They just want to make sure you're not a threat to Oak Creek. Just be honest and it'll all be fine."

If it weren't for the watermelon-sized lump in her throat, she would have laughed. Being honest never worked for her, but she didn't know the right lies to tell. She remembered the fear in the guard's voice when he talked about the president. Lying worried her far less than what would happen to her if the president determined her unfit to remain in Oak Creek, but knowing an argument wouldn't help, she smiled.

"I have to check on another patient, but you have an appointment in nine days to get your stitches out. I'll see you then if not before." Aaron started walking toward the door. He was leaving her, just like that? His distance seemed more than just irritation that she had left them. In fact, she wasn't sure he was angry about that at all. He seemed almost too eager to tell her that Oak Creek matched the stories he'd told himself about the future he should have. Despite the changes, he was still a familiar source of comfort.

"Aaron, wait."

By the time he turned around, she had crossed the space between them and pulled him into a tight hug. She didn't want to be alone, didn't want to be questioned, but human contact made her feel better.

"Thank you for helping me."

"Anytime," Aaron told her, and then he was gone.

Lareina washed her face, brushed her teeth, and dressed in the slacks and blouse that had been carefully folded in the gray bag. After months of wearing stiff, mud-splattered clothes, she felt overdressed, but the type of clothing Aaron had brought gave her the impression that meeting with the president was an event to be taken seriously. With shaky hands, she carefully tucked her pendant under her shirt so it wouldn't be visible.

Her socks slid on the tiled floor as she walked to the black dress shoes waiting at the foot of her bed. At least she wouldn't be barefoot anymore. Trying to quiet her thoughts, she took some deep breaths and stared through the window. The view included several identical buildings, all four stories tall with hundreds of windows. Beyond that the wall, and, what captivated her attention the most, a train slowly sliding by. She dreamed of being on that train and watching Oak Creek vanish far behind her. But first she wanted to talk to Nick. When she had left him, she thought he would soon be in Dallas where Aaron would help him find Ava. Now she wanted to know that he would be safe whether he chose to remain at Oak Creek or continue the search for his friend. She was surprised Aaron hadn't talked to Nick, but he did seem busy.

A loud knock shattered her thoughts, and she opened it for her visitor. The boy in the hallway stood about six feet tall and wore black slacks with a shiny black raincoat. A nervous grin froze on his face.

"You look like you're feeling much better than last night. I'm glad, I was a little worried." His voice sounded familiar, but she couldn't place it. "I'm sorry, you have no idea who I am," he said, holding out his hand. "Tony Acosta. I work security here and I found you outside last night."

She shook his hand, seeing a possible ally in this Oak Creek security guard. "I'm Rochelle Aumont. Thank you for rescuing me."

"Of course. You probably want to put on a jacket. It's still raining outside."

She grabbed the jacket Aaron had brought in the bag and slipped it on. With Tony leading the way, they walked through a maze of twisting hallways and steep stairways before emerging into the cool, misty morning. The sidewalks were empty of people, and Tony whistled a tune in complete contrast to his tenseness the night before.

After leaving the hospital, they followed a path that felt like a tunnel transporting them between single-story brick buildings on both sides. A dead end forced them to turn left toward a wider sidewalk that appeared to be the main walkway through the community. Lareina noted every turn in the sidewalk, every building, every open space, and every possible nook where she could hide.

Careful landscaping surrounded each building and perfectly manicured lawns lined the sidewalks. As they turned up the wide walkway, a monstrous structure came into view. Quadruple the size of any other building and covered in turrets and spires, it appeared to be a castle nestled among the dozens of plain structures.

Tony looked over at Lareina, who stood with her head tilted back to take in the entire building. "That's where the president lives," he explained.

Imagining the owner of such a house brought all of her anxiety back in a rush. A desire to run pulsed through her body, but she fought it and kept in step with Tony. "What is the president like?" Tony's response and body language would hopefully give her some tips on how to handle her interview.

He pushed his hands into the pockets of his raincoat. "He's very controlling and stubborn, so once he makes up his mind about something there's no changing it. He can be kind of paranoid, and new people sort of put him on edge." Tony shrugged. "We all think he's worried about sabotage from the outside," he whispered.

"Why would someone sabotage this place? And if he's so worried, why does he let anyone in?"

Glancing over his shoulder, even though they hadn't passed any people, he shook his head. "As much as he hates it, he knows the community can't expand without an inflow of new workers. We need them in the factory." Tony swallowed. "And to replace workers who are sent to the barracks. Plus we keep security pretty tight so there isn't really anything to worry about." He continued to scan the deserted sidewalks, as if someone would hear him mention something secret.

"What exactly do people at the barracks do?"

"I can't tell you much," he whispered. "It's kind of a military secret. But everyone knows they're digging tunnels."

"What are the tunnels for?" She had been so focused on escape that the possibility of being assigned a job hadn't even occurred to her until that moment.

Tony tensed as they neared the president's castle. "Don't tell anyone I said that—we shouldn't talk about it. Look, just answer the president's questions and agree with what he says. Tell him about your injury and maybe he'll assign you to work in the kitchen or something."

He pulled the front door open and held it while she passed through. The room sprawled around her with vaulted ceilings and a huge fireplace against the back wall. Chairs with red cushions and checkered throw rugs gave it a semblance of cozy welcoming.

"This way." He sounded far less cheerful than he had outside.

She followed him across the lobby to a hallway and through a second door. The box-sized space with gray walls didn't share the inviting quality of the lobby. A table with one chair on one side and two on the other furnished the room. Lareina hesitated in the doorway, but Tony walked in and pulled out the chair on the lonely side of the table.

"Go ahead and sit down. He'll be in soon." He said it mechanically, as if he had spoken those same words many times.

Although she wanted to retrace her steps back through the front door, she obeyed and took a seat. In the silence she focused on breathing to keep her fears to herself and project calm. Only minutes passed before two men strode in, followed by Tony, who closed the door behind them.

One man wore a carefully ironed shirt and matching tie. He was a tall, thin, harsh-looking man in his early twenties. His eyes were too close together for him to be handsome, but his lack of a smile didn't improve his attractiveness either. The other man, probably twenty years older, wore clothes similar to Tony's and had blond hair that sat far back on his head.

The man with the close-set eyes sat down and leaned forward, studying Lareina intently. "I'm President Whitley and this here is my head of security, Officer Storey. All we ask is that you answer our questions honestly."

Officer Storey didn't sit, but paced behind the president from one side of the table to the other.

"What is your name?" the head of security asked.

Her heart rate thudded to the rhythm of his footsteps. "Rochelle Aumont," she answered in a calm, steady voice. The false identity jumped to her tongue more quickly than her own name. So far so good.

"What brings you to Oak Creek?" The president revealed a slight smile.

Unable to ignore the way he studied her, she averted her eyes. "I didn't come on purpose." There was the truth, but it would need some embellishment. "My parents died of the fever two weeks ago, and we hadn't kept up with rent, so the landlord kicked me out. I'd been walking for several days when I was mugged and the few possessions I had left were stolen. I got disoriented and then I ran into your wall. I was only looking for a way around it to continue on my way."

She nodded toward Tony, who stood tall in front of the door. "That's when your guard found me."

The president leaned back, nodding, but Officer Storey didn't seem impressed.

"Is that how you ended up with a gunshot wound to your arm?" Storey demanded.

She nodded in reply. "I thought they just took my stuff; I didn't even hear the shot. I didn't notice the blood until I stopped running." Choking, she tried for tears.

"Let's stick to the issue," Storey said without sympathy.

"Whoa, give her a minute, she's not on trial." President Whitley looked up at Tony and any hint of the warm smile he had for Lareina faded from his face. "But this young man is."

Tony stiffened more, if that were possible, but he didn't seem surprised by the shift of attention.

"He brought an absolute stranger into our community without even considering that it could have been a trick, leaving us open to sabotage," the president continued.

It wasn't her battle to fight, and although she'd only known Tony for a few hours, she felt a gratitude and more importantly a debt to him that she wanted to repay immediately.

"I apologize, sir, but that's not even close to the way it happened," she interrupted.

Officer Storey's eyes widened, his mouth opened a little, but he seemed to have lost the capability to form words. President Whitley shook his head disapprovingly. Lareina didn't dare look at Tony. She had failed to keep her mouth shut and just answer the questions.

"Is that so?" Whitley's eyebrows lifted. "Please explain."

"Officer Acosta noticed that I was hurt." She turned to make the bandage more obvious. "He checked my arm himself while his partner checked the area. I was freezing and starving, and I owe him my life."

"Well," the president said, leaning forward again, his eyes more intense than ever. "We're lucky Acosta made a good choice this time, but one more reckless decision could mean the deaths of hundreds of people who rely on us for safety."

Lareina shook her head. "Wait a minute, are you even listening to me—"

"Are you listening to me?" Whitley interrupted. He leaned forward with his hands on the table, fingertips almost touching hers. A single blue vein throbbed in his forehead. "You may just be an ignorant little girl, only aware of your own problems, but war is coming to Texas and it's coming soon. We don't take chances of security breaches around here."

Storey looked uncomfortable, staring down at his hands as they rested on the table. He didn't make eye contact with her and neither did Tony. *Just tell them the truth and everything will be fine.* She wasn't following Aaron's advice and she definitely wasn't following Tony's. The sinking feeling of a huge mistake engulfed her, but she couldn't turn back.

The president's eyes burned into hers, but she didn't flinch. Despite the thick tension, he smiled. "Maybe you need to learn some respect for authority."

The words made her stubbornness flare. She pushed her hair back from her forehead and twisted it around before tossing it over her shoulder. "Maybe you need to worry less about punishing your guards for showing normal human empathy. Mr. President, sir."

The smile on Whitley's face widened, became softer and more genuine. "Well would you look at that, Acosta," he said, losing his smile and turning his glare to Tony, who remained at attention in front of the door. "Rochelle here isn't backing down from this one. I'll give you one more chance, so don't mess up tomorrow."

Officer Storey looked from Tony to the president as if trying to figure out a puzzle. "Sir, are you sure . . ."

"No worries, Storey," the president interrupted. "Acosta, take Rochelle to Louise. Tell her she has a new roommate and trainee in the library."

"Y-yes, sir," Tony stammered. "Thank you, sir."

The president stood and so did Lareina. For a few long seconds, they only looked at each other.

"Rochelle, I look forward to talking with you again. We'll have lunch one day." With that he left the room, Officer Story storming out behind him.

"Are you insane?" Tony exhaled the words in a hushed voice. "Do you know what could have happened to you?"

She had no idea what could have happened and decided that was for the best. "You saved my life. I couldn't let you lose your job for that." Her voice came out smooth and relaxed, but she kept her hands hidden under the table so Tony wouldn't see them shaking.

CHAPTER 18

"**A**ll of those books have to go back to the shelves upstairs. Now," Louise ordered from her chair at the front desk.

Lareina rested her broom against the wall. She would get back to sweeping eventually. After almost a week of working at the library, she had no complaints except, of course, about her boss, who also happened to be her roommate. Louise enjoyed giving her the most undesirable tasks possible. Every time Lareina passed by the main desk, Louise tilted her thin face to the side so her long blond bangs revealed cold blue eyes before ordering her to scrub the floor or thoroughly dust hundreds of bookshelves. Outside of work, Louise ignored her entirely.

If she didn't enjoy her job, Lareina wouldn't have so pleasantly accepted orders from her boss, who couldn't be more than two years older than her. However, shelving books on the second floor was her favorite part of the day. Louise never missed her on the main floor, so she took a little extra time and read while she returned books to their proper places in the room of endless shelves.

"No problem." Lareina responded to the order as if it had been a polite request. Before Louise could give her another job, she gathered a towering stack of books into her arms and shuffled to the staircase. Stretching her foot out in front of her to feel for the first step then the next, she read the top title. So many books existed in the world. Even if she dedicated the rest of her life to reading, she doubted she could finish every book in the Oak Creek library.

Upstairs, sunlight streamed through the east windows, illuminating every empty space on the shelves. Examining covers for authors, she walked from one end of the room to the other and filled gaps between books. Her favorite time to be at the library was during the morning, when it was quiet, since everyone was at work. The rush usually came in around two o'clock when the factory closed for the day. The library stayed open until five, then she was off to supper at the cafeteria. The meals weren't overly creative, but it was food that she didn't have to steal. After supper, she had nowhere to go except the tiny room she shared with Louise and nothing to do but stare through the window until lights out at nine.

That part of the day, between supper and lights out when she had time to think, was the worst. Sometimes she feared Galloway would find out she resided at Oak Creek, and she imagined what it would be like if he just walked into the library to arrest her. There would be no escape and she would be forced to surrender. Nick was also a constant in her thoughts, and she wondered if conditions at the barracks were as terrible as Tony had implied.

During lunch breaks, she had walked every sidewalk from the library to the wall, which was only about a mile in any direction. While every path ended at the wall, one corner of the community was hidden behind a thick screen of pines. The walkway ended fifty feet from the line of trees, and signs warned against trespassing. No one ever walked beyond the paved pathways, so she didn't either.

The president's mansion stood next to the library. From a second story window, Lareina watched young men dressed like Tony walk in and out of a little building nestled between the library and the president's house. Once she even saw them drag a handcuffed man inside. It seemed to be the guards' headquarters. Would they take her there if she were caught exploring that last corner of Oak Creek? She memorized the locations of windows and shrubs just in case.

Nick never appeared in the cafeteria or the library or on the pathways between buildings. His absence from the places everyone visited at least once a day, combined with the mechanical, obedient way people shuffled through their day, made her uneasy. Although they were warm and fed, no one seemed particularly happy to live at Oak Creek. Clearly there were other dangers for them to fear. Though she hadn't seen anything to make her think Nick was in immediate danger, the secrecy surrounding the barracks made her anxious to verify his well-being. Guilt still haunted her for leaving him and Aaron on the train, though she knew separating was the right choice with Galloway still after her.

She needed a plan to communicate with Nick since she couldn't attempt to find him without attracting unwanted attention. Despite her persistent pestering of Tony when they ate supper together, he never revealed anything more about the barracks, and she didn't trust him to take a message for her. The only remaining option was to break the rules and find him herself.

The night she decided to go to the barracks, she stared at the ceiling after lights out, listening to the steady tick, tick, tick of the clock hanging above her bed. Initially the sound had annoyed her, but it now felt like a comfort, something she could rely on to remain constant. Louise's steady breathing signaled that she was asleep on the other side of the room.

Cautiously, Lareina sat up and swung her feet off the bed. A spring squealed with her movement, and she froze, waiting for a response from Louise, but the room remained quiet. Tiptoeing across the room, she pulled her jacket over the t-shirt and sweatpants she had been provided with for pajamas, pushed her feet into her shoes, and slipped out the door.

Bright lights in the hallway made her blink several times before she could see clearly, but no one stood in her way. Avoiding the front door, the only allowed exit, where an official sat twenty-four hours a day, she walked into the first-floor bathroom. It was a long room of showers and toilets shared by everyone who lived on the floor. One of the showerheads dripped, but otherwise the room was silent. Unlatching the window by the sinks, she lifted it just high enough to slip outside, then turned and slid it almost closed, leaving space to pry her fingers under it upon her return. She dropped behind evergreen bushes surrounding the building and made her way to the shadow of the next structure.

Dark windows and deserted sidewalks, exactly what she had hoped for so late at night. She had completed this walk dozens of times in her imagination. Through all of those envisioned scenarios, guards stood in her way at every turn, trying to prevent her from finding Nick.

With her hands shoved deep in her pockets, she slipped through silent darkness like a shadow drifting through the night to the opposite corner of Oak Creek.

The wall of evergreens separating the barracks from the rest of the community trembled in the breeze. For a minute she hesitated to step off of the pavement, but she had to talk to Nick if she wanted to leave Oak Creek with a clear conscience. Her feet bounced across spongy grass and hands nudged needled branches aside as she forced her way through thick, untrimmed conifers.

As she emerged from the dense green cover, perfectly trimmed lawns transformed to a field of knee-high weeds. At the bottom of a gradual slope, a run-down three-story building with dirty windows and peeling paint stood illuminated in the moonlight. Behind the dilapidated structure, two sides of Oak Creek's ten-foot wall met at a corner. Her eyes followed its perimeter until she discerned the outline of a gate, just wide enough for one person to walk through, sealed by iron bars. From her vantage on the hill, she could see large dark mounds of dirt, she supposed, sprouting from a field that stretched away from Oak Creek.

Careful to keep her footing as she crept down the gentle slope, she approached the lonely building. Deep puddles stood everywhere, hidden by overgrown weeds, surprising her with icy cold water up to her ankles.

Tony had provided one very useful piece of information after three suppers of persistent questions and pleadings for help on locating Nick. After determining they would not be overheard, he had whispered that she should check the northeast corner of the lowest floor of the barracks. With that, he made it clear there was nothing more he could do.

The windows on the second and third floor contained cracked glass, but those at the basement level had been broken out and replaced by iron bars like prison cells. She couldn't imagine what the conditions must be like inside and although she wanted to find Nick, she hoped she wouldn't find him there.

Determining which side of the building was north, she slid along the wall past ground level windows that only stood as tall as her knees. Balancing on her toes to avoid sinking into the mud, she squatted in front of the corner window.

Lareina took a silent breath and gripped the window bars. "Nick," she whispered into thick darkness. "Nick, are you in there?"

CHAPTER 19

A cold breeze swept through the grass with an eerie rustling that sounded too much like approaching footsteps. Lareina looked back to the trees, but no one approached. Loosening her grip, she slowly released the breath she had been holding and turned away to leave.

"Rochelle, is that you?"

She turned so quickly she almost lost her balance, but managed to wrap her hands once again around the window bars. Nick's face slowly rose into view. His sunken eyes watched her without blinking, as if he thought she would vanish at any second. Nick leaned forward into the moonlight so she could see the grime streaked across his face.

"Are you alone?" In her surprise, she could barely speak.

"Yes, the cells are only big enough for one person. If it were thirty degrees warmer, I'd say I was lucky to get a window." He shook his head, eyes wide with disbelief. "But how did you get here?"

"By accident. I talked to Aaron and he told me you were here too."

Nick rubbed a hand back and forth across his forehead, smearing the dust into a gray smudge. "I shouldn't be surprised. You always seem to be around when things go bad."

Her worry bubbled into annoyance. "What is that supposed to mean?" she started a little too loudly before adjusting her voice.

"Don't get all upset," Nick said without emotion. "I just

mean that I've almost died at least four times since I met you. I'm sure it's just a coincidence."

Lareina squeezed the bars so tight her knuckles hurt but focused on keeping her anger—and more importantly, her voice—under control. "You better not be counting the pit. You got yourself into that one."

Nick half smiled. "But you showed up soon after. Kind of like this, I suppose. How do you keep finding me, anyway?"

"I'm not trying to find you. I'm trying to get away from you. You just keep showing up."

"That's an odd assessment considering I'm locked up and you're the one who, of her own free will, came to talk to me."

Her eyes narrowed and forehead wrinkled as she scowled at Nick. "I didn't come to Oak Creek looking for you, but when I found out you were here, I thought I would be nice and find out if you wanted help escaping."

"That's why I'm glad you're following me." He grinned. "You always come to my rescue. So what's the plan?" His voice grew serious and urgent. "How do we get out of this place?"

"I-I . . . don't know."

Nick stared down at his hands, scraping thick dirt from beneath his fingernails.

"I just need time to figure it out," she assured. "Is there any way you could slip away during the day?"

Nick rolled his eyes and sighed. "I'm not that helpless, Rochelle. If I could just *slip away*, do you think I'd still be here?"

"Okay, I'm sorry." Her apology held little sincerity. Wind hissed through bordering grass and she turned to scan the surroundings. Arguing with Nick had turned into a distraction, and she realized she'd spent far too long standing in one spot.

"You really shouldn't be out here, should you?" Nick observed. "If you get caught . . ."

"It's okay." She whispered close to the bars, feeling a need to conceal her voice from invisible ears. "No one knows I'm here."

"Until they find out. Then they won't hesitate to lock you up in this place. We can spend the rest of our lives shoveling dirt and enjoying our rationed bowl of potato soup together."

Lareina thought she noticed a slight waver in Nick's voice, but she couldn't be sure. "I never imagined you to be so sentimental."

He pressed his forehead against the bars. "I'm being serious. If you get caught, we're never getting out of this place."

Despite the flutter of fear in Nick's voice, she rolled her eyes and smiled, trying to lighten the mood. "I've told you before, I never get caught."

Reaching through the bars, he clutched her wrist in a rough, cold hand. "Promise me you'll be careful, Rochelle, and that you won't do anything stupid."

Instinctively, she pulled her arm back, but Nick didn't let go. His tired eyes remained focused on her, and Lareina understood escaping Oak Creek wouldn't be a simple game.

"I promise." She certainly intended to be careful, but so much of the community remained a mystery to her. She didn't quite know what kind of precautions to take.

Nick nodded and released his grip on her wrist. She pulled her arm back and tried to ignore the numbness in her ankles.

"Good," he whispered. "Now get back to where you came from before they notice you're missing."

"But I still have so many questions. I don't know what you're doing, or—"

He held up a hand, stopping her words. "It's manual labor, nothing exciting. I'll tell you all about it when you get us out of here. Now *go*."

Her walk back seemed shorter than it had on the way out. She followed the same path, slipped behind the evergreen bushes, and hoisted herself through the bathroom window. Sitting down against the wall, she caught her breath and shivered as she thought of Nick, hungry and trying to sleep in a cold, moldy prison. Imagining herself in Nick's position made her stomach turn cartwheels. She felt trapped enough already without being locked behind bars.

CHAPTER 20

The week-old Dallas newspaper flopped against Lareina's hands as she tried to turn the first page past a backward crease left by a former reader. The hospital waiting room was silent except for the bubbling of an aquarium and the tapping of the receptionist's pencil. She scratched absently at her arm where the stitches would be removed today as she scanned the headlines.

Flooding across Texas Leads to Major Evacuation, Property Loss, and Crop Damage. Persistent rains have fallen across the plains, but nowhere as severely as Texas.

She scanned the first lines of the article, but it was information she knew all too well. Her eyes skipped to a new article.

A new political group known as The Defiance continue to inspire riots and violence in parts of Kansas and Missouri. Local authorities and politicians worry these extremists will soon control the region.

The paper rustled as she turned to the next page to continue the story. She'd heard of The Defiance before, mostly whispered among her fellow runaways on the streets of San Antonio. They were groups of disgruntled orphans who joined together and survived by any means necessary.

The abandoned, ignored, forgotten children, coming of age in a broken society. People worried when these armies of teenagers robbed businesses, houses, and trains. That worry grew into fear when murders connected to The Defiance became common across Missouri.

Two schools of thought existed among teenagers haunting city streets. The first dismissed any possibility of association with The Defiance, citing their activities as appalling. The second expressed admiration that young people could establish a voice in a world that had turned on them. Lareina understood the fever was creating a vacuum in leadership and a shifting demographic in the ages of those who kept the world running, but it was unclear how these new leaders would affect the communities they led.

Defiance supporters have destroyed several railways in an attempt to gain control of the Texas-Oklahoma border.

The news didn't seem to contain a glimpse of hope in a world collapsing around her, but it also seemed far away and irrelevant. She tried to focus on her most immediate problem: escaping Oak Creek with Nick. She felt confident she could steal enough food from the kitchen to get them through three or four days of travel. In fact, just the night before she had examined the simple lock keeping her out of the cafeteria and determined she could get in once she improvised some tools to pick it. But none of that mattered if she couldn't come up with a plan to break Nick out of the barracks. Since exploring locked buildings seemed far more risky than sneaking around Oak Creek at night, she decided to limit her excursions to visiting Nick for the time being. She had, after all, promised she would be careful.

The fish tank filter hissed, and the low murmur of voices from deeper within the building seemed to move to the room next door. The tapping pencil sounded like a drum. A month seemed to pass in that one minute, and she decided the waiting would drive her mad. She was constantly waiting—waiting to talk to Aaron, waiting to free Nick, waiting to escape.

She started reading the newspaper again.

Shortages of medicine and medical supplies have been reported due to riots and railroad bombings.

Pages and pages of bad news bombarded her in tiny black type. Each story reported a severe problem, an unavoidable problem, an unsolvable problem. The thin newspaper grew heavier and heavier until she tossed it onto the chair beside her and turned away. Three other people sat in the waiting room, but she tried to ignore them by staring out at the gray morning.

"Rochelle Aumont," a woman's voice snapped.

Lareina jumped out of her seat and walked toward the nurse, who watched her approach with an annoyed frown. How many times had her alias been called? She smiled, hoping it would be enough to apologize for her inattention. It wasn't the time to get lost in thought and make careless mistakes.

The nurse switched her clipboard to the other hand. "Follow me."

Neither of them said a word as they walked down the hallway, which Lareina found preferable. In the exam room, she cooperated as the nurse took her weight and blood pressure then instructed her to wait and Doctor Swanson would see her soon.

Sitting on the exam table, she tried to plan what she could

say to convince Aaron that they had to get Nick and leave. Aaron seemed determined to be happy at Oak Creek, but maybe she could give him a sense of the danger she was just beginning to discover. Signs in the cafeteria threatened a life sentence to the barracks for taking food, and signs posted on the front door of her residence building informed there would be serious consequences to anyone outside without permission after lights out. Why would such strict punishments be enforced for seemingly small infractions? And he would definitely be upset when she told him Nick's condition.

The door squealed loudly on its unoiled hinges. "Hey, Rochelle. How's your arm?" Aaron asked as he pushed the door shut.

His familiar face brought her a sense of calm, but something about his demeanor set her on edge. "It's a lot better. I barely notice it anymore."

"Are you getting enough sleep? You look really tired."

She studied the room, examining every corner and surface without knowing exactly what she expected to find. Oak Creek gave her an uneasy feeling, as if someone watched and listened to every minute of her life. "I went to see Nick two nights ago." She held her voice at a nearly inaudible whisper, leaning as close as she could to Aaron without falling face-first off the exam table.

Aaron's eyes darted around the room, but when he didn't find the invisible threats she feared, his eyes settled back on her.

"Do you know how the people in the barracks have to live, Aaron?" Her voice shook, though whether from worry about Aaron's response or memory of her visit to Nick, she couldn't be sure. "They barely feed them and there isn't even glass in the windows. Nick is a prisoner over there. They all are."

Turning away, Aaron faced the door for a full minute, holding his hand to the back of his neck. His head, starting slowly and gaining speed, shook from side to side. He spun around, jaw set, and held her gaze. "No way. That can't be right. You must be mistaken."

Tightening her grip around the edge of the exam table, she felt her only chance of a partnership slipping through her fingers. How could he accuse her of lying about this? Nick was their friend. "Aaron, I was there," she protested. "I saw it all myself. Don't you believe me?"

He looked down at her arm and didn't answer as he began his work on removing her stitches.

"I can take you there to see it later tonight. To talk to him. Then you'll understand."

"Is that why you're so tired? You're sneaking around this place at night, looking for trouble?" Compared to the curious, interested Aaron she had become friends with, this one sounded aloof and disapproving.

She tried to swallow, but her throat felt constricted. Over the weeks she spent traveling with Nick and Aaron, she'd occasionally allowed herself to think of them as her family, the people she could count on to be there even when civilization seemed to collapse around them. Stinging betrayal quickly bubbled into anger.

"Looking for trouble," she spat back at him. "I'm trying to save my friend, and your friend. I thought you wanted to help people, but you're just going to settle for this?" She gestured to the little white room with her free arm.

So gently that she barely felt his touch, Aaron continued to remove stitches. She thought in a reversed situation, she would have poked a little harder had someone spoken to her the way she had spoken to him. Remorseful for her quick temper and disheartened by his lack of support, she sat still and silent.

"Your arm healed perfectly," he said after long minutes of silence. "I can write you a note to get a few days off work so you can catch up on your sleep."

Her feet landed on the tiled floor. "No, I'll be fine." She managed to keep an even tone, but her voice held a hint of disappointment and not a trace of warmth.

Aaron nodded and tried to smile as he walked her to the door, but their eyes didn't meet. "If you need anything, you know where to find me."

Of course, she thought as she stormed away. *Anything but rescuing Nick from dying in prison. Anything but helping me to save all three of us from possible imprisonment or death.* She left the hospital in such a distracted daze that she was halfway to the library before she heard someone calling her name and realized how hard rain pelted her face.

"Rochelle, wait, you'll get soaked out here."

Lareina stopped so abruptly she almost lost her balance. She turned to see the president jogging over to her, umbrella lifted. When he reached her, he held it higher so it would shelter both of them.

"Thank you. I didn't even notice the rain, I guess." She forced herself to smile. The last thing she needed was to raise the president's suspicions of her. Drawing too much of his attention could be the most dangerous move in the entire game.

"Where can I walk you to?" He smiled a genuine smile that made him look friendly, even kind. Any trace of the stern leader she'd met the week before had vanished.

"I'm just on my way back to the library. I had a doctor's appointment." A sick feeling started in her stomach. Why would the president be out walking, alone, in the rain? Had he been waiting for her?

"I hope you're feeling well."

"Yeah, just getting the stitches removed from my arm."

"Good, good." He smiled again then glanced down at his watch. "You know, it's almost lunch time. Do you want to join me for some soup and sandwiches?"

Was this some kind of test? "I should really get back to work. Louise is expecting me before lunch."

"Nonsense. Louise will be fine, don't worry. I'll vouch for you." He winked.

"All right, then. Let's go."

So much for not drawing attention to herself. She walked with the president past the library, past the guard station, and up to his house. They entered the big, cozy lobby and he directed her to a chair near the fireplace. When he went to make arrangements for lunch, Lareina closed her eyes and rested her head against the cushioned back of her chair. She felt sleepy, and the soft chair combined with warmth from the fire created the perfect atmosphere for a nap. Then she imagined Nick working out in the cold rain and sat up straight again.

"All right, lunch will be ready soon." President Whitley crossed the room and sank into the chair next to her. "So, how are you liking Oak Creek so far?"

"It seems nice," she lied. "The rest of the world is falling apart, but everything here is so well maintained. I like following all of the different pathways, but I haven't had a chance to walk on all of them yet."

"That's understandable with this record cold, rainy fall wo're having. In the spring you'll have more reason to explore, especially when the trees are flowering."

"That sounds nice." She decided not to waste an opportunity to acquire information. "This place seems so organized compared to the outside world. How do you keep everything running so smoothly?"

The president stiffened for a minute and Lareina worried she had asked the wrong question. But then he relaxed and leaned forward. "I like to think it's the rules and structure. There's nothing to fear when everyone knows their place and what to expect. Most of the people here have come seeking safety, and we're more than happy to improve our community with the skills they have to offer."

"But you don't let everyone in?"

"No, we're very selective. I have to determine who we can trust." A huge smile swept across his face. "You don't have to worry, though. We don't have many people show up the way you did, but I'm sure glad you found your way here. I've thought about our conversation at your orientation meeting every day since you arrived."

"Dinner is ready, sir," a woman announced from the doorway, then disappeared.

"Excellent." Taking her hand, Whitley led her down a hallway. She forced herself not to pull her hand back from his, smooth, dry, and gripping hers too tightly. He'd been thinking about their conversation every day?

Through a wide set of double doors, they entered a large dining room. Two places were set at a table capable of seating fifteen. The serving woman waited until they were settled then ladled soup into their bowls and placed sandwiches on their plates.

"Is there anything else I can get for you sir?"

"No, that will be all, thank you."

Lareina ate her sandwich, trying to come up with

another way to lead into a conversation about the barracks while Whitley talked about the flooding and responses from different governments throughout the state. She replied when necessary and played the part of an appreciative dinner guest.

"It might sound odd, but I knew there was something different about you from the moment I saw you." The president smiled, but seemed to be lost in thought. "You're different from any girl I've ever met." He chuckled as if just realizing he was talking out loud. "I mean that in a good way."

"Thanks." She smiled trying to be polite, but she wasn't sure how to react. From everything she had heard, she expected President Whitley to be threatening and hot tempered, not the kind of man who would shelter her from the rain and chat over lunch. It was almost nice to be appreciated after Aaron's direct rejection of their friendship.

At the conclusion of lunch, the president walked her back to the library, holding doors open for her at every exit and entrance, and promised they would have lunch again soon. She agreed and returned to the front desk where Louise sat at her computer typing furiously.

"I'm back," Lareina announced. "What would you like me to do?"

"Where have you been? Since when do doctor appointments last through lunch?"

"They don't. After my appointment I had lunch with President Whitley." She felt smug as she watched Louise's anger fade into shock, then disbelief.

"Lunch with the president, Rochelle? I'll be verifying that. Now go upstairs and dust—the shelves on the north wall are dirtier than I've ever seen them."

The last few hours of work raced by and at five she rushed around performing her closing duties of pulling shades over windows and turning off every light except the one over the main desk. Louise sat at her small desk, writing, glancing from one piece of paper to another. She didn't acknowledge Lareina's presence, so she pulled her jacket from the hook along the wall and rushed out of the building before Louise could find another job for her to complete.

Taking a breath of icy air, she shoved her hands into the deep pockets of her jacket as she walked to the cafeteria for supper. It was time to see how much they could hold without anyone noticing.

CHAPTER 21

All food must be consumed inside the cafeteria
Anyone who takes food out of this room
Will be sentenced to life in the barracks

The signs posted outside and throughout the cafeteria held a more ominous meaning on this particular evening. Taking food had always been a crime, but it had never stopped her before, and she wasn't about to let a few posters stop her now. She stood in line, watched food pile onto her tray as it passed from one server to the next, then carried it to an unoccupied table. Watching the others fascinated her, but she didn't intend to become friends with any of them. Making friends would only lead to two possible outcomes: they would either discover the truth and report her or be incriminated themselves.

Everyone around her was caught up in conversations. Free of their work and enjoying the small window of social time allowed each day, no one wasted a minute paying attention to her. At least, that's how it seemed at first glance. Four years earlier, Lareina had almost been caught stealing apples from an outside market because she failed to notice a man partially hidden beneath the shade of a nearby tree. On that day, she created a rule of her own: always double-check for witnesses. She glanced around more carefully, trying to feign casual observing, before quickly slipping her apple and dinner roll under the table then into her pocket.

"Hey, Rochelle." Tony sat down across from her. His voice sounded marching band loud to her ears.

She jumped. How had he approached so quickly? Did he see what she'd done with her food?

"Sorry, I didn't mean to startle you. It's been a few days since I've seen you."

Safe for now. Smiling, she scooped some pudding onto her spoon. "No need to apologize. I guess I'm just a little jumpy."

Tony leaned across the table. "Is it because of your lunch with the president today? Did he threaten you?"

How did he know about that already? "No, nothing like that. He just wanted to know what I thought of Oak Creek." She still wasn't sure how she felt about the lunch and didn't want to publicly commit to any particular emotion.

"That's it?" Tony sounded surprised and confused. "That's strange."

Of course the invitation seemed strange to her. Even more strange was the president coincidentally being outside in the rain at the very moment she left the hospital. If he were paying attention to her schedule, she would have to be extra careful. But she would need to visit Nick as often as possible to plan their escape and to pass on food.

"Tony," she asked absently, "how long have you lived here?"

"Since we moved from the other campus, so . . . two years now."

"The other campus? There are other Oak Creeks?"

Tony laughed and took a bite of his apple. "By other names, yes. Four of them, all within fifty miles of here."

Taking a drink of water gave her a minute to process the new information. "The other campuses," she said, repeating Tony's terminology, "are they just like this one?"

Tony shook his head. "Not at all. Oak Creek is relaxed compared to Rose Valley where I grew up. The others are military training camps. We're just here for production support."

"Production of what?" She hadn't bothered to learn what was produced in the factory buildings that lined one side of Oak Creek. It hadn't seemed important.

"Uniforms," he laughed, "and weapons, of course."

Lareina nodded, beginning to understand. "Because The Defiance is coming to take Texas next."

Tony twisted the stem from his apple. "The Defiance, someone else, it doesn't matter who. Unless a miracle happens, it's only a matter of time until the state government collapses, but we have a good chance of holding our ground and expanding."

"Exactly how many . . ." she searched for the right word, "troops are training at the other campuses?"

He leaned forward as if sharing a secret. "I can't give you an exact number, but it's in the thousands."

"And all of the digging over at the barracks," she continued, trying to put the pieces together. "It's for the war?"

Tony sighed. He had made it clear he wouldn't talk about the barracks any more, but he seemed to understand she would never stop asking. "If I tell you about the tunnels, do you promise to never ask about them again?"

She nodded and gave Tony her most reassuring look.

"Okay. We're building our first underground facility with a hospital, living quarters, and production centers. It'll give us a vast advantage over the enemy."

"Of course, I see how that would." Now that she knew the purpose of the barracks and tunnels was so, well, mundane, she felt a little disappointed. She had hoped that knowledge would give her the critical key to help Nick escape. "Do people from the barracks ever get out?"

Tony shrugged, and any enthusiasm faded from his expression. "Most of them deserve to be there." His voice wavered with uncertainty. "They're thieves and traitors. The last guy was a stowaway." He stared down at his lunch tray and she wondered if he would have been sent to the barracks for rescuing her had she not protested. "We shouldn't be talking about this. It's dangerous."

She shifted her jacket across her lap, so the apple's shape wouldn't be obvious beneath the material. Tony knew nothing of danger or starvation or cold or desperation. He did, however, understand one thing that she never could: how to follow orders, so he would always be safe and warm and fed.

Over the course of the next week, Lareina established a consistent schedule. She worked at the library by day, snuck whatever food she could at supper, went to bed early and dozed until midnight, then snuck out to visit Nick. He felt like an old friend, though he really hardly knew anything about her. Although their meetings always ended with him telling her it was too dangerous for her to come back, he never turned down a scrap of the stolen food.

They tried to form an escape plan, but none of their ideas were feasible. She wanted to sneak him out at night, but she couldn't find tools to cut through the bars on his window. Plus, Nick informed her that in addition to his locked door, there were guards posted just inside the building's exits. Every glimmer of hope fell short.

Sneaking around at night turned out to be the easiest part. The Oak Creek security didn't bother to set up any precautions against occupants breaking curfew beyond the attendants at the main entrances of residence buildings. People simply feared the consequences enough that they didn't attempt to break the rules, and most probably didn't see a reason to leave their rooms after nine.

Louise remained grumpy and distant despite anything Lareina tried, so she just avoided her roommate and boss as much as possible. The president invited her to lunch three times that week, always treating her with kindness and respect, but never revealing information of any importance, even when she tried to direct the conversation. Although she enjoyed the best meals of her life, and even found herself enjoying the president's wit and conversation, she felt frustrated that she hadn't come any closer to freeing Nick.

Twice, she arrived at the library to a vase of a dozen red roses on her desk. They didn't come with a card, but she knew who was responsible. The other residents of Oak Creek had started to notice her, and some whispered behind their hands after she passed. But none of them confronted her, and she was perfectly happy not interacting with any of them. Despite everything happening around her, she was committed to rescuing Nick and getting both of them out of Oak Creek.

CHAPTER 22

Sneezing and sniffling, Lareina pulled herself out of bed one morning. Ten days of sneaking out had caught up with her. Although she wanted to sleep for a while longer, she shuffled to the bathroom where she washed her face and brushed her teeth as she did every morning. She hated that she had been in Oak Creek long enough to have a morning routine.

Back in her room, she noticed the clock indicating she only had fifteen minutes to get to work. Louise went in early to open up and set up for the day. In front of the tiny mirror above her small dresser, she quickly examined her appearance. During the past three weeks her face had filled out so she no longer looked gaunt and her hair, washed and brushed, fell over her shoulders down to her waist. She would be pretty if it weren't for the dark circles beneath her eyes. The president had commented on them at their last lunch when she convinced him she was just tired from having a cold, which wasn't entirely a lie.

After stifling a sneeze in the sleeve of her pajamas, she pulled on the khaki pants and plain gray shirt that everyone except security wore. When she had been shown to her room after her orientation meeting, the clothes had been there on her bed, three pairs of pants and seven shirts. Her feet slid into shoes as she pulled her coat on and hurried down the hallway. She ran across campus, despite the ache of cold air in her lungs, and made it to her station at the front desk with thirty seconds to spare.

The room felt warm and Louise was nowhere in sight. Lareina sat down and rested her throbbing head in her hands. She didn't intend to rest for long, but every time she began to lift her head, she decided one more minute couldn't hurt.

"Hey, are you all right?" a loud voice boomed behind her.

She spun around in her chair to find Louise standing over her with her hands on her hips.

"Fine. Great. What do you want me to do today?" It took every ounce of willpower to keep the sarcasm out of her voice, so she only succeeded halfway.

A strange expression came over Louise's face. It resembled sympathy or at least the closest Louise had ever come to expressing concern. Just when she thought her boss might give her a break, Louise gestured to the mop and bucket by the supply closet.

"People have been tracking mud in all week. The entire place needs to be scrubbed, but I want you here on the first floor where I can see you."

She had no other choice but to nod in agreement and get to work.

At noon the president came and, as she had done before, Lareina walked with him to his house. As usual, he chatted about whatever came to his mind. She had opened up some, sharing forged memories from Rochelle's life, but today staying awake proved to be difficult, and keeping a conversation going, when she couldn't even comprehend what President Whitley said, became impossible.

"You're still fighting that cold, I see." Lunch over, they sat in front of the fire drinking tea. His voice was full of concern.

Despite her misery she tried sit up straight and keep her sniffling to a minimum. "Yeah, it's relentless."

"Are you sure you don't want to take a few days off work? Until you feel better?"

"Oh, I'll be okay for today, and I'm sure I'll be feeling better by tomorrow." There was something comforting about the concern he always showed for her.

President Whitley didn't respond, but also didn't take his eyes off her as she sipped her tea. She had grown used to the way he looked at her so intently, but today his gaze seemed more intense. She pretended to be absorbed looking at the fire.

"You're too pretty." The whisper was so quiet she almost didn't hear it. The president cleared his throat and drank some of his tea. "You're too pretty to be bothered with working at all. You should be wearing beautiful dresses and posing for paintings."

Lareina felt her cheeks burning as she decided how to react. On one hand she had never been paid such a compliment, but on the other she barely knew this man who everyone else feared.

"Excuse me?" She knew it was a weak response, but she needed more time to think.

President Whitley cleared his throat. She noticed the way his cup shook with his hand and wondered what could possibly make the all-powerful leader of Oak Creek nervous.

"I don't want to rush into things, but I've been trying to tell you I'm in love with you." His voice trembled slightly, but she felt a jolt as the weight of each word hit her. "I've never met anyone like you before, but I think I knew from the first day you would be the only one." He knelt next to Lareina's chair and took her hands in his. "I guess what I'm trying to ask is, Rochelle Aumont, will you marry me?"

His blue eyes studied her, searching for an answer. Her

heart pounded so fast it matched the throbbing in her head, but she forced a smile as she considered the man before her. She certainly didn't feel the same affection toward him, but she also believed he wouldn't hurt her. Saying yes could put her in a position to access information and maybe even resources she needed to free Nick and put Oak Creek behind her.

She had fooled people before. In the last three months, she hadn't had a problem introducing herself as Rochelle to every person she met. It couldn't be all that hard to play the part of devoted bride to be. Fighting every instinct in her body, she nodded, not trusting her voice.

President Whitley breathed for the first time since he posed the question and grasped her hand between his. "I'm so relieved! I mean, I've known since the day we met that we belonged together, but I didn't know if you would feel the same." He beamed at her. "My brother is coming for a visit in two weeks. We'll have a party the night before to announce our engagement and then get married in the summer." He paused. "If that's all okay with you, of course?"

Pretending to be an excited new fiancée, Lareina intertwined her fingers with his. "It's all perfect. I can't wait."

CHAPTER 23

By the time she returned to the library, people crowded every table and couch and a long line stretched from the checkout counter. Louise was nowhere to be seen. She'd lengthened her lunch break by three hours, leaving her boss alone for the entire afternoon. Tiptoeing to the main desk, she pushed through the swinging door, and slipped into the cushioned chair before beckoning to the first person in line. She'd only checked out books for two people when she heard Louise's footsteps coming down the stairs.

"Rochelle," Louise said calmly. "I need to see you in the back room right now."

Knowing she didn't have a choice, she stood and walked into the room behind the front desk. Louise followed and closed the door behind them.

Lareina smiled, hoping to disarm her boss. "We should probably be out there—you know it is the busy time right now."

"We," Louise laughed, a harsh sound. "I'm doing all of the work. Everyone knows that you and Whitley have some kind of thing going on, but the president wouldn't excuse even his closest friends from three hours of work. I'm reporting you, and you're fired."

The words rolled off of her as an involuntary smile formed over her lips. "He might consider firing his closest friends but never his fiancée."

"Excuse me." Louise's face reddened in confusion and anger.

"I'm engaged to the president. He'll fire you before he fires me." In books, she had read about people's jaws dropping in surprise or disbelief, but she had never experienced it in real life until that moment.

"You're . . . you . . . you're . . . *what?*" Louise held the palm of her hand against her forehead and stared at her employee as if she'd spoken a newly discovered language. After a moment of stunned silence, Louise whispered, "Go back to work. Just go."

She did as she was told and returned to the front desk to resume checking books out. A few minutes later Louise came out of the storage room, but she walked straight to the stairs and didn't reappear until they closed the library.

By the end of the day, the adrenaline rush of being proposed to by the president and then standing up to Louise had faded, leaving Lareina drained and nauseated. She forced herself to the cafeteria to get food but could only swallow three bites of applesauce. Though no one sat at her table, she noticed several people watching her and had to be particularly discreet when stuffing her ham sandwich, banana, and baked potato into her pockets. Louise had probably told everyone the news.

Looking forward to the warm, comfort of her bed, she remained in the cafeteria just long enough to ensure any observers would believe she had eaten the food on her tray. She hurried through the chilly evening air and stumbled into the warmth of her building and then her room. Louise hadn't returned yet, which was a welcome treat. Steadying herself against a wave of dizziness, she kicked off her shoes and hung up her jacket, then fell into bed to rest her eyes for a minute.

Rain pounding against glass tore her from a sound sleep. She sat straight up, struggling to orient herself in the darkness. Louise breathed steadily from her bed on the other side of the room. Unable to see a thing, Lareina brushed her hand over the surface of her nightstand until she felt the cold metal exterior of the flashlight she kept there. Aiming the light above her bed, she clicked it on and adjusted the beam until it illuminated the clock.

Two in the morning.

She should have been out to meet Nick two hours ago. Stumbling around in the dark, praying she wouldn't wake Louise, she slipped into her shoes and pulled her jacket over the shirt she'd worn all day.

Following the usual pattern, she slid through the bathroom window and outside into torrential rain. On the positive side, no one would be able to see her even if they were looking. She battled a torrent of precipitation slamming into her face harder than needles from the evergreen trees, and wind that threatened to sweep her off her feet with every step she took.

By the time she reached the barracks, the rain had thankfully slowed down to a light mist, but the chilly wind sliced through her soaked clothes that hung from her body like wax dripping from a candle.

"Nick," she whispered outside the barred window. "Nick, are you awake?"

Immediately his face rose into view on the other side of the bars. "Rochelle, where have you been? I thought they caught you." His voice shook and his wide eyes followed every flutter of her eyelids. "Are you okay? You look awful."

"I'm fine, everything's fine. I just fell asleep." Reaching into her pockets, she pulled out the banana, baked potato, and now soggy sandwich and handed them to Nick. Water cascaded through downspouts with a metallic rush, pooled all around the barracks, and streamed through the window in mini waterfalls.

"You shouldn't have come out in the rain," Nick scolded in an admonishing whisper. "And how can you bring so much food? What are *you* eating?" A thin crease formed a V in his forehead.

She rested her cheek against the bars to relieve her throbbing head, hoping Nick would think it was to muffle her voice. The small cell contained moldy walls with cracked paint, a bed, and inches of water rippling across the floor.

"Your room is flooded." She let her eyes close for a few seconds to ease the sharp ache behind her eyes.

"My bed is tall enough, the water can't get to me," he assured. "Now quit changing the subject. Where did you get all of this food?"

Usually Nick didn't miss an opportunity to complain, so his insistence on ignoring the rising water accentuated the seriousness of his question.

"I didn't have an appetite today, so I had extra."

He sighed and the crease in his forehead tightened. "You know you're shivering, right?"

Lareina rolled her eyes and clutched the bars to keep her balance. "Of course I'm shivering. I'm soaked and it's like forty degrees out here. Quit worrying about me."

Nick's dirt smudged face pressed closer in the dim, wavering moonlight. "My escape depends on you staying out of this place . . . and staying alive. You promised you would be careful." He sighed. "That you wouldn't do anything stupid. Remember?"

Despite her tired, watery eyes, the chilling wind that made her shiver, and the despair of Nick's flooded room, she smiled. She imagined Nick reading the warning posters hung around the cafeteria. The clarity of his imagined reaction reminded her of the day they met and his insistence on following the rules in lieu of comfort. For Nick, black and white morals triumphed over staying alive.

"What's so funny?" His eyebrows lifted enough to erase the crease. Wind whistled across the cavities of broken windows and pulled Lareina's hair across her face.

Every time I bring you food, I'm stealing it. Even though it's my own food, it's a crime to take it. What do you think of those rules? She gathered her hair, twisted it, and dropped it behind her shoulder. "Nothing. I'm just tired."

Her decision to marry President Whitley gnawed at the edge of her mind. How would Nick react to the news? A shiver overtook her body and she pulled her thin coat closer, wrapping her arms around herself to hold it in place.

"You should go get some rest." Nick traced the edge of the windowsill with his finger. "I don't want you to catch pneumonia or something."

Although her teeth chattered, she laughed. "That's the most touching thing I've ever heard."

Nick grinned back at her. "I'll think of something better for next time." He pushed his wet hair off of his forehead. "Rochelle." A serious tone returned to his voice. "Take a few nights off from visiting. Stay where it's warm and get some rest."

How many others had given her similar advice? She shook her head, ready to protest, but Nick folded his hand over hers.

"I'll be all right for a couple of days."

His hand steadied her trembling fingers and she nodded in agreement. "I'll be back as soon as I'm well."

"Be careful." He squeezed her hand then sank down below the level of the window.

Walking away from the barracks without Nick pulled at her soul as the mud pulled at her shoes. Guilt ached across her shoulders and worry clawed at the pit of her stomach. Just below the thick trees, she turned her head back to the building that seemed to deteriorate before her eyes. For the time being she couldn't do any more for Nick. She had spent hours walking around Oak Creek, exploring every hidden corner whenever she didn't have lunch with Whitley. She had located two sections where a tree could help her over the wall, but she couldn't leave Nick behind. Hadn't he cared about her? Hadn't he helped her survive? The moon shimmered in the dark sky, refracting in thousands of rippling puddles. Soft voices drifted on the wind and Lareina stiffened as movement near the barracks swept across the still night.

"I think there's someone over here," a voice shouted. "Yeah, I see someone. Right there!"

CHAPTER 24

Darting across the swampy ground, she scrambled deep into the trees. Behind her, feet splashed through puddles made invisible by the darkness. Instinctively, she dropped to the ground and used her elbows to propel her through the mud and under a protective screen of needled branches. Shivering, she positioned herself near the trunk of a large evergreen tree, pulled her knees up to her chin, and waited.

Minutes passed and the shouting voices faded then vanished, replaced by the soft *whap, whap, whap* of raindrops dripping onto the mushy ground. Silence returned, but she didn't move. Time closed in around her, heavy and ominous. Leaving meant the possibility of being caught and staying meant trying to cross the campus in daylight.

Lareina stood and held a branch until the ground stopped swaying. Drifting silently through the darkness, she tried unsuccessfully to brush mud from her clothes. She watched the buildings closely as she weaved down sidewalks. The only squares of light came from hallway windows where lights remained on at all times. Soon every room would be glowing to life.

The first glimpse of light appeared in the eastern sky as she reached her building. Pressing herself close to the cold bricks, she slid behind bushes and crawled until she reached the point directly beneath the bathroom window.

Her fingertips pressed flat against the glass. She shoved her arms upward. Her hands slid along the glass, but the window didn't move. Thinking she may have miscounted, she glanced around to verify she stood beneath the third window from the right. Once again, she pressed her hands to the glass. Shoulders, back, and legs all slid upward, but the window remained in place. Panic tightened her chest. She tried to pry her fingers beneath the window's seal. She picked at a crack in the outer trim around the glass. Nothing worked. Someone had locked the window from the inside. Did they know? Had someone learned of her secret? Were they waiting to arrest her?

The only other way inside was through the front door where the building monitor would be sitting at her desk ready to question Lareina's reasons for being out without permission. She rubbed her forehead and examined her mud-covered clothes. Pink light spread across the horizon, birds chirped on the roof, and her mind failed to spin a believable lie.

With no other options and time collapsing around her, she snuck up to the door and peered inside. The front desk sat vacant. Unable to believe her luck, she pulled the door open and darted down the hallway to the stairwell. Climbing four flights of stairs in only minutes, she strode down the empty hallway, allowing herself to anticipate the relief she would feel when she could collapse into bed. Still trying to catch her breath, and hoping Louise would still be asleep, she reached toward the door to safety, comfort, and rest.

"Hey, stop right there," an authoritative voice ordered.

Her hand slipped from the doorknob. Her legs wobbled as if the floor shook and for the second time that night, the ground appeared, for a second, to rise up toward her. Slowly, too exhausted to consider escape, she turned to face her accuser.

A tall woman with straight blond hair stood in front of her. Lareina recognized her as the building monitor who glared at her every evening when she returned from the cafeteria. "What are you doing out at this time?"

The stern voice demanded an answer, but when she opened her mouth no words came out. The lies that always formed so easily were gone, her mind blank and fuzzy.

"Answer me," the woman ordered.

The fluorescent lights buzzed inside Lareina's head, the hallway dimmed as if someone slowly lowered the light switch, and she steadied herself against the wall. She didn't even notice her door open until she felt the cool breeze of someone stepping up beside her.

"What's going on out here?" Louise's frightening tone would have definitely won in a competition with the building monitor's.

"Is this your roommate?"

"Yes, Ella, this is my roommate, Rochelle." Louise's voice was a low growl. She took a step forward so she stood in front of her like a protective shield.

Lareina wanted to run, but the room had become lopsided and blurry. Blinking, squinting, closing her eyes—nothing helped. She bit back a groan.

"Maybe you can tell me what she was doing out in the rain at this hour," Ella demanded.

"I'd be happy to. I sent her to the library to check the basement," she explained, so casually it sounded like the truth. "I couldn't sleep thinking of the disastrous flooding we had last year, so she volunteered to check it out."

Ella looked around Louise's shoulder letting her eyes burn into Lareina's. "And how was it?"

"Everything is f-fine. N-no water inside."

"So where did you encounter the mud that's plastered all over you?"

"I slipped . . . on my way back where the rain washed some mud over the sidewalk." She had noticed the poor drainage issue the day before and knew anyone who investigated would find the scene just as she reported.

Ella's posture, expression, and voice remained stiff and cold. "That better be true. I'll be watching you." She tossed her threats down the empty corridor then stalked away.

Louise turned her attention to her roommate, placing a hand on her arm and guiding her back into the safety of their room. By that time the blurriness in her head and trembling in her legs transformed standing into an impossible torture.

"Where have you been? It better have been worth it for me to lie for you like that."

Lareina tried to answer, but stumbled forward as everything went dark. When she opened her eyes, Louise stood over her. Somehow she ended up in a chair instead of on the floor.

"Are you all right? Rochelle, can you hear me?" Louise's exasperation collapsed into bemused concern.

As the room came back into view, she nodded.

Louise helped her to her feet and out of her muddy jacket. "We'll talk about this later. Go take a shower. I'll wait until you get back."

In a daze, she gathered a towel and some clothes, walked down the hall to the communal bathroom, showered quickly, and returned to her room.

Louise nodded toward Lareina's bed where the pillow had been fluffed and the blankets folded back. "Go to sleep. You're too sick to be of any use at work. Don't leave this room today. We'll talk when I get back."

Lareina agreed and crumpled onto the bed, sinking into sleep before Louise even opened the door.

Late in the afternoon, she woke to gray skies obscuring any glimmer of sun. A lack of light emphasized the dinginess of her small room with its dark corners and scratched furniture. Drifting in and out of sleep, she listened to angry rain patter on the roof and clank through downspouts outside her window. No matter how she tried to preoccupy her mind, her thoughts continually circled back to Nick being forced to live in a flooded room. A week and a half had passed since she promised him they would leave Oak Creek, and still they had no workable plan.

The barracks were similar to her own building except each room was half the size and a locked prison cell. Guards were posted inside to watch the exits. Nick shot down any plan she came up with to sneak in and pick the lock. He was right; it was too dangerous. Maybe she could teach Nick and he could unlock his own door? But no, Nick would mess it all up somehow.

When the doorknob jiggled, she burrowed under the covers and closed her eyes.

"I brought you supper," Louise announced. Shoes squeaked against the floor. She pictured Louise pulling them off and dropping them as she did every day. "Don't pretend you're asleep. We have a lot to talk about."

Lareina opened one eye, then the other. "How did you know I was awake?" She sat up and leaned against her pillow.

Louise handed her a sandwich and a stack of five crackers. "Lucky guess."

She looked down at the food in her hand, remembering the rules from the cafeteria.

"Don't think you're the only one who can sneak food." Louise walked back toward the door. "If you like that, just wait until you see what's in the hallway."

She propped the door open and carried in a vase loaded with white daisies and pink carnations, sat it on the desk, and pulled a card out. "I hope you feel better," she read. "Get plenty of rest and I'll see you soon. Love, Marcus." Louise sat down on the foot of the bed. "So, you're on a first-name basis with the president?" Her sarcastic tone indicated she didn't believe it.

"That's generally how it works when you're engaged to someone."

Louise smiled. "I understand why you don't trust me. I don't know if I should trust you, but I want to stop you from doing something entirely stupid and extremely dangerous."

Lareina took a bite of her sandwich. She didn't trust Louise, but then again she didn't trust anyone. Sitting back against the wall, she shook her head. "Thank you for helping me this morning, but I can take care of myself."

"That obstinate attitude of yours reminds me of my little sister." The first few words came out as a snarl, but her voice softened by the end of the sentence.

Louise's ever-changing emotions annoyed Lareina, but she worried how much more her roommate might know. "What do you want me to say?"

"I want the truth. I want to know why you're stealing food and sneaking out to the barracks at night. I want to know why any of that is necessary when you're engaged to the president."

Lareina felt the color drain from her face as if blood

stopped pumping through her body. She thought she had been so careful and yet Louise had complete knowledge of her actions. How? She meant to ask, tried to ask, but her vocal chords refused to make a sound.

"I've done it before just like you're doing now." Louise studied her as if trying to determine whether she could continue. "A year ago my sister tried to escape from this place. She almost made it to the train. When they caught her, they locked her in the barracks and forced her to work but gave her very little food. I snuck out every night to visit her. We spent hours planning her escape." Louise's smile vanished. "We were to meet at the tree line after she took the lock apart. I could see her running toward me from where I hid and I thought it was really going to work. Then I heard the gunshot. We didn't get far before she collapsed. I held her hand and listened to the searchers shouting and watched their flashlight beams getting closer." Louise's fist clenched. "I had to leave my own sister to die by herself with those brainwashed guards." Louise's tear-filled eyes looked out the window.

"I'm really sorry." The words sounded flat and meaningless, but she couldn't think of anything else to say. Louise had only ever been rude and aloof to her, and the idea of her having a sister, a sister who she had snuck out for and watched get shot, was too much to comprehend. She thought about the girl who gave her the pendant. She'd barely known her, but seeing the wound, knowing that she would die . . . For days she'd woken up in tears.

Louise nodded, composing herself. "Now, what's your game? What's your business at Oak Creek?"

Glancing over at the flowers, she twisted her hair and pushed it behind her shoulder. She told Louise about Nick and

Aaron, saving the story of her impulsive decision to marry the president for last.

Louise stared at her and tried to speak twice, but no words came out. "Why?" she finally managed to utter.

"Why did he ask me or why did I say yes?"

"Yes," Louise answered, then added, "Both."

Lareina sat back and smiled. "Apparently I'm the love of his life. I thought at the very least I would stay on his good side and perhaps gain an upper hand at escape."

Tapping her fingertips together, Louise leaned forward, looking off into empty space. "It could work. This could be the advantage we've been waiting for."

"We?"

Louise looked at her roommate as if she had forgotten she was in the room. "There's a whole group of us here who want out. People living in the barracks and people living in the general population. Do you think you could steal something from the president's house?"

Although she didn't yet know the layout of the president's house, she knew she would be spending more time there, and maybe she could ask for a tour. "I think I could manage."

Louise clapped her hands together, becoming the first person who was excited to share a room with a thief. "How about Nick? Can he help us from inside?"

"Nick is kind of helpless." She tried not to laugh. "When I first met him, I had to rescue him."

Louise nodded thoughtfully. "Well, if you can get a key to free others from the barracks, then I have a plan. If you're willing to work together, that is. What do you say?" She held out a hand.

Did she really have another choice? Lareina was out of

ideas and Louise seemed sincere. She gripped her new ally's hand. "I'm in."

CHAPTER 25

As she had promised, Lareina stayed away from the barracks until she felt better, which ended up being three days. On her second day back to work, the president came to take her to supper. She exchanged a knowing glance with Louise before following him through the door. Outside they walked arm in arm, but in the opposite direction of the cafeteria.

"I thought we were going to supper?"

"We are, but it's a surprise."

Although she played the part of spy and con artist, she enjoyed the sun on her face. Early November brought the warm dry weather they should have had the month before. President Whitley led her to his house, but instead of going inside, they went around to the backyard where a checkered blanket and picnic basket waited.

A real smile spread across her face. She'd never been on a picnic before. This would be more fun than she thought.

For hours, they ate and talked. The president told stories about his dad who had been the creator of the first two Oak Creek–like campuses. Sadly, both of his parents died three years earlier when the fever swept through. At that time his older brother took over, and then one year ago put him in charge of developing Oak Creek for production and support purposes. He only saw his brother twice a year but talked about him the way a child talks about his favorite superhero.

When Lareina thought about the plan Louise had shared with her, she felt a twinge of guilt knowing the humiliation she had set in motion for President Whitley. It would all occur right in front of his brother.

Trying to distract herself, she glanced around the backyard. A garden shed sat back against the outside wall that shielded the president's yard from the rest of the world. About twenty feet away, a tree from the outside reached its branches into the isolated world of Oak Creek. It would be easy to climb from the shed to the wall and into the tree. Her thoughts were interrupted by the president taking her hand.

Feeling peace there on a soft picnic blanket next to someone who cared about her, she imagined what a future with the president would look like. Being married to someone who loved her, living in a mansion, maybe having children, and never running from anything ever again held a stronger appeal than she expected. The thought brought a smile to her face and the president, leaning against a tree, noticed.

"We'll make this a tradition," he suggested, squeezing her hand. "We'll have picnics on abnormally warm November days and remember our first and all the wonderful years since."

A warm, sweet feeling of hope started in her chest and surged through her body. Her head rested on his shoulder. Never had she known what love felt like, but perhaps it wasn't a feeling at all. Perhaps it was a promise between two people. No person had ever promised to protect and take care of her for the rest of her life.

As they talked, the sun set, releasing the expected November chill. President Whitley placed his jacket around her shoulders and insisted on walking her back to her building. Arm in arm, they strolled down the sidewalk under buzzing lights mounted on iron poles. All of Oak Creek seemed transformed by the change in weather. For the first time, it shimmered with new hope.

Before they reached the front of her building, the president stopped and held her hands in his. "Will you join me tomorrow for lunch?"

She smiled and nodded.

He leaned in closer. "I'll be there by eleven thirty."

Leaning toward him, she whispered, "I'm looking forward to it already."

The space between them vanished and their lips met in a quick kiss.

Heart racing, Lareina bounced up the stairs to her room and fell back onto her bed.

Louise, who had been sitting at her desk writing, turned around. "How was your date?"

"We had a picnic and I've never done that before." She hesitated, unsure if she should share anything personal with her roommate, but needed to talk to someone. Telling Nick about her relationship with Whitley was something she wanted to avoid indefinitely if possible. Taking a deep breath, she closed her eyes. "I feel safe when he's taking care of me and I'm not sure if I'll ever find that again in my life."

Louise crossed the room and sat down next to her. "Yes, you will. You'll find someone far better than a ruthless leader like Whitley and instead of playing a game you'll have something real."

"But I think I already felt something real." She stared up at the ceiling. "I've been pretending for so long, what if I don't even know the difference?"

"You'll know." Louise returned to her desk.

Lareina felt dizzy and her head ached. She didn't understand her excitement for lunch the next day. Perhaps she had let herself get carried away with a fantasy. Perhaps she felt something real for this man who claimed to be in love with her. Confused and not quite over her cold, she decided to skip visiting Nick for another night. Instead, she fell asleep dreaming of a life as Rochelle Whitley.

CHAPTER 26

Seconds ticked by slowly and hours refused to elapse on the library's clock. Lareina spent the morning returning stacks of books to shelves. Little bursts of dust rose into the air, spinning in squares of sunlight. Silence filled the library and President Whitley filled her thoughts. Though she knew she had to go, she couldn't help but daydream about this other future. What would life be like at Oak Creek? The president's house would be warm in the winter and cool in the summer. Meals would be served three times per day every day. She would have clean clothes, medical care, leisure time to read, and a safe hideout from Galloway. Everything she could possibly wish for. Stretching her arm over her head, she pushed a book onto the top shelf. Her future, like that book, was right there at the tip of her fingers. It felt warm, soft, comfortable.

At lunchtime, as usual, the president showed up right on time to walk her back to his house. Unseasonably warm sunshine wrapped around her shoulders and danced across her face. They held hands, birds sang in the trees, windows glinted in the sun, and the sky stretched in all directions, endlessly blue.

When they arrived at the house, two men in security uniforms waited in the lobby. They stood at attention when the door opened. One removed his hat and raked a hand through his hair. The other clenched and unclenched his hands but kept his eyes on the floor.

"We're sorry to bother you, Mr. President, sir," the first

said with his hat still clutched in his hand, "but we really need a few minutes of your time for advice on an issue." The men seemed to lean backward, as if gravity pulled them away from their boss.

President Whitley smiled the wide grin that Lareina had become accustomed to. "Of course," he replied. "One moment."

He led her to a chair in front of the fireplace. "Make yourself comfortable. This will only take a minute."

Whitley directed the men to his office down the hall. For a dozen seconds she sat, listened to the silence, contemplated the reflection of blue sky on clear glass. Why had those guards been so nervous? What advice did they seek? Curiosity won. Cautiously, she stood, walked to the hallway, looked around, and found herself alone. Tiptoeing, she crept down the hall to Whitley's office and stood, with her back to the wall, outside his closed door.

She had to strain to hear the timid voice through the thick barrier. " . . . men have developed a cough and refuse to work until they receive medical attention."

"We won't stop work for anything," responded a gruff voice. The president? She had never heard him speak in that tone before. "I want the underground living quarters done before next winter."

"But, sir, if the men won't work, what are we supposed to do?"

Holding her breath, she waited for his answer.

"If they don't want to work, fine. But no food to any man who doesn't earn it. If you have protests after that, use whatever means necessary to put an end to it." Pause. "Am I clear?"

"Yes, sir. Of course."

"And if you want to take any more of my valuable time, you better have a real problem."

"Of course, sir, it won't happen again."

At the sound of chairs scraping against the floor, she darted down the hallway and back to her chair by the fireplace. As she landed on the spongy cushion, heart pounding, a door groaned open, and low voices disrupted the hallway's silence before footsteps echoed in the lobby. They joked about the weather in friendly tones that didn't match the dialogue of their meeting. Before they left, President Whitley led the two men over to the fireplace and introduced them in a light, cordial manner. Lareina smiled, shook their hands, and pretended to believe she would interact with them for years to come.

"What was that all about?" she asked as the security guards seemed to run out the door.

Whitley shrugged, took her hand, and shook his head. "Work issues—nothing to worry about."

"Lunch is ready, sir," announced a woman from the doorway.

During lunch, Lareina's heart sank through her chest while she choked down food she didn't taste. She focused on maintaining her fake joviality and selling the lies she'd practiced. Whatever brief delusion she had of a comfortable life married to the president vanished. She could never be at peace knowing that her husband inflicted misery on others, and she couldn't spend the rest of her life pretending to be oblivious of his cruelty. She had to steal the barracks master key and stick to the plan she'd formed with Louise to free Nick, and to escape. That meant, first, continuing to convince the president she loved him and wanted nothing more than to marry him in order to gain access to keys and information. Next, she had to play her part at the engagement dinner: smile, dance, then vanish into the darkness. She slid food around on her plate, but the president seemed too preoccupied to notice.

"I'm thinking about starting a school," he told her as they walked back to the library. "We can't keep this place going without children. I'm even going to begin recruiting some young families. What do you think?"

She forced a smile. "That sounds like a wonderful idea."

"I'm so glad you think so. It's been on my mind all day." They stopped in front of the library and the president took both of her hands in his. "Unfortunately, I have to leave later this afternoon for business outside of Oak Creek, but I'll see you for lunch on Wednesday."

"That's four days away. I'm going to miss you." She tried to sound disappointed instead of relieved.

President Whitley smiled then kissed her. Lareina didn't feel light, but light-headed; instead of a warm fluttering in her chest, she felt a stabbing chill. She focused her attention on being Rochelle Aumont as she smiled at the president and slid her hand slowly out of his before returning to work.

One overheard conversation had caused Oak Creek to lose all traces of the shimmering brilliance it had held earlier. The afternoon sun appeared dim, and cracks in the side of the library were more pronounced. Any dreams of a new life shattered like thin ice beneath a five-hundred-pound weight.

As the afternoon passed, her worries turned to Nick. *Some of the men have developed a cough.* Was that the extent of the danger, or were they reducing the seriousness of the situation due to Whitley's mood? Was Nick safe? Once again, the clock's hands moved achingly slow as they made their rounds.

Cool evening air and lack of wind brought a wispy fog that thickened into a wall by the time Lareina slipped through the bathroom window. Oak Creek became an unfamiliar place with only the ghostly outlines of buildings visible. Her feet followed the sidewalk until each familiar turn led her to the screen of evergreen trees.

One foot in front of the other, she made her way to the barracks. The fog and President Whitley's absence from Oak Creek gave her a sense of security and confidence that she could avoid the type of close call she'd encountered on her last visit to Nick. In an attempt to appease her guilt for delaying her return, she had stuffed her jacket with every scrap of food from her tray plus Louise's unwanted leftovers.

"Nick," she whispered through the bars. "Nick, are you awake?"

From some of the windows above she heard a deep, raspy cough, then the same sound echoed from within Nick's cell. He appeared slowly, rising bit by bit, on the other side of the bars.

"Hey." His voice wavered, but he managed a half smile. "I was worried maybe you got in some kind of trouble and they had you locked up somewhere."

Throat muscles tightening, her body understood that something felt wrong before her head could decipher the exact problem. "Nothing like that. I just had to get some rest."

"I think I caught your cold." Nick coughed that agonizing, chest-rattling hack. "Some of the others haven't been feeling well either."

His hand brushed hers as he reached out to grip the bars. It felt hot, too hot to match the chilly night. He started to speak again, but dropped his head below the window and coughed for almost a full minute.

"That sounds like something worse than a cold." A dull ache crept across the front of her skull. Feeling powerless, she rubbed the back of her hand in circles against her forehead to ward off a coming headache.

Nick rested his cheek against the two middle bars so she couldn't see his eyes. Lifting a shaking hand toward his face, she stopped, then gently pressed it against his forehead. Touching his skin felt like touching the sidewalk on a hot summer day.

"It doesn't matter. They won't let us see a doctor, and if we don't work we don't eat." He spoke the words as if simply discussing the weather.

"I brought you food." The words tripped over her tongue, vanishing into the fog. Reaching into her pockets, she handed Nick the stolen supper one item at a time. "You can rest and I'll make sure you have enough to eat."

"There would be other consequences when I don't die of starvation. It would be worse to sit here shivering all day anyway."

"You just need a day to rest," she protested. "Then you'll feel better."

He tried to stifle his cough, but another fit shook his body. "Being sick isn't an excuse here. This isn't third grade." Shaky sarcasm filled in for fading bravado.

"You need medicine," Lareina said more to herself than Nick.

"Did you even hear anything I just said?"

She remembered perfectly well what the president told the guards in their meeting. Maybe she could steal medicine, but what kind? She didn't know if Nick had the fever, or something worse, and her mind scrambled for a shred of an idea. If Aaron would cooperate, this would be easy, but he had been lulled into complacency by the regular meals and a chance to fulfill his dream. She hadn't seen him since getting her stitches out, but he'd made it clear he wasn't willing to risk those things for anyone, not even his friends.

Discouraged, she leaned her head against the bar next to Nick's face. A tear tickled her cheek as it followed the outline of her nose and plunged off her chin. She watched it shatter on the back of her hand, and then the idea came.

"You have to kiss me," she exclaimed in a whisper.

"What?" Nick pulled his face away from the window. "Have you completely lost it, or am I starting to hear things?"

Under different circumstances, she would have laughed. "Based on your reaction, I think you heard correctly."

He narrowed his eyes. "First of all, why? Second, I don't want you to catch this—"

"Yes, you do," she interrupted. "If I get sick, I can go to the doctor and get medicine and bring it to you. It must be contagious if so many people are coughing." Excitement clambered through her voice and expanded with each word.

Nick shivered. "What if it's the fever? What if there's no medicine?"

She swallowed hard, trying not to show any fear as she remembered the man in Austin, dying alone on his front yard. The reality of death had attached to her that day, but hadn't she been afraid of getting sick even before? She avoided people, tried not to bump into them, and held her breath if she heard anyone cough.

"Don't be so dramatic," she told him in a steady voice. Taking a deep breath, she leaned her face as far through the bars as she could.

"Can't we just drink out of the same bottle or something?" Nick suggested.

"Do you have a bottle?" she asked, the bars pressing against her face from each side. She looked ridiculous enough to make him smile.

"No, I guess not."

"This'll work the best anyway. Come on, don't be afraid," she teased. She closed her eyes and puckered her lips.

"I'm not afraid."

She raised her eyebrows, eyes still closed. "I don't bel—"

Nick's lips pressed against hers. The muffled coughing, dripping water, cold, and darkness swirled, blended, disappeared, returned again. When Nick stepped back, he looked down at the windowsill, and Lareina studied her knuckles turning white from her tight grip on the bars. Minutes passed, filled only with the trickle of water through gutters and silent fog that curled around trees and crept through the hazy darkness in search of a clear space to obscure.

"You should probably . . . get back before . . . they notice you're . . . missing," Nick said, clearing his throat after every few words.

"You're right. I hope you feel better. I'll see you tomorrow, right?"

Nick successfully held back a cough. "I'll be here."

Blind in the fog, she relied on her feet to carry her back to her building. For a moment when their lips met, she had been somewhere warm and safe. She tried to hold onto it, but the further she walked from Nick, the faster the warmth faded. Moisture collected on her cheeks as a few stubborn tears mixed with misty air.

The silent raising of a window. Tiptoeing through vacant hallways. A muffled clicking shut of a door. She arrived safely in her room, left her shoes on the rug, hung her coat on the hook, and got into bed.

"You were gone a long time. How's Nick?" Louise's groggy voice asked from across the room.

"He's getting sick." Her voice shook as she cocooned herself in blankets.

"Nothing serious, I hope?"

When she closed her eyes, Nick's pale face haunted her. When she opened them, nothing but the outlines of a dark room that never should have become so familiar.

"I don't know. I kissed him . . . to find out."

"You don't think he has the fever?" Louise's voice was much more alert.

Still shivering, Lareina pulled the comforter up to her chin, but she knew she wasn't cold.

"I hope not. I want to get him medicine."

"Oh, Rochelle, please tell me that wasn't your first kiss?" Louise's question, for a brief second, undermined the seriousness of the situation. Lareina closed her eyes and let herself believe they were just two teenage girls talking about boys.

"No, that would be when I kissed the president so he would believe our engagement was real."

Silence, then Louise stifled a laugh. "Don't count either one of those. The third one will be the guy you're really in love with."

A brief smile faded quickly. Where did the game of deception stop and the reality of her life begin? Her head sank deeper into her pillow and her memory fought to recover something familiar. It wasn't far away, but it was buried under layers of dust. Something unimportant or more important than everything else.

Sighing, she pressed her face against the cold pillow. What did it mean to be home? Was it Oak Creek where she had a roof over her head and a routine, the house that she must have once shared with her parents, or a place like Maibe where she had friends? At least she believed them to be friends, people who cared about her, but they had only been children. In the rest of her world, people were incapable of love. They might form alliances for protection, but no one wanted to carry extra weight or slow down for someone who couldn't keep up. She wondered whether Nick or Aaron could add insight to her question, but she realized she had no time for testing theories. Only three things mattered: escaping Oak Creek with Nick, protecting the pendant, and finding a family—people who would take care of her, people she didn't have to lie to, people who would never abandon her.

CHAPTER 27

The next night, Louise spread out a hand-drawn map of Oak Creek on Lareina's bed. She pointed at a building near the center. "That's where everyone will be gathered for the engagement party."

Lareina peered over Louise's hand to read the label above a little square sketched out in pencil. "Really? The cafeteria?"

Louise raised her eyebrows. "You didn't think we had some kind of fancy banquet hall you'd never seen?"

"No, I guess not." She glanced out the window but only darkness greeted her. All day she had waited for a tickle in her throat or that first chill to indicate an oncoming fever, but she felt normal, physically anyway. At work or in conversations, she could barely focus long enough to make sense of anything. Nick had entirely replaced any thoughts of Whitley that had preoccupied her mind only a day earlier, but what she had felt for Whitley and what she was feeling for Nick now weren't the same. She had been drawn to Whitley because she had confused the possibility of a stable life with falling in love. She thought about Nick because she knew he was sick and she had promised to get him out of Oak Creek. She told herself she didn't care about him more than anyone else, but felt guilty imagining him shivering in his cell, hungry and miserable.

"If prisoners in the barracks can cause enough confusion to keep half of the guards busy, the rest of us can take care of the guards at the party." Louise waved a hand in front of Lareina's face. "Hey, Rochelle, are you listening?"

"Yes, yes we have to keep the guards busy."

"Do you think Nick can handle getting the message to everyone?"

"Yes." *If he's well enough to move,* she thought, but didn't allow herself to put that thought into words.

"And you can get the key to the barracks? We have less than a week now."

"I'll get it before Saturday." She didn't even know what the key looked like or where President Whitley kept it, but she wanted to hug Nick and she couldn't do that with bars between them. Rubbing her forehead, she tried to remember how much he annoyed her.

"Good, you should probably get going to see Nick then. But first, I have a surprise." Louise walked over to the closet, pulled out two backpacks, and held them up. "I packed enough clothes from the supply closet for you and Nick. Plus a few extra just in case you can convince the doctor to come with you."

Lareina thanked Louise before she left on her nightly trek to the barracks. Those backpacks brought a slight relief to her anxious thoughts. Preparations made the escape plan feel concrete instead of something she just imagined in a hopeful dream.

Taking a deep breath, she whispered Nick's name into the dark space beyond thick, cold window bars. His face appeared almost instantly.

"Hey, are you feeling better?" Any solace from his quick response to her voice didn't last long.

Nick glared at her with an intensity of expression she'd never witnessed. "The big news around here is that the president is engaged to a Rochelle Aumont. What's wrong with you?" He spat the words at her.

She felt the question like a slap and took a step backward.

I'm not Rochelle Aumont, she wanted to scream, *so technically I'm not engaged to anyone.* Instead she closed her eyes and squeezed her hands around the bars until her knuckles ached. "I'm doing what I have to in order to get us out of here. I need you to trust me." Her voice remained even and calm, as she fought back the instinct to admonish Nick for his inability to see the big picture.

Nick's eyes rolled dramatically as he slowly shook his head back and forth. "Since when does dating the evil dictator help us get out of here?"

"I don't know, Nick, let's think about this." Her patience dissolved. "He has the key you need to get out, he has the power to imprison me if he gets suspicious at all, knowing when he's away gives me the opportunity to prepare supplies . . ."

"You mean to steal supplies," Nick scoffed.

"Do you want my help? Because I could have been out of here a month ago if I didn't have to find a way to get you out of jail," she snapped.

He didn't answer. She leaned against the building and looked at silhouettes of trees trimmed in moonlight. All of the secrets she'd kept from Nick danced through her head. How could she blame him for not trusting her?

"I'm sorry," she whispered, "but I don't know what you want me to do."

"I want you to say you'll stop lying and stealing the minute we get out of this place. I want you to try being honest for once in your life." He took a breath then bent over coughing before he could continue speaking.

Lareina brought her face close to the bars and waited for the wheezing to stop. "Nick, are you okay?"

His face reappeared. Shadows darkened the contours

beneath his eyes. She grasped his hand and he didn't attempt to pull it away.

"I'm sorry. I didn't mean that. I never wanted to leave you behind." Her words came out rushed and pleading. "I'll do better. I'll stop lying once we're out of this place."

Nick nodded. His expression softened with regret. "I'm sorry too."

She took a breath, relaxed her white knuckles, and took a minute to organize her thoughts. "Nick, if I get you the key would you be able to unlock your door?"

He nodded. "The window's broken out, so yeah, I could unlock it, but I couldn't get past the guards at the exit."

Tilting her head back, she let her eyes sweep over rows of windows covering three stories of the monstrous building. "Once you unlock your door, you're going to unlock the other doors too."

Nick sucked in a nervous breath. "You want me to start a riot?"

"I'm counting on it. For the plan to work, the guards have to stay busy. Saturday night is my engagement party. It's going to be a big event and most of the community will be distracted. Any additional security will be there. Can you let everyone out of their cells?"

For a minute Nick didn't move or respond, then he nodded. "Yes, I can do that."

"It's settled then." She smiled. "Saturday night, we're getting out of this place."

After coughing into the crook of his elbow, Nick groaned. He tried to smile, but hope drained inch by inch from his dull eyes.

"I'm packing. Anything you want me to bring?"

"Soap," Nick answered immediately. "All I want is a warm shower."

"You've got it," she promised in an overly cheery voice, then raised her eyes to Nick's. In the moonlight she could see every gaunt, tired feature of his face. The dusty grime across his forehead and under his eyes stood out against his pale skin. "We're friends again, right?"

"Of course." Cold stars shivered in the sky and his hand gripped hers tightly. "Do you remember when I chose flying as my superpower?"

Leaning closer, Lareina searched for hope in his eyes, but she couldn't find it. "I remember." The warmth of a rainy summer day in the olive-green house brought her fifteen seconds of peace. She would trade anything, even her pendant, to travel back to that moment and remain there forever.

"I changed my mind." He grinned and closed his eyes. His grip slackened. "I'd rather have the ability to walk through walls."

Hold on a little while longer. She pushed the thought at him, knowing she had to leave but unable to pull herself away. What if he wasn't there the next night? What if these were the last words she ever said to him?

She squeezed his hand and he let go. "Just hold on for a few more days and you'll be able to walk right through the door." Reluctantly, she returned to the sidewalks of Oak Creek and turned her feet toward the unguarded cafeteria to steal some food for the upcoming journey.

PART 3

WINTER OF 2090

CHAPTER 28

Blank white walls surrounded Lareina as she waited for Aaron. She swallowed a few times, trying to relieve the scratchy feeling in her throat without coughing. It had only taken forty-eight hours for the kiss to have its desired effect, and now, after one day with a fever, she was so exhausted she couldn't imagine how Nick could be working.

She had to focus on doing her job. If Nick could dig tunnels, she could steal a key. It was Wednesday—*the* day Whitley said he would be back for lunch, but what if his travels delayed him? What if he decided she was too sick for lunch and took her back to her room to rest instead?

She coughed into her elbow and rubbed her warm forehead. Almost a month had passed since she first arrived at Oak Creek. Despite its miniscule perimeter, compared to the wide prairie she'd been walking, she had stumbled right into its wall. Her life continued to put her on a collision course with Nick and Aaron, and now she couldn't bear the thought of leaving either one of them behind.

"You're not leaving much of a mystery for me," Aaron announced on his way through the door. "I can hear you coughing from the end of the hall."

"I think it's getting worse." She studied Aaron, looking for some sign of unhappiness as he checked her heart, lungs, and temperature. From all observable signs, he seemed as content as he had been the last time she saw him.

Arms folded in front of him, he studied her the way she'd

been studying him. "You have the flu, but you're only the second case I've had."

"It's just the flu and not the fever or something even worse?"

Watching her suspiciously, Aaron pressed the back of his hand against her forehead. "Yeah, but I don't need a thermometer to tell me you're burning up. How did you get so sick?"

She turned away to cough and avoid answering his question.

Aaron looked down at his hand. "You're still visiting Nick over at the barracks, aren't you?" He didn't wait for her to answer. "The only other case of the flu, so far, was a guy who works security over there. I've been investigating what you told me the last time you were here. About the barracks being a prison. Is Nick just as sick as you are?"

Lareina opened her mouth to answer, but that relentless cough returned. She waited a long while for her chest to stop burning while Aaron brought her a glass of water. "I can guarantee we have the exact same thing."

His eyebrows furrowed and a deep wrinkle formed across his forehead. "I was actually planning to come and find you today. I want to help you get Nick out of here. You're still doing that, right? Even though you're engaged to the president?"

"You didn't really believe I'd be engaged to someone I just met?"

"I doubted it, but I worried maybe you really did . . . you know . . . fall in love."

A shiver passed through her body. She didn't know if it was her fever or the memory of a day she really did think she fell in love. "We're leaving on Saturday night."

Aaron nodded and studied her expression. "I should be pretty worried about Nick, shouldn't I?"

"I know I am."

Looking around the room, slowly, inch by inch, he seemed to be memorizing every detail. "I'm coming with you then."

"You're what?" She stifled a cough. "But all you want is to be a doctor . . ."

"And as long as I stay here, I won't be a real doctor." Aaron looked down at his white shoes. "I haven't had any of the training they promised. They just send me to the patients that they don't want to deal with. I'm not really practicing medicine." He took a long breath and forced a smile. "You and Nick are real and this is all just a fraud. I'm sorry I couldn't admit that earlier."

Lareina could see the struggle trembling in his hands and pulling his eyes to the floor. "You're not a fake doctor, but you can definitely do better than this place."

Aaron nodded and finally lifted his head revealing blue eyes dulled by regret and the loss of a position too good to be true. "And I will. But if you're going to be well by Saturday, you need to get back to your room and get plenty of rest."

"But what about Nick? I need medicine."

He nodded. "The best advice I can give you is to get plenty of rest and eat some chicken noodle soup—"

"No, that can't be it." She couldn't tell Nick to rest more and eat soup. He didn't have those options any more than he had the right to see a doctor. Frustrated and exhausted, she pressed her face against the palms of her hands.

Aaron's hand rested warm and heavy on her shoulder. "I don't have anything that will magically cure either of you, but I can get you something to bring your fevers down, so you'll feel a little better." His voice held a comforting tone of authority and the confidence that he could solve any problem. He left the room and returned with a tiny box that rattled when he shook it. "Tell him to take one every six hours. Do you need me to do anything to get us out of here on Saturday?"

"Bring more medicine that'll help Nick after we escape."

"Done. Come back on Friday for a follow-up and we'll talk to make sure I'm clear on the plan." The unsettling cheeriness Aaron had displayed during her earlier visits had vanished as if he'd been jolted from a trance. His eyes met hers with the familiar gentle concern she missed.

Lareina threw her arms around Aaron and hugged him tight. She felt as if she'd just met a friend she hadn't talked to in years.

"Thank you" was all she could think to say, but she never meant it more in her life.

Aaron smiled, helped her down from the exam table, and walked her to the end of the hall, where they parted as if they'd never met. In the waiting room, a woman with a cough sat in one corner, a younger boy read a magazine in the other, and President Whitley jumped up from his seat the minute he saw Lareina.

He watched her as she approached. His eyes darted in all directions as if he feared some unseen enemy would come and carry her away, and he wrung his hands as he spoke. "Are you all right? Louise told me you're really sick."

She decided if any part of his concern was an act, she would give him an award. "It's just the flu," she groaned as miserably as she could. "I'll feel better after I get back to my room and get some sleep."

"Is it a good idea for you to be alone? What if you need

something? You shouldn't be walking out in the cold to get lunch."

"I'm not all that hungry anyway . . ."

"Nonsense," the president interrupted. "You can rest on the couch in my office until Louise is off work."

Holding her sleeve up to her face, she tried to stifle a cough and squeezed her eyes shut against the wildfire in her throat. "Are you sure I won't be in the way?"

The president put his arm around her. "Of course not. You're never in the way."

Leaning into him with her eyes half closed, she let him lead her the short distance back to his house. The gray sky and threatening cold rain had become so common she barely noticed as they followed silent sidewalks.

Whitley guided her into his house and down the hall to his office. He helped her to sit down on the couch and kissed her forehead. "I'll be back in just a minute."

Resting her head against the couch, she closed her eyes and listened to a murmur of voices in the hallway.

A few minutes passed in the quiet office before Whitley's footsteps padded back into the room. "All right, I have everything you need to get some rest." He carried a pillow and a pile of folded blankets.

Forcing a smile, she sat up and shivered.

Whitley sighed sympathetically. "Here, let's get you comfortable." He helped Lareina out of her jacket and tossed it over the back of the couch, fluffed the pillow before she laid down, and tucked four blankets over her.

He kissed her forehead again. "Are you warm enough?"

"Mmmhmm." She didn't open her eyes.

During the next fifteen minutes, she heard Whitley moving around the room.

Finally, the sound of crinkling paper and sliding pen indicated that the president had settled in at his desk.

Keeping her eyes closed, she pretended to be asleep, but forced her foggy mind to stay awake. Any visitors met with Whitley in the hallway. Their muffled conversations came through the thick door as indecipherable as a code scrawled on paper. The hallway meetings gave her an opportunity to inspect the room from where she lay. Shelves filled with books covered one entire wall. File cabinets stood near the door. Behind the president's desk, a large bulletin board displayed family photos, notes and flyers—and, in the bottom left quarter, keys. So many, in fact, that it tilted slightly to accommodate the extra weight.

All morning she waited for an opportunity to investigate, but Whitley never traveled beyond the hallway. Some meetings lasted for minutes and some much longer, but she didn't want to risk getting up with the president close enough to hear her footsteps. Papers ruffled, letters opened with a clean slice, and his chair squeaked with the slightest shift of weight. Each time she coughed, he asked if she was all right. Soup and orange juice arrived for lunch.

Lareina tried to suppress her cough, tried to remain completely still, didn't dare to sniffle. As long as the president worried about her being alone, he wouldn't leave the room long enough for her to steal the most important object she'd ever swiped. The clock thunked loudly. For a while she counted, trying to determine how much time had passed, but soon gave up. She kept herself awake by trying to attribute the building's groaning to footsteps or the wind outside. A new clicking sound echoed in the hallway.

"Sir, the factory manager is here for your two o'clock meeting," Whitley's secretary announced.

"Take him upstairs. We'll meet in the sitting room," he replied softly.

Papers shuffled and metal slid against unoiled tracks. She imagined Whitley gathering up a pile of papers from his desk, sliding one of the file cabinet drawers open, pulling out a folder, and pushing it shut once again. Soft footsteps—the kind that took effort—retreated. The door creaked but didn't click shut.

Opening her eyes, she glanced around the familiar space. Muffled light shone through thin white curtains. Keeping her eye on the sliver of light showing through the barely open door, she sat up and waited. She didn't want to make a sound to alert the secretary in the room across the hall. Dropping to her hands and knees, she slowly crawled across the floor, hid behind the desk, and waited. No one came to check on her and the building remained quiet.

Pushing herself to her feet, she squinted at the bulletin board. Whitley's ruthlessness could only be matched by his organization. Each key hung on its own hook with a white label revealing its purpose in uniform black type.

Factory Storeroom
Factory Boiler Room
Residence Hall #1
Residence Halls Master Key

She glanced over each label, not sure what she was looking for, but sure it had to be there. Steps clicked out in the hall. Lareina dove behind the desk and pulled her knees up to her chin. The clicking paused outside Whitley's office. She held her breath, but the door never moved and the footsteps diminished gradually.

Feeling a sense of urgency, she sprang back to her feet, then clutched the desk chair as the room swirled around her.

Barracks Main Entrance
Barracks First Floor Rooms
Barracks Master Key

Carefully, she slid the last key from its hook and examined it as it rested in the palm of her hand. It looked dull, tarnished, old. Duplicate keys dangled from several of the hooks. She selected one labeled **Administration Boiler Room** and slid it onto the empty hook. In her hand she held the power to open all doors in the barracks. Squeezing the key so tight it cut into her hand, she turned to walk away, but something in the middle of the bulletin board caught her eye.

The top of one flyer stood out in a mess of overlapping papers. Big, bold, black letters spelled out **WANTED**. She shifted flyers advertising flood relief shelters, soldier recruitment, and notes about scheduled meetings from October.

Beneath a newspaper clipping of the fall temperature and precipitation outlook, she uncovered a picture of herself. The mug shot had slightly shorter hair and appeared a little thinner, but the recognizable image of her hung among reminder notes and old letters. Her heart sped up and her breathing became a silent, staccato choking. She remembered the winter day less than a year earlier, when cold rain coated the smooth pavement. It had been exactly seventy-four hours and twenty-nine minutes since she'd eaten anything and then she spotted baskets of cookies displayed inside a bakery window. In less than a minute she darted inside and fled from shouts behind her as her feet skidded over the sheen of ice.

She knew she would fall before she hit the pavement, and she watched cookies slide down the street with her cheek against slickened concrete.

A detective pulled her to her feet and loaded her into the back of his white car. At the station they took her fingerprints and her picture. The arresting officer introduced himself as Detective Galloway. He told her stealing would get her nowhere and recommended she go to the nearest Home for Children because the next time the law wouldn't be so lenient. Lareina had promised to do so with no intention of ever setting foot in another Home for Children.

She reached for the pendant and twirled it between her thumb and index finger. Under her picture the poster read: Have you seen this thief going by the name of Lareina? Contact Det. Russ Galloway with any information. $3,000 reward for information.

The chill she felt had nothing to do with her fever. Did Whitley know about this? Could he possibly have looked at it without realizing it was her? Working quickly, she removed the poster and rearranged the other flyers so no one would ever notice it went missing.

Feeling weak and dizzy, she crossed the room and sat down on the couch. Looking at the poster one last time, she folded it in half twice and shoved it into the pocket of her jacket along with the key to the barracks. She rested against the pillow and pulled blankets over her head.

The remainder of the day passed agonizingly slow. She dozed in Whitley's office, then napped in her own bed after Louise walked her back to their building. Resting all day gave her enough energy to wake just before midnight. Never had she been so relieved to arrive outside Nick's window, but the relief didn't last long.

Nick, pale and drenched in sweat, watched her through hollow eyes.

"It's the flu," she told him. "Aaron sent medicine for you." She pushed the box toward him.

"It won't help." His voice shook. "Everything I swallow comes back up. I haven't been able to keep anything down since this morning."

"It'll be okay—"

"No," he interrupted, "it won't. I'm going to die here. I saw them take two people out this morning on stretchers, and that wouldn't happen unless they were . . ."

Nick didn't finish. He didn't need to. The hopelessness and lack of any emotion in his voice brought tears to the corners of her eyes. She sniffled and blinked a few times, hoping he wouldn't notice her crying.

"Come on, Nick, you're not going to die." The confidence in her tone didn't match the uncertainty thudding in her chest.

He stared past her, not listening to a word she said. "Do you remember when we first met? I was trapped in that pit and I thought that was the absolute worst things could get. Now those seem like the good old days."

She took his hand because she couldn't think of anything else to say.

"We keep thinking things will get better in the future," Nick continued, "but it's always the past that seems to be better. Nothing improves—it only decays with time."

"That can't be true." Although her entire life supported his argument, she wouldn't give up the possibility of a brighter future. "Everything is going to get better. We just have to get out of here, then you'll see."

Nick looked down at something resting in his hand. "I was stupid to come to Texas thinking I would find Ava. We were supposed to go to a dance together, but she moved away the week before. I never even got to say goodbye—they were just gone. She left me a note saying she would call, but she never did."

"You two were really good friends?" She hoped to get Nick focused on better times.

"We were best friends for most of our lives. A few years ago she gave me this for my birthday." Nick placed the small, smooth object in her hand. "She found two of them in her dad's desk and said they were kind of like friendship necklaces. I told her that was for girls, but I kept it anyway."

Lareina stared down at the black pendant, shaped like a tear drop. The temperature plunged five degrees and she squeezed her eyes shut so Nick wouldn't see her react. She ran her finger along the familiar outline, already sure it was identical to the one dangling around her neck. But then her fingers felt different contours on the pendant's face. Her pendant had the letters *S P E R O* written across the rounded side. In the exact same place, Nick's pendant said *O P T I M U S*. Ava, Nick had called his friend. Her throat constricted, tightening to the point she felt herself gasping for air.

My dad had two of these pendants, but I took them for friendship necklaces. Susan's voice echoed in her head. *My friend is out there and he has no idea what kind of danger he's in because of me.* She wasn't the only one who decided to lie about her name. Did Galloway know about Nick's pendant? He couldn't possibly, right? Only Susan/Ava knew and now Lareina, but all of that meant . . .

"My entire family is gone. Without Ava I don't have anyone left anyway, and I'm so tired of digging tunnels."

Forcing herself to breathe, she pressed the pendant back into Nick's hand, squeezing it between his palm and hers.

Her feverish hand couldn't even detect any abnormality in his temperature. She shivered, too sick to be out in the cold, but what about Nick?

"No, you've come too far." The force in her own voice surprised her and wind that howled like a train whistle filled any silence. "Ava is out there somewhere and I'm going to help you find her." Usually the lies came so easily, but this one burned her throat and tasted like sour milk in her mouth.

Nick nodded. His fingers slid through hers, but she held on. Letting go felt like losing him forever. Her feverish, irrational thought process told her that as long as she could feel his hand, warm in hers, he couldn't be sick, he couldn't be hurt, he couldn't die.

"I got the key." Her voice shivered. She pushed the box of pills into Nick's hand. "I'll bring it to you on Friday night. Take one of these. Just try."

He nodded, but still she held on. In cold moonlight she searched for the boy who argued about entering a stranger's house during a storm or dug potatoes with his bare hands to win a bet, but she didn't recognize him.

Silence ached in her throat, her hunched shoulders, and the arches of her feet. It swirled misery through the trees and into Nick's prison cell. Nothing remained but swampy ground, gray light, and the trembling secrets between two silhouettes holding hands.

"You should go. It's cold." His voice was the last wisp of smoke from a dimming ember. "And don't come back tomorrow night. Wait until Friday." He shivered. "We can't risk your engagement party being cancelled because you're sick."

"Do you promise . . ." The words stumbled across her tongue. "Do you promise you'll be here on Friday when I bring the key?" Nick looked away. "The plan won't work without you." She squeezed his hand until she couldn't feel her fingers.

"I promise." He didn't look at her and she didn't let go. "I'll be here." This time his eyes met hers, and for an instant the stubbornness she missed flashed across his face.

She released her grip and his hand slid away. He vanished from the window, and she forced her stiff muscles to straighten. She held onto her composure until she was hidden in the tree line, then gave in to her shaking knees and allowed gravity to pull her to the ground.

"My real name is Lareina," she whispered to the wind. "I have a pendant just like yours, Nick, because Ava is dead." The secrets and the truths of a professional liar quivered with the pine needles. Warm tears turned cold against her cheeks. She pulled the pendant off and held it close to her face, searching for a clue in the dark. Susan, Ava, or whoever she was, didn't know why the pendant was so valuable. Neither did Galloway. It felt hot in her hand, like a firecracker about to explode, but she couldn't throw it away. She could only hope it didn't blow up before she found the answers no one could give her.

CHAPTER 29

"Your blood-pressure is kind of high," Aaron told Lareina at her follow-up appointment.

She had spent the previous day in bed and stayed in that night as Nick had requested. Her fever had broken, but she felt queasy every time she recalled the truth about Ava and the lie that she could help Nick find her.

"If it wasn't, there would be something wrong with me. Between this engagement party, getting the supplies we need to leave this place, and Nick . . ." She couldn't tell Aaron about Ava without telling him about the pendant.

Aaron sat down on the exam table next to her. "What can I do to help?"

She slumped forward, elbows into thighs, face into hands. "Tell me Nick is going to be okay and we'll escape without getting caught."

"Nick is going to be fine and we'll escape without getting caught." Aaron believed it and she didn't. The part about Nick, at least. She knew the escape plan so well she could execute it in her sleep. But what if Nick wasn't okay? She wanted the hours to rush by so she could get to the barracks and check on him, but at the same time she wanted the clock to freeze because she was afraid he wouldn't come to the window when she whispered his name. How could she have left him alone last night?

Lifting her eyes back to the light, she turned to Aaron. The paralyzing mixture of apprehension, fear, and dread she'd battled every day at Oak Creek puzzled her. She'd been afraid most of her life, but usually it felt more like a tremble of excitement and only lasted until she swiped the food she needed or outran the authorities. Then came the calm, the clarity of thought, the plan for a new risk. At Oak Creek, anxiety frosted fear until her focus became slush.

"Aaron, I'm so scared all the time. I don't want Nick to die."

"He won't." Aaron's eyes traced his shoelaces. He couldn't make such a promise and he knew it.

"What if I can't get all three of us out? What if Nick is too sick to help? What if we have to . . ." The words died before they landed on her tongue. "I've never been so worried in my life."

"That's what it feels like to have a family." His gentle smile lit the room in a glow of comfort.

She always imagined a family would feel more like warmth, safety, stability.

Aaron tilted his head and his eyes smiled as he read the confusion on her face. "I was always worried that my family didn't have enough money for food. That's why I left—to make money, to make everything better for them."

Her thoughts collapsed and twisted. She jumped off a moving train in the dark. Aaron let his family believe him to be dead. She crossed Oak Creek every night in the cold and the rain even when Nick didn't want to see her. Why?

"Do you wish you would have stayed?"

"I miss them, if that's what you mean. But the next place we settle, I'm going to get a job and send them some money and a long letter."

"We," she repeated. "Are we going to the same place?"

He laughed. "Do we have a choice? Last time you tried to lose us, we all ended up here."

Her smile held up for exactly five seconds before it drooped and vanished. *Some family we are,* she thought. Galloway knew more about her than Nick or Aaron, starting with her name. A squeaking whoosh passed by in the hallway. The blindingly white walls made her head ache. "There's no telling how long the riot at the barracks will last as a distraction. We have to move quickly, so you have to be in the tree line by the barracks before midnight." Lareina closed her eyes and pictured the train schedule Louise's friend had stolen from the factory loading dock. The schedule she had studied every night by flashlight until she knew it by memory. "We'll slip out through the main gate and sneak onto the twelve-thirty train. Got it?"

"Try not to worry," Aaron told her. "I won't be late."

Everything will be fine. She let it repeat over and over, a silent reassurance only she could hear. Everyone knew their part in the plan and Louise had helped her to meticulously plan every detail. With Aaron's guarantee that she was recovering as quickly as could be expected, she returned to her room to rest until night returned to camouflage her visit to Nick.

Just before midnight, she buried the two backpacks of supplies from Louise beneath leaves and pine needles inside the tree line, then snuck over to the barracks for what she hoped would be the last time. *As long as I don't end up locked in there,* she thought, then shoved the thought away.

It took longer than usual for Nick to appear at the window, but when he did, his head lolled to the side and expressionless eyes barely noticed Lareina's presence.

She took a breath, let it out, hoped her face didn't reveal disappointment. "Hey, feeling any better?"

His forehead pressed against the bars as he watched

streams of water carve mini trenches through the dirt. "I can't do this, Rochelle," he whimpered. "I'm too sick."

A low, wailing whistle echoed off in the distance. Two sets of eyes snapped to the nearest tree, but not one twig stirred. She smiled and wiped a smudge of dirt from Nick's searing forehead with her thumb.

"Do you hear that?"

"Mmmmhmmm," Nick agreed with his eyes closed.

"This time tomorrow night, you, Aaron, and I will be on that train, getting far away from here. Just hold on for twenty-four hours."

"I'll try," he promised.

She pulled the key out of her pocket and folded it into Nick's hand. The feeling of cool metal against his skin revived him a bit and he opened his eyes.

"Tomorrow night at midnight, I'll meet you over there in the evergreen trees. Find a way to get all of the doors open. We're all counting on you."

He smiled weakly for the first time in days. "I won't let you down."

Returning to her room, she sank into her bed, and closed her eyes against the throbbing headache that hadn't eased since she'd been sick. Sleep, however, escaped any attempt she made to catch it. Instead, she watched shadows crawl across the ceiling, clutched the pendant in her hand, and visualized each detail of her escape second by second.

"Wake up, Rochelle. You have to see this." Louise was shaking her shoulder.

She sat up, rubbing one hand across her eyes, the pendant still clutched in the other. She slid her pendant hand beneath the blanket and blinked at her roommate, who held a sparkling blue dress up in front of her.

"This came for you with lunch today. There's shoes too," Louise exclaimed.

Lareina pushed matted hair out of her eyes, but some invisible curtain remained. "Lunch?"

Louise laughed and pointed to a box on her desk. "Since everyone has the day off, we all get delivery pizza."

The warm smell of dough and sauce tickled her nose. Somehow she'd slept through it. How could she not wake up at the smell of food? "What time is it?"

"Eleven o'clock. You were sleeping so tight I didn't want to wake you up. You better eat something though, and start getting ready for tonight."

She reviewed her plan while she ate pizza, while she showered, while she brushed her teeth. It would work. It had to work because she wouldn't get a second chance. She thought about Nick and her hands shook. She looked at the curling iron on her dresser; its solid red light indicated it was warm. In the mirror, she watched one shaky hand lift a strand of her hair then let it drop in front of her. "I don't know how to do this."

Louise crossed the room and reached for the curling iron. "Here, let me help you. It's hard to reach the back by yourself anyway."

"Where are you going to go when you get out of here?"

"There're five others who are going to travel south with me," she explained as she expertly twisted Lareina's hair around the barrel.

"Are you sure you don't want to come with me? I'm taking the train to Dallas."

"Maybe you should come with me." Louise untwisted one curl and started another one. "I hear things are getting pretty dangerous to the north with riots and train derailments."

Sitting in front of the mirror, Lareina studied her reflection. To anyone else, she would look so different from the unkempt, hollow-cheeked image on the wanted poster, but she still saw the resemblance. She'd been running from something her entire life, and she didn't like who she'd become for it. Going south with Louise, who had become like a protective big sister, appealed to her, but she knew she couldn't go back to San Antonio.

"Thanks, but I have to get back home."

"I understand. Just be careful. The world is dangerous," Louise warned.

"I'll be okay." She smiled. "I'm more nervous about tonight."

Louise set the curling iron down. "Speaking of tonight, I have something for you." She walked over to her desk, took something out of the drawer, and brought it back with her.

Lareina took the vial in her hand and examined the clear liquid inside.

"Mix this in his drink thirty minutes before you want to get out of there and he should be asleep by the time you leave," Louise instructed.

Her muscles tensed, the vial rested limply in her hand. "This won't hurt him . . . or anything."

"No, nothing like that. He'll be well rested in the morning to face his brother."

With Louise's help, Lareina brushed on some makeup. The dress was a shimmering diamond, a glittering jewel sprawled across her bed. How many hours had she spent staring into the windows of dress shops? How many dresses found in abandoned houses had she wished to try on? This dress surpassed them all and it belonged to her. When Louise left the room to visit a friend, she slipped it on and carefully hid her pendant beneath the rippling blue material. Three months had elapsed since Susan pressed the pendant into her hand and since that moment, not a second passed that she didn't feel its deadly touch.

At exactly six o'clock, Louise answered a knock at the door, revealing President Whitley standing in the hallway with a bouquet of roses.

"I'll be ready in one minute," Lareina said from across the room. She slid her feet into the silver high-heeled shoes delivered with her dress and glanced into her purse at the vial stashed inside an otherwise empty compartment.

When she stepped forward a smile spread across Whitley's face. "You look stunning," he whispered and extended the bouquet toward her. He had always treated her with kindness and she would repay it by abandoning him, starting a riot that could destroy Oak Creek, and making him look like a fool in front of the brother he admired. She froze.

"Those flowers are so pretty." Louise accepted them from the president. "I'll put them in a vase and I'll see you two at the party."

A second to breathe helped her to refocus on the part she had to play. "Thank you, Louise." She linked her arm through Whitley's. "I suppose we should get going."

Together, they followed the network of wide sidewalks lined by perfect landscaping that she could navigate with her eyes closed. Despite the familiarity, she could only think, *This is the last time.* She would never again walk those perfectly smooth sidewalks because on her way out of the party, she would be running.

When they arrived at the cafeteria, two men pulled the doors open for them to enter.

"Are you ready?" Whitley whispered.

Lareina clutched his arm tighter as they walked up the stairs to a mezzanine looking down over the party. From below she could hear a cascading waterfall of voices and laughter. White lights gleamed on the banister and along the balcony rail, then reached up in strands to meet in the center of the domed ceiling. She'd stepped into the polished silver shoes of a princess and any of the runaways from San Antonio would call her a fool for running away from the best opportunity she would ever find in her life. The voices sounded distant, like the ringing of a pebble dropped into a well. Whitley stopped walking and she realized they stood at the top of the stairs.

"Should I make the announcement, sir?" Officer Storey asked.

Whitley looked over at her and she nodded. There would be no turning back. "Yes, we're ready."

Storey walked over to the railing. "Can I get everyone's attention?" he repeated three times before all chatter from below stopped. "Introducing President Whitley and his fiancée, Rochelle Aumont." Storey stepped aside. Somewhere below, a door squeaked on protesting hinges to admit late guests. The room was a collection of held breath, an accumulation of reverent anticipation.

Together, hand in hand, the newly announced couple approached a railing enveloped in white lights. Hundreds of people, clustered in a shapeless mass, stared up at them. The trickle of a cheer crescendoed to minutes of applause and inaudible toasting that bordered on hysteria. Lareina waved. What else could she do?

The commotion below tapered out and changed focus. People dispersed, forming circles of conversation, visiting the buffet, or dancing in the open spaces. Still, she noticed one person near the buffet table look up at her contemptuously then turn back to his group of friends, who broke out in obnoxious laughter. As her eyes glanced from one individual to the next, she was met with a glare from anyone still paying attention to her. Anyone oblivious of the plan hated her. They only cheered under the heavy obligation of fear that forced them to conform to Whitley's rules, orders, and opinions. She depended on anonymity, the convenience of being invisible and disappearing into a crowd. If Galloway walked in, he wouldn't even have to pass out his posters.

"Are you okay?" Whitley whispered.

She watched the people below. None of them looked at her. Forced laughter and fake smiles shimmered through the crowd. She closed her eyes and felt the missing joy of Oak Creek vibrating around her. "Never better."

For the next four hours, they ate and danced and laughed. Each strawberry and deviled egg reminded her she would soon be hungry, each glance through the window that these were her last moments of warmth, each dance with Whitley that he would soon want her captured as desperately as Galloway.

At eleven he took her hand and led her back up to the balcony. They sat together on a bench, listening to music and laughter below. Lareina rested her head on his shoulder and looked at the rising moon outside, sensing the quickly passing time.

"Your hot chocolate, sir." A man set a tray with two steaming mugs, a bowl of whipped cream and a cup of marshmallows on the side table next to her.

"Thank you," the president responded, waving the man away.

He stood and stretched. "I have a surprise for you. Give me a moment?"

"I'll get the hot chocolate ready. Whipped cream as usual?"

"You know me too well," he responded with a wink as he walked away.

Looking around for observers and determining she was alone, Lareina slipped the vial out of her purse, dumped it into one of the cups, then returned it to hiding. Quickly she scooped in some whipped cream, stirred it, and topped it with marshmallows, leaving her cup plain.

Whitley returned with padded footsteps and a slightly shaking hand. His eyes and mouth pinched into a nervous smile. He held his other hand behind his back. "I know we're already engaged and everything, but I never got to give you the ring."

She took the small gray box he held out to her and closed her eyes. Her pounding heart ached like her legs after running from Galloway.

"Aren't you going to open it?"

Opening her eyes, she clasped the box tighter. "Just enjoying the moment." She took a breath and, with the flick of her thumb, pushed the box open. It glimmered brighter than the lights and she couldn't breathe. The contents of that little gray box could buy her tickets to anywhere in the world; she could travel the world if she wanted. President Whitley reached past her, picked it up out of the box, and slipped it onto her finger.

"There, it looks even better than I imagined." He held her hand in his.

Looking down at the ring on her finger overwhelmed her with thrilling elation and sinking guilt. Her mind brought up images of every proposal she ever read about in her lifetime, and yet nothing she imagined could ever match the excitement and dread she felt. The music below stretched, softened, and her words jumbled until she remembered her plan.

"It's perfect. I'll never take it off." She handed him his mug and took the other in her hand. "Let's toast." The mugs clinked and she sipped her hot chocolate as Whitley drank his. "This is really good. Did I get the cream-to-marshmallow ratio right?"

The president tipped his mug and swallowed more of the warm, sweet liquid. "It's perfect. We should dance."

Lareina took his hand, and there on the balcony they danced to a series of slow songs. The moon lifted higher into the sky, taking precious minutes with it.

"Our wedding is going to be amazing," the president said as they turned in slow circles. "You get to plan it just the way you want. Nothing is off limits."

Smiling as they spun through drifting notes, she could already picture her lacey white dress and the church filled with summer daisies. "We definitely have to have chocolate cake."

Whitley yawned. "You've got it." He yawned again and stumbled forward.

She caught his arm. "Are you okay?" Together they walked over to the bench and sat down.

He looked at her through bleary eyes with his forehead rested against his hand. "I guess I'm just getting tired." He leaned his head back against the railing. "I did get up pretty early to make sure everything would be perfect."

"Here, close your eyes for a few minutes and you'll be as good as new." She guided his head down onto the cushion of the bench and sat with him. The ring sparkled with each movement of her finger, music bounced across strands of light, and Whitley breathed in an even rhythm.

"Can I wear a yellow dress for our wedding?" she asked the chest that rose and fell, rose and fell.

Whitley didn't answer. She stared down at the sparkling ring on her finger and visualized thick bundles of cash in her hands. It would buy food and shelter for a lifetime. It would be irresponsible to leave it behind. She stood, took a step toward the stairs, swallowed back a wave of nausea, then turned around.

"I'm sorry it couldn't work out," she said to the sleeping president. "But I feel claustrophobic living inside of a wall and you're more of a pathological liar than I am." With her eyes closed she slipped the ring off her finger and placed it on the cushion next to him. *This is your fault, Nick Ziel,* she thought. Then, turning on her heels, she forced herself to walk away on betrayed feet that clung to the floor.

Kicking off her shoes, she snuck down the steps, and exited through a back door. She crossed the sidewalks, barely touching the cold pavement beneath her feet. Icy air collided with her face and sent tingles down her bare arms and legs. Unintelligible shouting, splashing, thumping, and cracking ruptured the usual facade of peace around the barracks. Her bare feet crunched over brown tree needles and discarded pine cones, too numb from the cold to feel them. Leaning into a tree, she focused on breathing, listened for Nick's footsteps, his voice. What if he didn't escape? Would she walk into the chaos to find him?

"Nick, are you here?" she whispered. "Nick?"

"We're over here."

Lareina spun around and noticed the movements of silhouettes under low hanging tree branches. Nick sat next to Louise in a circle with five other people.

"What took you so long? We've been waiting forever." He stood, looking a little wobbly, but smiling. He came toward her, ducking under prickly branches, then stopped. A goofy grin spread over his face. "Wow, Rochelle, you look so pretty . . . not that you don't always look pretty, but . . ."

Closing the gap between them, she threw her arms around Nick and held him in a tight hug, the way she'd wanted to for the month prison bars stood in her way. Touching him was like touching the outside of an oven door, and he smelled like unwashed gym socks, but she'd never been so happy to see anyone in her life.

"All right, you two." Louise laughed. "Shall we get out of here?"

Lareina let Nick go, but kept one hand on his arm, still afraid he might disappear. She examined the faces, squinting through darkness, and gripped his arm tighter when she felt the plunging absence of a comforting face and confident voice.

"Where's Aaron?"

Louise shrugged. "Either he changed his mind or he didn't make it."

"He promised not to be late." She pushed her heavy feet forward, scanning the shadows of trees. "I can't leave without him."

Louise caught her wrist and pulled her back. "There isn't any time. If we're going to make it through the gate, we have to go now while the guards are distracted."

Aaron said he would come. He said he would bring medicine. He couldn't have changed his mind. She turned to Nick. "You go with Louise. I'll get Aaron and meet you outside."

"Not a chance," he protested. "I'm coming with you."

"You can barely stand up. I'm not dragging you back across this place."

"And I'm not letting you go alone."

The previous peace between them evaporated. Louise and the others shuffled from one foot to the other.

"Come on, Rochelle, we have to go," Louise begged.

Two options and no time. It would be so much easier to take Nick through the main gate, but she knew Aaron wouldn't have failed to appear unless something got in his way. "You guys go. Come on, Nick, we'll get out a different way."

The others left. Lareina brushed dirt and needles off their hidden bags and handed the lighter one to Nick. She pulled socks and shoes onto her feet and led him across the deserted sidewalks. He gaped at the buildings, his first view of Oak Creek, as they jogged to the guard station. He could only be described as awestruck when they approached the president's house. Remembering warm sunshine and a picnic in the soft grass, she stopped and listened but only heard Nick's ragged breathing.

"You all right?" she asked with her eyes on the shed she'd observed during the picnic.

"Just catching my breath . . . I thought we were going to find Aaron?"

She nodded and pointed at the shed. "If I'm not back here in ten minutes, climb onto the roof of that shed, then walk along the wall to that tree and use it to climb down on the other side. The train will come by in less than twenty minutes and take you all the way to Dallas."

He clutched her shoulders and held her there. "Stop telling me what to do. I'm coming with you."

"We don't have time for this." She pulled free of his grasp. "Quit arguing with me and go hide in the bushes."

"Quit arguing with me. I'm following you and you can't stop me."

Her eyes burned into his, willing him to give up. She knew in a reversed situation she wouldn't let him go alone either, but it didn't diminish her frustration. "Fine, just stay behind me and do what I say."

Together they snuck across the yard and peeked over bushes at the guard station. The entire building glowed with light and the front door stood wide open, spilling a yellow rectangle onto the lawn.

"If they caught him, he's in there," she whispered.

Nick stood. "Great, what are we waiting for?"

Grabbing his wrist, she yanked him back down. "That place could be swarming with guards. There's no way to know who we'll encounter inside."

"How many guards do you think are in there?" He rubbed his wrist.

"I don't know."

"Do you think we could look in the window?"

Nick's swarming questions teetered at the top of her forced calm, threatening to topple it into panic. They had to get out in time or they'd miss the train and never get far enough away on foot. They couldn't leave Aaron behind, but walking into the guard station blind could get them all thrown in the barracks for the rest of their lives.

"Just let me think," she snapped and immediately regretted it when Nick recoiled and nodded down at his hands. He swayed slightly and Lareina thought she could easily push him over using one finger.

"All right, let's go."

With Nick close by her side, they crossed the small lawn between the bushes and the guard station, then remaining close to the building, snuck around to the front door. They listened for voices from within, but silence enveloped them.

Sweating despite the cold, heart slamming against

her chest, she plunged into the building. An empty room surrounded her. The pounding of her heart in her head, Nick breathing, and more silence.

"Is anyone here?" he called out.

She clapped a hand over his mouth. "What are you doing?"

"I'm back here." Aaron's voice called from deeper in the building.

"See, it worked," Nick mumbled.

Pulling her hand away, she walked in the direction of Aaron's voice. Light spilled from a room at the end of the dark hallway. Aaron slumped against the wall of a jail cell with his legs stretched in front of him.

"Rochelle, Nick, I didn't think you'd come." Blood covered his face and matted his hair. His hands gripped the bars of his cell tightly, and he used them to pull himself to his feet. "They've been questioning me for hours. Then they got a call about a riot."

"You're welcome," Nick exclaimed from the desk chair he rested in.

"I think they took the key," Aaron groaned.

Lareina picked up two paper clips off the only desk and straightened them between her fingers. "No worries, we don't need keys." She focused on unlocking the door, feeling time scurry away, pulling the train along with it.

Nick buried his face in his hands and coughed. Aaron rested his forehead against his arm, and Lareina didn't dare glance up at the blood. She worried that between Nick's fever and Aaron's injuries, she would never get both of them out of Oak Creek.

"Your medicine is in that bag on the desk," Aaron told Nick. "I almost got out with it but they caught me at the door."

She moved the pins carefully until one slid forward and the

door pulled open. "Well Aaron Swanson, it looks like you're free once again."

He scrambled out of the cell and gave her a one-armed hug. "Thanks, I owe you."

Nick hovered near the door shifting his weight from one foot to the other. He held the bag of medicine tightly in his right hand. "Can we get out of here before they come back?"

Ignoring him, she pulled the top drawer of the desk open. A key remained stuck in the lock indicating that it held something important. Inside she found a handgun shoved to the back.

"Nick's right, we should get going, Rochelle," Aaron urged.

She picked up the gun, ejected the magazine, and, satisfied that it was loaded, clicked it back into place.

"What are you doing? Put that back," Nick ordered from halfway out the door.

"There's not a chance I'm going back out into the world with no way to defend myself."

Nick stood in her way as if he wouldn't let her pass until she returned it. Aaron put a hand on Nick's shoulder and guided him through the doorway.

"We'll talk about this later," Aaron decided. "Right now let's get out of here."

Lareina followed her friends back out into the darkness, three shadows jogging across the lawn. At the shed, she put the gun and Nick's medicine into her bag before replacing it on her shoulders. Using a neglected flower pot for a stepping stool, she pulled herself up onto the roof then helped a lethargic Nick as Aaron gave him a leg up from below.

She walked across the top of the wall, one foot in front of the other, like a tightrope walker, arms straight out for balance. Behind her Aaron slowly stumbled forward, stopping every few minutes to regain his balance. Between them, Nick crawled along the wall, unable to keep his balance at all. Finally reaching the safety of the large tree, she tossed her bag down and pulled herself into its sturdy branches. For the first time since being discovered by the guards, she touched something outside of Oak Creek.

The boys followed more slowly, but all three of them made it safely to the ground, although Nick stumbled forward and collapsed into the grass.

Aaron helped him up and sat next to him against the wall. "Maybe we should rest for just a second.

Too anxious to sit, Lareina rifled through her bag until she felt the jeans she packed and slipped them on under her dress. Careful not to lose anything in the dark, she pulled socks and tennis shoes back onto her feet. While the boys rested, she went to the other side of the tree, pulled off her dress, and slipped into a t-shirt and jacket.

She held her beautiful dress draped across her hands. As much as she lamented leaving it behind, she couldn't justify carrying an item unnecessary to her survival that would only take up precious space in her bag. Holding it in front of her one last time, believing it would be the only beautiful dress she would ever own in her life, she tossed it over the wall.

"Are you guys ready to go?"

Nick and Aaron both looked up but remained still, as if just moving their eyes was exhausting enough. Nick, pale and listless, sat with his head back against the wall. Aaron leaned forward with his head in his hands.

"How are we going to get tickets for the train?" Nick groaned.

She felt the pinch in her forehead that always accompanied

his questions. "We don't need tickets. This train doesn't exactly stop here."

Aaron, always calm and logical, sat up straight and gaped in panic. "You said we could board a train."

"We can . . . we will," she assured. "It'll slow down as it passes the town and then we just have to jump on." She had imagined it a thousand times during the past week. Run along the train and dive inside without being swept under. Barring desperation, she would never attempt it, but they had no other options. She could run fast enough, but what about Aaron and Nick?

"We can't do that." Nick propped his head up on his hands. "Stowing away is how we ended up here in the first place."

"This time will be different because I'll be with you." She picked up one bag and secured it around her shoulders.

The boys didn't disagree but didn't jump up to join her either. They became two statues decorating the wall's exterior. A train whistle blared in the distance.

"I'm not making you guys do anything. Stay here, come with me, it's up to you." She pushed her way through the knee-high grass, knowing they would follow her. A rustling snap of feet moving confirmed her prediction and she smiled. Periodically she turned to encourage them and make sure Aaron still had the other backpack.

Three hazy flashlight beams wavered near the wall. "Check over there. They'll probably go for the tracks," a gruff voice ordered.

CHAPTER 30

All three of them froze in place. Nick's half-closed eyes glanced at Lareina while he tried to muffle his scratchy breathing. Instinctively she reached for his hand and squeezed. He replied with a weak press.

"We have to go," she whispered.

None of them moved.

After one last calming breath, she darted forward, pulling Nick along with her through the undesirable open area and across the tracks. They dove into a ditch and flattened themselves in the grass. Aaron slid down next to them. The approaching train light sent shadows dancing through overgrown pastures, and shook the ground beneath them with increasingly violent intensity.

"We'll get on a car toward the back," she shouted over the deafening roar. Chilly air rushed by her face as she watched open doors pass in slow motion. Standing, she took a step toward the train. "That's the one."

She jogged along the tracks, caught the side of the train, and pulled herself inside. Immediately turning around, she gripped the doorframe for leverage, caught Aaron's hand, and helped him into the empty box on wheels. Nick staggered through the grass, struggling to keep up. All three of them shouted at the same time but couldn't hear a thing over the clamor of their transportation. Lareina and Aaron each caught one of Nick's hands and hauled him inside.

They landed in a heap on the floor. All three of them

breathed heavily but Nick coughed so desperately he could barely breathe at all.

Aaron put an arm behind him and helped him sit upright, and Lareina rummaged through her bag until she found a bottle of water. It took a few tries for him to swallow any, but the water seemed to chase his cough away for a while. Pulling a sleeve of crackers out of his bag, Aaron held two out to Nick.

"No way." Nick shook his head. "Anything I eat makes me sick."

"This is going to help," Aaron assured. "You only have to eat two."

He took them, stared at them in his hand, and began nibbling at the edges. Aaron dispensed one of the pills to Nick when both crackers were gone.

"How long are we on this train, Rochelle?"

Folding her legs under her, she pictured the schedule. "We'll be in Dallas within a half hour, but we have to jump before the train gets into the city."

Aaron nodded in response, offered his bag to Nick so he had something to lay his head on, and joined Lareina where she sat looking out at the dark landscape.

"Is he going to be okay?" she asked without turning around.

Aaron pressed his fingers against his own forehead, massaging in small circles. "He'll be just fine. Give him a few days and you won't believe he was ever sick."

"Are you all right?" she asked. With the immediate worries of escape resolved, hundreds of others climbed up to take their place.

His smile exuded its usual assurance and confidence. He splashed water from his bottle onto his face and wiped it away with the bottom of his shirt. "Is that better?"

Lareina looked at him without her peripheral vision for the first time that night. Even in the pale light she could see darker spots on his forehead and along the left side of his face. "It's going to bruise really bad."

"Bruises won't last forever, but I'm beginning to think this headache will."

She nodded sympathetically. "Close your eyes for a few minutes. I'll keep watch."

He didn't move from his spot beside her. "Rochelle, I'm sorry I didn't listen to you when you first told me about Nick. I guess I just wanted to believe Oak Creek was the place I'd been looking for."

"For a while, I wanted to believe it too." She turned back to the dark sky dotted with stars.

Aaron's hand touched her shoulder then slid away. Resting her chin on her knees, she watched darkness speed by until houses slid across a conveyor belt—some abandoned and rundown, others kept up with lights shining inside. The train slowed, and she leaned out of the car to see the tracks curve to the left where a city sparkled with light in the near distance.

"Aaron . . . Nick," she yelled over the clacking train as she crossed the car to where Nick slept.

Aaron sat up, blinking groggily. "Are we there?"

She touched Nick's arm. He opened his eyes but didn't move.

"Yeah, there's a big curve coming up. We're slowing way down. Come on, Nick." She shook his shoulder until he sat up.

"I'm too tired," he groaned.

"You'll be able to sleep again soon," Aaron promised. "We just have to get off the train."

They slipped backpack straps over their shoulders, then pulled Nick to his feet as the train pitched and slowed. Holding onto each other for balance, they crossed the car and stood in the doorway, watching dark outlines pass against the horizon.

"You want to jump out as far as you can then roll on the ground. Don't try to stay on your feet," she shouted through the air swishing around them.

Aaron nodded.

Nick watched the ground rush by.

"On three," Aaron shouted. "One."

Lareina tightened her grip on the backpack strap.

"Two."

She set her feet and looked out for a good landing point.

"Three."

She jumped and floated weightlessly on the air for a breathless moment before crashing to the ground. Two thuds joined her a little farther along the tracks as she rolled then sprang to her feet. The train rumbled away with its whistle blaring, warning Dallas of its arrival. Aaron popped up out of the grass and together they found Nick and pried him off the ground.

"Everyone okay?" Aaron asked casually as if jumping from trains was a part of their normal, daily routine.

"Yeah," Lareina and Nick responded at the same time.

"Now what?" Nick asked.

"Now we find an abandoned house." She pointed across the railroad tracks toward a sprawling neighborhood down a steep embankment.

Thrilled that she could move in any direction without being trapped by a wall, she jogged down the hill and found herself in the backyard of a blue house with white shutters and well-kept landscaping. A hose lay stretched across the grass as if the owners had just watered the lawn.

Next door, a deteriorated fence introduced an overgrown

yard. Momentarily forgetting about the boys, who still struggled down the embankment, she slipped through an open space in the fence and waded through the waist-high grass to a cobblestone patio that jutted halfway into the yard and was surrounded by bushes. Overturned patio furniture and a half-rotted umbrella flapping in the wind were the only evidence of any enjoyable evenings and peaceful mornings that once occurred there.

"You could've waited for us, you know."

Nick's voice startled her and she spun around. Aaron shrugged. Nick righted a lawn chair and sat down.

"I'm sorry. I just want to find us some shelter." She walked up to the sliding patio doors. A curtain covered the window, but through a sliver of space she could see drawers dumped and strewn across gray linoleum.

"The place has been looted." She set her bag down and pulled out the gun. "You two stay here and I'll make sure it's empty."

She braced herself for an argument, but it didn't come. Perhaps her companions were too tired to continually protest. Taking her time, she walked around the house where she found a shattered window leading into the two-car garage. She pulled herself up and inside where one car remained. Any tools that once hung above a bench had been carried off.

Grasping the gun in her hand, she found the door leading inside and crept into the kitchen she'd observed from outside. Every cupboard hung open, revealing dishes and empty shelves. Open drawers hung lopsided beneath countertops. Paper clips, refrigerator magnets, and papers littered the floor. She flipped a switch on the wall. No electricity. She tried the sink. No running water.

Continuing her tour, she checked the living room, two

bathrooms, four bedrooms, and dining room, all equally torn apart by looters and empty of people. Feeling confident they were safe, she returned to the dining room and slid the patio door open.

Aaron jumped up, but Nick remained seated on the lawn chair.

"Aren't you coming?" Aaron asked him.

"No, I'm done with breaking into people's houses and using their stuff. We're going to get caught and I'll end up right back in prison."

Lareina noticed Nick cringe as she slipped the gun back into her bag. "We aren't going to get caught. Someone else has already stolen everything valuable."

"I suppose there's no running water," he continued. "The only thing that could possibly convince me to enter that house is a warm shower."

She groaned and turned away, ready to leave Nick outside, but Aaron caught her arm. "We can't leave him out here. It's cold."

"You once told me that I'm old enough to make my own decisions." Nick pulled his chair against a wall that sheltered him from the wind. "I'll just stay outside where I still have my freedom."

Focusing on breathing, she kept her expression neutral, remaining tolerant of his impractical notions. "You're sick and it's freezing out here. I thought you were starting to understand that we need shelter for survival."

Slouching into the chair, Nick blinked up at her. "I thought you figured out the difference between right and wrong. It was around the time you kissed me."

Aaron stared at each of them in turn, switching his attention from one to the other.

"You mean when you kissed me." Annoyance twisted through her voice. "And gave me the flu."

"You said it was the only option we had." Nick sat up straighter. "I told you it was a bad idea."

"Yeah, well, I thought getting you out of that prison to somewhere warm was the right thing to do." What more could he want? "But I guess I was wrong, because here you are, free and perfectly content to sit out in the cold."

With one hand flat against the back of his neck, Aaron took a few steps toward the house. "You know, you two aren't so fun to be around when I have a headache."

Nick's eyes remained locked with Lareina's. "You saved us by lying and stealing. You're a real hero."

"Why do you always have to be so stubborn?"

"Why do you always have to get your way?" He crumpled into an intense fit of coughing.

She waited for it to stop, but even after it did, he stayed hunched over. Shaking her head, she turned and walked into the house. Aaron followed and flopped down on the couch.

"Why did I bring him along again?" She rubbed her forehead.

Aaron rested his head against the couch pillow. "It must have been for the twenty-five percent of the time you two actually get along. It was only yesterday you were worried about him."

She sank into a chair, feeling guilty for arguing with Nick and leaving him outside when she was well and he was sick. His cough sounded worse, and the temperature outside continued to drop. There had to be some way to trick him into coming inside.

After Aaron fell asleep, she explored the house, finding blankets and some clothes. Despite her attempts to distract herself, her mind continually returned to Nick: cold, sick, and alone outside. Then she remembered the hose in the neighbor's yard. The lawn next door was trimmed and the house kept up. It appeared that someone lived there, so maybe they had running water.

Lareina walked onto the patio carrying a blanket and a bar of soap she'd stolen from Oak Creek. She dropped the blanket onto an empty patio chair and tossed the soap at a sleeping Nick. It slammed into his chin.

"Ow, what are you doing?" he groaned, looking at her through watery eyes, trying to clear his throat.

"I know a way you can take a shower, but I'll only help you if you'll agree to come inside after."

He shivered and picked at a patch of dirt on the back of his hand. "You just said this house doesn't have running water. Is this some kind of trick?"

"No tricks." She held her hands out in front of her. "Just the chance to wash that dirt away. And all you have to do is agree to come inside where it's warm and comfortable."

Nick looked down at his filthy clothes, then back up at her. "Fine, if you can come through with your side of the deal then I'll come inside."

She smiled. "I'll be right back."

Slipping through the fence, she went to the neighbor's front door and knocked loudly. When no one answered, she tried again with the same results. Just to be safe she peered into the windows. No lights and no movement assured her temporary safety.

Lareina turned a handle where the hose connected to the house and let out a relieved breath when water spilled onto the grass. She pulled the hose across the lawn, over the fence, and through the bushes. Nick looked doubtfully at the thick stream of water swerving over patio stones.

"It's going to be ice cold," she warned, "but it's the best I can do unless you want to break into another house."

He forced a smile. "No, this will be fine. I'll be quick."

On one side of the natural screen of bushes, she held the hose so water spurted up and over onto the patio.

"Do you have water?" she asked through last summer's whispering leaves.

"Yeah, perfect."

"Great," she said sarcastically. "Hurry up and shower, then tell me when you're wrapped in the blanket."

With every passing minute her arm tingled in protest then eventually went numb from holding the hose in position. "Are you almost done?"

"Almost," Nick stuttered through chattering teeth. It felt like hours before he finally shouted, "Done."

She let the hose drop and made her way back around the bushes. The blanket covered Nick from head to toe, so she could barely see his eyes but couldn't miss how the loose material trembled.

After walking him inside and handing him a pile of clothes, Lareina opened the bathroom window and used the neighbor's hose to fill the bathtub and every container in the kitchen before returning it to its original position and turning the water off.

Back in the house, she found Nick dressed and shivering in the living room. After a search of the hall closet, she discovered a heavy blanket folded in the back and draped it around his shoulders then gathered some pillows from the bedroom and brought them to the love seat.

He didn't waste a second sinking into his new bed and a deep sleep. She covered him with several more blankets then settled herself on the floor and rested her head on the cushion next to Nick's pillow. Every muscle in her body ached from a combination of her earlier illness and arduous escape from Oak Creek. Fighting to keep her heavy eyelids open, she listened to Nick's raspy breathing.

When she opened her eyes, gray light illuminated the room. She lifted her head from the love seat, shrugging her shoulders to relieve some of the stiffness. Nick slept with his face turned toward the love seat's upholstery and blankets tangled around his ankles. Lareina pushed herself to her feet, stretched twisted blankets back up to Nick's chin, and brushed her hand across his warm forehead. In the kitchen she poured herself a bowl of cereal, sprinkled some raisins on top, and ate as she looked through the patio doors at an overgrown garden. Closing her eyes, she drifted back in time to flowers bordering the fence and vegetables growing in neat rows.

Returning to the living room, she noticed Aaron's absence from the couch where he had been sleeping the night before. She padded down the hall and peeked into the first bedroom where he slept soundly on the bed. Even in the muted light, she could see dark bruising along his jaw line and swelling near his eye. She covered him with a blanket folded over a rocking chair. Satisfied that both of her friends were safe, she continued to the next room, stepped over piles of clutter left on the floor by looters, and curled up on the bed's soft, green comforter.

A low rumble reverberated through her sleep. *Clank, pop, clank, pop.* The ghost of a giant hailstone smacked her in the face and she sat up in bed. Light flashed outside the window, followed by booming thunder that shook the house. She shivered and felt a tightening clench in her throat and her chest. As much as she wanted winter to pass, she dreaded the inevitable spring storms. Pushing the curtains aside, she peered out the window but couldn't see a thing through sheets of rain that slammed against the glass.

Shaken and knowing she would never fall back to sleep, she paced the room for a while, waiting for the storm to subside. Unfortunately, it only grew louder and continued to pelt the house from all sides. Too anxious to remain still, she crept down the hall to the kitchen. She stepped up to the patio door just as a small branch slapped against the glass. Jumping back, she let out a stifled yelp.

"Rochelle, is that you?" Nick called from the living room.

Taking a deep breath, she followed his voice and found him sitting on the love seat.

"Nice storm, right? What a soothing sound to wake up to."

She listened for sarcasm in his voice, but couldn't detect any. "I don't know if I'd put it that way exactly."

Nick leaned forward and Lareina felt him studying her in the dark. Thunder echoed above and she shuddered.

"You're afraid of the storm, aren't you?" He didn't ask in a cruel way, but as an observation.

"Ever since I was a little kid," she confessed. It took effort to control her shaky legs as she walked over and sat down next to Nick. "I . . . I know all the scientific stuff that thunder is the sound from the lightning traveling so fast . . . but . . ."

He leaned back and raised his eyebrows. "Didn't anyone ever tell you about angel's bowling and water fights in heaven?"

She looked at Nick and his expression told her he could see the confusion playing over her face.

"Those are the stories my mom used to tell me when I would wake up during a thunderstorm."

"And they made you feel better?" She cringed with the next crack of thunder followed by a gust of wind.

Nick laughed. "Yeah, when I was six. Then I learned all the scientific stuff and I guess I just wasn't scared anymore."

Scrunching herself against the back of the couch, she pulled her knees up to her chin. "When I was six, I was in a Home for Children in Oklahoma. They kept us locked on the second floor and I thought a tornado would carry me away one night." Lightning illuminated the room like a strobe light, prompting her to cover her head with her hands.

"No wonder you're afraid." Nick gently pried her hands away from her head so he could see her face. His skin didn't feel hot.

She pulled one of her hands free and held it to his forehead. "Your fever broke." Sheets of rain bombarded the front door. "Do you think it'll flood here? What if there is a tornado?" She hated that her voice shook, but she couldn't control it.

"We'll be fine," he said in a calm, soothing voice. "Jumping off trains and stealing from Oak Creek are far more dangerous than this storm."

Lareina moved closer to him. "You're probably right."

Nick laughed. "Probably?"

Another roar of thunder shook the house.

"How can it just keep going?" she grumbled. "It's like the endless storm."

His hand held hers. "Just listen to the rain. It's not so scary. Think of it this way—we're safe from everyone out there. I mean, who would want to go out in this weather?"

Leaning her head against the couch, she listened as rain pattered loudly against the roof. Galloway wouldn't look for her, she was free from Oak Creek, and she had shelter from the violent storm. Thankful for her temporary fortune, she closed her eyes.

In the morning she woke up with her head resting against Nick's shoulder. Slowly she moved away and stood without waking him. The storm had ended, leaving a foggy mist in its place.

Lareina scooped a cup of water out of the bathtub and washed her face, arms, and feet, still dirty from crossing Oak Creek barefoot. She noticed the chain from her pendant showing against her neck and slid it back under her t-shirt. It only served as a reminder of guilt, a reminder of a girl she couldn't help and a promise she couldn't keep. The time to tell Nick about Ava and the pendant had come, but she worried. Would he give up hope? Would he blame her? Would he believe her? None of it affected her survival, but the answers to those questions mattered more to her than survival.

By the time she hobbled to the kitchen, Aaron and Nick already sat at the counter eating granola bars and crackers. She took a seat next to Aaron and pulled the blue-and-white wrapper off a granola bar.

"I don't know if the rain will let up today." Aaron nodded toward the patio doors streaked with raindrops. "We're hoping tomorrow morning we can be on our way to Dallas."

Nick traced over something written on a pad of paper with the pencil in his hand. "I lost that original notecard, but I have Ava's address memorized. You were right, Rochelle, I'm actually going to find her."

Lareina looked at her granola bar then dropped it on the counter. "Nick." She paused to swallow, to find the right words. "I have to tell you something. Can we talk in the living room?"

He shrugged. "Sure."

Aaron turned to her. "You look a little pale. Are you feeling all right?"

She nodded and followed Nick into the other room where she sat down next to him on the couch.

He looked over at her with the most sympathetic expression she'd ever seen on his face. "Rochelle, what's . . . what's wrong? You look . . . like you're going to cry."

"Nick, I wish I didn't have to tell you this." She reached her hands back to unclasp the chain around her neck. "I knew Ava." Her shaking hands slipped off the clasp and she tried again. "I didn't know it until you told me about . . ." She unhooked the chain and held the pendant out to Nick.

For a while he just stared at it, then finally took it and held it in his shaking hand. "This is it. This is hers." He looked at Lareina's face then back down at the pendant. "I don't understand. If you have it . . . That means . . ."

She knew he understood all too well what she didn't want to say. Holding back tears, she told him the highlights of the story leading up to Ava's death. They wouldn't allow Nick to visualize what she had experienced, but she didn't want him to see those images. He listened and nodded with the pendant clutched in his hand. Sometimes he shook his head and sometimes he remained uncomfortably still.

"She told me to protect the pendant. She told me to find the other one and warn him . . . you . . . but I believed her name was Susan and then you told me your story . . ."

Feeling a warm spot on her cheek, she reached a hand up and wiped away a tear as others pushed at the back of her eyes. "I'm so sorry, Nick."

"At Oak Creek you promised I would find her . . . but you already knew . . ." His voice trailed off and he turned away.

"Ava is dead, and you knew and you said . . ." He shook his head, stood, and left the room.

Lareina stayed where she was, face bent forward, tears trickling along her nose. A hand settled lightly on her shoulder and Aaron sat down next to her.

"Please tell me you heard all of that," she sniffled. "I don't want . . . to explain it again."

"I heard it." He wrapped an arm around her. "It's uncanny the way you two kept finding each other. It's like you were meant to tell him."

She looked up at Aaron. "It's a terrible, sad coincidence." The force in her voice surprised her. "I could have kept it to myself and Nick would still be happy right now. We would all just be chatting over breakfast."

"You did the right thing." Aaron's voice was soft and soothing. "Telling Nick that story took a tremendous amount of courage, but he deserves to know. Otherwise he would have found out when he went to that address, or he would have spent his entire life searching for Ava. It was better that you could break it to him gently."

She rubbed tears away with her hand but new ones replaced any she had removed. "And now Nick is never going to talk to me again."

"Of course he will." Aaron hugged her tighter. "You just have to give him some time."

CHAPTER 31

When the rain stopped later that afternoon, Lareina stepped out into the cool fresh air. She couldn't stand the stuffy house where Nick remained closed in one of the bedrooms and Aaron tried to convince her she had done the right thing. She hadn't saved Susan. If she could have only kept her hidden from Galloway for another week, Nick would have been there . . . Did that mean he would have found her? She tried to align the details. If Susan had lived, Lareina wouldn't have crossed the flooded bridge and Nick would have never been freed from his trap.

Glancing around the patio for a distraction, she noted six chairs tipped over and scattered throughout the yard, the table rested on its side nearby, tree branches covered the brick surface, and strewn flowerpots cluttered a walking path. Deciding to clear the branches, she collected a few at a time and piled them near the broken fence. She became so focused on her task that she didn't even notice Nick until she looked up and he stood right in front of her.

Startled, she jumped back, dropping the branches she held.

Nick bent down and quickly gathered them up. "I'm sorry, I didn't mean to scare you. I just needed to get out of that house."

"It's okay. I'm just a little jumpy." She pushed her hair away from her face. "I've been worrying about you."

Nodding, he dropped his branches on the pile. "Yeah, that's what Aaron told me."

"You don't have to help if you don't feel up to it."

He returned a chair to an upright position. "It's okay. I think I'll feel better if I have something to do."

Lareina didn't reply but joined Nick in righting the grimy patio furniture and stacking terra cotta pots near the shed.

"I understand why you lied to me at Oak Creek." He rolled a twig back and forth under his shoe. "I needed hope then and you knew that."

"That was the hardest lie I've ever told in my life. I never imagined . . ."

Nick sat down to watch the sun sinking behind the garden fence. "I know what you mean. All this time we've known each other and we had no idea . . ."

She pulled a chair up next to Nick and sat down.

He leaned forward. "That's really why the detective is after you? He's wanted Ava's pendant the entire time?"

"Yes . . ." She brushed her hair together over her shoulder and dropped it behind her back. "It's such a relief to tell you the truth about it. I was just trying to protect you and Aaron . . ."

Nick watched her with wide eyes. "How worried do I have to be about the detective wanting my pendant?"

"You'll have to be careful, but I don't think he knows about it. If I had never met Susan . . . I mean Ava . . . I would have never known someone else in the world had one too."

"I'm glad you met her though, so she didn't have to be alone at the end. Without you, I might have never known the truth."

Lareina watched clouds on the horizon burn bright pink against the hazy blue sky. How ironic that she, the one Nick constantly accused of lying, had been the one to reveal the truth. "I wish it could have been different."

He nodded. "After everything we've been through to

get to Dallas, I guess I never needed to go there in the first place." Minutes passed in silence. "Are you still on your way to Nebraska?"

Closing her eyes, she pictured Maibe as it had been when she was eight. A vibrant Main Street with a grocery store and bakery and playgrounds with green, freshly cut lawns. Those places didn't interest her so much anymore, but the images offered warm comfort and security. Then doubt swept in to wipe the image away and she was back on the patio next to Nick.

"Yes, but I'm a little afraid." A cool breeze made her shiver and draw her knees up under her chin. "When things are bad, I think I'd be happy if I just had the basics: warm meals, a warm shower, and a warm bed. But I had all of that at Oak Creek and it wasn't enough. I want a family, Nick, a real one with people who genuinely care about me."

"And that's what Maibe represents, right?"

She nodded. "But what if it's gone? What if I get there and it's abandoned? What if no one remembers me and they don't want me there? Why would they want me there?"

Nick held his hand out to her. She took it and felt any remaining uncertainty between them melt away.

"What if it's all of the things you remember?" He squeezed her hand. "You have to find out."

"I'll be alone in the middle of nowhere again . . . if it's not."

A loose board on the fence squeaked with each gust of wind.

"I could come with you. I mean, Nebraska is my home too. Only if you want me along though." He spoke quickly and kept his attention on the sunset.

"Of course you can come." A smile spread over her face. "We'll leave for Dallas tomorrow and Nebraska after that."

For a long time they sat together watching the sunset. Lareina leaned back in her chair and for the first time she could remember, her thoughts didn't race through a montage of worst-case scenarios. She had been afraid to travel a thousand miles just to find out no one wanted her around, but now all of her fears melted away. She would have Nick. Even if they arrived in a crumbling, abandoned town, she wouldn't be alone. Bright pink clouds faded to sparkling stars and the chilly breeze became uncomfortably cold. Nick stood and helped her to her feet.

"We should probably get some rest if we're going to walk to Dallas tomorrow." He laughed. "That is, if it doesn't rain."

She slid the glass door open. "Maybe, just this one time, it won't rain. You know, maybe luck will be on our side."

"Luck has never been on our side," he reminded her.

"That's not exactly true. We are still alive."

Nick smiled. "Rochelle Aumont, ever the optimist." He reached into his pocket and pulled out the pendant she had been wearing since August. "You should keep this one and protect it like she asked. You've done a good job so far."

She took the pendant but didn't feel the usual chill. Knowing she was going home and Nick was going with her overpowered any negative feelings the pendant could inflict. In her bedroom, she clipped it back around her neck and curled up in a blanket. Imagining a future of comfort, warmth, and no reason to run lulled her to sleep. In a dream, she walked up the flower-lined walkway to Rochelle's house and knocked on the door. But before anyone could answer, a loud clap of thunder startled her awake. She sat up in bed and listened to the roar of a downpour pelting the roof.

Disappointed that their travel plans would be disrupted by the weather again, Lareina trudged to the bathroom. She washed her face and brushed her hair, wishing she could make herself look so different that Galloway's wanted posters would be useless.

In the living room, Nick and Aaron sat across from each other at the coffee table playing a game of checkers. She picked up her jacket from the back of the couch, slipped it on, and sat down.

Aaron skipped a checker across the board. "You can't be cold?" The bruises on his face stood out in deep purple splotches.

"A little." She glanced at raindrops streaming down the window. "Do you think it'll rain all day?"

Nick stared at the board in front of him, clearly running out of moves. "I predict it'll stop by lunch time."

Aaron laughed. "I hope weatherman Nick is right. Our food isn't going to last much longer than a day or two."

Leaning back against the couch, Nick scooped up a piece of paper half hidden under the coffee table. "What's this?" he asked curiously as he unfolded it.

Lareina froze in place, unable to move, blink, breathe. She felt in her coat pockets—empty.

The color drained from Nick's face.

"What's this?" He turned to her and dropped the paper onto the coffee table for Aaron to see. She was aware of Aaron looking at the poster, but she couldn't tear her eyes away from the angry betrayal in Nick's eyes. "Rochelle, what is this?" He sounded out of breath as if he had just run five miles.

Aaron turned to her, anticipating a response to Nick's question. She tried to answer, but words became a jumble of webs in her brain never making it to her tongue. Nick stood and for the first time she noticed how much he towered over her.

"Maybe you'll answer my question if I call you Lareina," he suggested. "What is this?" His voice was low and soft. Anger? Betrayal? Both?

She swallowed, but it didn't help. Her throat felt like sandpaper baking in the sun, and she knew there wasn't an excuse or a lie that could explain away the facts on that creased, white background. She should have destroyed the poster, but she hadn't.

"It's the truth," she confessed in the loudest whisper she could manage.

"You lied about your name." Nick stood frozen in place, watching her through betrayed eyes.

Aaron stood and took a few steps toward Lareina. "Nick, give her a minute to explain."

"Fine, explain."

She stood, tired of feeling as if she were under interrogation. "I lied about my name. That's the truth. My real name is Lareina, not Rochelle Aumont. I don't have a last name because I was an orphan found wandering around by myself and no one has ever cared about me enough to give me a last name."

Nick didn't sway. "Why is your face on a wanted poster?"

"I already explained that to you. I don't know what makes the pendant so valuable but Galloway wants it."

"I don't believe you." His voice broke. "The things you've been telling me don't add up. What else are you lying about?"

She took a step toward him, and he backed away. "Nick, please. You know more about me than any other person on Earth; my name was the only lie. When I told you my name was Rochelle, I didn't think I'd ever see you again, but then I did, and you always hated dishonesty, so I didn't know how to tell you. It's just a name." She took another step toward Nick and held a hand out to him, but he backed away.

Shaking his head slowly back and forth, he looked at the window. "Who is Rochelle Aumont anyway? Another criminal? Some name you read in a newspaper?"

"My friend from Nebraska."

Nick's scowl deepened. "All of this time, I've watched you con every person you met, and for some reason I let myself believe I was somehow immune, but I've been just as stupid as all of them."

Shoving her hands into her pockets, she stretched to stand as tall as her body would allow. "I guess I was stupid for letting you slow me down. I thought maybe I cared about you, but you're just like everyone else."

Nick turned on his heel and left the room. Lareina sank, slowly melting into the couch cushions as if she didn't have the strength to combat gravity. Aaron sat down next to her and for a long time they stared at a dark square where a painting once hung on the wall in front of them.

"It might take a while for me to remember your name," Aaron finally said.

She leaned forward and rested her chin in her hand. "It doesn't matter. For all I know, my name isn't even Lareina. I'd rather not be—I've been Lareina for two minutes and look how everything unraveled." She gestured toward the hallway where Nick had gone.

Aaron put a hand on her shoulder. "He'll come around."

"Why are you still talking to me? I lied to you too."

"So you told me a different name." Aaron shrugged. "You're just trying to protect yourself. I believe everything else you told me. Especially the part about the pendants. Not even you could make that up."

Sighing, she squeezed her eyes shut. "I wish I would have just stayed in bed. Everything was fine ten minutes ago."

"I'll talk to Nick. He's probably already feeling stupid about overreacting."

Maybe Aaron was just trying to make her feel better, but she knew Nick. He could forgive her for calling him a wimp and breaking into empty houses, but he could never forgive her for a breach of trust that started the moment they met. She couldn't blame him; after all, she'd had plenty of opportunities to tell him the truth. When she met him for a second time, she lied to both him and Aaron, and then at Oak Creek, through all of those conversations at the barracks, the truth about her name never came out.

She leaned back into the couch and held her hands over her face. Somehow she handled breaking the news about Ava, the worst news of Nick's life, but couldn't manage to throw in a "By the way, I lied about my name." Letting her hands drop from her face, she realized Aaron had also disappeared from the room. Outside the rain slowed to a steady drip, drip, drip.

"She could be a murderer for all we know." Nick's muffled voice sliced through the wall.

Moving quietly across the room, Lareina stopped in the hallway.

"We know better than that. We've never seen her hurt anyone," Aaron reasoned.

"She always has a gun."

"The one time she used it, it saved your life. Come on, Nick, just talk to her."

"No. If you still trust her, fine. But I'm not fleeing the state with a wanted criminal who can't even trust me with her real name."

CHAPTER 32

Sitting cross-legged on the living room floor, Lareina divided the last granola bars and crackers between two bags. Nick wouldn't talk to her but he had told Aaron he planned to leave at the first break in the rain. Through the patio doors, she could see that it was still cloudy, but the rain had stopped and the outside world appeared a little brighter.

She pictured Nick sitting outside on a patio chair watching the sunset with her. They had devised the perfect plan and for the twelve hours it had been in place, she believed that she could escape Galloway for good and leave all of her problems behind. She had the assurance that Nick would be by her side for more than a few weeks. He could have been part of the family she wanted, but now she would never see him again. The truth had made both of them miserable. She figured lies made people miserable too, but they also bought time. Regrets, however, wouldn't change anything, so she did her best to push such thoughts out of her mind.

"Do you need any help?" Aaron stood over her.

"No." She tossed two granola bars and a sleeve of crackers into Nick's bag. "Does he know this food won't last him more than a day? What is he going to do when he runs out?"

Aaron leaned back against the wall. "I told him the food won't last. I told him I'm staying with you. I told him he's being childish. Nothing is changing his mind."

"He's made his choice then." She rolled a t-shirt into a tube and shoved it into the bag. "I guess we can't help him anymore."

"I guess you're right." He sauntered to the patio doors and stepped outside.

Lareina stuffed her extra clothes into the bag she would share with Aaron, tried to zip it, rearranged, tried again. She remembered when she first met Nick how she wanted to keep moving, and he tried to stall her. Now he couldn't wait to walk out that door. But he wasn't any less defenseless than he had been back then.

The zipper caught on a shirt and she pulled it backward. How could he stay alive, even a week, on his own? Reaching down to the bottom of her bag, she grasped the heaviest item and pulled it out. For a second, she balanced the gun on her hand then looked at the backpack she had filled for Nick. In a final effort to protect him, she buried the gun under extra clothes and the little food that made up his third of what they had left. She tossed one extra granola bar into his bag and zipped it shut.

I never should have met him in the first place, she reminded herself. It was only by a serendipitous turn of events that she'd gotten to know him at all.

A door creaked and she listened to Nick's footsteps approach until he stood in front of her. She pushed herself to her feet and picked up his bag.

"Here." She didn't look at his eyes. She didn't want to cry.

Nick took the bag, unzipped it, glanced inside, closed it, and swung it over his shoulder. He nodded then turned away and walked out onto the patio. She followed, but lingered in the doorway.

Aaron turned when he heard Nick approaching. The boys shook hands.

"It's been great knowing you, Nick. Take care of yourself out there."

"I'll be fine. You never know, we might run into each other again someday." There was a slight catch in his voice. Sadness? Regret?

Aaron turned toward Lareina. "Maybe we will. It has happened before."

Nick nodded, but kept his eyes diverted from hers.

Taking only a few steps forward, she stopped as if a wall stood between them. "Bye Nick." She turned away so he wouldn't see the misery she couldn't disguise.

"Bye Lareina," he replied in a flat, emotionless voice.

For a moment he looked at the place where the sun had set behind the fence and she wondered if he was thinking of their plan. He shook his head and took a step and then another. Standing with Aaron, she watched Nick move farther and farther down the road that would take him to Dallas. She wanted to shout at him for being arrogant and stubborn, but instead told herself she couldn't wait for him to fade into memory like all of the others who had been so quick to abandon her.

Trudging back into the house, she leaned against the wall, and let the imagined weight of her pendant pull her down to the dining room floor. There had been a time when she believed she could escape Galloway, but she realized now that hope had evaporated. Too many times he had found her when she thought it was impossible. There wasn't anywhere he wouldn't follow her to get his hands on the pendant. If he knew Nick had one too, would he want it just as much? How many more pendants were out there? The questions haunted her, but she didn't have any answers.

The patio door scraped shut and Aaron sat down next to her. "I guess it's time for us to get going to Dallas."

"We'll give Nick a head start. I don't want to run into him

ever again." She turned to Aaron, who slumped forward with his legs stretched out in front of him. He looked defeated and she realized she'd been so preoccupied with Nick she hadn't really talked to Aaron about anything else. "Is everything okay?"

"Fine, I'm just tired."

She wasn't entirely convinced but didn't want to push any further. Instead she remained quiet so he would know she was there for him if he decided to share what was on his mind.

He pressed a hand to the bruised side of his face, as if he'd forgotten, then winced and pulled it away quickly. "I'm a little worried, I guess, that I won't be able to find work at a hospital in Dallas."

"Of course you'll find work. You're great at being a doctor."

Aaron smiled. "I'm not really a doctor, Lareina. I don't even know if I have what it takes to get into a training program, and if I do it'll still take years. What if I can't make it?"

"You've convinced me that you know a lot about being a doctor, so why wouldn't you be able to prove the same to everyone else?"

He studied her as a rectangle of sunlight materialized across the floor. "How do you manage to do that? Despite everything that happens, you always believe that tomorrow will be better than today."

She wished that his observation were true, considered pretending that it was, and then decided to be honest. "I do believe that things have to get better," she admitted. "But ever since I started wearing this pendant, I've been afraid that they won't." She looked down at it, accentuated against her blue shirt, where it shivered with her every breath.

"It looks harmless to me." Aaron shrugged.

Lareina tried to find words that could explain the heavy

feeling of dread, but as usual she couldn't. "There are so many unanswered questions and so many things that don't make sense. It gives me a bad feeling."

"Because of the detective . . . and how it's connected to Nick?"

The pendant slid back and forth between her thumb and index finger. "It's something more than that."

"Let me see it."

She held it out into the light and closer to Aaron.

"Do you know what *spero* means?"

"I don't even know what language it is," she admitted.

"It's Latin—I picked up a little learning medical terminology." Aaron's natural confidence returned to his voice. "It means something along the lines of hope or to hope for. How threatening can it really be with a message like that?"

Closing her eyes, she pictured Nick's pendant. "What does *optimus* mean?"

"Optimus," Aaron repeated, stressing different syllables than she had. "The best. I don't think it's conjugated quite right for them to form a grammatical sentence. But I think the message is hope for the best."

She stared down at the pendant, but Aaron's translation didn't reveal anything new about its meaning. If anything, it only intensified the foreboding mystery. "Or maybe it's a warning. Maybe it's dangerous for the two pendants to be near each other. But I guess we don't have to worry about that anymore."

He nodded in his usual understanding way. "Let's take an hour to regroup then we'll get out of this place. We'll both feel better when we get to Dallas." He stood, stretched, and walked outside into the sunny backyard.

Hope for the best.

What did that have to do with Galloway, Susan, and Nick? Despite Aaron's encouraging words, her thoughts circled back to fear that she and Nick carried something far more valuable, more dangerous, than they could ever understand. Nick. She wanted to warn him to toss his pendant into a river and pretend it never existed. But there would be no helping Nick as long as he didn't want her help. She knew he had never fully trusted her. *Why won't he ever believe me?*

Because of Galloway, she decided. Who wouldn't be suspicious of someone who had to run hundreds of miles to escape a detective? Closing her eyes, she envisioned Galloway plastering her picture all over Dallas. She felt like the entire world knew her name and what she looked like. How could she ever hide with all of those people searching for her, motivated by the promise of money?

Forcing herself to her feet, she trudged into the bathroom. Sun streamed through the window. She searched every drawer and cupboard until she finally found what she looked for in the medicine cabinet. Using her hands, she brushed her long hair over her left shoulder. Gathering all of it in one hand she raised the scissors, then dropped them back to the counter.

"It's temporary," she scolded herself. "It'll grow out long again."

Twisting her hair into a long rope, she raised the scissors, and sawed through it at the level of her chin. Then she brushed hair forward over her forehead and cut long, jagged bangs that hung down to her eyelashes.

CHAPTER 33

"The town in Nebraska where you're going—what's it like?"

Lareina shielded her eyes from the sun that had slipped so low she felt she walked right into it. "Maibe is a small town like most others." She shrugged. "Main Street is lined with stores and shops. There's a bakery right in the middle of downtown where you can buy a huge chocolate chip cookie for a quarter." She closed her eyes, imagining the delicious aroma of fresh bread and warm cake. "During the summer everything is green wherever you look and as far as you can see . . ."

"And there's a hospital there?" Aaron interrupted.

"Yeah, a small one." She could barely visualize the old brick building that she had never been inside. "Why do you ask?"

"I'm just a little worried about you traveling all the way to Nebraska by yourself, and I thought maybe I could go with you, and get some more medical experience in a small town before I start my career in some big city."

An involuntary smile spread across her face, but she tried not to let Aaron see. "Of course you can come along. But you're sure that's what you want? Don't change your mind because you're afraid." Her last sentence came out as a weak plea. She didn't want to lose him but also didn't want to hold him back.

"No, of course not," he insisted. His eyes met Lareina's

and his expression softened. "I'm a little bit afraid, but I'm mostly worried about you." He smiled.

She quickened her pace to keep up with Aaron's long strides, and fought back the impulse to insist that she could take care of herself. Being capable and independent didn't have to equate to being alone. Just because Aaron would be watching out for her didn't mean she wouldn't be doing just the same for him.

"Do you see that up there?"

Maybe a few miles in the distance, she could see buildings stretching toward the sky. Surrounding the shimmering magnificence of the city, in spirals that stretched away from it for miles, stood rows and rows of what appeared to be small black dots. So many houses they would pass on the way back to civilization. What happened to the people who once occupied all of those houses? Shivering, she pulled her hood up to block the wind.

"That's Dallas," Aaron shouted. His pace quickened so Lareina jogged forward to catch up. "We can be there before dark if we hurry."

The thought of real food and dry shoes enticed her. She wanted to run until buildings surrounded her on all sides. No more empty land. No more grass and sky with nothing in between. The goal of running toward Dallas felt so much better than the fear of running away from Galloway. She gladly settled into the faster pace Aaron set and stayed at his side.

Her soaked shoes sloshed against the pavement, but her worries eased with something manmade beneath her feet. That, coupled with houses lining the street on each side, gave her hope that people still had some power over nature. She had grown weary of seeing concrete crumbled by newly growing trees, buildings attacked by vines, and nothing but disintegrating foundations when she needed shelter the most. Starvation, she knew, was as much a possibility in the city as in the wilderness. Plus, entering the city added new risks of disease and the dangers that came with overpopulation during desperate times. Despite all of that, it was a relief to be back in a game with familiar rules. She understood how the city worked; she knew how to survive there.

"Hey, where are you going?" The two of them had been following the curving sidewalks of a neighborhood for the last half hour, but now Aaron stepped into the waist-high grass of a former front lawn. Lareina stood firmly on the street, refusing to move within three feet of the rippling grass surrounding a large yellow house.

"The street is going to loop around and through those houses. If we cut through these yards in a straight line, we'll get there faster," he explained.

She didn't want to take any shortcuts, any unnecessary risks, and she felt safer with concrete beneath her feet.

"Come on, Lareina, I've been watching for lights in these houses, and I'm pretty sure no one lives here." Aaron took a few backward steps deeper into the yard.

She stepped up onto the sidewalk but couldn't bring herself to set foot on the lawn. "That's not what I'm worried about. Before they left home, a lot of people built traps so no one would bother their houses. It's especially dangerous this close to the city."

Aaron rolled his eyes and walked back toward her. "I know you're used to danger around every corner, but these houses look to have been abandoned for years now. I highly doubt there are any traps still in working order if there ever were any in the first place."

He has a good point, she thought. Dallas was more populated than San Antonio and if those traps were going to be sprung, they would have been years ago. She wanted to get to Dallas before dark as much as Aaron, and her hesitation only slowed both of them down.

"All right." She took her first steps onto the overgrown lawn. "But let's keep our eyes open for anything suspicious just in case."

The hood of her jacket had slipped, so she pulled it over her head to repel water dripping from tree branches and followed Aaron around the side of a house. Scanning the ground for suspicious wires, mounds of dirt, or unusual piles of leaves, she tiptoed across the yard. Every step took incredible courage as she imagined a net dropping from above to trap her, or her feet tripping some wire that would shoot an arrow through her leg. The walk only took seconds but stretched into slow motion for Lareina. Finally, she reached the end of one yard, prevented from entering the next by nothing more than a chain-link fence.

Letting out the breath she had been holding, she looked up at Aaron. He grinned back at her and his eyes said *I told you so.* She wanted to jump up and down, to celebrate their victory of crossing the yard unharmed, but she wouldn't give him the satisfaction of knowing the extent of her fear. Instead she placed a foot in a space of the chain-link fence and hopped over. Aaron followed and they crossed the next yard without difficulty.

As they continued to make their way across back patios and over fences, the sun sank, leaving the world shrouded in darkness. It didn't make sense, but the less she could see, the more secure she felt. Her increasing courage decreased her need to scan every inch of ground in front of her and allowed them to travel faster. *Nothing bad is going to happen,* she decided. *We've made it too far for anything to go wrong now. And Nick is the only one I've ever seen actually get caught in one of the traps. There probably aren't that many.* She focused her attention on the houses they passed instead of worrying about any imagined hidden dangers. None of the houses seemed worth mentioning until they landed on the other side of a tall wooden fence. Moonlight outlined an all-brick mansion with a wraparound deck. Despite the overgrown lawn and untrimmed shrubs, she couldn't pull her eyes away.

"Look at that house." Her voice was a whisper of admiration.

Aaron made a soft whistling sound. "That place had to be difficult to abandon."

Her imagination carried her inside. She visualized each large room with plush carpets and chandeliers that sparkled in sunlight. Staring up at a bay window on the second floor, she imagined sitting there, looking out at a green yard, watching raindrops drip from leaves and splash into the pool. It stood obstinate to the changing world around it. A fortress against storms, riots, wars.

"I want a house just like that someday."

Aaron stopped and turned around to face her. Despite the darkness she could make out a look of surprise on his face.

"I never imagined you would want fancy things."

Lareina's cheeks grew warm, but the night hid her embarrassment. For a while she didn't say anything, but her shame faded quickly. "I've never owned anything more than the clothes on my back. Is it so wrong for me to dream of more than that?"

"No, of course not. I guess I just didn't think you'd ever be able to settle down in one place. You can't have a house like that and run like this."

Shaking her head, she approached the next sturdy wooden fence. "I've done enough running for three lifetimes. All I want now is to find a place where I'm allowed to stay."

Aaron reached the fence first and hoisted himself to the top. "Hmmm, that's funny. Nick always guessed that you would never be able to stay put for more than a year."

She stiffened at the mention of Nick. Her hands, already on the fence, gripped so tightly her knuckles ached. "Why were you guys talking about me?"

Aaron just smiled and slid over the fence, dropping out of sight. Lareina hoisted herself up halfway to follow.

"I want an explanation when I get over there," she demanded through cracks between the wooden planks.

Instead of the teasing refusal she had expected from Aaron, an agonized shriek echoed through empty darkness.

CHAPTER 34

Ducking back down, she plastered herself against the fence and braced her feet against the ground, ready to push off and run to safety.

"Aaron?" she whispered.

A whimpering like an injured animal continued on the other side of the fence. Instead of running, she peeked over the fence, surveying the grass, a swing set, and a trampoline all glinting in the moonlight under a coating of heavy raindrops. Aaron huddled below her against the fence, clutching his leg. Satisfied that no other people or animals waited on the other side, she scaled the fence and lowered herself to the ground near him.

"What happened?" she asked, trying to control the panic in her voice.

"I can't get it off," he groaned through clenched teeth.

Lareina followed his gaze. A metal contraption was clamped tightly around his leg from his ankle to his knee. It reminded her of the bear traps her Montana replacement parents hung on the wall in their living room.

Aaron, desperate to remove the crushing pressure that cut deeper into his leg every second, tried to separate the jaws.

She pushed his arms away. "Stop, you're going to make it worse. Just give me a second."

He tried to hold still and remain quiet, but involuntary spasms and whines shuddered through his body. He clenched the thick grass in both hands as she examined the trap with her cheek against the ground.

"Can you get it off?" he whimpered. His breathing was speeding up.

Unzipping her bag, she rummaged until she found a screwdriver. "This thing is spring activated." She leaned down toward the trap. "If I can get these two screws out, it'll release the spring and the whole thing should open up."

The darkness forced her to work mostly by touch as she struggled to open the trap as quickly as possible. Even though it hadn't seemed practical at the time, she commended herself for taking a screwdriver and a couple of Allen wrenches from a kitchen drawer at the last house. She wanted tools she could use to pick locks, but she had thrown the others in, unsure of what she might face in coming days. *It pays to prepare for everything,* she thought.

One more turn and the spring popped free. The trap lost pressure and pulled open. Aaron gasped. His breathing filled the silence in rough, uneven gulps. A passing cloud slid along its course and moonlight trickled down. She squeezed her eyes shut and turned away.

"Lareina, you can't be squeamish right now. I need your help," he pleaded.

Taking in a slow breath, she forced herself to turn her attention back to his leg. Blood soaked the bottom half of Aaron's pants. Swallowing back the nausea that threatened to overtake her, she nodded.

"I need you to use your knife and cut my jeans away, up to my knee, so we can get a better look," he instructed.

She didn't want to see the rest of the hidden wound. How could Aaron remain calm when she could barely breathe? With a trembling hand she pulled out the pocketknife she'd found at the last house and sliced the denim away as instructed.

Aaron looked down at his injured leg and groaned. The

sharp edges carved a deep gash from his knee to his ankle. Even worse, bone protruded just below his knee. With wide eyes he assessed the damage to his mangled leg. She could tell he didn't know what to do; even with all of the medical training in the world, he lacked the equipment to fix something so serious.

Her breathing sped up again, so she forced herself to take normal breaths, in through her nose and out through her mouth.

"I need you to push the tibia so it lines up with the bone above it," Aaron groaned. "It's just a broken leg."

Lareina stared down at the bone, the leg covered in blood, everything covered in blood. *Just a broken leg?* Reviewing the names of bones she'd read about helped to calm her a little, she tried to remember which one was the tibia. Where did it belong?

I can't do this. I have to do this, she told herself. *I can't leave him here.* Her hands shook as she lowered them toward the injury. Breathing in shallow gasps, she placed her hands on Aaron's leg, and despite his muffled yelps, pushed the bone back into the skin.

Aaron leaned back, taking in shaky gulps of air. "You did it, Lareina." She averted her eyes from him, then noticed her bloody hands. She couldn't fight the queasy feeling in her stomach any longer. She crawled a few feet away and threw up in the grass—all six of her rationed crackers.

"You okay?" He asked when she finished retching.

It isn't fair for him, she thought. *He shouldn't be comforting me.* But she couldn't look at the blood and bone where a healthy leg should be. Aaron would have been better off with Nick. Tears streamed down her face, but she ignored them. She spit a few times and wiped her mouth with her sleeve before crawling back over to Aaron. She sat down next to him with her back to his leg so she could only see his face.

"Don't cry," he comforted. "It's going to be okay."

"How?" she sobbed. "What are we going to do now? I can't leave you here and you're not going to be able to walk."

Aaron reached for her hand and squeezed it in his. "Hey, one thing at a time. First, I need you to help me clean this wound and splint my leg. Then we'll figure out the rest."

Lareina gagged, bit her lip, and failed to breathe. She wondered which of them appeared paler and decided she would probably win that competition.

He squeezed her hand tighter. "You can do this. I'll tell you exactly what to do, and then when I have some money, I owe you a brick mansion."

She shook her head. "I would give up every brick mansion in the world if this had never happened."

Aaron nodded. The regret in his eyes reflected back in her own. "I should have listened to you. If I had just stayed on the road like you told me . . ."

Using her free hand, she wiped tears from her face. "We have to stop," she sniffled, "and deal with this. What do I have to do first?"

"There's a first aid kit in the bag."

Reaching both hands into the backpack, she searched for the little white box by touch. An absolute silence engulfed them again. She closed her eyes and pictured the city. Lights shone through every window revealing restaurants and shops. People bustled in the streets, dressed in their best clothes for an evening out. The aromas of food lingered on the breeze, the melodies of music bounced through a window, the sidewalks and buildings radiated heat absorbed all day from the sun.

Her hand found the first aid kit, and she opened her eyes to harsh moonlight.

CHAPTER 35

"Please, can you help me? My friend is hurt," Lareina pleaded. The woman passing by pretended not to hear and crossed the street. She had asked at least thirty people for help, but not one of them would even stop to talk. They all seemed preoccupied, wrapped up in their own problems, watching for some invisible force lurking nearby.

"Fine, pretend we don't exist," she shouted after the woman.

"Hey, it's all right," Aaron said. "Let's take a break." He leaned heavily against her, unable to support any weight on his right leg. It had taken another day and night for them to hobble into Dallas. They moved as one slow, lumbering person, receiving suspicious glances from everyone they passed. A building dread permeated the air. The city remained quiet in the middle of the day. People hurried down sidewalks, eyes downcast, avoiding conversation. Music didn't play, children didn't shout, doors didn't slam, and half of the shops remained shuttered.

Helping Aaron to a building with steps that opened up to the sidewalk, she lowered him to the second step, and sank down beside him. Her eyelids weighed fifty pounds. In her worry and rush to get Aaron to a hospital, she had barely slept in two days. She couldn't think clearly anymore, but she couldn't rest until she found help. Why didn't Dallas function like every other city? Even fever-ridden Austin had maintained some sort of normalcy. She tried to hope for the best like Aaron suggested, but optimism felt like an unrealistic emotion in their situation.

Lareina pressed her hands against her aching eyes. It would be easy to leave Aaron. To walk away and never return. To be free and keep moving. To pretend someone would eventually come along to help him. It would have been cruel to leave him outside of the city, but here . . . She knew no one would come, and if the situation were reversed, he wouldn't abandon her. Would he? Her real parents, replacement parents, Home for Children directors, and Nick had all decided she wasn't worth the trouble of keeping around. She couldn't do that to Aaron.

"What are we going to do?" She spoke into her hands, which muffled her voice.

"Lareina, I think you need to leave me here."

She pulled her hands away and turned to him. He was still very pale, but he looked serene in his decision. "What? No."

He remained serious, looking down at his outstretched leg wrapped in bloody bandages. "Don't argue. There's no reason for both of us to die."

The pendant's cool surface burned into her chest, reminding her of the day she'd left Susan alone and bleeding outside of San Antonio. She couldn't do that again. Before she could protest, she spotted a man coming down the sidewalk toward them.

"Hey, can you help me, please?" she called. "My friend is hurt."

The man slowed down. He noticed Aaron's leg and gave them a sympathetic look. He pointed down the street. "There's a hospital two blocks that way," he said, then bent his head forward and walked away quickly.

"Thank you," she shouted after him. It wasn't much, but it

was better than nothing. Leaning her head against her knees, she closed her eyes to rest for just a minute.

"Are you sure you're up for two more blocks?" Aaron asked.

"Of course I am. We can both rest at the hospital."

She stood, then pulled Aaron up so he balanced on his good leg. They continued with their halting walk to the hospital. Signs pointed them toward their intended destination, but no ambulances sped by, no sirens ordered everyone to clear a path. The cool air pressed against them, silent, stale, heavy.

Aaron hopped on his good leg, but he couldn't move or even balance without support. She doubted he could even crawl on his own, but only a few more steps and they would arrive at the hospital. Automatic sliding doors would welcome them into a comfortable lobby, doctors would fix Aaron's leg in a sterile white room, and nurses would present him with crutches so he could complete the journey.

"We're almost there. Just a little further," she encouraged. Ahead, a wide archway with the word HOSPITAL engraved in it spread across the entrance to a two-way driveway leading up to a sprawling building. A closed wrought iron gate fit into the archway.

As they got closer, she noticed two teenage boys standing on either side of the archway. They did not move to help as she and Aaron staggered up to the gate.

"We need a doctor right away, it's an emergency," Lareina explained, nodding toward Aaron's leg. Neither of the boys moved to unlatch the gate. They turned to each other and chuckled.

"How much money do you have?" one guard, tall with black hair, challenged.

She looked at Aaron and he shrugged, unsure of how they should respond.

"If you give me a second, I can scrape together a few dollars," she offered.

That sent the guards into a fit of hysterical laughter. Every time they looked at each other, the laughing started up again.

"Let's get out of here and find another hospital," Aaron urged, trying to pull her away from the gate, the frenzied cruelty, and their final hope.

She noticed the guns swinging from each guard's belt. Any other day she would have backed away, but she was too tired and desperate to fear their weapons. "No, wait, I want an explanation."

"It doesn't matter what you do," the other guard, short and blond, snickered. "No hospital is going to let you in for less than fifty dollars. This city is now a territory of The Defiance. Join our movement and we'll think about helping you."

"Let's go," Aaron insisted. He leaned forward, applying all of his force to move her forward, but she had more leverage with two feet on the ground.

"You think we would join a movement that allows people to die on the streets?" she shouted. "Maybe you should rethink what you're fighting for."

The short guard took a few menacing steps closer to her. "We take care of our own. Otherwise, hospitals are for those who can pay for care. If you can't pay, then we can't help you," he growled. "Now get out of here."

She wanted to scream at them, lunge at them, and force her way through the gate, but a sinking feeling in her stomach and the tightness in her throat zapped any strength she had left. She could do nothing but turn and walk away.

Defeated and out of options, Lareina wandered down the empty sidewalk, pulling Aaron along with her. Any hint of November sun hid behind the buildings, allowing a winter chill to sweep through the city. She despised the cold weather, the constant rain, and the cruel, selfish people taking over everything around her.

"Where are we going?" Aaron asked, trying to hide the pain in his voice that she couldn't ignore. Every step they took had to feel like fifty nails stabbing his leg.

"I don't know," she admitted. "I don't know what to do anymore." She wanted a safe place to rest, but everything she thought she knew about city life no longer applied if The Defiance ruled. The dread and caution of everyone she'd met made sense now. Terrified people on high alert filled the city. Breaking into a home or business, where citizens of Dallas lived, could be dangerous, but choosing a structure seized by The Defiance would be a deadly mistake.

"Let's find a bridge or something," Aaron suggested. "It'll probably rain again tonight."

After three more agonizing blocks, they found an overpass. Too exhausted to be picky, they hobbled under the concrete shelter and chose the highest section, where there were no puddles, as a place to rest.

Leaning back against the cold concrete wall, Lareina reached into her bag for something to eat before she remembered they were out of food. They had finished everything they had on their slow journey into Dallas. If she didn't do something soon, the two of them would end up starving before anything else could kill them. Shadows slanted across the road as light quickly vanished. The wind whistled as it funneled under the overpass.

"We're out of food," she apologized. "I'll get us something to eat tomorrow."

"It's okay, I'm not hungry anyway." He sounded brave, but his voice rose in pitch slightly at the end of his sentence.

Although her body didn't complain, she knew she had to be hungry too. She just nodded and leaned her head against Aaron's shoulder. He sighed and rested his head against the concrete wall behind him.

"Aaron," she whispered after a few minutes. But the slow even breathing of sleep was his only response. She propped their backpack behind his head to act as a makeshift pillow and closed her eyes. Despite her exhaustion, the steady *drip . . . drip . . . drip* of water from above kept her awake. Squeezing her eyes tighter, she listened for the distant rushing of trains, a blaring whistle. Nothing. Had The Defiance suspended the trains? Maybe trains were being diverted around Dallas because of The Defiance.

Lareina pulled her hands into her coat sleeves and drew her knees up to her chest. She imagined thousands of people lying awake in darkness. Hunger, fear, and desperation stalked the streets. Everyone had their own family and friends, their own little world to fortify against collapse. A thin cloud revealed the outline of one twinkling star, dimming and brightening, laughing at her huddled on the cold concrete until she closed her eyes.

CHAPTER 36

Pale pink light stretched across the horizon, announcing a new day. The world blurred into patches of dull color through Lareina's half-open eyes. Her body begged her to rest for a few more hours, but they needed food and transportation out of the city. She sat up and rubbed her eyes with the back of her hand. Fuzzy colors became roads, bridges, buildings. Not wanting to wake Aaron, she slid away from him and stood up. Fear gripped her until she noticed his chest moving steadily up and down with every silent breath. He slept sitting up, his back against the concrete wall, head tilted toward his left shoulder, injured leg stretched straight out, blood crimson against white bandages. Their backpack had slipped to the ground beside him.

Kneeling down, she pulled the bag toward her, and silently dug through the contents, feeling for the smooth cylindrical outline of a pencil. She had always carried pencils and paper in her old bag, but minutes of rummaging resulted only in a pen with a crack in its plastic body. Painstakingly, she scraped the pen against the cement. It didn't work at first, but after dipping it into some water and scribbling on her arm, she eventually managed to scrawl *went for food* on the smooth pavement near Aaron's hand.

Taking a few steps out of the monstrous shadow cast by the road above, she stopped, unable to convince her feet to venture any further away. Aaron coughed, and she darted back to his side. His eyelids fluttered slightly but didn't open; his even breathing indicated a deep sleep. Leaving him behind, out in the cold, unable to protect himself or even run, felt like a betrayal, but she had to get food soon or they would both be too weak to move at all. If she waited much longer, the city would be swarming with people and she couldn't even guess what kind of obstacles The Defiance might create. Aaron needed rest and even if she waited for him to wake up, he would only slow her down and make stealing impossible. Taking a step away from him, she stopped and for a second held her hands over her bleary eyes. In slow motion, she let her hands slide back down until they dangled at her sides.

"I won't be gone for long," she whispered. Aaron didn't stir and she decided he would be safer asleep under the overpass than he would be in the city with her.

As her feet traced cracked sidewalks, she thought about how she had planned to be out of Texas months ago. Meeting Nick and Aaron slowed her progress to that of a snail making a cross-country trip. A snail would be faster, she decided, which brought a smile to her face. Despite all of the complications they had caused, she owed both of them a little bit of credit for her survival.

Her smile sagged as worry for Aaron returned. She knew the severe injury to his leg wouldn't heal on its own, and every minute that ticked by tugged him closer to death. The bellow of glorious train whistles serenaded her as she walked, announcing they came to the city after all, and as if hypnotized she followed the much-anticipated sound to its origin.

With any luck, she thought, *we'll be able to sneak onto a train heading north.* Her feet crunched over glass scattered across sidewalks from shattered display windows, doors to shops hung open on broken hinges, and a thick, acrid smoke curled up from the next street over. Trying to hold onto any shred of hope, she ignored the sick feeling in her stomach and kept walking.

Blaring whistles, warning everyone in Dallas to clear the tracks, grew louder. She followed those sounds to a set of tracks and then followed those tracks to a train station. The station, unlike the rest of the city, turned out to be a bustling place. She watched, fascinated by the hundreds of people boarding and exiting trains. Trains with more cars than she could see lined six sets of tracks.

"Tickets, present your tickets here," men in uniform yelled at the base of steps leading up to the train cars. Train security guards walked up and down the platform, watching the trains to prevent stowaways. Nearby, teenage boys, members of The Defiance, supervised the commotion, mingling near the ticket booths, the lines of people boarding trains, and the workers unloading boxes and crates. The Defiance had seized the railroad and control of all shipments entering and exiting Dallas.

Curious and cautious, she walked along the train. Toward the back, she passed cars with large open doors and watched men and women swarm in and out, rolling carts full of boxes. The entire scene reminded her of an anthill with constant activity and confusion. But the cargo cars gave her hope. If they could board one after it was fully loaded and hide behind some of the goods, they might not be caught. Of course sneaking injured Aaron and herself into the car fast enough that no one would notice made her rethink that plan.

"Can I help you?" a deep voice threatened from behind.

Lareina turned quickly, not sure at first if the man spoke to her in the bustle. He wore the blue uniform of the railroad security and stared down at her with an impatient glare.

"I'm sorry, sir," she said, forcing herself to be polite. "I've never been to the train station before. I'm supposed to meet my sister here, but I can't seem to find her."

"So you weren't thinking of sneaking onto one of these trains," the man accused. Three boys dressed in the signature uniform of The Defiance stepped forward, closing a tight circle around her.

"No," she lied, smiling, forcing her voice to remain steady. "I'm just looking for the ticket booth. That's where my sister said she would meet me."

The man stared at her but didn't say anything. His hand moved at his side, and for a minute she thought he might strike her. Instead he lifted his arm and pointed over her head. "You can buy tickets down there."

"Thank you, sir," she replied, striving to retain her smile a little longer.

She backed away then hurried in the direction the man had pointed. Crowds of people surrounded a short building with glass windows. Everyone who had the money to travel scrambled to escape the city under siege. Standing at the back of a line, she stared up at large signs plastered against the window. Each square of the chart listed a destination and below it a train number, time of departure, and stops along the way. She scanned the timetable for a train passing through Nebraska.

Dallas, TX to Sioux Falls, SD
Today
Train #16 2:00 P.M.
Train #25 9:00 P.M.
Tomorrow

Train #1 8:00 A.M.
Train #19 8:00 P.M.

Stepping up closer to read the tiny black print, she poured over a list of cities and towns where the train would stop. After Dallas there were a few more destinations in Texas, several in Oklahoma and Kansas, but only a few in Nebraska. *Please be there,* she thought over and over. *Please still exist.* The third stop in Nebraska brought a smile to her face. She couldn't take her eyes off Maibe, NE, it's listing insignificant to most travelers but essential to keep her hope alive. The only home she'd ever known still existed and the train could take her there.

Lareina repeated the numbers and times over and over but wished she had paper to write them down. People in front of her gave destinations and train numbers to smiling women behind the glass.

"Two tickets to New York City," a tall man in a black suit requested.

"That'll be one hundred and three dollars," the smiling woman prompted from behind her shield of glass.

The man pulled five crisp, green bills from his pocket and slid them through a slot under the window.

The woman's blond curls bounced slightly as she thumbed through the money. Satisfied, she turned and tore two white rectangles of paper from a roll behind her and slid them under the window.

"Be sure to board fifteen minutes early, sir. How can I help you, ma'am?" the woman asked with a smile as the man moved away.

Lareina glanced in both directions. She had been so

preoccupied with the activity around her, she didn't realize she had reached the front of the line. Doing her best impression of the others she walked up to the window.

"What would two tickets to Maibe, Nebraska, cost?"

The woman looked down at some numbers printed on a sheet of paper. "That would be sixty dollars."

She took a sharp breath. "Do the tickets ever get any cheaper?" She had a dollar in her pocket, and maybe a few quarters in the bag she'd left with Aaron.

"No ma'am, I'm sorry." The woman sounded sincere.

Nodding, she walked away from the window before the impatient customer behind her could shove her out of the way. She found an empty bench near the platform and sat down. For a long time she watched people and trains, contemplating how she would get herself and Aaron out of Dallas. His injury, combined with their lack of money, made the entire situation impossible. Hundreds boarded trains, few disembarked. Workers loaded boxes, unloaded crates, paced up and down the platform. She didn't move.

She barely noticed the commotion, the vanishing clouds, or the passage of time until she felt warm light on her face. The sun gleamed directly above her. Noon. Lareina jumped to her feet. She had left Aaron before sunrise. Her stomach growled as she drifted away from the chaotic train station toward the inevitable peril of a desperate city.

For five blocks, she surveyed shattered windows, smoldering skeletons of buildings, and abandoned belongings scattered in the streets. Among the belongings were discarded signs protesting The Defiance. Together, the scene suggested there'd been a riot recently. She wandered the maze of a broken city for hours searching for food until she heard whispering on the breeze, a barely audible hint of faraway voices. Straining her ears, she tried to identify the exact direction they came from. One block forward, two to the left, a right down an alley, then straight ahead again. Indiscernible conversations lifted over rooftops and skipped down sidewalks. Verbalizations of civilization mixed with the familiar aromas of baking bread, ripe fruit, and meat on a grill. One more block and she entered a stretch of the city that swarmed with people. The only operating market area she'd encountered, it consisted of several buildings lining the street, all specializing in different types of food. Signs above doorways and display windows announced: Bakery, Fresh Fruit, Soup and Sandwich Shop.

Someone bumped into her, shoved her out of the way, and murmured in annoyance. She decided soup would be comforting for Aaron. A bell tinkled above her when she pulled the door open. Warm steam, smelling of vegetables, wrapped around the little room with its clean tile floor and dainty white tables and chairs. Lareina shivered when she noticed a table surrounded by four teenagers, members of The Defiance, who glared at her as if to say *Follow our rules or you'll have a problem*.

Ignoring the suspicious stares, she approached the counter to view a menu above her. Soup of the day: $6.00. The cheapest sandwich cost $4.00. She couldn't find anything on the menu priced below $3.00. With The Defiance commandeering everything in town she knew the lone dollar in her pocket held the same value as a single sock.

Frustrated, she left and continued down the street. She stopped in front of a window with clothing on display. Cupping her hands against the window, she stared in at the rows and rows of shirts on hangers and shelves of jeans. She looked down at her dirty jacket and torn jeans then back at the crisp blue shirt and flawless skirt in the window. She wanted the new clothes more than anything, even food, but with price tags of $25.00 and $42.00 that wasn't going to happen. Remembering Aaron, she felt guilty even contemplating the risk of being arrested for stealing a shirt.

Taking one last look at the outfit in front of her, she turned away and followed the aroma of freshly baked bread across the street and into a bakery. Glass cases all around the room displayed loaves of bread, decorated cakes, cookies, and brownies. *I don't need anything fancy,* she thought. *A simple loaf of bread can't be expensive in comparison to all of that frosting.* She gazed into a display case filled with different shaped loaves of bread.

"Is there something I can help you with?" a man's annoyed voice declared behind her.

Lareina spun around to face a tall man in a white apron and hat. He glared down at her but kept a fearful eye on a teenage boy slouched against the wall with his hands in his pockets. The boy looked about her age, wore jeans and a jacket like she did, but like every teenager in The Defiance, his eyes watched the world with resentment.

"Do you sell anything that costs less than a dollar?" she asked, ignoring the man's obvious agitation.

He laughed. "Of course not. I would go out of business for selling anything that cheap. If you can't pay then get out of my bakery."

The man blocked her from walking any further into the shop, so she had no choice but to turn back toward the door. Frustration and anger increased her courage with every step she took toward the exit. In small green print, $3 was written on a sign above a basket next to the door. She had to get back to Aaron and she couldn't go without food. Looking around to make sure no one watched her, she reached a hand into the basket and pulled out a bag of rolls. Holding it in front of her, against her jacket, she thought no one had noticed.

She reached for the door. *Almost there. Don't look suspicious.*

"Hey, stop right there," The Defiance guard yelled.

She didn't stop, but pushed the door open and darted out onto the crowded sidewalk. Dodging people, occasionally bumping into them, she pushed her feet across the pavement, but the guard's shouting always echoed right behind her. *He's better at this than Galloway,* she decided, regretting ever seeing the rolls. Thieves in San Antonio were hung for their crimes, but stealing from The Defiance wouldn't result in such an easy death. She swallowed hard remembering the stories of beatings, lost fingernails, and blinding that could never be verified since no one ever survived. It couldn't be true. A knocking in her head matched the rhythm of her feet, and the sky blurred with concrete and gray buildings. She had to hurry. If they locked her up or put her to death, Aaron would die alone, believing she'd left him behind on purpose.

Ahead, she spotted a gathering of people waiting outside the door of a building labeled Carrie's Coffee. Seeing her chance, she pushed through the crowd despite people's protests, ignoring demands of "Watch where you're going." She dropped the bag of rolls amongst the crowd and turned into an alley that ended in a brick wall. Two dumpsters, countless bags of trash, and a pile of rotting pellets offered her only options for hiding. Knowing the guard couldn't be far behind, she hoisted herself up to the edge of the dumpster and slid inside.

Lareina hunched in a dark corner that smelled like rotten fish and sour milk. Nearby and getting closer, the guard's loud, angry voice questioned people in the crowd, but she couldn't hear their responses, only the rising grumble of frustration in the interrogator's voice. For the first time since she'd been in the city, she felt grateful for the self-centered attitude the majority of people had adopted. Still, she waited tensely, hoping The Defiance guard wouldn't decide to check the alley. He had his bread back; what more could he want? She held her breath, closed her eyes, and willed herself to remain absolutely motionless.

"Did you see which way she went?" the threatening questioning passed the intersection of the alley.

Voices rose and faded. Soon she couldn't distinguish between individual conversations as the roar of a crowd gained volume. Five minutes, ten minutes, twenty minutes passed and her legs shook, unable to support her crouching stance any longer. Not wanting to sit amongst the trash, she stood and peered over the edge of the dumpster. Her ears hadn't deceived her. People filled the street, shouting and hoisting signs into the air. *Down with The Defiance*, one sign screamed in bold black letters. *End the Occupation in Dallas, Save the City,* another announced in dripping red paint that reminded her of blood.

If the guard hadn't given up his search, he would never find her in that crowd, and it appeared he had bigger problems to deal with. Lareina hopped out of the dumpster and pulled her hood up. Plunging her way into the crowd, she pushed past men shouting their resistance, women thrusting signs high into the air, and occasional children crying in the chaos.

"Clear the streets. You have one minute to clear the streets," a loud voice thundered from above and echoed over her.

She froze and stood on her tiptoes, trying to find the origin. Some of the people around her looked up and she followed their gazes to the roof of a three-story building just down the street. Six teenage boys and one girl, no older than herself, glared down at the crowd, shoulders back and heads high with an air of evil rebellion.

"This is our city now, just as St. Louis and Kansas City are ours." The assumed leader spoke into some kind of megaphone, amplifying his voice, bringing the crowd to a silent attention. "Join us and we'll bring an end to the injustice of our broken country."

"Never," a voice shouted from below in the street. People backed away from the resister and she spotted him. The brave boy couldn't have been older than twelve and she watched as he raised a gun, aiming toward the roof. A shot reverberated down the street, bouncing between buildings, and the boy crumpled to the ground. Another shot echoed, followed by a deafening cadence of gunfire.

CHAPTER 37

The crowd became a stampede and Lareina a part of the shoving, scrambling confusion. She pushed forward, stumbling, but unable to fall with people packed so tightly around her. Someone's knee jabbed hard into her leg, an elbow slammed into the side of her skull, and despite welling tears, she continued to move with the wall of former protesters. Somewhere in the deafening roar her ears popped, and the gunfire mixed with panicked shouting that thundered all around her.

Something warm splattered across her face and the woman beside her fell to the ground with a yelp. Rubbing a hand across her forehead, Lareina examined the sticky red substance on her fingers. She pushed forward faster, trying to get out of the crowd, but always finding herself roughly shoved back into her bubble of space. People continuously vanished, succumbing to their injuries and sinking to the ground. The pavement below her feet grew slippery, but she didn't dare look down to verify what stole traction from her tennis shoes.

The crowd thinned. She didn't stop, stared straight ahead, avoided looking back. Soon no one ran beside her and she found herself alone on an abandoned street as the setting sun filtered through the clouds, shimmering against windows on the top floors of buildings and casting shadows at the ground level. A narrow alley beckoned between two skyscrapers. She ducked inside and slid to the ground, unable to stand on her wobbly legs any longer. Blood covered her hands and stained her clothes. She felt sick and dry heaved against the wall, but nothing remained in her stomach for her to expel.

Tears spilled down her face and her breath came in gasping sobs. Afraid to move, she cried alone, watching shadows shiver across the opposite wall. Fleeting images of the scene replayed in her mind, preventing her from catching her breath. Her instincts screamed at her to run far away from the city and never look back. But she had left Aaron behind in the morning, and if she didn't hurry, darkening twilight would find him all alone, lying on the cold concrete.

Her legs throbbed, her jaw and forehead burned, and she had as much control over her arms as wet noodles, but she managed to pull her stiff, numb body to its feet. A wave of dizziness passed as she pressed herself against the wall then forced herself out onto the sidewalk. Silence replaced the cacophony of chaos from earlier. Edges of yellow lights seeped past shades in windows, sealing the world out, leaving her alone. She limped, impeded by her injuries from the stampede, past boarded up windows and glass on the sidewalks that glittered like snow under half lit street lights.

"Rochelle? . . . I mean, Lareina?" The voice floated on the air faintly behind her. Aaron couldn't have moved, so she dismissed it as a delusion.

"Lareina?" the voice said again, closer and a bit sharper.

If someone intended to hurt her, she didn't have the energy to fight him off. In her last act of disapproval for all she had seen that day, she spun around to face her death.

One lone figure stood ten feet away, hands stuffed in the pockets of a baggy coat, only a silhouette against the half-light of dusk. She strained her blurry eyes to make out the familiar features of messy blond hair, straight thin nose, and sleepy eyelids.

"Nick?" She whispered his name. Logic told her he couldn't be standing there in front of her. She blinked. She squeezed her eyes shut and shook her head. He didn't fade.

Nick stepped forward, close enough that she could see his expression, then stopped and took a step back. His mouth opened as if he would cry out then twisted into a cringe. It was a look of disgust and horror. She remembered her blood-splattered clothes and waited for him to make a judgment.

"Lareina, what happened to you? You look . . ."

Awful, disgusting, like a monster. She could think of plenty of words to finish his sentence, but he didn't utter them. He looked so clean and neat, but his eyes darted from side to side, constantly scanning the empty street. She shivered. She wanted Nick to take her hand in his, needing the comforting touch of another human, but everything from his posture to his expression warned her to stay back.

"I got . . ." The words jammed in her throat so she swallowed and took a breath. "I got caught up in the protest. They . . . I couldn't . . . I tried . . ."

Nick pulled his hands from his pockets and let them rest at his sides. He moved forward, bridging the gap between them until she could smell bitter coffee on his breath.

"Are you hurt?" His cold contempt melted to genuine concern.

She shook her head. "What are you doing here? How did you find me?"

"I got worried when I saw you at the train station without Aaron." His words sounded sincere, but something in his eyes told a different story. If she had more time and less worries, if she wasn't so tired, she might have evaluated his honesty further, but the darkening sky indicated that she had accomplished nothing in an entire day.

"Aaron," she exclaimed. "Nick, he's hurt and I didn't even get him any food." Her knees wobbled and she wanted to sink into the sidewalk, sink into darkness where she could sleep for a week.

"I have a room at a hotel by the railroad tracks. We can all stay there until we catch a train out of here."

She stared at him. "How can you afford a hotel?"

"I sold the gun you left in my bag. You didn't think I could make it without your help, but I can handle things." His tone sounded ominous to Lareina, but she just figured he wasn't ready to trust her yet. *It'll all be better once we have time to talk*, she decided not wanting to push away her only ally.

"I'm glad you're here."

"How bad is Aaron hurt?" Nick asked. A late street light buzzed to life.

"Bad." She pictured the trap around his leg then forced herself to breathe.

"Where is he?" His eyes narrowed, watched her reaction, created a barrier between them. Did he suspect her of lying? About this?

She led the way, and Nick followed her eight blocks to the overpass. Silence threatened to obliterate her forced calm. She wanted to talk about something, anything, but he didn't say a word. He walked an arm's length away from her, but she could feel his eyes scrutinize her with an aversion that burned right into her thoughts. The scared Nick, the judgmental Nick, the arguing Nick—each would have been preferable to the silent, aloof Nick.

When the overpass came into view, she ran toward it, and Nick did the same, never letting her out of his sight.

"Aaron," she shouted into the darkness before her eyes adjusted. "Aaron." No one responded. Soon her vision cleared enough for her to realize that Aaron, the backpack, everything was gone except for her message scrawled on the pavement. She ran her fingers over the words then patted the concrete around her as if she expected her friend to materialize there.

A sudden breeze whistled overhead and swept her hair over her eyes. "He's gone." Her despairing voice wasn't loud enough to compete with the wind. "I left him right here this morning and he's gone."

CHAPTER 38

"**A**aron," she yelled. It didn't make sense. He couldn't go anywhere on his own. Who could have taken him?

"Lareina," Nick shouted. "Listen."

"I'm here," Aaron's muffled voice announced.

It didn't come from under the overpass but from outside. Lareina darted out from under the bridge, closely followed by Nick.

"I'm here," Aaron repeated.

Following his voice, she and Nick turned toward the embankment alongside the overpass. Aaron sat there, half hidden by the tall brush, but he looked no worse than before. Running over to him, she collapsed into the grass, and wrapped him in a hug. He hugged her back, squeezing tighter than she expected.

"What are you doing out here? Are you okay?" she asked. Neither of them pulled away from the embrace.

"I could hear people walking by and I thought I would be safer out here. I was afraid maybe you wouldn't be back," he admitted.

Little by little, Aaron released his grip and she leaned back. The dewy grass felt cold against her knees. "How could you think I wouldn't come back? I left a note and I left my backpack."

For the first time, he got a good look at her and his hands lifted to her face, gently feeling along her swollen jawline and pushing her hair back from the lump on her forehead. "Lareina, what happened to you? All of that blood . . ."

She shivered, remembering all that she had survived, not ready to relive it. "We have to get out of Dallas right away. The Defiance is in control now."

Nick stepped forward. "Guys, if you haven't noticed, it's getting dark, so how about you finish this conversation at the hotel."

"Is that Nick?" Aaron's voice brightened. "Where did you find him?"

"He found me," she explained. "He's going to help us."

"It's about time he took his turn," Aaron joked. A wide grin spread over his face; Lareina hadn't seen him smile since the accident.

Nick rolled his eyes then smiled. He knelt down next to her, and she watched his reaction progress from emotionless stare to horrified shudder at the sight of bloody bandages securing a piece of picket fence acting as a splint. His cringe faded to a guilty frown as he realized the danger and urgency of the situation. For a second he turned away, took a few heaving breaths, then looked back to his friends.

"Oh man, what happened to you?"

"I won the lottery and found the trap hundreds of others managed to miss," Aaron admitted, forcing a weak chuckle.

"I know what that's like," Nick reassured. He positioned himself so he wouldn't be able to see Aaron's leg in his peripheral vision. "Don't worry, Lareina and I will find a way to fix this."

They pulled Aaron to his feet and began their slow walk through cold fog that materialized between buildings, transforming distant sounds to ghostly echoes. Aaron tottered from side to side, leaning against Nick as they moved toward the train tracks. Limping along beside them, Lareina hoped no one would notice three teenagers hobbling through the darkness. Her head ached, her feet protested every step, and her eyes watered, but just when she decided the promise of rest had to be a cruel joke, a false hope, Nick pointed out the hotel from a block away. She stared in amazement up to the top of the building stretching at least twenty floors toward the sky.

"Wow, that's where you're staying?"

"Yeah. Don't slow down now, we're almost there," Nick snapped.

Aaron looked over at her, but she just shrugged and continued walking.

They entered through clear glass doors into a clean lobby with a black-and-white tiled floor and a spiral staircase in one corner. Nick looked over to a desk at the right, but no one waited there, and for the first time he seemed to relax. Nonetheless, he rushed his friends through the lobby and into an elevator. Lareina had never been in an elevator before, and although she preferred the stairs to the tiny room that felt like a trap, she knew that wouldn't be an option for Aaron. The ride seemed endless, and she hated the feeling of her stomach sinking through her body. She held tight to a rail along the wall and focused on glowing numbers above the door as they clicked up to eight.

Finally, the elevator dinged and the front wall opened to a long hallway of white doors. Nick directed them halfway down the hall, then pulled out a key and pushed his white door into room 814. On the way in, he flipped on a light switch illuminating the most beautiful room she had ever seen. Two beds covered with pillows and fluffy gray comforters lined one wall. A long wooden dresser and a glass door leading out to the balcony occupied the other two walls. To the right of the main door, she noticed another door that she guessed led to a bathroom. The soft tan carpet beneath her feet and gentle gray tones of the room's color scheme relaxed her pulse to a normal rate. She dropped her backpack on the dresser and helped Nick settle Aaron on one of the beds.

"There's a twenty-four-hour cafe downstairs. I'll get us something to eat," Nick offered. He picked up his key off the dresser and disappeared through the door.

Lareina situated herself on the bed next to Aaron, being careful not to disturb his injured leg. A clock, hanging near the door, ticked loudly.

Closing her eyes, she rested her forehead against the palm of her hand. "This place is pretty nice, huh?"

"It's too nice." Aaron glanced around the room as if searching for something he'd lost. "How can Nick afford this place?"

That same question bounced around in her mind, but she ignored it in her relief to see Nick and a chance to get Aaron to real shelter. The details of the last week swirled and blended into an indecipherable smudge in her memory. She no longer cared how or why, but Aaron didn't relax, his dirt-smudged face still concerned. Dried blood still smeared his shirt from the night he wounded his leg.

"I put the gun in his bag. He told me he sold it. Maybe he's better at haggling than I am."

Aaron nodded, but the crease of worry in his forehead remained.

"I'll be back in a second," she told him and walked into the bathroom. Letting a stream of warm water cascade from the faucet, she washed her hands and face, looking away so she wouldn't see red-tinged streams slide down the drain. On the counter she found a washcloth and held it under the warm water until it soaked through. Pushing Aaron's questions out of her mind, she returned to the main room. Carefully she washed Aaron's face, hands, and arms, then helped him into a clean shirt. The bandages on his leg would have to be changed, but she decided Nick would be far more qualified for that task. While they waited for Nick, she fluffed the pillows behind Aaron and pulled a blanket over him.

"Now get some rest." She brushed her hand over his forehead then took a step away.

The horror of everything she'd witnessed that day returned as the feeling of boulders on her chest and oxygen that never quite seemed to reach her lungs. Not wanting to alarm Aaron, she stepped out onto the balcony, leaned her elbows against the rail, and buried her face in her hands. She closed her eyes and tried to focus all of her attention on breathing, but her mind wouldn't shut off so easily.

Alone on the balcony, in the cool darkness, she found herself jumping through time. She looked down at a mysterious pendant in Susan's bloody hands, called to a boy trapped in a muddy pit, slipped a key off a wall of keys, and fought her way forward as people collapsed on a crowded street. Her legs buckled beneath her and she sank to the balcony floor, resting her forehead against cool metal.

"It deceives you, doesn't it?" Nick asked.

Lareina's eyes snapped open. She hadn't heard him come in, but there he was standing in the doorway behind her. Using the railing for support, she pulled herself to her feet.

"What do you mean?" she asked, disregarding her pounding heart.

He stepped forward, leaned into the rail, and looked out at the city. "At first all you see are the pretty lights. They draw you in before you know what you're getting yourself into, then you notice the darkness a little bit at a time. A part of you always knew it was there, but it's so much easier to believe the lies."

Brightly lit windows illuminated the buildings in some neighborhoods while others were invisible, cloaked in darkness. A minute ago the cool breeze felt good on her face, but suddenly it sent a shiver through her body. She looked over at Nick, but he wouldn't make eye contact with her.

"I know you don't trust me and I don't blame you, but I do regret lying to you." She leaned heavily against the railing, and awaited his response.

He let out a long breath and shook his head. "Am I talking to Lareina the orphan, Rochelle the con artist, or someone else entirely?"

Swallowing hard, she considered Nick's question while his icy stare drilled into her soul for answers.

"I suppose I'm both of those people and some I don't know yet. I've been trying to figure that out my entire life." A chilly gust of wind slapped at her face and she gripped the railing tighter. "Do you know what I've decided?"

The memories of cruelty and misery ran laps at the edge of her mind and the air seemed to thin once again. Nick's expression softened and he took a step forward, but held back.

Lareina forced a quick smile that faded immediately. "I'm nobody. I don't even have a last name. My existence means nothing to anyone and when I'm gone, the world won't miss me because it never even knew I was here."

Tears burned in the corners of her eyes and she turned away from Nick. The city loomed beautiful, mysterious, and deadly below. She felt the rail sway slightly, indicating his presence beside her, but she didn't turn her head to acknowledge him.

For minutes they stood there together, silent, alone in their own thoughts.

"You should go inside and get cleaned up." Nick's voice wasn't comforting, but it wasn't icy either. "We can talk later."

She nodded, too exhausted to argue or search for some kind of hidden meaning in his tone. Vision blurred by stubborn tears, she walked straight into the bathroom, locked the door, and peeled off her clothes without examining them. Sobbing, she stepped into the shower and remained still as the steaming water mingled with her lukewarm tears. Eventually she calmed down enough to dry herself with a soft white towel and dress in the last clean outfit left in her bag.

For a long while she stood in front of the mirror staring at her own reflection. Any weight she had gained at Oak Creek seemed to be melting away, leaving her face drawn and tired. When her puffy eyes returned nearly to normal, she combed through her short, uneven hair and pushed the annoying bangs out of her eyes. She pressed a cold washcloth against the lump on her forehead and examined her pupils to assure herself she didn't have a concussion. Five minutes ticked by, and she contemplated sleeping in the bathtub—anything to avoid conversation with Nick—but she had to check on Aaron and hunger urged her to leave the room. With one last look in the mirror, she watched her reflection take two slow breaths, then opened the door.

"The weather changes every five minutes. People are really nice though and help each other after blizzards and floods," Nick was saying. The bathroom door groaned. Both Nick and Aaron turned toward her.

She put a smile on her face for Aaron's sake. "What are you guys talking about?"

"Nick was telling me about Nebraska," Aaron explained.

He seemed tense, disappointed, maybe a little worried, and definitely paler. Lareina hoped he wasn't in too much pain. Sitting down on the other bed, she rested her elbows on her knees.

"There are no words to give you a realistic impression. You'll like it when you get there," she reassured him.

Aaron forced a weak smile. His eyelids hovered half open as if he struggled to stay awake. She looked over at Nick and the worried expression on his face mirrored what she felt.

He sighed. "I can't get him to eat anything and I think he's running a fever."

"Don't listen to him," Aaron protested. "I'm fine, and I did eat a little." His head lolled to the left.

She glanced over at the full bowl of soup and nibbled sandwich on the nightstand by Aaron's bed. "Come on, you can do better than that." She picked up the soup and sat down next to him. "You haven't eaten for days. You have to be hungry."

Aaron struggled to lift his arm, gave up halfway, waved his hand toward her, then let his arm drop back to his side. "Maybe later."

"That's exactly what he told me." Nick kept his voice even, but the panic showed in his wide eyes.

Lareina looked from one of her friends to the other. The air around them felt still, dense, suffocating, but she had to breathe, had to remain calm.

"Nick, it's okay," she reassured, keeping her voice smooth, speaking slowly to prevent it from rising in pitch. "I need you to find all of the first aid stuff in my bag." At first he only looked at her, as if debating whether he wanted to obey. So she added a "please" and he finally gave in.

Turning to Aaron, she held a spoonful of soup near his

mouth. "Just a few more bites. You have to keep your strength up for the train ride," she coaxed.

It worked and he swallowed the contents of the spoon. Despite her own hunger, she spent the next hour persuading Aaron to finish his supper, then held his hand while Nick changed the bandages. Watching Aaron squirm and feeling how tightly he squeezed her hand disheartened her so completely that she couldn't even imagine how Aaron must have felt.

After Nick finished with the bandages, he left to take a shower. Lareina sat with Aaron, giving him her best sales pitch for Christmas blizzards, spring lilacs, blazing summer days, and football games on crisp fall nights. He listened, nodding occasionally, while his eyelids hovered halfway between lethargy and sleep.

"All right, it's time for you to get some sleep." She brushed her hand lightly across his forehead. It felt warmer than normal, or maybe her hands were just cold.

Aaron didn't protest as she rearranged his pillows and helped him lie down. He closed his eyes and sighed. "Lareina, I think it's infected and without antibiotics . . ."

Huddled beneath the comforter, he looked so small, like a frightened child. She took his hand in both of hers, not sure how to comfort him but compelled to try. She wanted to run back to the hospital and shout, threaten, throw things until the corrupt guards let them in. She wanted to haul Aaron across the street and load him on a train to anywhere. But she couldn't do either of those things.

"Shhh. Just rest." She spoke in the most reassuring voice she could muster. "You're going to be just fine. I promise."

"Lareina," Aaron mumbled as his eyes began to close. "I started a letter to my family. The address is on it, in the front pocket of the backpack. Can you send it for me?" His blue eyes were pools of pleading fear.

"I'll find you a stamp. You can send it yourself."

Aaron slipped into sleep. Despite his peaceful appearance, she couldn't bring herself to leave his side. She felt an obligation to protect him, to comfort him if he found himself trapped in a nightmare. After pulling a blanket up to his chin, she leaned back in her chair, closed her eyes, and listened to water rushing through pipes in the wall.

Her eyes barely opened at the feeling of a light warmth against her shoulder. Nick pulled his hand back the second she moved. Droplets of water dripped from his hair to the shoulders of his t-shirt. Aaron breathed silently. Lareina rubbed her stinging eyes.

Nick handed her a white paper bag. "Here, you didn't eat anything yet."

She thanked him and took the bag. It contained a bowl of soup and a sandwich, just like Aaron's. Removing a plastic lid from the Styrofoam bowl, she took a bite of soup. It was cold, but she was too hungry to care.

"He's going to be okay, right?" Nick whispered, looking over at Aaron.

"We have to get him to a hospital as soon as we can," she mused more to herself than Nick. "Thank you," she said when she noticed him watching her, "for helping with the bandages and everything."

He nodded then sank down onto the second bed. "Lareina, can you tell me about Ava again, the whole story? I have to know everything, even the worst details." Color drained from his face, he slouched forward a little, and for a moment he seemed familiar again.

It wasn't the conversation she wanted to have, but it was

better than not talking to him at all. As she ate, she recounted every detail she could remember, beginning with meeting Ava who introduced herself as Susan, to the search for Dr. Iverson, to hiding in alleys, to Ava's death. "She told me to protect you, although I didn't understand her words until I thought about them later." Her eyes met his for the first time since she'd started the story. "She told me she loved you."

Nick remained frozen in place the entire time she spoke. Sometimes he closed his eyes as if he couldn't handle the images she described, but the rest of the time he watched every movement of her lips and scrutinized every facial expression and gesture. He seemed . . . quiet? Lost in thought? Distracted and conflicted, perhaps, were the closest words could come to describing his behavior.

"And that's the entire truth? You didn't change any details for my benefit?" he probed after a minute of silence.

She leaned back into the cushion of her chair. Fatigue prevented her from telling anything but the absolute truth. Actually, it seemed to sharpen her memory to the impressions she'd spent months trying to forget. "That's exactly how it happened. I'm done lying to you about anything ever again."

Nick nodded and locked his eyes on hers. "And you only took the pendant when Ava offered it to you? You only have it because you're trying to keep your word?"

Sliding her empty soup bowl onto a stand nearby, she shifted in her seat, feeling like she was under interrogation. "Yes, Nick. I didn't want it in the first place and I don't want it now, but because of what Susan . . . I mean Ava, told me, I'm afraid to give it up."

He sighed and nodded. A long silence passed between them, but she no longer felt tired.

"Okay," he finally said. "I have some work lined up for us

tomorrow. Together, I think we can make enough money for tickets out of the city."

"Great." Lareina yawned. "What kind of work?"

"We should really get some sleep. I'll tell you all about it tomorrow."

He flipped the light off and her mind hurtled toward sleep. What had they been discussing?

"You're right. We'll talk about it tomorrow." She picked up an extra blanket and curled up in the chair next to Aaron's bed. From outside, a muffled train whistle danced through her ears.

CHAPTER 39

The fog only thickened as Lareina followed Nick across gray sidewalks, between gray buildings, and through gray mist. He told her they were going to help unload trains for a different railroad not far from the hotel. He told her they would receive free tickets in exchange for their work. She didn't question him. She was out of ideas, and without his help there was no hope for Aaron.

A motionless calm enveloped the streets. She questioned whether the previous day's mayhem really occurred. Perhaps it had all been a nightmare created by her restless mind. She touched her hand to the lump on her forehead and shivered. Wispy fog drifted by, wrapping around buildings and floating over cars, making any other pedestrians inconspicuous. She zipped her jacket and slid her hands into her pockets. All she could think about was Aaron's deteriorating condition. Until that morning she hadn't been sure he was running a fever, but the minute her hand made contact with his burning forehead she knew. Every instinct screamed against leaving him alone all day, but she couldn't save him unless she could get him out of Dallas, and she couldn't get the tickets without leaving him behind. Gently, she had tucked blankets around him, not wanting to wake him up, and left a note of explanation on the nightstand.

She clutched her pendant, hidden inside her jacket pocket. That morning she had watched her reflection struggle with the clasp to remove the pendant from its usual place. For the first time since she'd received the unwanted gift, she slipped it into her pocket instead of wearing it. A new worry that she might lose it while unloading train cars harassed her thoughts. *We're almost home,* she thought. *We're almost home and everything will be okay.*

"Here we are," Nick announced.

She hadn't been paying attention, but it only took a second for a startling realization to creep through her. She had followed Nick into a dead-end alley. There wasn't a train or the hustle and bustle of people that she had anticipated. Nothing but red brick walls surrounding her on three sides.

Taking a step back, she fought the urge to run. Did Nick know how to spin a believable lie? What could he possibly know of deception? "Where are we? I don't understand."

He stepped around to face her. "This is it." His voice held a chill deeper than any winter she had ever known, but his eyes studied her with uncertainty.

Her only escape beckoned behind him, but instinctively she took another step back. He leaped forward and clasped her arm tight in his hand, pulling her toward the side of a building. Cold metal swallowed her wrist and secured her to the bars covering a window. Nick backed away and she tried to follow, but the handcuff dug into her wrist and held her in place.

"What are you doing?" she choked. Fear, anger, and disbelief mixed until she felt nothing at all.

"This is justice for what you did to Ava. The detective will be here any minute to collect you." His voice quivered, and she glimpsed his doubt. Enough doubt to change his mind if she had enough time.

"No, Nick. I only lied about my name and the pendant. You know who I am—I wasn't pretending." She shouted the words, speaking quickly as time sped away.

"Stop lying to me, Lareina. Galloway told me the truth," Nick growled. "You shot Ava because you wanted her pendant. He'd been following you for months on suspicion of robbery and murder and that was when he caught up with you. But after you stole Ava's pendant, he rushed her to the hospital, and she made it. She's alive, and in exchange for you, he's giving me two train tickets back to San Antonio so I can find her."

Blinking back tears, she lunged forward, but her wrist jerked her back. Galloway had given Nick the lie he wanted to believe. She couldn't construct any truth to compete with that.

"You didn't tell him about your pendant?" she whispered, worried Galloway could be lurking around any corner.

Nick's frown deepened. "That's none of your business."

She bit her lip to fight back a rising hostility toward Nick. "Don't tell him," she pleaded. "We can't let him have both."

Rolling his eyes, he shook his head slowly back and forth. "I don't know what kind of scheme you're trying, but I'm not letting you go."

She tried again to move toward Nick, but he backed away and the handcuffs prevented her from getting any closer.

"Well, well, well . . . It looks like you came through for me after all." Galloway's gruff voice boomed through the alley. The detective's words had been directed at Nick, but he couldn't take his eyes off Lareina.

"You're absolutely sure that she did it?" His voice held the hesitation of deepening uncertainty, but it was too late for that.

Galloway held out two yellow, rectangular pieces of paper to Nick. "I wouldn't have spent so much time chasing her if I wasn't sure, now would I?" Galloway spoke with a confident arrogance.

Nick nodded and took the tickets, stepping away from her. Galloway walked up to her and clutched the front of her jacket in his fist.

"Where's the pendant?" he demanded.

She pulled away from him. She wanted to run, but the handcuffs prevented her from getting more than two steps away. "Take three guesses." She spat the words at him, but he reached out, grabbed her arm, and pulled her closer to him.

"Where is it?" He emphasized every syllable of every word. His hot breath on her face smelled like cigars. Nick hovered at the opening of the alley.

She needed to buy some time if she were to have any hope of escaping, but she also had to protect the pendant. "I sold it. I needed the money and that poor naive man believed it was a valuable family heirloom." She shrugged as if it didn't matter and wondered how long she could prevent Galloway from checking her pockets.

"Excellent." Galloway rolled his eyes. "You're going to tell me where." He took out a key and moved toward the handcuffs.

"Wait," Nick shouted. Galloway and Lareina both turned toward him. Nick's feet cemented him in place. *Get out of here, Nick,* she thought. *What are you still doing here?* He didn't understand how dangerous Galloway could be, and she wouldn't be able to protect him. In less than ten minutes, she'd failed to keep both of her promises to Susan.

"What do you want?" Galloway grumbled.

"Can I at least . . ." Nick swallowed. "Say goodbye?" He took a few steps back from Galloway, and stuffed his hands into his pockets. "Please?"

"Fine. I can spare one minute," the detective said. "Be quick."

Lareina couldn't believe he granted Nick's request, but she didn't complain as a new plan seeped through her thoughts. Galloway stepped back but continued to watch her closely, and Nick stepped right up to her. They stood there looking at each other for a second before Nick surprised her by pulling her into a hug.

She lowered her free arm down into her pocket.

"I'm sorry," he whispered. "I wish we'd have never met."

Her fingers brushed souvenirs she'd taken from the last house until she finally clutched the pendant in her hand. Keeping her arm hidden in front of Nick, she raised it out of her pocket. "I know, me too." Inch by inch, she slipped the pendant into his pocket. She had picked hundreds of pockets without the owners feeling a thing, but the reverse operation proved far more difficult. "You tricked me and I didn't even see it coming. Well done." She slid her hand expertly back to her side.

"Enough," Galloway ordered. "You've had your minute."

Nick reluctantly let go of her. Glimpsing his face as he backed away, she decided he never looked so miserable. Fog drifted between them and a forlorn bird cooed loudly from above.

"Take care of Aaron," she called over her shoulder as Galloway led her out of the alley. "He needs a doctor right away."

Nick didn't respond, but she knew he heard her. Shock and disbelief blurred her thoughts, and she waited to wake up. It felt so much like the familiar nightmare that haunted her sleep, but Nick had never been part of it.

With a firm grip on her shoulder, Galloway propelled her forward, through the streets. "Here I thought you were smarter than to believe you had a friend." He laughed.

Strangers with wide eyes gawked after them. She watched them whisper to each other and imagined their conversations. *"It looks like they caught another one of those criminals." "I'm glad they caught her." "I hope she gets what she deserves."* None of the devised dialogue offered her the slightest empathy or pity.

She stared forward, trying to ignore the detective, disregard any suspicious stares, and avoid panic.

CHAPTER 40

Cold metal burned into Lareina's wrists as she strained forward, testing the strength of the support beam she'd been handcuffed to. It was sturdy, unlike the rest of the long-forgotten park shelter where she now found herself. A half-collapsed roof surrounded by overgrown trees and brush hid her from any curious passersby, not that she'd seen any people around.

Galloway had checked the handcuffs twice before he felt confident enough to leave her behind. Initially he didn't believe a word she said, but when he searched her pockets and didn't find the pendant, his face flushed bright red, beginning in his cheeks then moving down his neck, creating an unbroken field of crimson. His hand clenched into a tight fist and he slowly brought it up to eye level, holding it there in front of him, but refraining from using it. He couldn't kill her yet, not until he held the pendant in his hand. She listened to him rant and yell at her, at the trees, and at the sky as she formulated a story.

"It's at the ticket booth at the train station," she told him, dropping her voice to a low whisper of defeat. "I convinced the man inside that it was worth something and he let me trade it for a ticket."

"So where's your ticket then?"

She let out a long breath. "At Nick's hotel room with the rest of my stuff. I suppose I won't be getting any of it back."

"Don't worry. You won't need it," he threatened. "I can

check your story a lot faster without you, but don't worry. I'll come back and you better not have lied to me."

Useless trinkets she had stuffed into her pockets at the last house lay scattered on the ground where Galloway had dropped them. A charm bracelet, a single golden earring, a refrigerator magnet painted to look like a slice of watermelon. None of it could help her, but the detective hadn't bothered to pull everything out of her pockets after determining the pendant wasn't there. She twisted her hand until she gripped the side of her jacket. Inch by inch she bunched the material together until her fingers wriggled inside of the pocket. Deep in the warm lining she felt something cool and gripped it between two fingers. She pulled the paperclip from her pocket, straightened one side so she could feel the shape of an L, then jammed it into the lock and bent it over to create the key she needed.

Arching her hand back as far as her wrist would allow, she twisted the paperclip counterclockwise, but her neck wouldn't allow her head to turn far enough to see her wrists. Birds squawked high above in the trees, flapping from branch to branch, dropping twigs to the ground. Panic stole her steadiness, and her paperclip scraped across the hand-cuffs.

Calm down, just calm down, she told herself. *You've picked millions of locks and you can pick this one too.* Taking a deep breath, she tried again. She knew she couldn't lie to Galloway indefinitely. The fact that he even believed her was lucky on her part and idiotic on his, but he wouldn't be gone for long, and when he returned he would be out of patience. Her wrist ached from bending the wrong way and the paperclip slipped out from between her fingers, pinging against the concrete under her feet. Frustrated, she kicked the beam with her heel then turned her head so she could see over her shoulder. The improvised key glinted against a clump of encroaching grass just behind her foot.

Time fluttered on the breeze that hissed through winter brush. The darkening sky and elongating shadows, vanishing behind a quickly rising fog, became ominous reminders of the haste with which the task must be completed. How long would it take Galloway to walk to the train station? Fifteen, twenty minutes? Once he learned the truth, he would be back in half the time.

Pulling her wrists in tight, she leaned back against the beam, and slowly lowered herself until she sat on the ground. Visualizing the pin's position, she extended her fingertips as far back as they would reach. Thumbs and index fingers fumbled along the cold concrete until her fingertip grazed smooth metal accentuated by the rough pavement.

"Come on, almost there," she whispered, ignoring the strain of muscle and bone as she bent her wrist back farther. "There it is, got it!"

Lareina rested her head back against weathered wood and contemplated her escape route. Directly in front of her, a few straggly trees competed with the weeds, but they weren't thick enough to offer a promising hiding place. A lake behind her blocked that route, and wide-open soccer fields to her right offered no cover. With the possibility of hiding looking bleak, she decided her only chance would be to get a head start long before Galloway showed up. Taking a deep breath to steady her hands, she thought her chances of sawing through the beam would be more likely than successfully picking the four locks on the handcuffs.

Just one more time. Get one hand free and the rest will be easy. Knowing the detective could be back any minute, she grasped the paperclip tight between her fingers, determined not to drop it again. Precious minutes passed as she scraped her pin along the rounded edge of the handcuffs, searching for the keyhole. Once again her hand slipped. "No, come on," she whispered.

Frustration led to anger, doubt, mistakes. She knew that, but she couldn't fight the frustration any longer. She needed someone to blame. There had to be a way to attribute getting caught to Galloway's luck or Nick's disloyalty, but every time she thought any deeper than that, she couldn't avoid the discovery that the catastrophic error belonged to her alone. She made the decision to break the number one rule of surviving as a runaway: don't trust anyone.

How could I have been so stupid? The last three months played out in her mind like a movie in fast forward. Every event linked together into decisions she had made, and after all of it Nick had betrayed her. Galloway was right. People like her didn't have friends, and this was why. *Nick knew how much I wanted to escape. He knew that Galloway would hurt me. I never should have told him the truth. I never should have helped him in the first place.*

Her hand slipped once again, and she screamed at the sky in aggravation. In the silence after, she regretted calling attention to herself. The last thing she needed was for someone worse than Galloway to come along and find her defenseless. Members of The Defiance could be lurking around anywhere and she didn't want to meet one.

Leaves crunched under invisible feet. Her muscles stiffened, but she continued her work.

Crunch, crunch. The footsteps continued and grew louder.

Her chest heaved and every instinct screamed at her to run away, but her flight response seemed to forget that she was chained to a beam planted firmly in concrete. Her only option was to sit, vulnerable, and hope she had enough cover that no one would see her. She fought the impulse to yell out. If she said the right words, she might be able to frighten the approaching individual away, but more than likely it would just help him locate her.

Staring ahead, she desperately tried to solve the lock, the only barrier standing in the way of her freedom. Scanning the tree line, she waited for someone to jump forward, but everything remained still.

Crunch, crunch, crunch. The footsteps echoed around her. Now she could see someone, just a silhouette in the fog around the lake. He wasn't tall enough to be Galloway, but that didn't offer much comfort. At least she knew how to deal with the detective. A stranger would offer far more difficulty and danger.

"Who's there?" she shouted, unable to remain silent any longer.

The figure walked toward her. A few more steps and she recognized the blue jacket and disheveled blond hair.

"It's me," Nick said when he got close enough for her to hear.

Leaning her head back against the beam, she sighed. Relief then anger swept through her as he strolled over to observe the trouble he had caused. She didn't need any distractions, especially not Nick.

"What are you doing here?" She spoke too loudly.

He didn't look like much of a threat standing there with his hands in his pockets. "I came to save you." He smiled as if that would be enough to earn her forgiveness.

"You came to save me?" She laughed bitterly. "You're the reason I'm here." The paperclip found one keyhole and slid inside. She turned it one way then the other and felt a click. Three more to go.

Nick blinked at her, speechless, as if he hadn't expected to be met with such hostility. She shook her head and ignored him to focus on picking the next lock. He couldn't help her anyway—he didn't have the key, and he had already proven his loyalty to Galloway.

"I made a mistake believing the detective. I'm sorry," he pleaded.

"Go away, Nick. I can save myself."

A crunching and snapping of branches, louder than that of Nick's footsteps, caught their attention. They turned in the direction of the sound, but the wall of fog blocked any visual indication of who approached. Lareina could tell by the heavy bootsteps that had followed her for months that Galloway approached and he was angry. Despite her disgust with the traitor in front of her, she didn't want to watch Galloway hurt him, or worse.

"Get out of here Nick, right now. He's coming back," she hissed.

But it was too late and he didn't even attempt to run. When Galloway stepped out of the gray mist, he didn't look surprised to see Nick, and it was only a matter of time before the detective discovered his great fortune in finding both pendants on the foolish, trusting boy in front of him.

"What are you doing here, son?" Galloway asked in a gruff voice.

"I m-made a mistake and I w-want you to let Lareina go."

"That's not going to happen. You know your little friend here lied to me again. She doesn't seem capable of telling the truth at all."

Nick stood straighter. "You're the one who lied."

She twisted the paper clip. The metal teeth of one cuff slid apart, freeing one wrist.

Galloway walked up to Nick until they stood only inches apart. "I'm going to give you one minute to walk away from here."

"No," he protested. "I won't leave without her." He stood up as straight as he could, but Galloway still towered over him.

With the detective distracted, she pulled her wrist in front of her and picked the other two locks with ease now that she could see what she was doing.

"That's too bad."

Lareina spun around in time to see Nick sprawling backward and Galloway reaching for the gun on his belt. Without time to think, she scrambled forward, picked up a thick tree branch, and swung hard, connecting with the back of Galloway's skull. He staggered forward and collapsed into the grass, clutching a hand to the back of his head.

"Come on, we have to go now!" She held out a hand. Nick opened his eyes and looked up at her, blinking, and confused. Precious seconds slipped by before he seemed to comprehend.

He lifted his arm and she pulled him to his feet and away from the detective. Before he had time to protest, the two of them ran hand in hand across the overgrown brush and into the park, putting feet of swirling fog between themselves and Galloway. Nick turned around once but there was nothing to see. Then the louder crunching of boots over dead leaves joined their fleeing sounds, confirming that the detective had only been stunned. Squeezing his hand tighter, she propelled him forward as the first bullet ricocheted off a tree, causing an explosion of bark splinters a foot away from Nick's head. The next one struck so close that soft soil peppered her legs.

As they distanced themselves from the lake, the fog thinned a little and she knew Galloway's shooting would become precise when he could actually see his targets.

"There, come on," she whispered and pulled Nick toward a bunch of abandoned playground equipment. They dove beneath a half-collapsed wooden bridge connecting the slide platform to the monkey bars platform. Grass and weeds had grown freely, providing cover. Lareina peeked through the screen of brush while Nick dug his elbows into the ground, trying to flatten himself out of sight. The grass wouldn't be any protection from a bunch of bullets, so they had to hope Galloway didn't see where they disappeared.

"Are you okay?" she whispered close to his ear.

He jumped, startled by the sound in a silence so absolute they would be able to hear a snowflake land on a blade of grass. "Thanks to you," he replied when he caught his breath. "How did you get away?"

"I picked the lock. I'm good at that, remember."

He stared at the ground, but she could sense the misery and guilt emanating from him. Her shoulder brushed his and she could feel him shaking, hear his shallow breathing. Holding a hand against his jaw, he stammered, "Do you think he'll find us?"

"Based on his past record, I'd say eventually." She squeezed his hand. "This is why I told you to run."

Nick turned his head, one centimeter at a time, until he faced her. "I couldn't leave you again. I found the pendant you put in my pocket, and I knew you never would have given it up unless your story was true and his was a lie . . ."

The detective stepped out of the trees, his head roving back and forth frantically. A smile formed across her lips.

He couldn't see them and, with any luck, wouldn't be able to distinguish their hiding place.

"Hey Galloway," a deep voice called out.

Nick and Lareina spied through the grass, at first unsure where the voice had originated. It didn't take long, however, for them to spot four men crossing the cracked blacktop to where Galloway stood. The men walked in formation, two in front and the other two directly behind them. They all wore the same gray suit and blue tie. Galloway reached for his gun, but the shortest man, who appeared to be the leader of the group, pulled his out first.

"Don't even think about it. Hand over the pendant and we won't have any trouble," the man commanded. The other three stood behind him, glaring at Galloway.

"I d-don't have it." It was the first time she had ever heard fear in the detective's voice.

The leader shook his head. "What do you mean, you don't have it? You told me this was it, you said you had the girl. Are you telling me some teenager has been leading you on a wild goose chase across Texas on the TCI's money?"

"Just give me one more day. She's here, I just had her," Galloway pleaded.

Lareina swallowed, but her throat felt dry anyway. She had never seen the four men. All of those months she thought it was only Galloway after the pendant. There were more though, at least four, and from what they said, a whole group of people. *TCI*. She stifled a shiver that raised the hair on her arms and the back of her neck.

"We've been giving you one more day for almost four months now. We even gave you equipment to find her," one of the other men accused.

Galloway put his hands up as if they could protect him from a bullet, and took a few steps back. "You guys have to believe me. She's here, I can get the pendant."

The leader held his gun aimed at Galloway, and the detective continued to back away.

Nick started to get up but Lareina grabbed his elbow and pulled him back down. "What are you doing?" she hissed. The last thing she needed was for Nick to give away their position and prove Galloway's theory to the others.

"We have to do something. They're going to kill him," he choked.

She couldn't look at Nick. His wide, childlike eyes pleaded with her to do something, but there was nothing to do. *His naivete would have gotten him killed long ago if he didn't have me,* she thought.

"We can't help him. If we go out there, we'll die too. Just close your eyes," she told him and she did the same. In the safety of her fabricated darkness she could hear her heart beating, Nick's ragged breathing, and the angry voices of Galloway and the other men, which she tried to tune out. She knew what was coming, but everything happened so slowly. It reminded her of a thunderstorm, seeing the lightning and then waiting forever for the thunder because she anticipated it. Expecting thunder to echo across the deserted blacktop any minute, she covered her ears. No one would hear it. No one would witness the murder except for Nick and herself, and they would be powerless to do anything about it.

Three loud cracks pounded in her ears. Nick's breathing sped up so she tightened her grip on his hand once again. "It's okay, we're safe," she repeated over and over again, unsure of whether she even believed her own words. She felt certain that the men would walk right over to their hiding place and demand the pendant, but after minutes of silence she opened her eyes. The four men had disappeared and Galloway lay crumpled and lifeless where he had stood only minutes earlier.

CHAPTER 41

"They're gone," she whispered.

"Are you sure?" Nick asked with his eyes squeezed shut.

"I'm sure."

He opened his eyes and looked out across the blacktop. "Is he . . .?"

"Yeah," Lareina answered, trying not to look too closely. "I have to get out of here."

"But I don't understand what just happened. What are these pendants? Do they know that I have one too? Are there other people who are going to come after us to get them?" His words hurtled through the space between them in rhythm with her heartbeat.

Building dread tasted stale in her mouth and bitter hostility burned in her chest, flooding over her, taking control of her thoughts, words, actions. She started to sit up, then changed her mind and ducked down again. "I don't know, but I'm done. This is your friend's mess, not mine." She couldn't breathe, her chest ached, and Nick's questions throbbed in her head. She crawled out from under the bridge, considered standing, but couldn't find the courage. Using her elbows, she propelled herself forward, ignoring her shaky muscles and the wet grass that soaked her clothes. Then she remembered Nick's accusations: *you're a thief, you're a liar, we don't really know anything about her.*

"Hey, wait." Loud rustling in the grass behind her indicated his irritating nearness. "Where are you going?"

She stopped and turned so quickly that Nick almost ran into her. A screen of grass waved between them. She didn't want to be alone; some part of her wanted to trust him. She could forgive him, promise to change, try to understand his perspective, but she had already done all of those things once. More than once.

"I can't do it anymore." She gasped for air. "Just leave me alone." She waved a hand at him the way she would shoo a fly.

"But what about Aaron and going back to Nebraska?" He sounded just confused enough to be pathetic.

"I'll take care of Aaron. He won't be able to escape when you trade him to The Defiance for an apple." Tears blurred her vision. She turned away and started crawling again.

The image of Galloway begging for his life swam across the inside of her eyelids. Her villain had his own enemies, but they weren't her friends. They wanted the same thing, and she knew they wouldn't stop searching. Had they believed him? Did they really think a seventeen-year-old girl named Lareina had continually evaded a detective and carried a seemingly valueless piece of jewelry across Texas?

A wall rose out of the grass to meet her, to slow her progress, to block her path. The trap was bigger than she had ever understood. Escaping Galloway had been difficult enough. She couldn't outmaneuver an entire network of people, a worldwide search tightening around her by the minute. Tears swerved down her cheek and her lungs burned with every breath. Giving into exhaustion, she sat up and rested her head against cool bricks. Disoriented, she looked for a familiar landmark. Crumbling buildings surrounded her. Spindly trees fought through the grass that threatened to engulf everything. What had this place been? She reached up to push hair out of her eyes, but her hands shook so much it took three tries to accomplish anything.

"Lareina, are you okay?" Nick's voice trembled. His face hovered close to hers, but she kept her forehead pressed against the wall so he wouldn't see her tears. She opened her mouth to answer him, but no words came out. Then his arms were around her, protecting her, comforting her.

"It's okay," she whispered over and over until she realized she was the one sobbing. "I don't want to do this anymore."

"You don't have to. We're going home," Nick promised.

She pulled away, but he held her tighter. "You didn't believe me. You listened to Galloway, a stranger . . . Your friend Ava lied to me . . . she's the reason . . ." Closing her eyes, she buried her face against his shoulder. She didn't have the energy to argue or move.

"He told me Ava was alive." Nick sniffled. "I wanted that to be true."

Taking a deep breath to get her voice under control, she looked up at her friend. Tears ran along the contours of his nose.

"I messed up," he choked, "and I'm sorry. It's not enough but I'm sorry."

She wiped her own tears away with the sleeve of her jacket. Nick had an infuriating way of making her feel sorry for him when he didn't deserve it.

"You came back."

He held the palms of his hands flat against the top of his head. A smile formed then vanished. "I only got in your way. You were right when we first met. I don't know what I'm doing."

A piece of tarp, caught in some trees, snapped in a gust

of wind and they both froze, expecting men in gray suits to materialize, but no one appeared. Pulling the pendant out of his pocket, he pressed it into her hand. She looked down at it, so familiar yet strange against her dirt-smeared skin.

"You keep that one and I'll keep mine. There's no reason for them to have both when they catch me." Nick spoke to his shoes. She said nothing.

He stood and took a few backward steps away from her. Then he froze, watching her where she sat, half hidden in the wind-ruffled grass. "I meant to tell you—I like your haircut." He smiled and so did she. Then he turned and step-by-step, the fog erased his presence.

Squeezing the pendant so tight her knuckles burned, she watched his back moving away from her. She brushed her bangs out of her eyes as he became a shadow then an outline. He had betrayed her in the worst way possible. He had abandoned her like everyone else . . . but he had come back and stood up to Galloway. Despite three months of Nick hurting her feelings with his judgments and Lareina insulting his pride, they'd made it to this point. Through the desperation at Oak Creek, bailing off trains, and even traveling in different directions, they'd always found each other. Watching his outline fade against the horizon stung like pins in her lungs, stealing her breath away again.

"Nick, wait," she shouted, pulling herself to her feet.

He stopped, a blurry blob in a colorless world. She waded forward through waist-deep grass, marking her progress as his features came into focus: blue jeans, blue jacket, blond hair, thin nose, hands in his pockets, face drawn in misery, eyes shining with hope.

Stopping in front of him, she smiled, and held out her

hand. "Hey, my name is Lareina. I don't have a last name, but I do have this mysterious pendant."

Nick grinned, breathed, understood. He took her hand and squeezed it. "Nice to meet you Lareina. I'm Nick Ziel. I'm trying to get home, to Nebraska. Where are you headed?"

A raindrop landed on her sleeve, and she watched it slide toward her wrist. "I'm going to Nebraska too."

He wiped rain from his forehead. "I can't believe it, everyone else I've talked to has told me I'm going in the wrong direction."

"Because it's cold and boring with no civilization?" she said without cracking a smile. He laughed and soon she joined him despite the cold rain. For a second, joy rose through the bleak mist that tottered between rain and fog. Laughter drowned out the fighting, hunger, loss, and despair. Then some loud pops followed by lower echoes of the originals shattered the silence. Jumping closer to Nick, she imagined Aaron alone and frightened in the hotel room. Smoke rose into the sky in a thick black plume.

"We should get back to Aaron." Without waiting for a response, she marched forward, lifting her knees, and propelling herself toward the city as fast as she could without getting tangled in the grass. Nick appeared beside her, breathing heavily with the burst of effort it took to catch up. Their eyes met, reflections of the same worry, and they started to run.

A light breeze sliced through thick fog. Buildings, bridges, and cars became visible once again. Bronze light filtered through the remaining clouds, giving the city an eerie glow. A pale sun fragmented in shattered glass and glittered across every shimmering surface.

Following Nick, she sprinted over deserted sidewalks. They rushed into the hotel, ignoring clusters of people in the lobby who stared at them. Relief at discovering the building still standing mixed with worry about Aaron's condition. She rushed to the elevator and Nick stepped up beside her, panting, hands on his head, elbows pointing out. She pressed a large button calling the elevator, then stared at the silver doors, waiting for them to slide apart. They didn't move. She pressed the button again, listened. Nothing. Lareina pounded the heel of her hand against the little glowing green arrow before Nick caught her arm. With his hand gently gripping her elbow, she watched the doors slide apart in a whoosh of air. Together they stepped inside and Nick pressed the right buttons.

"So, what's the plan?" he asked as the elevator rumbled up the shaft.

"We're getting on a train to Nebraska one way or another," she said with a determination so strong she surprised even herself.

"But all I have are two tickets in the wrong direction," he reminded her.

The elevator dinged and the doors slid open. She stared at the light blue wall of the hallway. "I promised not to lie to you anymore, so here's the truth. We're not buying any tickets."

The doors started to slide back together. Nick stepped onto the threshold, sending them back into hiding. "You mean you're going to steal them." His smile sank into a frown, head into his shoulders, hopes into the elevator shaft. "Lareina, stealing, lying, stowing away . . . it's going to get you in trouble or worse. I don't want you to end up like me at Oak Creek."

She looked over at the disapproval on his face, but she

noticed something new. A gentleness remained in his eyes, not accusing but pleading.

"I'll be careful," she promised. "But we have to get Aaron out of here."

Nick nodded, but his smile didn't reappear. He stepped off the elevator and she followed him into the hallway of one hundred white doors. What kinds of lives did the people staying behind those doors lead? Most of them probably weren't pretending to be someone else. More than likely they weren't afraid to greet people on the street in case they were recognized from a wanted poster. In all likelihood they didn't steal all of their food and break into houses when they needed clean laundry.

Before opening the door to room 814, Nick stopped and turned to her. "I understand that we don't have another choice. I trust you."

He pushed the door open and disappeared into the room. She wanted to say something comforting, but she knew neither of them would feel safe until they were aboard a moving train. Maybe they wouldn't be safe anywhere, but leaving Dallas might buy them a few more days, and that was all they ever seemed to have anyway.

CHAPTER 42

Twenty-four. Twenty-five. Lareina counted the cars of a train chugging by, picking up speed on its way out of Dallas. Workers had spent the previous hour loading the last fifteen cars with boxes and bags of goods. With The Defiance taking over Dallas, people flocked to the train station. Crowds bustled everywhere. Everyone wanted a ticket, but few could afford them. People pushed through the crowd, pulling suitcases and wagons or pushing wheelbarrows and strollers of their hurriedly packed possessions. Men and women begged for money; children shrieked in their mother's arms.

"Out of the way, clear a path to the ticket booth," one man shouted. No one moved, and he made slow progress pushing through the shoulder to shoulder crowd.

"I want to go home," a little girl whined.

"I want to ride the train," her brother exclaimed excitedly.

"Everyone move in an orderly fashion. One line to the tickets and one line to board." A man in a long black coat spoke through a megaphone, attempting to bring about some kind of order, but no one listened.

About the time the final cars were being loaded, passengers had arrived and piled into the first ten cars. Those cars were guarded with the heaviest surveillance. Two guards waited at each entry point, taking tickets before anyone entered, and turning away or sometimes dragging away anyone trying to board without a ticket.

Lareina had her eyes on the freight cars. From what she

had observed, two guards walked up and down the length of those cars and shooed people away to prevent theft of the cargo. But during that time workers, dressed in plain clothes, bustled in and out of the cars, carrying boxes and often asking the guards questions regarding the placement of goods.

Now the track was empty, awaiting the arrival and loading of the next train to Nebraska. She didn't know what the train would carry, but considering that its departure was scheduled for eleven o'clock and it was nine, she figured it should have been there already. *I should be looking at it right in front of me,* she thought. Her head ached and she rubbed her forehead. *Trains sometimes come behind schedule. As long as they keep running, everything will be okay.*

"Are you going to eat something?" Nick asked, interrupting her plans.

She looked over at the boys beside her. They nibbled at bread and cheese Nick had purchased with the ten dollars he made from selling the gun. Sitting against the side of the ticket booth in shadowy darkness kept them clear of the bustle but gave them an unobstructed view of the constant train traffic.

"I'm not that hungry," she replied and turned back to the empty tracks.

"You should eat before we get on the train. It's going to be a long trip," Aaron suggested. He seemed a little stronger and more optimistic than the night before. *Maybe all the rest helped*, she thought. But his leg was still infected and he needed medical care.

Nodding, she reached over for a chunk of cheese and crumbled it absentmindedly between her fingers. "The train should be here by now. What if it doesn't come?"

"It'll be here." Nick didn't sound so sure.

"I think I can hear it coming right now." Aaron looked down the tracks, eyes bright.

They both turned to him. *Please don't start hallucinating,* Lareina thought. *That's the last thing I need right now.*

"I don't hear anything." She tried to smile. "Maybe it was some other noise."

"Shhh. Just listen," Aaron insisted.

Although it seemed a hopeless task, they stopped talking and strained to hear the urgent warning of a train approaching. Silence. She could hear nothing but silence. *What am I supposed to say to Aaron?* A muffled whistle sounded off in the distance, no louder than someone playing a flute down the block. At first she thought she was only hearing what she wanted to until the whistle blared again, louder and closer.

Nick nudged her arm with his elbow. "I hear it. It's real, Lareina."

"I hear it too." She smiled.

"See, I'm not completely useless," Aaron joked.

All three of them kept their eyes on the tracks until a train chugged into the station and stopped with a hiss. Doors opened and people spilled onto the platform, talking, laughing, and disappearing into a thinning crowd around the ticket booth. Workers swarmed around the train, checking it for mechanical problems and carrying boxes up ramps and into freight cars at the back. *This will be my last chance to get us out of here,* she thought.

The night remained warm and calm with a bright moon to illuminate everything below. Clear, perfect weather in early winter. Hadn't she wished for those conditions thousands of times over the past months? Finally her wish had come true, but it wasn't ideal for a night of undercover operations.

Timing is always off, she thought as she walked parallel to the train, far enough away to avoid the crowd.

Peering around the ticket booth, she observed stacks of brown boxes waiting to be loaded. Luckily the people who loaded boxes in and out of the train didn't wear uniforms. Most of them wore jeans, sweatshirts, and tennis shoes. It provided the perfect opportunity for the chaos that she planned to use to her advantage.

She had tasked Nick with sneaking Aaron onto the train. Wanting them as close to the train as possible, she sent them down the tracks to hide behind another small building. They would still have about one hundred yards of wide-open space to cross to reach the boxcar they had chosen.

"How are you going to get on the train?" Nick had asked her.

"I don't know yet," she had told him. "I might not, but I'll meet you in Maibe as soon as I can."

He shook his head when he heard they might be separated. She thought he might argue or refuse to go through with the plan. Instead, he swallowed hard and said, "Be careful, and I'll take care of Aaron."

"Everything will be okay," she had replied, and she believed it. The plan would work now that they all trusted each other. They were truly in it together, working for a common goal. She wouldn't let anyone hurt her family. Before leaving she leaned in and kissed Nick on the cheek, then walked away quickly.

Holding onto that memory, she left the safety of darkness and strolled into the well-lit area of stockpiled boxes. She knew if any part of her plan failed, she probably wouldn't see Nick or Aaron ever again. Yet she moved forward. The faster she completed the mission, the faster they would all be safe. With as much confidence as she could muster, she walked right up to the loading area only to be overwhelmed by the massive number of boxes. She stopped and stared up at the pile.

"Hey there, no dawdling. We have to get all of this on the train in the next twenty minutes," a stern but not unkind voice ordered.

Quickly, she turned to see a woman, not much older than herself, standing next to her with a clipboard. "I'm sorry."

The woman just smiled. "The last three cars are all loaded. Start with these boxes and fill the next three."

Before Lareina could say another word, the woman had moved further down the line to give another set of orders. Watching the area, expecting someone to stop her, she hoisted a box into her arms. It wasn't heavy, and the contents made a slight crinkling sound every time she tilted it forward.

The last three cars were entirely loaded. That was the information she really needed to activate her plan. As she walked toward the train, she picked at the two staples holding the flaps of her box together. It didn't take long to pop one free then the other, so the flaps of the box bounced slightly with every step she took.

Lowering her box, she surveyed the scene around waiting boxcars. One of the freight guards made his way from the back of the train toward the front. The other guard was on his way from the front to the back. There would be no way to avoid both of them, but she would only have to distract one. She waited for the guard heading toward the front of the train to pass, then lifted the box up in front of her face and walked right into the other guard's path.

He barely bumped into her, but she didn't let him know that. She fell to the ground, dumping the box over and spilling its contents on her way down.

"Are you okay? I'm so sorry. I saw you and tried to stop." The guard stumbled through an apology.

"It's my fault. I shouldn't have had that box in front of my face." She groaned and sat up slowly. The mess around her consisted of hundreds of individually wrapped candies scattered all over the platform. Perfect.

Turning the box right side up, the embarrassed guard began to scoop candies back into it. He was young, maybe even a year or two younger than her. "Are you hurt?"

She reached for some stray candies by her hand. "No, I'm okay," she told him. "I've always been a klutz. They didn't want to give me this job, but I promised I would be more careful."

The guard smiled, and his blue eyes sparkled. "Don't sweat it." He laughed. "I won't tell them."

She looked down the tracks to the last car. Nick and Aaron hobbled slowly toward the train. *Only a little further. Hurry up, Nick.* Dropping a handful of candy into the box, she smiled. "Thank you. It's awfully kind of you to help."

The guard raised his eyes and looked down the track toward the front of the train. He scanned each car, moving his eyes slowly toward the back where Nick and Aaron still stood outside in plain sight.

"Wait, is that one by your knee!" she exclaimed. It worked. The guard dropped his eyes and felt along the ground near his leg.

He picked up a rock and held it out for her to see. "Nope. Just a rock."

Lareina scooped any remaining candies into the box. "Oh, I'm sorry. I just didn't want to miss one. You know they count these and it comes back on us if any are missing." The fabrication came easily.

"Of course. I understand," the guard replied. He picked up the box and lowered it into her arms. "Now be careful. You don't want to pick those all up again."

She smiled and walked toward a car that other workers rushed in and out of. Before entering, she glanced toward the back of the train. No sign of Nick and Aaron.

Leaving her box next to several others, she followed some workers back to shrinking piles of cargo then cut around behind the ticket booth once again. She watched as people arrived to board the passenger cars, waving their tickets impatiently in front of busy guards who struggled to keep the crowd under control. The scene at the back of the train was much quieter with two guards continuing their pacing and the occasional worker carrying a cardboard box.

Too close to her ears, the five-minute whistle blared, cutting through the calm night air like a siren. Trains didn't always enter the station on time, but they almost always left according to schedule. *I'm running out of time,* she thought. *I need a distraction—everyone looking in the wrong direction.*

Scanning the platform, she looked for something new, something she had missed, something she could use. Unfortunately, the entire scene looked identical to how it had minutes before. The amiable guard she talked to earlier made his way to the back of the train, about to turn around and continue his pacing back in the other direction. Before she thought it through, Lareina sprinted around the ticket booth and toward the guard.

"Help," she yelled at him, trying to sound alarmed. "Help!"

She stopped in front of him, breathing heavily after the sudden burst of running. He placed a gentle hand on her shoulder and asked with concern, "What's wrong? What happened?"

"There are . . . looters," she gasped trying to catch her breath, "over by the loading area . . . They're stealing everything."

"Stay here," the guard ordered. As he hurried away, she could hear him calling all guards to the shipment area on his walkie-talkie. With news spreading down the platform, chaos erupted. People scattered and ran in all directions.

"I'm sorry," she whispered after the guard, but no one was close enough to hear her. Knowing she had limited time, she hurried toward the train. Close enough to touch it, she reached her hand out to pull herself into the last car.

"Stop right there," a gruff voice yelled. The volume of his command indicated that the owner stood right behind her.

How many times has someone said that to me in the last year, she wondered, then turned around to face the most recent hindrance to her plan. An overweight guard stared back at her, and he wasn't smiling.

"Where do you think you're going?" he demanded.

She couldn't think of a single answer that would be enough to get her on the train before it departed. The best she could do was escape the current threat and catch another train later. She took a few steps back, then darted around the guard.

"Hey," he yelled after her, but she ignored him.

Running along the train led her to realize that it moved with her, only slower. Lareina timed a jump through the space between two of the cars and doubled back. She could see her pursuer in the openings between cars as he ran along with her.

"Stop," he yelled. "You can't get away."

She ran in the opposite direction that the train moved, but only had four cars to go before it ended and she lost her cover.

Desperate for an escape, she reached for a bar that protruded high above the link between two cars. Picking up speed, the train swept her along with it and she clung to the slippery metal, bracing her feet against the hitch between her car and the one in front of it.

"Hey! Hey!" the guard screamed, running alongside the train. He tried to hold onto the edge of the same car, but his hands slipped and he fell face-first onto the platform along the railroad tracks. As the train continued to gain speed, she clung to the side of the car and watched as the guard stood and stomped his foot into the hard ground. He didn't take his eyes off the departing train but didn't attempt to follow.

She knew she couldn't make the entire trip outside and with every second that passed, the speed increased. Sliding her feet along a ledge near the bottom of the car and clinging to the bar, she eased her way to the side. Wind ripped at her hair and clothes while every bump threatened to throw her from the barreling train. She reached for the open doorway, only a few feet away. A panel covered the bottom to prevent anything from sliding out, but that left the top wide open for her to climb into. Her foot slipped as the train hurtled over a bump. She hung from the ledge, feet dangling toward rushing tracks for a second before she managed to swing her lower body into the open part of the door. That left her hands clinging to the side of the train, afraid to let go, but unable to hold on for much longer.

"Nick," she yelled against the roaring wind. "Nick!" He'd never be able to hear her over the roaring clatter.

Her muscles ached after only minutes of hanging on. Hope faded when she realized the next stop would be miles away. Her hands slipped slightly with each jolt. "Please don't let me fall onto the tracks," she prayed. Looking down at the ground speeding under her only terrified her further, so she squeezed her eyes shut.

"Lareina, can you hear me?"

Nick's voice? It can't be real. She kept her eyes tightly shut.

"Lareina, give me your hand," his voice demanded.

She looked toward the open doorway. Nick stood with his head sticking out so he could see her.

"I can't let go. I'm scared," she shouted.

"Just one hand." He reached as far as he could. "You can't stay out there."

He had a point. She decided if she was going to fall, she might as well attempt to save herself rather than wait for gravity to win. Tightening the grip of her left hand, she let go with her right hand and reached for Nick. She felt her hand in his and then his other hand tightened around her elbow.

"Okay, I've got you. Now let go."

I can trust him, she told herself, and let her hand slide from the train. In one quick motion, he pulled her in through the opening and they crashed against a stack of crates.

The boxcar smelled of dust and wet cardboard. It tickled her nose as she lay with her cheek against the floor, stunned, breathing stale air, waiting for her heart to beat at a normal rate. Ankles, wrists, and left ear jolted against the solid platform beneath her as the train bumped along, carrying her with it.

Careful hands gripped her shoulders and pulled her up through the darkness. "Lareina, are you okay?" Nick's voice sounded like raindrops in a drought. His face hovered close enough that she could pick out every familiar feature.

A tingling sensation of near death and returning life surged through her fingertips, elbows, shoulders. Mounting realization spread a smile over her face. She lunged forward, wrapped her arms around Nick, and toppled them back into a wall of boxes. They both laughed, and despite a sharp corner smashed against her spine, she couldn't compel herself to let go of him.

"Never let me do something like that again." Her voice shook so intensely she didn't recognize it.

"I didn't think you were going to make it." He hugged her so tight she couldn't breathe, but she didn't protest. "When the train started moving, I thought for sure we were leaving you behind."

"Hey, are you guys all right over there?" Aaron's hoarse voice swerved through a maze of crates and cardboard.

The train lurched, threatening to toss them both back to the floor, but Nick kept them balanced. Finally, she loosened her grip and the two of them crawled over to where Aaron rested against the opposite wall. Bandaged leg stretched in front of him, jacket unzipped, head lolling at the mercy of the train, he grinned at her.

"I missed it. How did you manage to get on the train?"

Lareina slid and shifted until she sat directly next to him. Their shoulders brushed and she leaned her head closer to his. "I wish *I* had missed it."

She felt Aaron smile.

"I can hardly believe it," Nick whispered and glanced back toward the door as if he expected someone to enter. "We made the plan work."

She couldn't believe it either. She had finally caught her train. The train that would take her home to food and shelter, warmth and belonging. The train that would carry the family she always wanted to safety. Glittering shards of light crisscrossing through trees and buildings outside painted flickering shadows across cargo of varying sizes, Nick's jacket, Aaron's face. Reaching into her pocket, she outlined the triangular perimeter of Susan's pendant. She traced each letter, S-P-E-R-O, on the smooth surface of the strange necklace that had brought her so close to death on so many occasions. *Hope for the best,* she thought, *but don't expect it just to happen.*

"What's wrong?" Nick asked.

"You still have your pendant, right?"

He reached into his pocket and held it up in front of her. She nodded and untied her shoelace.

"What are you doing?" Aaron asked.

Pulling her shoe off, she dropped the pendant inside. "Just taking a slight precaution, in case things don't go according to the plan. It might be a little uncomfortable, but they'll search our pockets before our shoes."

Nick pulled his shoe off and did the same. "There are far worse discomforts. I don't think our plans ever work exactly the way they're supposed to."

Sliding her foot back into her shoe, she took her time tying it tight. She closed her eyes, sank into the boxcar's cold wall, and laughed.

"What's so funny?" Nick watched her with his head tilted to the side, his expression trying to decide whether to smile or check her for a fever.

Aaron coughed, his breath serrated, and his head drooped to Lareina's shoulder. She slid her arm around him, and Nick dug out a half full bottle of water.

"I'm all right," Aaron assured after a few swallows. "Go back to laughing."

Holding the back of her hand against Aaron's hot forehead,

she reminded herself that they were on their way to help. "After everything that's happened, this doesn't seem real."

"It better be real." Nick laughed. "Otherwise we're all looking at the same mirage."

"Maybe that bread was moldy." Aaron's voice had the strength of a fading echo. "It could cause hallucinations."

"Lareina didn't eat any of the bread, so as long as she sees what we're seeing, it's real." Nick crumpled his jacket into a pillow and stretched out near her feet. He curled his arms around the jacket and casually rested his blond curls on the homemade cushion, as if he swung on a hammock in his backyard. "Everyone get some rest. We'll be on this train all night. We can figure out how far we got in the morning."

Moonlight broke into long rectangles then floated through the car just to be replaced by the same monotonous pattern. Her eyelids slid toward sleep, but in the darkness Galloway's ghost paced in the shadows of towering boxes. The reliable rhythm of the train clacking forward mixed with his voice. *I'll always find you.* For months she had feared he could see her every step, and now the thought of his presence, there on the train, made her shiver. The pendant burned against her heel as if its shimmering surface picked up energy in the pocket of air between her sock and shoe.

Lareina opened her eyes. The moonlight replayed its usual pattern, clacking metal swallowed silence, cargo vibrated with a whoosh of scraping cardboard. Aaron's head bobbled against her. His cheek burned through her jacket, a hot coal dropped onto her shoulder. Nudging Nick's arm with her shoe, she whispered his name. He flinched, drawing his knees halfway to his chest before slipping back into sleep. She held Aaron's hand in hers, tried to cushion his head from the worst of the bumps, and willed the train to move faster, the seconds to race by, his fever to drop. Each click against the rail represented progress.

"Almost there," she whispered. "We're so close now."

When they finally stopped in Maibe, would they be welcomed or turned away? Could anyone be following them? Was Aaron's fever getting worse? The questions were a constant torment that cycled through her head as if they rode a looping conveyor belt. They were going home, but she didn't know what that meant or what to expect. Would anyone remember her? Would it be better if they didn't? The people she remembered, Rochelle and the others, they couldn't have changed in the way the rest of society seemed to be altering. In Maibe, people didn't leave family members out in the yard to die of the fever. They didn't charge admission fees into the hospital or sentence newcomers to forced labor digging tunnels. Did they?

The train lurched and slowed; Lareina felt her thoughts stay behind in the icy darkness as momentum shifted her body forward then motion caught up and ripped her back into place. For the fifteenth time, a blaring whistle announced their approach to another town. She looked from Nick to Aaron, both sound asleep in the shadowy corner of the boxcar, the only speck of the world that she could be sure of. Every glittering minute carried them farther away from murdering pendant thieves, infected cities, and cities under siege. The train picked up speed once again, racing through darkness toward hope for a better future and the only place that had ever felt like home.

ABOUT THE AUTHOR

Vanessa Lafleur is a full-time high school English and creative writing teacher, competitive speech coach, and middle school volleyball coach. She lives in Nebraska and teaches at the school she graduated from.

Her absolute favorite part of teaching is helping her students discover their writing talents and hone their skills.

When she isn't in the classroom, grading research papers, or coaching at a speech meet, Vanessa enjoys spending time outside, reading, and of course, writing. Thanks to her amazing students and their encouragement, Vanessa was inspired to draft a story for them and anyone looking for an adventure about finding your place in the world.

Hope for the Best is her debut novel.

For more information about Vanessa and her book, visit www.vanessalafleur.com